Captain Gannon spoke with a conviction that led Colin to believe the man had seen action against the aliens. "There are those who believe that a war with the Chodrecai is one we cannot win, that it will be over before you complete your training. Those people are wrong. We will fight this threat, not only the militaries of this world but also with the assistance of our friends, the Plysserians."

Turning, Gannon indicated the alien standing behind him. "This is *Zolitum* Teqotev. *Zolitum* is a rank designation, comparable to that of sergeant. Teqotev and other Plysserian soldiers will be working with your drill instructors. To date, seven platoons of Marine recruits have trained alongside Plysserian soldiers. We have adapted their weaponry and other technology. We have infused our training with knowledge they've shared with us. Platoon 3003 will be the eighth such unit."

It required physical effort for Colin to keep his slackening jaw from falling open. *Oh, my God. What the hell have I gotten myself into?*

Counterstrike: The Last World War, Book II
is also available as an eBook

COUNTERSTRIKE
THE LAST WORLD WAR

BOOK II

Dayton Ward

POCKET **STAR** BOOKS

New York   London   Toronto   Sydney   Jontashreena

Pocket Star Books
A Division of Simon & Schuster, Inc.
1230 Avenue of the Americas
New York, NY 10020

This book is a work of fiction. Names, characters, places, and incidents are products of the author's imagination or are used fictitiously. Any resemblance to actual events or locales or persons, living or dead, is entirely coincidental.

First Pocket Star Books paperback edition May 2010

POCKET STAR BOOKS and colophon are registered trademarks of Simon & Schuster, Inc.

For information about special discounts for bulk purchases, please contact Simon & Schuster Special Sales at 1-866-506-1949 or business@simonandschuster.com.

The Simon & Schuster Speakers Bureau can bring authors to your live event. For more information or to book an event, contact the Simon & Schuster Speakers Bureau at 1-866-248-3049 or visit our website at www.simonspeakers.com.

Art and design by Alan Dingman

Manufactured in the United States of America

10 9 8 7 6 5 4 3 2 1

ISBN 978-1-4391-6774-8
ISBN 978-1-4391-6797-7 (ebook)

First and foremost, this book is dedicated to the men and women of the United States Armed Forces. Thank you for your service and your sacrifice. For those of you in harm's way, I wish you a speedy and safe return to your families.

This book also is dedicated to the readers and ardent fans of *The Last World War*. Without you, this book would not have been possible. For everyone who supported the first novel and kept after me to write a sequel, and who remained patient and supportive throughout the long journey it took to get here, I offer my sincere and undying gratitude. Here's hoping it was worth the wait.

August 6

ALIENS ON EARTH

NEOSHO, MO. Residents of this small southwestern Missouri town are still coming to grips with the realization that their community was one of the first battlegrounds in what is quickly escalating into a war between two worlds.

"We could hear explosions and gunfire," says Hal Kirchoff, a Neosho business owner who has lived here all his life. "I thought they were making a movie or something. At first we didn't think anything of it, because you always hear that kind of thing on the base."

Initial encounters with the aliens occurred on the grounds of the Camp Growding National Guard Reservation, located just south of town. A unit of U.S. Marine reservists conducting annual infantry refresher training discovered the two groups of aliens, identified as "Plysserians" and "Chodrecai."

Sources have confirmed that while the Plysserians have so far proved to be friendly, the Chodrecai instead are believed to be responsible for several attacks on civilian and military personnel. During the first of several press conferences held over the past few days at the Pentagon, the Secretary of Defense confirmed two sizable engagements between the Marine reservists and a Chodrecai military unit, with the reservists receiving assistance from Plysserian soldiers. Casualties are believed to be significant.

So far, no government or military official has provided any explanation as to how the aliens arrived on Earth, or what has brought them here.■

September 9

REPORTS OF ALIEN ACTIVITY INCREASING

More "Portals" Found; Chodrecai on the Move

LOS ANGELES, Calif. Even as the damage here is still being assessed, reports of similar attacks by alien soldiers are coming in from around the world.

Witness accounts of the attack during yesterday's morning commute mirror those already received in Toronto, Rome, Philadelphia, Sydney, and Seattle, with unconfirmed reports starting to trickle in from many more cities across the planet. General descriptions of the incidents are virtually identical, with the aliens emerging from mysterious doorways that seem appear from nowhere.

This aligns with the information being released by the Department of Defense. At the Pentagon's daily press conference, DoD officials reported that incidents involving contact with members of the Chodrecai alien species are being reported around the world with mounting frequency. In some cases, the assaults are isolated and result in few injuries before the aliens withdraw from the area. Others, such as yesterday's attack in downtown Los Angeles, take place in more crowded regions with greater potential for mass casualties. Despite several reports of people seeing "spacecraft" of varying size and description, none of these sightings has been confirmed.

During his primetime news conference last night, President Leonard Harrington revealed many details the government and the military have gathered in what was described as "weeks of alien activity" taking place around the world. More startling were the revelations of how and why the aliens came to be on Earth.

"The Plysserians and the Chodrecai have been at war for generations on their own planet, Jontashreena," the president said last night. "Their presence here appears to be accidental; an unfortunate happenstance resulting from the use of experimental technology intended to transport personnel and equipment between two points on the aliens' home planet."

Instead, the "portals," as they've come to be called, have somehow connected both worlds. The Plysserians, having developed the portal technology, were the first to use it, with Chodrecai forces following after seizing several sites on the other planet that housed the equipment needed to generate the portals.

What remains to be seen is whether the aliens will continue to fight their war even though it has spilled over from their own planet to ours. ●

CHODRECAI OFFENSIVE TURNED BACK!

Human and Plysserian Forces Counter Three-Pronged Assault

WASHINGTON, D.C. Facing what has been described as a massive campaign against Earth on the part of the Chodrecai, armed forces around the world have worked in concert to repel an invasion targeting the centers of human military power.

"I don't know if I'd call it a clear victory," said General Andrew Grayson, chairman of the Joint Chiefs of Staff, during a press conference held at the Pentagon mere hours after alien forces were seen retreating from the battle that had all but consumed the National Mall here in Washington. "But we'll take what we can get."

The offensive, what Grayson called "as bold in scope as it was audacious in execution," was launched against three prime targets: Beijing, Moscow, and Washington, D.C. Video footage captured by reporters embedded with military units at all three points of attack shows wave after wave of Chodrecai soldiers emerging from portals. Eyewitness reports of the invading alien armadas describe ground vehicles and light airborne attack craft, which, by all counts, far surpass the capabilities of anything used by military forces on Earth.

General Grayson acknowledged these limitations along with those already known with respect to alien weaponry and other equipment, at the same time offering his views on how human forces, working in concert with Plysserian units who had pledged their assistance, were able to counter the assaults.

"First, we had good intelligence," the general offered during the press conference. Though he would not elaborate, he did hint that he, along with other military leaders around the world, benefited from information delivered to them by sources on Jontashreena. "Assets on the ground there alerted us to the coming invasion, allowing us to plan a response. Without that intel, I think it's fair to say the Chodrecai might well have caught us totally unprepared for their attack."

Those preparations enabled Earth's forces to repel the Chodrecai invasion at all three of the targeted cities. Despite the inability of the aliens to gain footholds during the campaign, damage to all three cities is extensive, with both sides suffering significant casualties. Small skirmishes continue even now, days after the assault was seemingly called off, with hundreds of Chodrecai soldiers being taken prisoner. President Harrington has ordered the humane treatment of all captured Chodrecai, granting them all the rights and protections as prescribed under the Geneva Conventions and pertaining to the status of military prisoners of war.

"We did not provoke this assault on our way of life," President Harrington said during a speech to the American people, given shortly after a cease fire had been declared in Washington. "We did not invite this battle, but we are confident that we have demonstrated our resolve to defend ourselves and our home from outside aggression." ○

ALIEN THREAT REMAINS

President, Military Experts Believe More Chodrecai Attacks Are Coming

THE WHITE HOUSE "There can be no question that the Chodrecai will return, and when they do, we must be ready."

This comment punctuated yet another speech offered by President Leonard Harrington during a primetime news conference held last night at the White House. The president, joined by the secretaries of defense and homeland security as well as key military advisors, dispelled any illusions that the danger posed by the Chodrecai remains a paramount concern for civilian and military leaders around the world.

"Though the battle was won," the president said, "the war is far from over. If the sacrifices of so many brave men, women, and Plysserians are not to be in vain, then we must look ahead to the next battle."

President Harrington's latest executive orders call for build-ups and expansions of military forces on a scale not seen since the Second World War. At last report, he was considering requiring national service of every able-bodied citizen. Falling short of calling such extreme measures a draft, the president did not rule out a return to conscription as a means of filling the military ranks.

"We must be vigilant," the president warned during his closing comments. "We must be strong of focus and—most of all—we must be prepared."

Even as those preparations get underway, the questions occupying our every waking moment are: When will the Chodrecai return, and what will happen on that day? •

CHODRECAI–PLYSSERIAN
LINGUISTIC EXTRACT

Amleq – "yes"

Bretloqa – model of pulse rifle used by Plysserian soldiers

Bretmirqa – handheld explosive launcher, like a LAW or other antitank weapon

Cenet – unit of distance, somewhat similar to a meter

Chodrecisilae – the continent on *Jontashreena* that is home to most of the Chodrecai population

Dekritonpa – title of Chodrecai elected officials. "First" and "Second" *Dekritonpas* are similar to "Prime Minister" and "Deputy Prime Minister"

Drakolitar – horseshoe-shaped Chodrecai attack craft

Esat – term for low-ranking Chodrecai soldier, similar to "private"

Fonsata – generic term for low-ranking Chodrecai soldiers, similar to "troops"

Galotreapiq – the continent on *Jontashreena* that is home to most of the Plysserian population

Gangrel – a brewed beverage, similar to coffee

Hneri – mountain range in the *Chodrecisilae* continent's western region

Jenitrival – Plysserian armored assault vehicle, featuring characteristics similar to tanks, Bradley fighting vehicles, and even the obsolete Ontos antitank vehicle

Jenterant – Chodrecai officer; rank held by supreme military commander

Jontashreena – "home"

Kentelitrul – Plysserian officer, similar to "general"

Koratrel – a mass-casualty explosive device

Kret – Chodrecai rank similar to "corporal"

Laepotic – Plysserian title, similar to "Professor" or "Doctor"

Lisum – model of Plysserian attack craft

Lotral – model of Plysserian troop transport

Malirtra – a Chodrecai officer, higher than lieutenent

Malitul – a Plysserian officer, higher than lieutenant; similar to *malirtra*

Margolitruul – mountain range in the Plysserian *Galotreapiq* continent's southern region

Misabril – a Chodrecai military-issue sidearm

Murigral – mobile pulse "cannons" similar to antiaircraft guns

Nomirtra – a Chodrecai officer equivalent to "lieutenant"

Paola – a type of fruit native to *Jontashreena*

Secratichal – a type of liquor

Tempra – like a cigar or cigarette

Tilopwat – a backless chair preferred by many *Jontashreena* natives

Tilortrel – generic Plysserian term for military officers

Weh otiquol atan – phrase meaning, essentially, "Freeze" or "Stay where you are"

Zanzi – a Plysserian profanity

Zolitar – Plysserian rank, similar to "sergeant" or *zolitum*

Zolitum – Chodrecai rank, similar to "sergeant"

Status Quo

1

Corporal Bradley Gardner did not see the lone Chodrecai soldier, at least not until the damned thing was ready to frag his ass.

"Gardner! On your nine!"

Reacting to the warning from somewhere behind him, Gardner spun to his left in time to see the wounded alien warrior rising from beneath smoldering wreckage, bringing up the pulse rifle it carried in its bulky, muscled arms. Its pale gray skin was darkened with ash and soot. Shreds of burned skin and muscle hung from its left arm, injuries no doubt resulting from the fuel-air bombs that had blanketed the area less than thirty minutes earlier. It appeared to Gardner that the alien's molded body armor had melted in places, perhaps even fusing to the Chodrecai's exposed, scorched skin. How the thing managed to stay on its feet was beyond him.

Then none of that mattered as the gaping muzzle of the soldier's pulse rifle rose to point in his direction.

Gardner fired without really aiming, the oversized Plysserian weapon bucking in his hands as it belched energy. The air whined in his ears and a bolt of displaced air crossed the space separating him from the Chodrecai, striking the wounded alien in its broad chest and sending it staggering backward. It tripped over a piece of flame-riddled debris and fell, toppling to the blackened ground.

"Get down!" another voice shouted, this time from somewhere to Gardner's right, and the corporal dropped instinctively to one knee as figures rushed past him. Leveling his pulse rifle at the fallen Chodrecai, he watched as fellow Marines closed on its position, training their own weapons on it. Someone yelled at the soldier in its native language, ordering the alien to remain still and offer no resistance.

"Nice shot, Gardner," a gravelly voice said from behind him, and Gardner looked up to see Gunnery Sergeant Kelley Owens, his platoon leader. The imposing African-American man's eyes bored into him from beneath the brim of his floppy green camouflage boonie hat. "Almost makes up for you sleepwalking through the area. You looking to get your ticket punched, or what?"

Rising to his feet, Gardner felt his face flush in embarrassment as he watched fellow Marines take the wounded Chodrecai soldier into custody. "Sorry, Gunny. I was too busy looking for anything we might salvage. I screwed up." It had been a boot mistake, the kind of error Gardner might have made what seemed like a lifetime ago, when he was nothing more than a full-time hospital payroll administrator back in Kansas City and a part-time Marine reservist.

A lifetime ago, before the war had come.

From somewhere off to his right, Gardner heard more weapons fire and turned to see other Marines—some wielding pulse rifles like his own while others carried M4A1 carbines—converging on another Chodrecai warrior, this one appearing uninjured as it lunged from behind the burnt-out shell of a collapsible shelter. The alien was firing on the run, lumbering toward the protective cover of the forest surrounding the glade where the Chodrecai had made their encampment. Gardner flinched as one Marine caught the full brunt of the alien's weapon, everything above his waist disintegrating in a cloud of blood, skin, bone, and clothing fragments. What remained of the man fell to the ground as his companions pressed forward, catching the Chodrecai in a cross fire until the alien soldier collapsed in the onslaught.

"Damn it," Owens said, shaking his head as he and Gardner made their way over to the fallen Marine. Gardner's stomach lurched at the sight, one he had already seen far too many times in the months that had passed since the arrival of the Plysserians and their enemies, the Chodrecai. Using the muzzle of his pulse rifle to turn the dead Marine's largely uninjured lower body onto its front, Owens reached down and moved aside a piece of shredded camouflage uniform to read the name tape stitched above one back pocket. "Meade," he read. "Shit." Looking to Gardner, he asked, "Did you know him?"

Gardner replied, "Not well. We played poker a few times." It was a reality of the life he now lived that he did not form close friendships with most of the people with whom he came in contact. That was a consequence of his frequent transfers from unit to unit around the country, as well as occasional trips abroad, thanks to the rather specialized knowledge he mostly by accident had come to possess.

Yeah. Lucky me.

Owens was walking across the scorched ground looking around the glade and the burnt remains of what had been the Chodrecai encampment. Wreckage still smoldered here and there, but some of the Marines already were seeing to the small fires, some kicking dirt on the flames while others used entrenching tools—military folding shovels—to take care of the larger fires. "Doesn't look like the Air Force left much of anything," the gunny said.

"Probably not," Gardner conceded, reaching up to wipe sweat from his forehead. The pair of B-2 stealth bombers dispatched to sanitize this target had done so with their usual effectiveness, all but obliterating the encampment with surgical precision.

"Recognize anything that might be a portal generator?" Owens asked.

Gardner shook his head. Very little of whatever equipment and materiel staged at this location had survived the B-2 bombardment. He pointed toward a larger, curved structure, similar in design to the old Quonset huts he remembered from boot camp at the recruit training base in San Diego. Only a portion of one curved wall still stood, the rest of the structure having been consumed by fire. "That looks like it was the only thing large enough to house it," Gardner said, "but it got hammered pretty good. I'll be surprised if there's anything salvageable in there."

The camp's location had been pinpointed less than a day earlier, deep in an expansive, largely uninhabited area of Pacific Northwest forest in Oregon. Orbiting satellites had detected the energy output of what was believed to be the power source for yet another in a series of portals that had been opened between Earth and *Jontashreena*.

"According to the satellite imagery they gave us," Owens said, "whatever generator they had here could only have been operational for thirteen or fourteen hours. Still plenty of time to move troops and equipment through." Giving the area another look, he added, "And I have to say, I don't see *that* much stuff lying around here."

"If they stuck to usual Gray tactics, they've scattered," Gardner replied, using the nickname bestowed upon the Chodrecai during his first encounter in southwestern Missouri with members of the alien race, in response to their pallid skin pigmentation. He waved his left hand to indicate the surrounding Oregonian forest. "They could be anywhere out there. Besides us and maybe Bigfoot, there's nobody for miles."

From behind him, a deep voice said, "We must also re-member that the Chodrecai who built the generator here had to have arrived via another portal."

Gardner and Owens turned to see the towering figure of Makoquolax, a Plysserian soldier. He was dressed in a formfitting dark uniform, over which he wore a vest comprised of interconnected armor plates, along with an equipment harness. Large, oval-shaped black eyes peered out from beneath a protruding brow, and small holes occupied the locations where ears or a nose would be on a human head. The pale gray skin of his exposed arms and bald head were covered with an intricate series of patterns and lines rendered in dark blue ink. Many Plysserian soldiers followed this same practice, as Makoquolax had explained to him, with each of the glyphs representing a significant battle in which the individual soldier had fought, or some other major life event the wearer wished to commemorate. Seeing the tattoos on various Plysserians had given Gardner cause to christen their newfound, unlikely friends as "Blues."

"Hey, Max," Gardner said, invoking the moniker he had given to the Plysserian. Indicating the destroyed camp with a nod of his head, he asked, "You thinking what I'm thinking?"

Nodding his large, oblong head in greeting, Max said, "I have surveyed the area and found nothing of use, but the size of this encampment suggests a larger contingent somewhere nearby."

That other camp, Gardner knew, likely had been the insertion point for a portal that had originated on *Jontashreena*. As they seemed to have been doing with increasing frequency during the past several weeks, Gray scouting parties had come to Earth and immediately set to the task of erecting a portal generation site. Once completed, it would serve as an anchor point for a stronger, more reliable conduit, one that would not have to be powered down due to the energy demands of maintaining a portal powered from only one end.

"Month after month of little to no activity," Gunny Owens said, "and now all of a sudden the Grays are on the move again? Why now? If the reports we've been getting are right, they're still rebuilding and reorganizing after their last big offensive, and we've heard nothing that says they're ready to try again."

Folding his muscled arms across his broad chest, Max replied, "Given the sporadic and often incomplete intelligence reports we have received from sympathetic sources on *Jontashreena*, it is entirely possible that at least some Chodrecai rebuilding and rearming efforts have been carried out in relative secret. However, with the threat of ever-dwindling resources on my home planet, such initiatives—covert or otherwise—would be plagued with difficulty."

Max's grasp of English was even better than Gardner's understanding of the Plysserian's native language, thanks to a wondrous translator device the alien had shown him during their first encounter. A band worn around the head, it interfaced directly with the wearer's brain, accelerating cognitive functions with respect to speech and language. Gardner had no clue how it worked, but had come to rely on the device as an unparalleled communications and learning tool.

Gardner had heard some variation of Max's explanation more than once. In short, the only reason Chodrecai forces did not keep pouring through countless portal locations across the world was the simple fact that Gray personnel and equipment, already stretched thin after the protracted war on their own world, were not sufficient to expand the campaign to Earth for any extended period. Chodrecai leaders had gambled on a massive three-pronged attack, targeting Moscow, Beijing, and Washington, D.C., in the hope of crippling three of Earth's major military powers. Only fortunate happenstance had made it possible for sympathizers on *Jontashreena* to get information about the coming assaults, providing just enough time for American, Russian, and Chinese forces—working in concert with Blue allies—to ready a counteroffensive. Though the Chodrecai campaign had failed, the battle had been costly for all sides. Forces on Earth were still recovering and attempting to prepare for what many experts believed would be a renewed campaign.

And who the hell knows what the Grays are really doing?

"This is the fifth instance of a portal opening in three weeks," Gardner said after a moment, "and the third one we've been able to confirm is due to Gray activity. I think it's safe to say they're on the move again."

Owens nodded. "If they're not ready to kick in the door, they're at least sniffing around."

Pausing a moment as though attempting to decipher the Marine's words, Max finally replied, "Agreed. We should pass this information on to your superiors and mine as well. I believe any respite we may have enjoyed to this point is coming to an end, and we still have many preparations to make."

"I'll see about getting us transport," Owens said. Looking to Gardner, he added, "Take another sweep, see if there's anything worth taking with us. Otherwise, we're out of here in fifteen minutes."

"Aye, aye, Gunny," Gardner said, shifting the pulse rifle so that it rested more comfortably in the crook of his right arm. The weight of the weapon now seeming more pronounced to him.

"I knew it," he mused aloud, releasing a small, humorless grunt.

"I do not understand," Max said, regarding him with what Gardner had long ago learned to recognize as an expression of confusion. "Something amuses you?"

Shaking his head, Gardner sighed. "It was all too good to last."

2

"You'd better quit eyeballing me, recruit! Head and eyes straight to the front!"

Colin Laney felt flecks of spittle on his face as the drill instructor, a lean, muscled Latino man introduced mere moments ago as Staff Sergeant Medina, screamed at him from a distance of less than twelve inches. The Marine's head, replete with the olive drab hat—"cover," as Laney and the other recruits had been instructed to call any and all headgear that was not a helmet—filled Colin's vision. Indeed, the cover's wide brim was so close it nearly rested on the bridge of Colin's nose. Despite his best effort, he was unable to keep from flinching as the drill instructor leaned even closer.

"Get your boots and get on line now!"

Even as Colin turned toward the mass of clothing and assorted items he had been forced to dump onto his bed, and reached for the two pairs of combat boots he had been issued two days earlier, Medina was behind him, the man's voice thundering off the cinder-block walls of the barracks. "Any day, recruit. *Any day!*"

Mindful to avoid actually running into the drill instructor as he grasped a pair of brown suede combat boots in each hand, Colin scrambled back to stand in front of the two-tiered bunk bed. Glancing down, he made sure the heels of his tennis shoes were on the edge of the inch-wide black line painted on the maroon-colored concrete floor and running the length of the barracks. He locked his body into what he hoped was a position of attention, mimicking the actions of other recruits who likewise had retrieved their boots and returned as ordered to their position in line. Across the ten-foot-wide aisle separating the rows of bunks behind him from those in front of him, another recruit whose name Colin could not remember stared back at him, his eyes wide with fear as he held out his arms and displayed two similar pairs of military-issue footwear. Looking at the other man—a boy, really, just like him—was almost like staring into a mirror: pale, shaved head, combat utility uniform that did not appear to fit quite right, white running shoes sticking out from beneath the cuffs of the uniform pants. Colin and his fellow recruits, fifty-seven men varying in age from eighteen to thirty-one, represented a variety of ethnic and socioeconomic backgrounds to be found east of the Mississippi River. Until their graduation from boot camp, they would be known collectively as Platoon 3003. They had been together for nearly three days and had not yet even had the chance to wear their boots.

"Hold 'em out!" a voice from his left boomed through the squad bay, a voice that Colin now knew belonged to his platoon's senior drill instructor, Staff Sergeant Blyzen. Like the other recruits, Colin extended his arms in front of him, the boots dangling from his hands. He tried not to tremble as Medina and another drill instructor moved down the center aisle, which had been deemed off-limits to recruits except upon explicit instructions to the contrary. The Marines' eyes darted from recruit to recruit, checking to see that each was in possession of two pairs of boots.

Colin nearly flinched as he saw, somewhere to his right at the edge of his peripheral vision, Medina turn to a recruit and scream at the luckless target about not holding his arms high enough.

"Stow them in your seabag, now. Move," said Blyzen, and Colin and his companions turned to shove the footwear into one of the two drab green duffel bags they each had received, along with the rest of their uniforms and assorted hygiene items, on their first morning as Marine recruits. With the frenetic pace of the past two days, this actually was the first real opportunity to see most of what they had been given. Almost all of it was green or possessed a pixelated camouflage pattern.

Colin returned to his place on line. It was the fifth or sixth iteration of the exercise, and already he could feel sweat on his head. The urge to wipe it away was all but overpowering, but Colin remained frozen in place.

What the hell am I doing here?

He had volunteered, of course.

During those first weeks after the failed Chodrecai offensive, citizens around the world had listened to statements from government leaders vowing retribution for the attacks, and the calls for able-bodied men and women to volunteer for service in order to face the global threat. In the beginning, media pundits had voiced concerns that American citizens might well reject such measures, given the prolonged conflicts in Iraq and Afghanistan and the costs they had incurred. In addition to indignation over the monetary expenditures that had taken a toll on the country's economy, there was widespread belief among a significant percentage of the population that an unwritten code of trust had been violated between the government and the country's armed services.

Supporting the ongoing operations had required the involuntary extensions of enlistment contracts, a legal yet unpopular measure levied against an all-volunteer military in the face of wars that many found unnecessary and even illegal. Further, the protracted use of reserve forces called to active duty had caused no small amount of strife, with reservists serving their second or even third tours in a combat zone. If they were lucky enough to come home uninjured or, more commonly, suffering from wounds that might heal in time, they returned to find their jobs eliminated as part of rampant downsizing and outsourcing of jobs to overseas locations. The military struggled to meet recruiting quotas because citizens, customarily vocal about "supporting the troops," had long since tired of wars that—in theory, at least—should have ended in short order. As the years dragged on and casualty counts mounted, and the reasons for those wars seemed to shift with the tides, the American people lost patience with the apparent lack of progress. Even the near total turnover of the American government following the most recent presidential and congressional elections did not seem to bring answers for ending the country's involvement in the conflicts.

Much of that changed the day the aliens arrived.

While it was unreasonable to say that all past sins were forgiven in the interests of uniting against a common foe, the Chodrecai threat did indeed have the effect of motivating many nations on Earth to set aside—for a time, at least—their various differences. Those governments that chose to concentrate on their own agendas soon found themselves marginalized as countries around the world pooled and exchanged resources in order to prepare to fight the alien invaders. Not since the Second World War had such effort been expended for so singular a purpose.

Though the dangers facing the planet had brought an influx of volunteers to military recruiting and induction offices around the world, experts believed that more were needed. Governments either reinstated or instigated military conscription policies. Colin had received a draft notice for the United States Army in his mail while attending college three weeks ago at the University of South Florida, but after discussing the matter with his father at the family home in Tampa, he had elected to withdraw from his studies and instead make his way to a Marine Corps recruiting office near the university campus. It was there that he learned the true scope of the call-up. Here in the United States, all men and women between the ages of eighteen and forty were being summoned for initial screenings. Those deemed unsuitable for the rigors of combat were reviewed for their ability to act in other areas—logistical support, communications and computers, mechanical and medical services, to name but a few. Still others, determined to be unsuitable for military service, were directed to the civil service and one of the myriad jobs that were being ramped up in order to support the war effort.

What had followed Colin's first visit to the recruiting office was a whirlwind of tests and paperwork, much of which—according to the recruiter—was being carried out at an even faster pace than at the height of the wars in Iraq and Afghanistan. Colin had already heard in the news that training cycles for new recruits were being accelerated. In the case of the Marine Corps, the normal fourteen-week boot camp cycle had been cut in half, the unspoken yet understood truth being that most of the newer recruits were little more than cannon fodder for the escalating conflict with the Chodrecai. Those surviving long enough after initial indoctrination would receive advanced training as time and resources permitted. As he stood in the squad bay, much like his grandfather had done in the aftermath of the attack on Pearl Harbor, Colin wondered about his place in the world he was about to enter, and how long he might occupy that position in the face of forces far beyond his control.

Though the first two nights at Parris Island had been hectic, they paled in comparison to what had transpired in only the first moments with the trio of drill instructors that would oversee Platoon 3003's training for the next three months. Introduced by First Lieutenant Ferris, an officer who had identified himself as their "series commander" and overseeing platoons 3000 through 3003, Staff Sergeant Blyzen had in turn presented Staff Sergeant Medina and 3003's third drill instructor, a scowling African-American man named Sergeant Stevens. Then, as Blyzen stood at one end of the squad bay, arms clasped behind his back and maintaining an unwavering military pose, he had unleashed the other two Marines on the platoon with a simple directive.

"Get 'em."

In response to that command, Medina and Stevens had bolted into action, wading into the gathered platoon and plunging the room into utter chaos. How long had it been going on? Several minutes, Colin guessed, though no clocks were in his line of sight. As for his wristwatch, it currently resided in a small blue satchel—a "money and valuables" bag—resting in the large cargo pocket along his right pants leg. The bag contained those few personal possessions he had been allowed to keep upon his arrival at I (for "India") Company, Third Recruit Training Battalion, Marine Corps Recruit Depot, located in humid Parris Island, South Carolina.

Colin had expected something like this, mostly due

to re-creations of similar scenes in movies. Unlike those fictional representations of drill instructors with their screaming and spitting and bug-eyed madness as they verbally and physically assaulted the men in their charge, these Marines had yet to utter a single profanity. Likewise, they had not laid so much as a finger on any of the recruits, except as a means of delivering instruction such as in the proper positioning of feet or arms while standing at attention.

"Show me six green T-shirts," Blyzen ordered, his voice once more carrying the length of the squad bay. "One in each hand, one across each arm, one on each shoulder. Do it now."

Once more, momentary calm disintegrated in a blur of frantic movements as the platoon scrambled to carry out the new order. Even as he reached into the mound of clothing and other flotsam in search of the required items, Colin saw Medina and Stevens swarming toward one hapless recruit. Thankful that he was not the subject of their ire on this occasion, he pulled six olive drab undershirts from his pile and returned to his place on line, and as he did so he caught sight of two figures standing at the end of the squad bay, behind and to the right of Staff Sergeant Blyzen.

Holy shit. The thought echoed in Colin's mind. *It's one of them.*

The alien stood nearly two heads taller than the officer next to it, with wide shoulders and a massive chest threatening to burst from the dark formfitting garment it wore. Colin recognized the creature as a Plysserian from the numerous pictures and video footage he had seen on television and in magazines and on the Internet for months. Much of its pale gray skin was covered with an assortment of unrecognizable patterns and shapes rendered in dark ink. Its garment was devoid of any insignia, but Colin knew that the clothing was meant to be the alien's version of a uniform.

Why's he here?

Colin knew that militaries around the world had allied with Plysserian forces, such pacts being a primary reason that Earth had been able to repel the massive three-pronged assault launched by the Chodrecai six months earlier. Since that time, Plysserian military units had been working with their human counterparts, augmenting training, weapons, and other technology for the next major offensive many believed was coming sooner rather than later. Did the lone Plysserian's presence here, now, mean that such enhancements had already been made to Marine recruit training? That would make sense, Colin decided, given what he had heard about the focus of military preparations in the months since that last costly battle.

"What are you staring at, recruit?"

The question, screamed into his left ear, had come a mere heartbeat after Colin had detected movement from the corner of his eye. Sergeant Stevens had moved with catlike grace across the squad bay to home in on him like a missile finding its target. Unable to help himself, Colin cringed in response to the drill instructor's query, all but cowering from the man as Stevens closed the distance, his long index finger poised directly before Colin's eyes.

"Get on line now!"

Arranging the T-shirts in the fashion prescribed by Blyzen and following the example of the recruits across the aisle from him, Colin locked his elbows at his sides and draped one shirt over each arm. With a shirt on each shoulder, he held the remaining two in his hands as Medina and Stevens repeated the process of verifying that each recruit had followed instructions.

"Stow them in your seabag now. Move," Blyzen barked, the command issued with the Marine's customary crisp efficiency. The platoon carried out the order and returned to the line, and as he took his place Colin detected movement on his left and heard the sound of the heavy metal door opening at the squad bay's far end. An instant later, Blyzen's voice thundered through the room. "Attention on deck!" There was a verbal exchange that Colin could not hear before Blyzen turned once more to face the assembled platoon. "Eyeballs."

"Snap, sir!" each recruit shouted in unison, turning their heads as earlier instructed toward Blyzen, who promptly frowned in disapproval at the reaction to his order.

"You'd better stop whispering," he retorted, his face a mask of disgust. "Get 'em back." He waited until each recruit returned his head and eyes to face forward, then with a louder voice added, "Eyeballs!"

"*Snap, sir!*" When the platoon responded this time, Colin was sure the windows of the squad bay rattled in their frames.

Satisfied, at least for the moment, Blyzen said, "Listen up. The company commander wants to talk to you." Stepping to his left, the senior drill instructor assumed a position of parade rest as the officer, a man dressed in an impeccably tailored green uniform, moved to where Blyzen had been standing. He had removed his cover, revealing a nearly bald head save for a patch of closely cropped blond hair, the "high and tight" style affected by nearly every Marine Colin had encountered. Over the man's left breast pocket were rows of brightly colored ribbons, silent testaments to an impressive military career. To Colin, the man represented everything the Marine Corps preached about—how it transformed children into adults and forged warriors from civilian flotsam. It was because of men such as this that Colin—like his grandfather before him—had opted for the Marines rather than answering his original Army draft notice.

In a deep, imposing voice, the officer said, "My name is Captain Gannon, India Company commander, and on behalf of the commanding general, I welcome each of you to the Marine Corps Recruit Depot, Parris Island. You now stand where thousands of Marines before you have stood. Many of those same Marines sacrificed their lives in service to our Corps and our country. If you successfully complete the training you are about to undertake, you will enter a brotherhood that has existed for more than two centuries—an elite fraternity unlike any other in the history of the world. You will have earned the right to be called a Marine."

As he spoke, Gannon began to pace the length of the squad bay, his eyes meeting those of each recruit as he walked past. "Now, you and many more men and women just like you are being called upon to do the same, not simply for the United States, but for this entire planet. A year ago, we may have sent many of you to Iraq or Afghanistan, but the world's changed. The conflicts we waged with those who might intend harm to our country have become insignificant. The enemy we face is not interested in political or religious ideology. They care about one thing: this planet and the resources it offers, in order to rebuild a world they destroyed through generations of war."

Gannon spoke with a conviction that led Colin to believe the man had seen action against the Chodrecai. In the time since the alien threat first became known, skirmishes and battles of varying size and scope had unfolded across the world. Many of those encounters had played out on live television or the Internet, narrated by journalists traveling with combat units and representing news organizations from countries around the globe. The specter of war now was a daily occurrence, an unshakable reality from which there seemed to be no escape.

"As was proven six months ago," Gannon said as he turned and began to march back up the center aisle, "the people already living on this planet had something to say about that. We still have a lot to say about that, but the simple truth is that we cannot do it without men and women like you. What I require from each of you is your utter commitment to your training. It will be hard—as unforgiving as anything you have ever attempted. It will tax your body and your mind to their limits, and once you have reached those limits, you will be pushed even further. Do not give up on yourself, and we will not give up on you. If you do as you're told, if you follow the orders put to you by your drill instructors and other Marines charged with training you, if you give one hundred percent of yourself, then you will succeed."

Colin, like everyone else in the room, tracked the captain's movements until Gannon once again stood at the front of the squad bay, staring back at them with an expression that seemed to challenge each of them to rise to the trials they soon would face. "There are those who believe that a war with the Chodrecai is one we cannot win, that it will be over before you complete your training here. Those people are wrong. We will fight this threat. We *are fighting* this threat, not only the militaries of this world but also with the assistance of our friends, the Plysserians."

Turning, Gannon indicated the alien standing behind him. "This is *Zolitar* Teqotev. *Zolitar* is a rank designation, comparable to that of sergeant. Teqotev and other Plysserian soldiers will be working with your drill instructors. To date, seven platoons of Marine recruits have trained alongside Plysserian soldiers. We have been adapting their weap-

onry and other technology. We have infused our training
with knowledge they've shared with us. Platoon 3003 will
be the eighth such unit."

It required physical effort for Colin to keep his slackening jaw from falling open. *Oh, my God. What the hell have
I gotten myself into?*

3

If there was one thing Bruce Thompson hated about being a general, it was the umbilical cord connecting his office to whichever concentric circle of Hell generated the endless, knotted streams of red tape. It consumed his days, along with many of his nights, and for every bit he hacked away, more stood ready to take its place.

Slumping in his high-backed black leather office chair, Thompson gazed across the chaotic mass of folders, binders, loose papers, and other detritus littering what was once the polished surface of his wide mahogany desk. Pushing away from the mess only seemed to make it seem larger than it already was, and Thompson was almost certain that the administrative flotsam might actually be reproducing every time he looked away.

Don't I have people to handle this crap? RHIP? Rank Hath Its goddamned Paperwork.

As if on cue, the intercom light on his phone flashed a bright, blinking green, accompanied by a single tone and the voice of his aide, Sergeant Amanda Carter. "General, Nancy Spencer is here to see you."

Thompson sighed as he glanced at his wristwatch and took note of the unholy hour, certain he knew at least the broad reasons for one of his most trusted assistants to be visiting him so early in the morning. "Send her in."

A moment later the door opened to reveal an attractive woman in her early forties, wearing a gray pantsuit over a pale blue silk blouse. Not for the first time, Thompson noted the odd strands of gray that had begun to intrude on her otherwise shiny brown hair. Had she allowed it to hang free, her hair might have reached the middle of her back, but instead it was held in a ponytail. Thompson also noticed the puffiness under Spencer's eyes, a testament to the long hours she and everyone else from Thompson on down had been working for longer than he could easily remember.

"Good morning," she said, closing the door behind her. In her left hand she carried a red file folder, while her right hand cradled her omnipresent cellular phone. Thompson smiled as he caught sight of the phone, which doubled as a personal digital assistant with access to e-mail and the Internet as well as the Pentagon's secure intranet. He had long ago come to think of the gadget as an extension of Spencer's body, and although he had joked with her about it early on in their relationship, there could be no arguing the effective use to which she put the device as she carried out her numerous, demanding duties.

Seeing the red folder, Thompson sighed. Red was the color designated for reports and other information dealing with alien contact. That particular hue had been all but neglected for the first several years of his tenure as commanding officer of United States Space Command, Operations Section 04-E — referred to colloquially as "4-Echo" — but such was definitely not the case these days. "What've we got?" he asked, holding out his hand and gesturing toward the folder.

"The portal in the Pacific Northwest," Spencer replied, moving without waiting for an invitation to one of the leather guest chairs positioned before Thompson's desk.

"Satellite imagery confirmed Gray activity in that area, and SR-71 recon photos picked up not only a portal generator under construction but also a sizable Gray contingent. B-2s neutralized the target, and a team swept the area but found nothing of use. Our people on the ground there are certain that the Gray unit had to have arrived from another portal opening in that area, after which they scattered into the wilderness."

Thompson nodded. It was the same story he had been hearing with increasing frequency over the past few weeks, told on each occasion with little variation, and each reaching the same conclusion: The Grays were back.

"Well," he said, rising from his chair, "it looks like our little break's almost over."

Even as he spoke the words, Thompson felt a sense of dread beginning to wash over him. In truth, he had experienced this same feeling every waking moment since that fateful afternoon when he had received a briefing about the initial encounter between a small unit of U.S. Marine reservists and a contingent of Chodrecai soldiers in southwestern Missouri. In the weeks that followed, the entire planet was plunged into near-total chaos as an increasing number of Gray military assets were transported through a still-unknown number of mysterious conduits that linked Earth with the aliens' own planet, *Jontashreena*, allowing the invaders to gain footholds around the world.

Following the failed campaign to launch simultaneous offensives against the American, Chinese, and Russian capital cities, large numbers of Gray military assets appeared to withdraw from Earth back through conduits to their home planet. Provided with a seeming reprieve of unknown duration, world powers set to the task of readying for what many believed was the inevitable return of the alien army. In short order, Thompson and his team at 4-Echo found themselves at the tip of the spear, leading the effort to see that the United States was prepared for the next chapter in what had escalated to interplanetary war.

"Nancy," he said, retrieving from his desk a coffee mug emblazoned with the Air Force logo, "have you ever wondered if the people who convinced Truman to investigate UFOs really thought we'd be where we are today?" He crossed his office to a counter set into the room's far wall, atop which sat a coffeemaker. Looking over his shoulder, he held up his mug, silently inquiring if Spencer was interested in her own cup.

Shaking her head in response to the offer, she instead replied, "I don't know if they believed it, but you've read the same files I have. They took it seriously, and given how skeptical the public was about the idea of extraterrestrials and alien invasion back in those days, that was no easy feat. I'm betting every single one of those bastards was an alcoholic by the time they quit that job."

Pausing as he lifted the steaming mug of fresh coffee to his lips, Thompson could not help smiling at the imagery Spencer's comments evoked. What must life have been like for the men and women tasked in 1947 by President Harry S Truman to form Project Sign? An exploratory group within the United States Air Force, Project Sign would grow and transform over the next six decades into the far-reaching organization that Bruce Thompson now commanded. Tasked with scrutinizing reports of alleged visits to Earth by beings or craft from other worlds, Project Sign and its string of successors also had been charged with developing procedures when encounters with extraterrestrials occurred, as well as creating contingencies in the event such contact was not deemed to be "peaceful."

4-Echo and its earlier incarnations had until recently existed almost entirely within the shadows, the notable exception being the "Blue Book" project of the 1960s. This latest iteration also had begun life as a small, covert operation hidden among other classified projects within an impenetrable maze of bureaucratic jargon, misdirection, and outright lies. All of that had changed now, with the organization being revealed to the world at the direction of the current president, in the hope of assuring a frightened public that the governments of the United States and other countries were not woefully unprepared for even this most outlandish of scenarios: war with another world. Unfortunately, such was not the case.

Not really, anyway.

"Okay," Thompson said, returning to his seat, "so that makes five new portal locations in the United States in the past three weeks."

"Six," Spencer replied, her gaze directed to the phone in her right hand. Thompson could see her thumb playing over the device's miniature white trackball as she scanned what he figured to be one of the hundreds of e-mail messages she received each day. "There was that one in Florida, but it was only a Gray scouting party, which we were able to capture within hours of their arrival."

Thompson released a single humorless chuckle as he settled into his chair, recalling the incident. "They were found wandering around the Tomorrowland area at Disney World." He shook his head, imagining what a scene that must have made. Of course, the legendary tourist attraction was closed these days, all but abandoned in the face of global panic as well as government-enforced curfews, the rationing of commodities like food and fuel, and even martial law in many of the country's larger cities. There had been an understandable outcry against the extreme measures, with fears heightened by the near-total assimilation of television and radio broadcasts by the different news outlets, which bombarded audiences with unrelenting coverage of the war and its myriad effects on every facet of human civilization. The Internet was not much better. Service was spotty in many areas, due to severed transmission lines as well as damaged or destroyed buildings in different locations around the world that once housed key systems and data storage facilities upon which the global network was dependent. Much of the equipment and bandwidth that remained had been co-opted by the government and the military, leaving precious little else from which the rest of the world might glean information. Thompson himself had no desire to see such drastic action taken, but as the president had communicated during the first of what had become nightly addresses to the American people and the rest of the world, these were not normal times. Despite the uncertainty many felt, there were reassuring lessons to be taken from recent history. Thompson remembered the stories told to him by his father of how the country had come together as America entered the Second World War, and efforts approaching that scale had been under way for months.

We're going to need all of that, he mused, trying to seek some measure of solace as he sipped his coffee, while finding none. *And more.*

"How many does that make worldwide?" Thompson asked.

Studying her phone's display again, Spencer replied, "Seventeen. In each case, the portal site was captured or destroyed. Gray personnel were either captured or killed. Of course, more soldiers were likely dispersed into the surrounding areas before the sites were taken, and those are just the portals we know about."

"It's obvious they're probing," Thompson said. "The question is: Are they just snooping around to see what we're doing, or are they reconnoitering in preparation for another major assault?"

He glanced at the computer monitor perched on the far left corner of his desk, its screen displaying the contents of his calendar for the day. As always, meetings with various 4-Echo department heads dominated the agenda, each one scheduled to provide him with the latest status reports from their section, as well as their progress with respect to finding new ways to combat the Chodrecai threat. With the capture of so many Gray soldiers as well as the recovery of weaponry and other equipment, 4-Echo's research and development division had received plenty of material for study. Plysserian military and scientific personnel were also contributing to the effort, assisting human counterparts to understand the advanced technology in order to replicate it as well as to devise defenses against it.

"Our intel reports have been sketchy from the beginning," Spencer said, allowing her hand and the phone to rest in her lap. "We know that one of the main reasons the Grays haven't launched another significant offensive is because Blue forces have kept them busy."

Though the Chodrecai offensive had inflicted damage to significant portions of Washington, D.C., Beijing, and Moscow, human and Plysserian military units had prevented the Grays from establishing footholds at any of those locations. Major damage to buildings and other property had occurred in a large area surrounding the point where the portal had opened on the National Mall, including historic structures such as the Capitol, the National Archives, and several museums. Both sides had lost significant numbers of ground troops, vehicles, and other materiel, though by all accounts the Chodrecai had fared worse from the exchange. Further, the bold gambit and the commitment of so many assets to see it carried out had also allowed beleaguered Blue forces to reclaim territory previously captured by the Grays on *Jontashreena*.

In hindsight, according to several Plysserian and human military analysts, the Chodrecai offensive had borne all the characteristics of a desperate gambit. Though the limitations of the portal technology could serve as a partial explanation for the notable lack of large-scale weaponry to support the swarms of foot soldiers sent from the alien planet, the actual attacks served only to strengthen theories that the Grays were simply running out of resources with which to fight this war. Might the addition of a new enemy—even a reluctant one, as Earth was—actually be the catalyst for finally bringing the generations-long conflict to an end?

Has a nice ring to it.

"What do we know about these Plysserian resistance groups on *Jontashreena*?" Thompson asked, swiveling his chair so he could place his feet atop the open bottom drawer on the left side of his desk. "Are they organized? What kind of numbers are we talking about?"

Spencer shook her head. "We don't know for sure. The intel we're getting suggests small, scattered groups, a mixture of civilians and renegade military, operating independently throughout Gray-occupied territory. Mostly guerrilla-style hit-and-run tactics, striking targets of opportunity and only rarely engaging Gray forces directly."

"That's what you do when you're outnumbered a hundred or a thousand to one," Thompson replied, "and all the hardware belongs to the other side." As a young pilot in Vietnam, he had seen such strategies employed by the Viet Cong to devastating effect.

"Plysserian military leaders have been attempting to make contact with some of the larger cells," Spencer said, "in the hopes of somehow getting them organized."

Releasing a dismissive grunt, Thompson countered, "That could take months. We're not going to have that kind of time."

"The Joint Chiefs are saying the same thing," Spencer said. "They're ordering stepped-up recon patrols through the portals we control, and they're accelerating plans to begin positioning personnel and assets at a series of strategic locations on *Jontashreena*."

Thompson had been expecting that, and was pleased that efforts to understand, replicate, and improve upon Plysserian portal technology would contribute to such planning. One of the drawbacks in the initial series of portals created by the Blues was the size of the conduits, which had proven too small for anything of appreciable size to traverse. The limitation had proven fortuitous, as both Blues and Grays had been prevented from sending through large numbers of military vehicles, such as their equivalents to tanks, planes, or helicopters. Such equipment was instead broken down to varying degrees, requiring reassembly upon its reaching the conduit's other end. It was during the coordinated attack against China, Russia, and the U.S. that the existence of a larger, more powerful portal generator had been revealed. That generator had nearly turned the tide of battle in favor of the Grays.

Now it's our turn.

"What about the recall beacon that group of Blue comm engineers was developing?" Thompson asked. "What's the status on that?" He had been fascinated by the preliminary reports regarding the device, which was capable of transmitting a signal from one end of a conduit to the other, using technology similar to that of the portal generators themselves, and actually supplying the signal's receiver with location information needed to establish a new portal endpoint. The tactical applications for such a gadget were obvious.

Spencer replied, "The prototype's been field-tested, with largely favorable results. There are still some bugs to work out, but it looks promising. JCS has already approved a recon mission to *Jontashreena*, where it would play a major role."

"I know about that," Thompson said, recalling the briefing memo he had read two days earlier, outlining a planned search-and-rescue mission to retrieve a Plysserian engineer from a Chodrecai prison. As one of the group responsible for its creation, the Blue scientist was believed to be one of the foremost experts on the portal generation technology.

"The knowledge this engineer is supposed to have is unmatched," Spencer said, "and no doubt the Grays are sucking him dry as they work to improve the portals they control."

Thompson nodded. "We're going to need that kind of brainpower if the plans for launching a major counteroffensive against the Grays have any hope of moving forward." He paused, reaching for his coffee. "Speaking of that, the JCS are still clamoring for the large-scale portal generators. What's the latest on those?"

Pausing to consult her PDA, Spencer replied, "Three of the six test locations are reporting successful transport tests. The problem is that the damned things use so much energy, and generate one hell of a lot of heat. They have to be powered down after only about forty-five seconds, and it takes nearly forty minutes for them to cool enough to be used again. Our people are testing new ways to deal with that, of course."

"A few minutes here and there won't be enough if we end up having to launch a full-scale offensive." Thompson recalled a book he had read, years ago, about an Army colonel who had commanded a company of soldiers during one of the earliest engagements of the Vietnam War. He and his men had been sent into a landing zone by helicopter, handfuls of soldiers at a time, against what eventually was revealed to be a numerically superior enemy force. Those men already on the ground and under fire had to wait for intervals of nearly thirty minutes for groups of reinforcements as the helicopters returned to base and picked up their companions to bring them to the fight. Unable to retreat and all but surrounded, the company held its ground for three days as casualties mounted while food, water, and ammunition dwindled to all but nothing. If personnel were deployed to the alien planet in similar fashion, the losses could well be devastating.

Fuck that. Shot down over Vietnam himself, Thompson had evaded the enemy for five days before finally being rescued. Therefore, he considered himself something of an authority on hanging your ass out in the wind while waiting for backup.

"Tell our people they need to work harder," he said, lifting his feet from the open drawer and sitting up straight in his chair. "That's not a commentary on their efforts to date," he added, seeing the expression on Spencer's face. "They've done phenomenal work so far, but if we're getting ready to send young men and women into combat on *another fucking planet*, we can't have them sitting there waiting for reinforcements because our equipment isn't up to par." Sighing, he reached up to rub the bridge of his nose. "They have to do better; it's as simple as that."

"Agreed," Spencer said, offering a single, curt nod. Then, looking at him, she asked in a softer voice, "Bruce, are you all right? Pardon my saying so, but you look like hell."

Chuckling, Thompson nodded. "I need a vacation. We all do."

"Is that an invitation?"

When she said nothing else, Thompson lowered his hand and regarded her. Nancy Spencer had been a valuable member of his staff even before the aliens' arrival. Since then, she had become indispensable. His respect for her professional abilities came without reservation or qualification; he could think of no one else he would rather have at his side during these trying times.

As for anything further, was there something there? Was he so blind, so buried in the work, that he had failed to see Spencer as anything other than a colleague?

"Maybe so," he finally said, allowing himself a smile before releasing a small sigh. The past several months had taken a toll on them all. For Thompson, this was the latest in a string of conflicts in which he had participated throughout his career, from Vietnam to Desert Storm to the conflicts in Iraq and Afghanistan. This war was on a scale surpassing anything the civilized world had ever seen, but for Thompson himself it was different in a smaller, far more personal sense; it was the first war in which he had fought where his wife, Nicole, was not at home waiting for him. Taken by cancer nearly seven years earlier, she had been his emotional rock throughout the three decades they had shared.

"You still miss her, don't you?"

Spencer's words broke through his reverie, and only then did Thompson realize he was staring at Nicole's photograph, perched in a cherrywood frame next to his computer monitor. Offering a weak smile, he nodded. "Every day." He had never remarried, had never so much as dated since her death. For much of that time, he had simply immersed himself in his work. Only now, as he and everyone else on Earth faced the possibility that their days might truly be numbered, could Bruce Thompson admit that while he always had acknowledged his wife's absence, he had until now never felt *alone*.

If you're up there, he mused, *I hope you're putting in a good word with the Big Guy on our behalf, because we're going to need all the damned help we can get.*

4

The shouts of alarm came as they always did, an instant before the first shots of automatic weapons fire, jolting Private First Class Simon DiCarlo from fitful slumber. Rising from the makeshift bed he had fashioned from his poncho and backpack, he adjusted his helmet and laid the barrel of his M16 atop the parapet of sandbags ringing his fighting hole.

"Son of a fucking bitch, D," hissed his companion, Lance Corporal Mike Bundy, his eyes wide with fear and his Tennessee drawl thickening with every word. "Fuckin' Charlie's fuckin' comin'. They're fucking *everywhere*."

Ahead of him, twenty or thirty meters into the jungle, DiCarlo saw light flickering through the trees, flares triggered by trip wires. Silhouetted by the fading illumination were slight, shadowy figures, darting from tree to tree and using the underbrush for cover as they advanced on the platoon's firebase. From his left came the staccato bursts of the M60 machine gun manned by PFC Tony Robinson, the new kid from Detroit who had been given the unenviable task of humping the heavy weapon while on patrol. Harsh orange streaks lanced from Robinson's hole into the jungle, tracer fire accompanying the machine gun's regular 7.62-millimeter ammo. Lighter, higher-pitched reports from various M16s to either side of DiCarlo joined in the fight, the rounds they fired tearing through the thick foliage in search of targets. His finger tightening on the trigger of his own rifle, DiCarlo peered down the weapon's length, looking for the enemy.

At the same time, he pissed his pants, commemorating his first firefight.

A figure emerged from behind a tree less than ten meters in front of DiCarlo, charging in his direction. His hands trembling, DiCarlo aimed his M16 at the approaching soldier and fired, his finger crushing the trigger as round after round exploded from the weapon. The first three or four shots missed, but the next four to six found their target, stitching across Charlie's chest. One round found his head, snapping it back as his body went limp and collapsed to the ground.

"Don't waste your fuckin' ammo, man!" Bundy shouted between shots of his own. "Pick your fucking target and put the motherfucker down!" He punctuated his point by firing again, followed as quickly by three more single shots.

His breath coming in deep, rapid gasps, DiCarlo forced himself to listen to Bundy's words, flipping the M16's selector switch to semiautomatic mode before taking aim at another Vietnamese soldier who chose that moment to emerge from the trees. Dressed in dark, loose clothing, Charlie was all but concealed by the shadows until he stepped forward into the feeble yellowish light cast by another tripped flare. He was hunched over, trying to make himself less of a target as he traversed the open ground, but by then DiCarlo had wrestled his breathing under control, and centered his rifle's front sight on the enemy soldier's chest. DiCarlo pulled the trigger and the other man jerked, stumbling and falling to his knees. He used one hand to keep himself from slumping to the ground, and DiCarlo's second shot took him in the face.

To his left, Bundy grunted, his breath expelling like air from a punctured tire as he dropped his rifle and reached with both hands for his chest. He staggered away from the parapet, stumbling over the pair of backpacks and falling to the ground, grimacing in pain. In the dim light, DiCarlo could see something dark moving around and over Bundy's fingers, staining them and his faded green camouflage jacket. Blood.

"Mike!" DiCarlo shouted, worried about the friend he had known for less than a week but unable to help him as still more enemy soldiers approached from the jungle. He saw three this time, all of them heading toward him, and DiCarlo fired at the closest one. Two bullets tore into the man's abdomen and he went down, followed by the man next to him as DiCarlo caught him with a head shot. As he pressed the trigger one more time, he heard the unwelcome sound of the M16's bolt locking to the rear. The weapon was empty.

Motherfucker!

He fumbled for the button to drop the rifle's spent magazine, but an earsplitting shriek halted his movements. At the same instant a figure blotted out what little light remained from the distant flares. DiCarlo caught sight of the AK-47's muzzle less than a meter from his face and swung his rifle, its barrel knocking aside the other weapon just as Charlie fired. The crack of the shot at this range was deafening but DiCarlo ignored it, bringing around his still-empty M16 and trying to hit the Vietnamese man's leg. The son of a bitch dodged the strike, jumping down into the fighting hole. DiCarlo saw the bayonet affixed to the rifle's barrel just in time to avoid having it jammed into his gut. He sidestepped the attack, nearly stumbling over Bundy in his attempt to gain some maneuvering room.

The Cong soldier howled in rage as he pulled back

the AK and tried again, but this time DiCarlo was ready, dropping his useless rifle and lunging at the other man. His hands found the soldier's throat at the same time that he butted the man's head with his helmet. A cry of pain echoed in the hole's narrow confines, but DiCarlo hit him again, driving forward with his head and slamming the crown of his helmet into the Cong's nose. DiCarlo howled in primal fear, one fist beating the other man's head as he fought to keep his other hand on Charlie's throat, digging into the soft skin with his fingers. Looking up, he locked eyes with the other man, seeing the hatred in the enemy soldier's eyes. The Cong reached for DiCarlo, his small hands finding no purchase as DiCarlo once more smashed him in the face with his helmet.

Then Charlie shifted. His light brown skin faded to a mottled gray, and his body stretched and grew, the loose pajama-like clothing replaced by formfitting body armor covering muscled arms and legs. His face contorted, twisting and broadening as his ears and bloody, broken nose seemed to recede into his skull. When the Cong opened his wide mouth, DiCarlo saw rows of jagged, sharp teeth, like those of a shark. The soldier reached for him again, and this time large, strong hands found DiCarlo's own throat. The gray monstrosity leaned closer, and DiCarlo felt its hot breath on his skin before the thing opened its mouth again.

Sergeant Major Simon DiCarlo jerked awake, muscles tensing and his heart hammering in his chest as he sat upright. Looking around, he saw no Viet Cong or Chodrecai soldiers. There was no jungle here, of course; instead, he saw only the familiar rock walls of the cave that served as his temporary home.

Forcing himself to inhale slowly and deeply, DiCarlo brought his ragged breathing under control. The cave's cool air chilled the perspiration on his back and chest, and he looked down to see goose pimples across his exposed skin.

"Bad dream?"

The voice, warm and soothing, was enough to ease DiCarlo's anxiety, and he slumped back down to the thick pad and collection of heavy woven blankets that formed the makeshift bed. To his right, his companion in the bed rose just enough to support herself on her left elbow and looked down at him.

"What was it?" asked Belinda Russell, and thanks to the soft light of a crude candle situated atop a crate a few meters away, DiCarlo could see the young woman's delicate ebony features darkened by an expression of concern. Reaching out with her right hand, Russell stroked the side of his face. He felt her fingers move across the beard that had covered his chin for the past several months.

Exhaling audibly, DiCarlo replied, "It was damned weird, that's what it was." He described to her the same dream he had experienced at irregular intervals for more than thirty years, since not long after the night on which that original firefight had taken place.

"It's always the same," he said. "I dream it almost exactly as it happened, though I always wake up before . . ." He paused, his mouth suddenly feeling dry. "Before I kill the guy." As he had countless times since that night, DiCarlo recalled the final moments of the brutal fight in that dark, dank hole, flinching as he did every time he remembered the sound of the Cong screaming and the blade of his combat knife plunging into the other man's stomach.

"Only this time was different," he added after a moment, highlighting for Russell the dream's new twist. "That's the first time I've dreamed about fighting a Gray, which, when you think about it, is pretty odd by itself, all things considered." He looked around the low-ceilinged cave, itself little more than a small alcove branching from a wider tunnel that connected a series of caverns. Above them was what had been identified to him by Plysserian soldiers as the *Margolitruul* mountain range. It was one of the prominent geographical features of the *Galotreapiq* continent's south-western region, providing thousands of square miles of terrain in which to hide. This was fortunate, as a considerable portion of the area—which, like the rest of the continent, had been home to the Plysscrian people for uncounted generations—was actually Chodrecai-occupied territory.

Living on an alien planet, DiCarlo mused. No matter how many times he considered that simple, blunt statement, and given all he had experienced during the months he and Russell had spent here, there were times when accepting this reality seemed like nothing but the very notion of insanity.

Moving her hand from the side of his face, Russell rested her open palm on DiCarlo's chest, her fingers playing with the fine, dark hair they found there. "What are you thinking?" she asked after a moment.

DiCarlo shrugged. "Same thing I think about every day: I wonder what's going on back home." He reached up and ran a hand over his head, feeling the long strands of gray-streaked black hair there. Like his beard, his hair also had grown out, now almost as long as it had been the summer prior to his reporting for boot camp a lifetime ago. Without a razor or scissors here, grooming had become something of a challenge in the months since his and Russell's arrival. Her hair, once straight and styled short, also had grown, returning to her natural curls.

Had it really been the better part of a year since he, Russell, and a Plysserian soldier named Kel had arrived on *Jontashreena*? Had it been that long since his unit of active and reserve Marines, while training at Camp Growding, a National Guard base near Neosho, Missouri, had encountered the Plysserians and their enemies, the Chodrecai? Following a brutal initial skirmish with the Grays at the compound where the Marines had made their base of operations—an encounter that had caused several casualties, including the officer in command of the unit—DiCarlo had taken charge if the situation, aided by a group of Plysserian soldiers who allied with the Marines.

Russell, a reservist with a communications occupational specialty, along with her team had discovered that certain radio frequencies had some form of debilitating effect on the aliens' weaponry and other technology. This revelation offered a meager advantage when it was decided they would attack an encampment harboring a portal opening, the one used by Chodrecai soldiers to travel to Earth. A contingent of Grays was fortifying its position in order to facilitate the transfer of weapons and equipment through the conduit. DiCarlo and his Marines, with the welcome assistance of a mysterious federal agent named Nichols, who had arrived via a black helicopter on orders from the Pentagon, attacked the compound, with DiCarlo and Russell maneuvering into position a supply truck laden with comm gear. The goal was to disable Gray weapons while the Marines and their Blue allies overwhelmed the enemy camp. DiCarlo had driven the truck into the portal, apparently disrupting the bizarre energy field before DiCarlo, Russell, and Kel were transported to *Jontashreena*.

Once here, they soon linked up with Javoquek, a Plysserian military officer operating with his unit behind enemy lines and doing his level best to disrupt the Chodrecai military. DiCarlo and Russell had fought alongside Kel and Javoquek's unit during a successful quashing of the Grays' attack on Washington, D.C., before retreating with their

Plysserian friends so that they might regroup to fight another day. What had followed were long stretches of little activity, during which the two Marines learned as much as they could about Plysserian and Chodrecai culture, and the truth behind the war that had consumed both societies for generations. Operating all but independently while receiving his orders from a central military authority, Javoquek moved his unit at frequent yet irregular intervals, either to engage or destroy a specified target such as a supply depot, weapons plant, or other sensitive military installation. In the time since their arrival, DiCarlo and Russell had not had the good fortune of coming across another portal generator that might offer them a way back to Earth.

"Hello?" a soft voice whispered in his ear as he felt a single finger tapping on his forehead. "Is there anybody in there?" DiCarlo smiled as Russell lay back down next to him, pressing her warm and remarkably naked body next to him.

"Sorry," he replied, wrapping his arm around her so that his right hand rested on the small of her back. "You know what's weird?" he asked after a moment. "While I wonder what's going on back there, I don't really *miss* anything, or anyone." He pulled her closer to him. "Of course, having you here makes up for a lot of that."

"I have that effect on men," Russell said, kissing his neck as her hand stroked his stomach.

Divorced years ago, his marriage yet another casualty of the long separations that come with military life, DiCarlo had not been in any kind of serious romantic relationship for years. Whether as a result of simple attraction or perhaps because of their odd circumstances—they were the only representatives of their species on this strange world—he and Russell had found solace in each other, their bond deepening with the passing months. Several years younger than DiCarlo, Belinda Russell was as self-assured as any woman he had ever known, a list that included his former wife. Her passion for literature and writing had been the topic of many late-night conversations. DiCarlo was no slouch when it came to reading, and if he had any regrets about being cut off from Earth, it was that he had not had the foresight to pack a few books for the trip. Still, he was no match for Russell in her command of the subject, be it classic literature or modern pulp fiction, including the science fiction stories she loved to read as well as write. For these and many other reasons, he was captivated by her.

And she's going to kill me, he mused as he felt her lips on his chest and her hand moving from his stomach toward other, more sensitive areas. If anything matched Belinda Russell's enthusiasm for the written word, it was her zest for what she called "morning calisthenics." *There are worse ways to go*, he conceded, rolling toward her and pushing her onto her back, his lips finding hers as his own hands began to wander over her body.

"DiCarlo. Russell."

Regarding each other with mixed expressions of amusement and irritation as they recognized the voice, they both looked in the direction of the heavy woven blanket that acted as a sort of privacy screen across the entrance to their alcove.

"Kel?" DiCarlo asked, rolling to his feet as Russell pulled up the blanket to cover herself while he pulled on the trousers he had made a few weeks earlier from a spare blanket, using a crude sewing needle he had fashioned from a piece of scrap metal. "What is it?"

The blanket across the entryway moved aside, and Kel's oversized head appeared. DiCarlo saw his reflection in the Blue's bulbous, black oval eyes. The two had met very soon after the group of Plysserians allied themselves with the Marine reservists in Missouri during those first, frantic days. In the weeks and months following their arrival on *Jontashreena*, the Blue soldier had proven himself to be a valuable ally and loyal friend.

The thin line of Kel's mouth barely moved as he replied, "Javoquek has asked to see you. He has received orders, and there also has been an interesting development he thinks you will want to see."

Sighing, DiCarlo turned to look at Russell, who still lay on the bed, the blanket covering everything below her bare shoulders. Her eyes narrowed in mock irritation, but she nodded.

"I'll be right there," she said. After a moment spent with no one moving, she nodded toward Kel and added, "In a minute, you know."

From the entryway, Kel replied, "I would have thought you would realize by now that I find nothing attractive about human females, nude or otherwise."

"You don't know what you're missing," DiCarlo countered.

"Out," Russell snapped, "before I shoot you both."

Having gained some understanding of the human concept of humor from his exposure to DiCarlo and Russell, Kel immediately withdrew, disappearing behind the privacy curtain. Chuckling at that, DiCarlo reached for his well-worn combat boots as Russell threw aside the blanket and retrieved her own clothes.

"Time to get back to work, I suppose," he said, already wondering what Javoquek might have in store for them, as well as his unit. Smiling at Russell, he asked, "Rain check?"

Pulling on an oversized dark shirt made from a burlap-like material, Russell stuck her head through the neck opening and leveled a mocking yet determined glare at him. "Absolutely," she said, her smile lingering in his thoughts as he turned and left.

The last thing DiCarlo expected to see upon entering Javoquek's command post was another human, let alone two of them.

"What the hell?" he asked, taking in the surprising sight of two men, both dressed in similar stark black combat utility uniforms, over which they wore matching equipment vests and harnesses. They carried M4 carbine assault rifles, each equipped with grenade launcher and infrared scope, slung over their shoulders. One man was Latino, the other was light-skinned. Their hair was short, indicating to DiCarlo that they were military, though probably not Marines. Neither of their uniforms bore any name tapes, rank, or service insignia. The Latino man, obviously the leader, stepped forward, extending his hand in greeting. He was a head shorter than his companion and perhaps eight to ten years younger, but to DiCarlo he looked capable of bench-pressing a decent-sized car.

"Sergeant Major DiCarlo," he said, "I'm Lieutenant Michael Gutierrez. We've been looking for you."

Taking the proffered hand, DiCarlo could not help smiling. "Good to meet you, Lieutenant. With all due respect, sir, you certainly took your damned time about it."

"Couldn't find a cab," Gutierrez replied, returning the grin. He nodded to his companion. "This is Sergeant First

Class Marty Sloane. He's saved my ass more than a few times over the years, and I've learned to never leave home without him. They don't come any better than him, and he has the spurs to prove it."

His eyes narrowing at the remark, DiCarlo regarded Sloane. "Cavalry scout?"

The sergeant nodded. "Roger that, Sergeant Major, though a lot of that was a long time ago."

Handshakes were exchanged before Gutierrez said, "We're with a special section of the Pentagon—the same section that sent you Agent Nichols back in Missouri."

"General Thompson's group?" DiCarlo asked, remembering the general's name from briefings provided by the mysterious Agent Nichols, who had arrived in the hours leading up to the Marine reservists' attack on the Gray encampment in Missouri. He recalled Nichols's descriptions of the think tank Thompson commanded from somewhere in the depths of the Pentagon, and the astonishing mission to which the clandestine organization was assigned. It was this group—acting on intelligence reports DiCarlo and Russell had helped to provide—that had spearheaded the response to the massive coordinated attacks on Washington, D.C., Beijing, and Moscow six months earlier.

Gutierrez replied, "That's him. As you can imagine, he and his people have been rather busy these past months."

From where he stood near the high bench that served as his worktable, *Malitul* Javoquek said, "They were found by one of our security patrols, though I still do not fully understand how they managed even to arrive in our general vicinity."

DiCarlo watched as Gutierrez nodded toward Javoquek, his expression one of respect. "Your grasp of our language is impressive, sir."

Releasing a small grunt, which DiCarlo knew was Javo-quck's way of expressing humor, the Blue military leader reached out to his worktable and held up a dull-metallic band. It consisted of a dozen rectangular components linked in a circle, each component featuring a series of inwardly protruding nodes. "Fortunately, I have benefited from technology developed by people smarter than I."

Like Kel and a few other Plysserians, Javoquek had learned to speak English, just as DiCarlo and Russell had acquired proficiency in several Plysserian languages thanks to translator headbands like the one Javoquek held. The humans had worn the bands almost constantly during their first weeks on *Jontashreena*, enduring the headaches and other discomfort that came with extended use. The won-drous devices, given to them at first by Kel and other Blues while still on Earth, had proven invaluable during the ini-tial days the Marine reservists spent acclimating themselves to the idea of visitors from another planet.

"To answer your question," Gutierrez said, "the truth is we've been trying to find you for weeks. It's taken us several recon jumps from Earth to even get close, acting on patchy and often unreliable intel we've been able to gather. Until recently, transit activity through the portals was sporadic, but it's been picking up, mostly by the Grays."

"They're on the move again?" DiCarlo asked.

It was Sloane who replied, "That's the thinking at the Pentagon, Sergeant Major. General Thompson wanted us to find you, since you've become the closest thing we've got to eyes and ears here. Your firsthand experience and insight are priceless, and the general wants to tap that for all it's worth."

Looking to Javoquek, Gutierrez added, "That goes for you and anyone in your unit, sir. You're all welcome to ac-company us back to Earth once I complete my mission."

Then, as if remembering something, the lieutenant reached for a pouch attached to his equipment vest. He opened the pouch and extracted a wrapped bundle, which he offered to DiCarlo. "General Thompson sends his regards."

Opening the parcel, DiCarlo smiled as he beheld a wondrous sight: five premium Cuban cigars, along with a box of wooden matches and a gold-plated cigar-cutter bearing the Marine Corps emblem. "The general has exceptional taste," he said, lifting one of the cigars to his nose and inhaling its aroma. His own meager supply had been depleted within days of arriving on *Jontashreena*, and his attempts to find a decent substitute made from the noxious substances Plysserians smoked had only made him ill. He had gone without smoking of any sort for months, and taking in the intoxicating scent of the fine cigar he now held felt as wonderful as the first night he had spent with . . .

"Whoa," Belinda Russell said from behind him. "Nobody said we had company."

Everyone turned to see her standing at the entrance to the command post, dressed in her worn camouflage trousers and an oversized shirt she had made from material given to her by one of Javoquek's soldiers. Over her clothing she wore her U.S. military issue web belt and suspenders, on which was arrayed an assortment of pouches. Her hair, which had grown well past her shoulders over the months, was pulled back away from her face in a functional ponytail.

"Sergeant Russell," DiCarlo said, gesturing toward the new arrivals as he placed the cigars in his uniform jacket's breast pocket, "meet Lieutenant Gutierrez and Sergeant First Class Sloane. Apparently, they've been looking for us."

Stepping forward, Russell held out her hand and shook the lieutenant's. "Glad to meet you, sir."

"Same here, Sergeant," Gutierrez replied. "As I told Sergeant Major DiCarlo, we owe you both a hell of a lot. The intel you managed to get to us before and after the attacks six months ago saved a lot of lives."

Russell said, "But we weren't able to stop the whole thing. How bad was it?"

"Pretty bad," Gutierrez answered, frowning. "We don't have exact figures or damage estimates for Moscow or Beijing, but there were hundreds of casualties on the ground in D.C., both military and civilian. They may end up rebuilding the Capitol from scratch due to all the structural issues."

Sloane added, "The area around the National Mall got the shit kicked out of it, to put it kindly. A couple of the Smithsonian museums were totaled. The exterior of the National Air and Space Museum took a pretty good beating, too. Damage to artifacts inside was minimal, but I did hear a report about a group of idiots breaking in one night and trying to make off with a model of the ship from the old *Star Trek* show."

Chuckling at the image that evoked, DiCarlo asked, "Tell me they didn't get away with that."

Sloane shook his head. "Their master plan was foiled by a nighttime security guard and a couple of soldiers from the unit sent to guard the museum."

His features returning to a more serious expression, Gutierrez said, "It could have been a lot worse, but it's still enough to keep cleanup efforts going for months, if not years. Even after the major offensive was turned back, skirmishes continued for weeks afterward. We've got a nationwide curfew in effect, and some cities are damned near in lockdown mode. The government has taken control of just about every major industry you can think of, enlisting manufacturing plants across the country to gear up for the war effort. It makes the mobilization for World War II look like the committee planning for a high school reunion."

"Given your presence here," Javoquek said, "it would seem that you have enjoyed at least some success acquiring portal technology."

"Yes, sir," Gutierrez replied. "We've taken control of nine portal generators just within the United States, with another eleven around the world. Most of them were in various stages of construction, or else were damaged during air strikes or other offensive action. We've also got Plysserian scientists working with our people to build our own generators, but it's slow going, mostly due to the massive power requirements as well as the apparent need for materials that don't exist on Earth. There's research under way to create substitutes for certain raw materials, but that won't matter if we can't find a way to adequately power the damned things." Shrugging, the lieutenant added, "That's actually why we're here."

"DiCarlo," said Javoquek, his inflection stilted as a consequence of his still incomplete grasp of English, "my superiors have tasked me with assisting Lieutenant Gutierrez to carry out his mission." Turning to the table behind him, the Plysserian reached for a small cylindrical device with a series of four bejeweled controls set into its surface. He aimed the device at an octagonal plate sitting atop the table and pressed one of the buttons, in response to which the plate's surface cast upward an expanding pale blue shaft of light. Within the conical beam appeared a three-dimensional representation of five structures standing within the confines of a perimeter wall.

"Cute toy," Sloane remarked.

"Just don't ask them to explain to you how it works," DiCarlo replied. He had been impressed by the holographic generator since first seeing it. The device could be programmed to display any geographical location merely by inputting coordinates from a map or geographical positioning system, using both archived and real-time satellite imagery along with computer graphics simulation to extrapolate details from the high-altitude pictures. Once, he had inquired about the dangers of using such a device, which required access to data transmitted from satellites, some of which might have been of a military or other classified nature. As with just about everything pertaining to computers or other high-tech gadgetry, and despite the best attempts of Russell and her Plysserian counterpart assigned to the communications team, the concepts behind the holoprojector's operation still made DiCarlo's head hurt if he thought too much about it.

"This is a Chodrecai prison facility," Javoquek explained. "It originally incarcerated civilian criminals, but in recent times its primary purpose has been modified so that it now houses political detainees as well as prisoners of war."

Gutierrez added, "For the latter category, they're usually officers, or other specialists believed to possess particular knowledge that might prove useful to the Chodrecais' ongoing war effort. According to my intel, they're holding a particularly valuable Plysserian scientist named Wysejral at this location."

"*Laepotic* Wysejral," Javoquek said, and DiCarlo caught the way the *malitul*'s eyes widened in recognition. "One of our foremost experts on portal generation technology. He was among the very first engineers to develop the concept into an operational prototype." Pausing, he nodded. "He was missing and presumed dead quite some time ago."

Gutierrez said, "Nope. Currently, he's a guest of the Grays, a situation I've been charged with alleviating. According to the higher-ups at the Pentagon, this guy's head is filled with just the info we need to fix the problems we're having with our portal generators: make them more stable, make them able to stay open longer, and allow the passage of larger equipment. Naturally, we don't want the Grays to have that info."

"Understandable," DiCarlo remarked.

Imitating one of those irritating late-night television infomercial pitchmen, the lieutenant said, "But wait, there's more! In addition to that info, our sources tell us that he also participated in the strategizing for what would've been their D-Day. That alone makes him valuable, and by all accounts, the Grays have no knowledge of his involvement in that planning. My bosses think it'd be nice if we could grab him before that situation changes, as well."

"Seems like an awful lot of trouble for one person," DiCarlo said. "No matter the knowledge he might be carrying. Must be something huge going on somewhere for you to be here like this." When Gutierrez said nothing, but instead simply regarded him with a small, knowing smile, the sergeant major nodded. "Yeah. Thought so." Even as he spoke the words, his mind began to fill with thoughts of what thousands of ground troops from Earth might look like, emerging from portals around *Jontashreena* and all possessing a single mission: Take the fight to the Chodrecai.

Jesus.

"If he's got the knowledge you say he does," Russell said, "and if the Grays have him, then it makes sense that they'd do everything they could to keep that knowledge secret."

"Indeed," Javoquek replied. "Just as it is logical for the Chodrecai to keep him at a facility like this one. It is not a high-profile installation, possessing no real value as a military target." He pointed to a large structure at the center of the base, which stood taller than the surrounding buildings. "Though the facility contains a high-security section within prison headquarters, this is a small base and as such maintains only a modest military presence. Our last reports indicate thirty to forty soldiers, and a leadership contingent of perhaps five *tilortrel*. About half of those are assigned to oversee the prison population, while the others are believed to serve in various support capacities."

"Tee-lor . . . what?" Sloane asked, frowning as he tried to repeat the Plysserian word.

Russell replied, "*Tilortrel*. It's their word for 'officers,' though as near as I can figure, it also can be used to describe high-ranking civilian personnel, as well."

"How many prisoners are we talking about?" DiCarlo asked.

"Several dozen," Gutierrez replied, "possibly as many as a hundred, though it's likely a much lower number."

DiCarlo was surprised to hear that. "So many? That seems like a lot, particularly for the number of guards we think are there."

"Chodrecai military prisons are known for their strict approach to discipline," Javoquek said. "So long as detainees obey all rules and regulations for the duration of their stay, they do not have a problem. However, and with few exceptions, the penalty for almost any infraction is death. Punishment is almost always carried out swiftly, with no chance for appeal."

"Note to self," Russell said. "Avoid Gray prisons."

Javoquek nodded. "It is advice repeatedly imparted to our soldiers during training." He gestured to the holographic image. "It is worth noting that this facility is not typical of Chodrecai military prisons, which are larger and possessing of more formidable security. The detainees held here are considered low-risk, low-security inmates. The purpose of this installation is not simply incarceration but rather knowledge gathering. Anyone taken there is usually in possession of information believed to be of some use. The scope and level of that usefulness varies with the detainee, of course, as do the methods used by the Chodrecai to obtain such information."

"I don't like the sound of that," DiCarlo said, a knot forming in his gut as memories long buried but never forgotten teased the edges of his mind. Forcing away the unwelcome thoughts, he crossed to where a small heating stove sat next to Javoquek's worktable.

"Nor should you," Javoquek replied. "The Chodrecai Security Division is well practiced in the art of information extraction. This facility is one of their primary locations for carrying out such duties. If any of our people are captured trying to infiltrate it, death would be a preferable alternative to a stay of any length."

Gutierrez asked, "What about the prison itself? How fortified is it?"

Shaking his head, Javoquek replied, "It is lightly defended, at least when compared to other prisons of this type." He indicated the holographic projection of the wall surrounding the buildings. "The perimeter serves as the most effective deterrent, standing high enough to prevent attempts at scaling. Towers at the corners of the headquarters building, as well as at the midpoints of each of the building's five walls, provide unobstructed coverage of the entire exterior. There are also various video surveillance and infrared tracking devices scattered throughout the compound."

"But if it's like most prisons," DiCarlo said, "its security is designed toward keeping people in, not out. Right? The sensors and cameras and everything else are inside the perimeter wall, or near entrances and such."

Javoquek nodded. "Indeed. The compound also sits in a largely open area, devoid of much that might provide cover or concealment. Infiltrating it will not be easy."

Frowning, Russell asked, "What about the rest of the prison population? If any of them are out of their cells or whatever is used to hold them, they're not going to just stand by while you go to all this trouble to break into the place and leave them behind."

"They're not a factor," Sloane replied. "We won't have the resources to help them. Our focus has to be on our primary target. If other prisoners get in the way of that, then our orders are to deal with them as I feel appropriate."

DiCarlo thought about that a moment. "You know, setting them free and giving them the opportunity to make their own break for it might be useful. If nothing else, they'd provide another distraction for the guards while you're trying to get out of there."

"Maybe," Gutierrez said, shrugging. "We'll evaluate the situation once we get some on-site intel, and go from there."

"What about this diversion?" DiCarlo asked. "What've you got in mind?"

Gutierrez smiled. "Let's just say I'm planning on calling in the cavalry. I haven't worked out the details yet, but at this point I'm sure it'll involve a lot of loud explosions and holes blown in stuff."

"What about getting out?" Russell asked. "Even if we get the guy, we'll still be outnumbered all to hell. What's your plan for that?"

By way of reply, Gutierrez reached for another of the pouches on his equipment harness and retrieved from it a black rectangular box, into which was set a type of keypad. At first, DiCarlo thought it might be some kind of cellular or satellite phone, both of which likely would be useless here, but the lieutenant set him straight.

"It's like a beacon," Gutierrez said, holding up the device. "Don't ask me to explain how it works, but my understanding is that it transmits a signal that's not all that different from the beam used to establish a portal. In this case, it sends a burst transmission back to the portal we used to travel here, providing our coordinates here for the calculations needed to relocate our end of the conduit."

"Beam me up," Russell said, smiling in approval.

Gutierrez nodded. "Basically, that's it. An R and D team consisting of Plysserian and human engineers came up with it, and my team and I were the guinea pigs." Pointing to what DiCarlo recognized as a standard personal computer data port set into the unit's base, the lieutenant added, "This lets us copy messages or pictures from a laptop or cellular phone, and fire them through the beacon as burst messages. It's how we get status reports and other info back to the other side."

"We've had nothing but success on all our tests," Sloane said, "which is why General Thompson green-lit this mission. We grab the scientist, hit the beacon, and get the hell out of there. That means you, too."

Exchanging glances with Russell, DiCarlo realized he was not sure how to react to that. Having been in the company of Kel, Javoquek, and the other Plysserian soldiers for so long, he had grown accustomed to living with them. Of course, the constant movement and living in primitive conditions had begun to take its toll.

I am getting a little old for this shit, but what would I be doing if I went home?

As though reading his mind, Gutierrez said, "Your firsthand experiences here offer needed insight, Sergeant

Major, experience we hope to exploit in the coming weeks and months. There are plans under way. I'm not authorized to tell you more, and to be honest I don't know any more."

"General Thompson's orders?" Russell asked.

"Absolutely," the lieutenant replied.

Looking first to Russell, then to Javoquek, who both nodded to him, DiCarlo returned his gaze to Gutierrez. "All right, Lieutenant. Let's roll."

6

If Colonel Matthew Holden never saw another serving of whatever it was that passed for food in this place, he decided he could die a happy man.

"And I thought the beef stew and veggie burgers were bad," he said, rubbing his nose as he nodded toward the assembly line. "Of course, I've never seen those being made, so I suppose there's still hope." The line was enclosed in a temperature-controlled area, separated from the rest of the plant by Plexiglas dividers. Inside the controlled sections, a dozen employees, including three Plysserians, and all wearing white coveralls, gloves, and masks, oversaw the largely automated process of separating the manufactured food—Holden was not about to try pronouncing the actual name—into individual portions. Those servings, vacuum-sealed into special packaging, would then be added to other components of larger meals being processed elsewhere in the facility and transported to military bases around the country.

Standing next to Holden, Jessica Parelli, the food packing plant's floor manager, replied, "Three things people should never want to see being made are laws, sausages, and field rations. If you think this is bad, come with me and I'll show you what passes for desserts so far as the Blues are concerned."

Holden scowled. "Pass." Reaching up to wipe sweat from his smooth, bald head, he asked, "I figured it would be cooler."

"Heat's being thrown off the fans on the refrigeration units. We like to call that irony around here." Her smile seemed to brighten her entire face. Parelli was in her mid- to late thirties, Holden guessed, with blond hair cut in a pageboy style. She wore khaki pants, comfortable shoes, and a dark blue blouse with the top three buttons undone, so Holden could see the black shirt underneath. She wore no ring on her left hand, nor was there a hint of a tan line or crease along her finger where a wedding band or engagement ring might have been. Her skin was smooth and pale, with the slightest hints of freckles around her nose. When she spoke, it was with a hint of southern drawl that Holden guessed originated somewhere in the Carolinas or perhaps Kentucky.

Nodding toward the assembly line behind Holden, Parelli regarded him with that wistful smile of hers, which he found delightful. "So, I'm guessing you're not up for a lecture on the ingredients?"

"Not ever, if it's all the same to you," Holden replied. "This place brings back too many memories of the lunch lines at school." His mother had worked on one of those lines, and because of that he had seen more of the inside of a Detroit-area elementary school cafeteria than should ever be forced upon an impressionable child. Looking around the plant, Holden nodded in approval. "I have to say, Ms. Parelli, the progress you've made in such a short time is extraordinary."

Parelli smiled again as they began the long walk toward the air-conditioned section of the massive building and her office. "All the pieces were in place. The biggest obstacle was hiring a staff to handle the workload, but you'd be surprised how a decent paycheck and benefits can lure people out of hiding."

Until a few months ago, the Corrac Corporation had been just another midwestern company hit hard by the tumultuous economic recession. Founded by Benjamin Corrac after his return from Europe following the Second World War, the company had begun life as a family-owned meatpacking plant located in the small town of Downers Grove, Illinois. The company grew as years passed, diversifying its production to include the processing and distribution of numerous prepackaged foods and meals, ranging from TV dinners to microwave popcorn to freeze-dried foods for camping. The company even supplied NASA with dehydrated fruit for the better part of the 1970s, until the end of the Apollo program curtailed the need—for a time, anyway—to feed astronauts in space.

With the recession of the late 2000s, the primary Corrac plant, home to more than seventeen hundred employees, was forced to take extreme measures in order to stay afloat. The company CEO, himself the grandson of Benjamin Corrac, reluctantly ordered the closing of one of the two primary processing facilities, reducing the number of employees by a third. That drastic action, while a short-term remedy, had begun to look like the first of several steps that would bring the company to bankruptcy.

All of that changed with the arrival of the aliens.

With the country—indeed, the entire world—on a war footing unmatched since 1942, many plants and factories that once were all but abandoned now were enjoying new life. World leaders, fearing a long, costly campaign to defend Earth against the Chodrecai, had directed the military machine of the United States and its allies on a path of expansion not seen for decades. Along with the first draft since the Vietnam War, voluntary enlistments were exceeding all previous records. All of those troops would need continuous resupply of ammunition, food, fuel, and other consumables. If the U.S. government did not simply take over the operation of abandoned facilities, it contracted with existing firms like the Corrac Corporation to convert as much of their production as feasible to military needs, all with the promise of generous payments and guaranteed business for the duration of the conflict.

Of course, if the Grays decide to show up and wipe us out in a single afternoon, those promises aren't going to be worth jack shit.

"What made you decide to go with preparing food for use by Blue soldiers?" Holden asked, genuinely curious. "Only a handful of companies put in bids for that."

Parelli shrugged. "Mr. Corrac has always been one of those forward-thinking yet outside-the-box types, you know. He thinks there'll be a market for Plysserian foodstuffs once the war's over. You have to figure at least some of them will want to settle here, right? They gotta eat, too."

"Fair enough," Holden replied. In truth, he had given little thought to what might happen with any Plysserians—or Chodrecai, for that matter—who might end up settling on Earth. A lot of how he might feel toward the issue naturally would depend on how the people already living here fared with respect to the war and whatever direction it ended up taking. "Still, I've read the reports you've submitted. Nasty phone calls, threats, hate mail. Not everybody wants the Blues to hang around, now or after the war's over."

Parelli clasped her hands behind her back as they walked. "I suppose a bit of that's to be expected. How many companies who supported the troops in Iraq and Afghanistan got the same kind of treatment?" She paused, frowning. "I mean, with the circumstances being so different this time around, I thought people would act differently, but I suppose that's what I get for thinking."

The detailed accounts of the harassing behavior were not unlike those Holden had read from other locations around the country. Earth for Humans was one group known to be operating in the Midwest, itself an apparent amalgam of several smaller groups that had come together, united in their common cause to—as their website described it—educate the public on the true story behind the Plysserian-Chodrecai War. According to the propaganda, the role of the United States and other countries that had allied with the Blues was to subjugate and eventually eradicate the victimized Gray civilization. In most cases, things had not progressed beyond this sort of passive resistance, and Holden could understand and even sympathize with such viewpoints. "There will always be a segment of society who feels war is never the answer, will never be the answer," he said. "It's a nice thought, and believe me the world would be a hell of a lot nicer place to live if it were true, but it's not as though we lay down our guns and everybody else goes home."

"If wishes were horses, yadda yadda yadda," Parelli replied.

Opening the portfolio he carried in his left hand, Holden retrieved a pen from one of its pockets and jotted down a note to again review the memos on such groups when he returned to his office at the Pentagon. There had been no reports of such activity during the two days he had spent inspecting the site and meeting with various members of company management, though he had seen the security measures currently in place to protect the plant and its workers. All of that, as well as any recommendations he had for improving that security, would be something upon which he would have to expound once he sat down to write his official report for the Army's inspector general.

"I think that should do it for the actual tour," he said as he continued to write, "but I'm still hoping I can meet with Mister Corrac before the day's out. Any chance of that still happening?"

Parelli frowned. "I know his schedule was booked solid when I checked yesterday and again this morning. I don't think he's trying to avoid you."

"I don't think so, either. I'm sorry this inspection was un-announced. It's typically not the way I like to do things, but things have been hectic lately." Though he had his suspicions about the sudden increase in inspection and readiness tours of various plants and factories around the country over which the Army had been given authority, Holden had been given no information to corroborate or refute his personal theories. He knew that plant managers and company CEOs now working with the military would be curious, as well, but speculating with them as to the reasons behind the more frenetic pace was out of the question.

Loose lips, and all that.

Shrugging, Holden said, "Well, I'm here for one more day. Maybe I can get on his calendar for tomorrow?" He pulled a business card from another of the portfolio's pockets and extended it to Parelli. "This has my cell number on it, so I can be reached anytime, day or night."

Parelli looked at the card before cocking her head and eyeing him. "Day or night? Maybe I should keep this, then."

Hello.

Caught off guard by the comment, Holden almost stumbled over his own tongue but instead managed to pull things together before disaster ensued. "Uh, absolutely." He paused, watching her expression, and wondering if he was reading the signals wrong.

Ah, go for broke.

"In fact, if you're not doing anything tonight . . ." he began.

"Would you like to have dinner with me?" Parelli said, almost talking over him. They stared at each other for a moment before chuckling. "Anything has to be better than being stuck alone in that hotel room."

Holden smiled. "I've spent twenty of the last thirty days living out of a suitcase. It's better than a muddy hole in the ground, but yeah, I wasn't really looking forward to another night of that."

"Maybe it's all in the company you keep," Parelli said, her expression playful. "So, is that a yes?"

"That's a yes," Holden said. "Show me some fine Downers Grove dining. Anything beats room service." He had not been on so much as a date in three years, following a short yet bitter divorce from his wife that ended their five-year marriage. He had not been good at dating even then. Contrast that with Jessica Parelli, the confident, capable, beautiful woman standing before him. What did she see in a bum like him? Though he had made a career out of the Army, advancing from the enlisted ranks to earn a commission and eventually attaining the rank of colonel, Matthew Holden had started out life on a different path. Growing up on the streets of inner-city Detroit, he might have been less than a year away from dying or going to jail if not for his mother's brother. In the absence of Matt's father, Uncle Morris had jerked a much-needed knot in young Holden's ass. Morris had taken him under his wing, teaching him to fix cars at his garage as well as other useful life skills, and it was because of his uncle's distinguished service career in Vietnam—including a Bronze Star—that Holden eventually decided to enlist. It was a decision he firmly believed had saved his life. As for recent dating, or lack of same, in the wake of his divorce Holden had channeled that energy into his career. Then the war had come, and there seemed to be no time for anything else.

Maybe she's a sucker for hard-luck cases.

The moment was shattered by a wave of blaring alarm sirens echoing across the plant. Holden flinched at the Klaxons, automatically looking around in search of an enemy or threat. Alert lamps mounted on various columns activated, casting harsh crimson around the vast chamber. On the plant intercom system, a female voice called out above the cacophony.

"Attention. We have a security breach at Gate One. Security breach at Gate One. An unauthorized vehicle has entered the premises. White panel van, looks to be heading toward Building Three. For the safety of all employees, remain inside."

Holden looked to Parelli. "It's coming here?" A number of scenarios flashed across his mind, all of them bad. Discarding his portfolio, he grabbed Parelli by the arm. "Let's go." Even as he spoke the words, he heard police sirens somewhere outside, faint at first but growing louder with every second as they drew closer.

Oh no. No no no no! Was it possible that one of the protest groups, which until this point merely had voiced their displeasure with companies like Corrac, was stepping up their game? It seemed plausible. He had been close to enough car bombs in Iraq that he long ago learned to trust his instincts.

"Everybody off the floor!" he yelled as loudly as he could in order to be heard over the alarm sirens. "Move! Move! Move!"

"What?" Parelli asked, her expression a mask of concern and confusion. "You don't think . . . ?"

"I don't know, and I don't care," Holden said, increasing his pace to a jog and pulling her along with him. Seeing

Corrac employees scurrying from various work areas, he waved his free hand and yelled, "Get out of the damned building. *Now!*" Seeing a phone mounted on one nearby column, Holden ran to it, ripping the receiver from its cradle and punching in the code stenciled on the column above it for emergencies.

"This is Colonel Holden," he said, not even giving the poor security officer on the other end of the line a chance to say anything when he answered. "Order Building Three evacuated now."

"Sir," the security officer began, "I—"

"Just do it!"

A thunderclap sounded behind him as something hit the building, and Holden jerked his head at the sound of tearing metal and the roar of an engine as a tall, garage-style door buckled and the front end of a white van punched through its aluminum panels. Holden heard the engine rev as the van's driver punched the accelerator, guiding the vehicle into the building. He caught only a glimpse of the driver, someone wearing a dark ski mask, his or her gloved hands spinning the wheel and causing the van to skid on the polished concrete floor. The driver eased off the gas long enough to regain control, the back of the van fishtailing into a support column before the tires once again gained traction. Then the vehicle accelerated, aiming directly for the cordoned-off packing area. Outside, Holden heard police sirens stop outside the building, followed by a chorus of shouts and orders and footsteps running in this direction.

"Get out. Now!" he shouted, dropping the phone and pushing Parelli toward the torn-open door just as the van crashed through one of the Plexiglas dividers separating the food packing area from the rest of the plant floor. The vehicle continued through the hole it had created and slammed into the bank of control switches, adding a new chorus of bent and twisted metal to the racket of alarms blaring inside the building.

The van's front doors opened and two figures emerged, both dressed in matching black long-sleeve shirts and combat fatigue trousers, their heads and faces covered by ski masks. Something about the way they ran from the wrecked vehicle sent a chill down Holden's spine.

"Earth for humans!" the passenger shouted, sprinting away from the van.

"You'd better run, traitor!" the driver called out as he pointed at Holden.

Son of a bitch.

The van's passenger got through the smashed door, but Holden intercepted the driver, shoving him into the wall. The man grunted, squirming in what Holden recognized was genuine panic. From the look in his eyes, he definitely wanted out of this building, and right fucking now.

"What did you do?" Holden shouted, flecks of spittle landing on the other man's ski mask.

"Let me go!" the man shouted, almost crying in desperation.

It was the last thing Matthew Holden heard before the explosion.

7

"Jenterant, Malirtra *Curpen and* Nomirtra *Farrelon have arrived.*"

Lnai Mrotoque heard the call from his aide as transmitted by the communications system, and chose not to answer. Instead, he continued to study the latest three-dimensional, computer-generated map of the planet Earth. Suspended above the oversized table at the center of his private office, the holographic image rotated on an invisible axis, offering Mrotoque an unfettered view of the planet it represented. The more he studied the map, the more he comprehended and appreciated Earth's simple beauty. With its vast oceans and sprawling landmasses, Earth was truly a wondrous sight, rendered as it had been by the team of engineers and analysts currently serving as his intelligence counsel. A sizable portion of the planet had remained uncharted for uncounted cycles, but covert operatives—often working with sympathetic humans or even Plysserians—had succeeded in collecting enough information to render the map in full. The landmasses and bodies of water of every size now possessed names, and the computer also had available for immediate reference nearly complete geographical and topographical information, as well as data pertaining to climate and population and even reports on technological levels.

How unfortunate that such a picturesque world is also the home of our enemy.

"Jenterant," his aide repeated, "*shall I have them return at a later time?*"

Sighing in resignation, not for those with whom he would be meeting but instead what he knew they would be bringing to him, Mrotoque reached for a control pad set into the table near his left hand and pressed a glowing green indicator. "Send them in." A moment later the door at the far end of the room spiraled open, revealing two of his most trusted confidants.

"Good day to you, *Jenterant*," said *Malirtra* Curpen, the senior of the two officers.

Mrotoque nodded in greeting. "I trust that your presence in my chambers so early in the day is not cause for concern?" The aides, knowing his penchant for rhetorical questions, said nothing.

Curpen and Farrelon were part of a larger team of advisors with the responsibility of collating and prioritizing information from numerous sources for Mrotoque's review. Since the discovery of Earth and the expansion of the conflict with the Plysserians to that planet and its inhabitants, the two young officers had distinguished themselves on many occasions by offering frank, often controversial counsel. Unlike other members of his staff, who were content to tell him what they thought he wanted to hear, Curpen and Farrelon instead chose to speak their minds. Always respectful of their positions relative to senior members of Mrotoque's advisory group as well as the *jenterant* himself, they nevertheless did not hesitate to offer a perspective that often was at odds with what others might tell him. At first Mrotoque had dismissed their opinions as being those of inexperienced officers who did not know their place, but over time he had come to rely on their keen eye when it came to seeing information and situations from different viewpoints, as well as their willingness to disagree with him.

"I have reviewed the latest readiness reports," Mrotoque said as the three of them took seats around the briefing table. "We are not progressing as I had hoped." ·

Nodding, Curpen replied, "Rebuilding and restructuring activities continue apace, *Jenterant*, but obtaining raw materials and resources for an effort of this scope is somewhat problematic. After all, we have not experienced a sustained buildup of this size since the very beginning of the war."

Mrotoque understood the harsh truths as spoken by his advisor. Acquiring the resources to keep the Chodrecai military functioning at required levels had been a growing concern for quite some time. The war had taken its toll not only on the people of *Jontashreena* but also the planet itself, and the failed campaign against Earth had been costly on a number of fronts. In addition to the losses suffered on the alien planet either as direct casualties or else those personnel and materials seized by human and Plysserian forces, Chodrecai units had come under attack here on *Jontashreena*, as well. "*Jenterant*," said *Nomirtra* Farrelon, "there is talk, not only among our staff but also our government leaders, about the use of larger-scale weapons against the humans."

"You speak of mass-casualty weapons?" Mrotoque hated that descriptor. "You cannot be serious."

It was Curpen who replied, nodding. "There are those who believe it an option worth considering, *Jenterant*."

"Only those who choose not to heed the lessons of our own history," Mrotoque snapped. Decisions to employ mass-casualty weapons, made early on and while Mrotoque himself was still a young officer rising through the ranks, had caused many regions to be rendered uninhabitable.

Entire cities and their populations had been all but vaporized, with further damage to water supplies in those areas as well as the very soil used to cultivate food. Though the use of such weapons had long ago been halted, the wounds inflicted upon the planet would take generations to heal.

Farrelon said, "Despite our advanced technology, conventional weapons have proven only partially effective against the humans. According to our intelligence reports, they already are devising countermeasures, either on their own or with Plysserian assistance. Even as we speak, human factories are in the early stages of producing weapons for their own soldiers that are not so removed from those our forces employ."

"Yes, I know this," Mrotoque countered, "but you are talking about personal arms for foot soldiers. They cannot yet be ready to construct larger weapons or vehicles of any measurable superiority to ours, can they?"

Curpen shook his head. "No, *Jenterant*, they are not advancing *that* quickly. What they *are* doing is learning to adapt their current technology to what the Plysserians can provide them. Indeed, adaptability would seem to be a hallmark of human behavior."

"I'd think fighting for one's own survival is a wonderful incentive," Mrotoque said. Seeing the look on Farrelon's face, he held up a hand. "I know, *Nomirtra*. This also concerns our leadership."

The younger officer nodded. "Yes, *Jenterant*. It is this concern that has fueled discussions of escalation with respect to battling the humans."

"If we are to survive this conflict and make any attempt at returning our people to a normal way of life," Mrotoque said, making an effort to keep his voice controlled and not offer any display of his rising irritation, "then rendering Earth useless to us is not a viable option. Our studies have shown us that the planet is already suffering the effects of countless generations of unchecked abuse. Toxic pollutants scar its land and taint its water and even the very air the humans breathe. Their energy needs are dependent upon all manner of raw materials they rip from the planet's depths, and many of those resources even now are beginning to wane. Despite all of that, Earth still has much to offer us, but not if we wreak even more havoc with weapons designed to cause widespread, unchecked destruction."

Curpen said, "We agree, *Jenterant*, which is why our attentions have been focused on other development efforts. A number of projects currently under way promise to provide weapons designed to specifically target human physiology."

"You mean aggressive biological agents," Mrotoque replied. "The problem with such weapons is that they do not discriminate between soldiers and noncombatants. We would be sentencing innocent parties to death merely for being human. Is that truly the legacy we wish to leave for our descendants?"

Leaning forward in his chair, Curpen said, "If we allow the Plysserians and their human allies to conquer us, we will have no descendants to honor any legacy, *Jenterant*. It is for this reason that our leadership has authorized the research and development efforts."

"Triumph by any means available and regardless of consequence is a hollow victory," Mrotoque said. "I will resign and submit myself for execution before I ever participate in any such action." He had not yet had the opportunity to discuss with his own superiors the possible use of such weapons, and it was not a conversation he relished. Shaking his head, he added, "Even if our leaders were to sanction such methods—a scenario I find unlikely—it does not matter. According to the briefings I receive, a prototype is far from completion and, for all we know, may well prove as dangerous to us as it hopes to be for humans. We cannot afford to spend precious time and energy contemplating the uses for such weapons. It is likely that the Plysserians and the humans are planning some sort of campaign, if not to defend Earth then to launch further counteroffensives here."

Farrelon made no attempt to hide the skepticism that clouded his features and laced the words he spoke. "That would require coming through portals from Earth. With all due respect, *Jenterant*, do you really believe the humans are capable of carrying out such a bold plan?"

"We already agree that the humans are quite adaptable," Mrotoque replied. Rising from the table, he began to pace around it, hands clasped behind his back. "When I next meet with our leadership, I intend to offer another possibility. Given that neither side seems ready to launch any sort of full-scale offensive, now may be the time to approach the Plysserians and the humans with a plan of equal boldness yet far lesser potential for casualties and continued destruction."

"You cannot mean surrender?" Farrelon asked.

Mrotoque grunted. "Certainly not, but I suspect that even with all that has happened, the humans—and perhaps even the Plysserians—will be open to the idea of a truce."

"Peace with the Plysserians, after all this time?" Curpen asked, the skepticism in his voice quite noticeable. "Is that really a possibility?"

"I did not say it would be easy," Mrotoque replied, "but, given the alternatives, I suspect that even the Plysserians cannot want to continue involving the humans in our war. We have already done lasting harm to our own world; shifting our conflict to Earth would sentence that planet to the same fate. Were we to seek peace, we might well be able to forge an alliance with the humans and save the people of both worlds."

Farrelon cleared his throat. "There will be those who disagree with such ideas. So far as they are concerned, the humans chose their fate by allying themselves with the Plysserians."

"And they are fools to think so," Mrotoque barked. "Yes, we have legitimate grievances with the Plysserians, but the humans were unwitting latecomers to our conflict. They do not deserve to die as a people merely for wanting to protect themselves from aggression, nor do I believe they think differently of us. In fact, there are groups of humans on Earth who support our cause. If for nothing else than that, we must find some commonality, some basis for uniting in mutual cooperation."

"I do not disagree with you, *Jenterant*," Farrelon said, "but I believe convincing others to believe as you do will be at best a difficult prospect."

"Nothing of worth is achieved without effort, *Nomirtra*," Mrotoque replied. There had to be a way to convince his superiors that seeking peace was not a foolish waste of time. Surely, the populations of two worlds and all the potential they possessed—individually and even working together toward common goals—were sufficient reason for exploring every conceivable possibility to end generations of unremitting conflict.

A sensible notion, Mrotoque mused. So, *why am I worried?*

Checking the display on the back of the digital camera to ensure it was set to record video, Paul Simpson stepped back from the unit and let his gaze wander over the impromptu set he had built in his cellar. He examined the small area with a critical eye, trying to imagine how it would appear to whoever watched the presentation he was preparing to create. There was nothing that might be of use to law enforcement or the military in determining his location. No windows offered glimpses of the outside world or any landmarks that might be identified via image or pattern recognition by some computer analyst toiling away in the lower levels of MI-5 or one of the other insidious government agencies tasked with prying into the private lives of citizens.

"The flag's a nice touch," said Amanda Hebert, nodding in approval from where she stood near a workbench occupying the cellar's back wall, her arms folded across her chest. "Don't you think it's a bit of a risk, though?" There was only a hint of nervousness in her voice, but Simpson still was able to pick up on it.

He shrugged as he regarded the Union Jack mounted on the wall before the camera. "I don't think so. There's nothing in the camera frame that'll indicate anything other than a flag hanging in the background." As always, he would be wearing a mask while recording the statement, and other than the standard itself, Simpson's own voice, which he would alter with digital enhancement when he set to the task of editing the recording, would offer the only clue as to the video's origin. He had considered not using the flag as part of the set's backdrop, but he was rather pleased with himself at how the display had turned out, with the flag partially burned and the remaining material painted over with the words FREEDOM FOR TWO WORLDS. The slogan—more of a plea, really—tied in quite well to the overall vision and mission statement of Humans for Interplanetary Peace and Equality, the organization he had joined several months earlier; far better than the moronic war cry put forth by one of the group's equally dim-witted American members: "Believe the HIPE!" Simpson had refused to use the slogan, dismissing it along with any other e-mails sent by that particular imbecile.

Life's too short to spend time dealing with anyone who thinks Star Wars *is better than* Doctor Who.

Walking back to the workbench, Simpson tilted the screen of his laptop computer so that he was better able to see its display. The document he had prepared for his script was set to the correct font size, which would allow him to use the laptop as a makeshift teleprompter. As for the script, it had been written to last no longer than three minutes, similar in length to the previous videos he had created, so as to keep the resulting digital file to a manageable size. It then could be loaded with relative ease to e-mail and file transfer servers across the Internet. He would probably have to drive to nearby Brighton in order to have a decent chance at uploading the file, as Internet access here in Hassocks had become problematic in recent months.

It was probably just as well, Simpson knew, owing to the government's increased scrutiny of electronic mail and

websites that could in any way be interpreted as supporting the Chodrecai, or anything else that might be viewed
as a security threat. Such snooping had escalated in recent
weeks, coinciding with frequent news reports of isolated
pockets of alien activity being observed around the country. Though England had been spared direct conflict during the last major Chodrecai campaign six months ago, the
British military had engaged small numbers of alien forces
from time to time, capturing several of them in the process.
Interrogation had revealed a common theme: advance or
scouting parties sent through the incredible passages link-
ing Earth with the aliens' home planet, only to be cut off
when most of the portals disappeared. Though many of the
captured soldiers appeared to have no real knowledge of
the overall situation, a few speculated that the Chodrecai
military leadership had retreated in the hope of regrouping
as they considered a new campaign.

"Did you see the news this morning?" Hebert asked,
reaching for the mug of coffee she had earlier placed on
the workbench. "They found another safe house, this one
in Twineham. Eleven Grays, secreted in some widowed
housewife's cellar."

Simpson nodded. "She's Jewish, you know. Smuggled
out of Germany in a suitcase when she was five, or something like that. Can't say as I blame her for trying to return
the favor."

Reports had been circulating for weeks: accounts of
sympathetic humans offering aid to Chodrecai soldiers
who had managed to avoid capture or other confronta-
tion with British military forces. Some people had seen fit
to offer food, shelter, and even safe passage to the aliens.
This much fit with other rumors Simpson had heard, with
other activist groups working together to form a network
through which Chodrecai refugees might pass, obtaining

assistance as they fled for the unoccupied countryside and possible safe haven. It was this development that currently had the government and the military scrambling as they tried to determine if there was any validity to such stories.

For that reason alone, Simpson was glad HIPE was not the sort of group to do anything that might run it afoul of the authorities. The grassroots activist organization had been staging a series of large yet nonviolent protests in recent months, calling for a quick and peaceful end to the war. Still, the group had voiced its support for the Chodrecai, whom many saw as the victimized party in their war with the Plysserians on their home planet. Even though it was the Chodrecai who had taken initial provocative action against humans here on Earth, HIPE and similar organizations around the world held to the belief that such acts simply were the next logical steps for the Chodrecai to defend themselves.

HIPE and groups like it had been speaking out against the continuing alliance with the Plysserians by the United States and other countries, trying to bring attention to the truth behind the war that had all but consumed the aliens' planet and that threatened to serve Earth with a similar fate if something was not done. Surely there was another way, which was the simple message put forth by HIPE as they urged governments to seek a peaceful resolution to the current dilemma. It was that message, and the promise of peaceful dissent to which every member of the group pledged, that had caused Paul Simpson to seek them out and join their ranks.

"Was there anything at the mail drops today?" he asked, glancing over his shoulder at Hebert, who shook her head.

"I checked all three on my way over here," she replied. "Nothing."

Simpson regarded her with a questioning look. "See anything suspicious while you were checking?"

"Not a thing," Hebert said before offering a frown. "Of course, that would sort of defeat the purpose, wouldn't it?"

"Never can be too careful," Simpson said, shrugging.

Due to worries that their e-mail and other Internet chatter might be under observation, HIPE had taken to communicating via more creative methods. Regular mail handled a portion of the correspondence and other packages, but none of the group members used it to exchange anything resembling sensitive information. At best, a letter Simpson sent to another member might contain one or more key phrases or other code words, hopefully appearing innocuous to uninitiated readers as well as spies or other eavesdroppers. The same rules were observed when corresponding via the Internet or even talking on the phone. No one rang up another member to discuss anything regarding group activities or other matters, and code phrases had been prepared for a number of contingencies, up to and including raids by law enforcement or the military on member homes or businesses.

Finally, a network of "dead drop" sites had been established around the West Sussex area as well as the surrounding villages and towns, along with signals to indicate the delivery of messages or other materials. A chalk line drawn on the side of a call box, a note posted on a bulletin board at one of the town's more popular pubs, or the placement of a particular stone in the garden outside one of the larger churches was an indicator that someone had utilized one of the three dead drop locations scattered around Hassocks. Activity on that front had been quiet of late, owing to mounting fears that the government might be directing increased attention to the village and at least a certain segment of its population. Simpson had yet to detect any signs of surveillance, covert or otherwise, but that did not mean the watchers were not lurking about somewhere.

Sneaky wankers.

Turning from the workbench, Simpson moved to where he had set out a nondescript green jacket and matching wool ski mask, his standard attire when standing before the camera to record a message. "I hate this getup," he said, shaking his head as he regarded the ensemble.

"Would you rather have your face plastered all over the news?" Hebert asked.

Simpson released a sigh as he reached for the jacket. "Not until they stop lumping all protestors into the same basket." The government's apparent policy toward activists and protest groups, at least publicly, was to treat them at best as nuisances and at worst as outright threats. To date, no member of HIPE had been arrested or even questioned by authorities, who had their hands full with their normal responsibilities as well as hunting for the Chodrecai and those who might be helping them. Still, Simpson saw no need to take chances, hence the disguise. Additionally, he always made a point to emphasize in his videos HIPE's commitment to peaceful dissent and support for ending the war.

"All right," he said, donning the jacket, "let's get on with it, then."

Hebert checked the thin gold watch she wore on her left wrist. "Depending on how long it takes you to edit everything, I can still make it to Netpama before curfew."

Buttoning the jacket, Simpson nodded. "We'll be ready." Netpama was one of the few Internet cafés still operating in Brighton. Economic downturn, as well as martial law, mandatory sundown curfews, and the curtailing of civilian access to the World Wide Web, had spelled doom for several such establishments, but a few holdouts still lingered. As a consequence, those cafés still operating were under routine surveillance by law enforcement, requiring utmost care whenever groups like HIPE wanted to use such locations for transmitting information to the Internet. Thankfully, Hebert had befriended a couple of Netpama's employees, one of whom oversaw the shop's network systems and was able to upload files she gave him in such a way that its transmission was camouflaged among the rest of the Internet traffic to and from the café. However, and as with anything else, Simpson preferred not to fall into routine or pattern.

"We'll send out a DVD at the same time we post it to the Net," he said, picking up the ski mask, "just to be on the safe side. I'll package it along with the article for the papers. It'll give us a chance to test out this new guy Jerry's brought on board, and see if he can make the delivery to our friends in Cardiff." Even though most newspapers and magazines had continued publishing, in many cases their output had been curtailed, and much of what remained was—many believed—simply operated under the aegis of the government. Still, some news publications, such as the *Cardiff Gazette*, were notable for their outspoken opposition to the war while remaining firmly neutral so far as their allegiance to any side. The *Gazette* was the largest such paper, and in the past had welcomed the opportunity to publish messages or articles from HIPE, as well as to stream the occasional video on their website. All that was needed was for someone to get the material to their allies at the paper's headquarters.

"Jerry speaks highly of him," Hebert said. "He says Carl's background will make him a real asset."

Simpson shrugged. The latest addition to the group, Carl Hosey, had been recruited by Simpson's and Hebert's friend and fellow HIPE member Gerald Cleef. Hosey, during the one or two times Simpson had met with the man, came off as rather dour and driven. Simpson chalked up such traits to Hosey's prior military service, which according to the new man had ended under less than favorable circumstances several years ago. When Hosey spoke, which was not often, it usually was to utter some complaint or other unfavorable observation regarding the government or the military.

Still, the man's apparent list of skills was impressive, even for a former soldier who had seen more desks than foxholes during his time in service. Computers and communications were Hosey's specialty, along with the preparation and dissemination of information to print, televised, and electronic media. Such experience would have landed the man a position with any major tech company of his choosing here or abroad, but Hosey instead had spent the interval following his discharge from service bouncing from one temp job to another. To hear him describe his situation, he was unwilling to subvert himself to the whims of an employer longer than was necessary to secure whatever funds he required to subsidize the minimal lifestyle he had established for himself. At first, such a naturally rebellious spirit seemed to Simpson incompatible with the needs and agenda of a group like HIPE, but as Hebert had pointed out, Jerry Cleef had vouched for the man.

Good enough for me.

"We'll find out soon enough," he said. He was bringing the ski mask to his face and preparing to don it when he paused at the sound of the phone ringing on the far wall. With cellular phone service ranging from erratic to nonexistent, depending on location, landlines had reacquired some portion of the business they had lost in recent years. "I wonder who that might be." Crossing the cellar, Simpson retrieved the phone's receiver from its cradle and held it to his ear. "Hello?"

"Paul? It's Jimmy," said a deep male voice, belonging to Jim Franks, a friend of both Simpson and Hebert and also a member of HIPE. Several years their senior, Franks was one of the group's founding members, his participation having drawn him out of the semiretirement he had enjoyed before the aliens' arrival. Offhand, Simpson could not recall the last time he had spoken with the man.

"Afternoon, Jimmy," Simpson replied. "Been a bit since we last chatted. What can I do for you?"

"I'm wondering if you have any plans for this afternoon," Jimmy asked. Despite the casual nature of the question, Simpson could not help thinking there was something else lurking behind the words. He also did not fail to remember that Jimmy knew full well what he and Hebert were doing today.

Acknowledging the possibility that the conversation would be monitored, either in real time or later if some word or phrase triggered an automated computer search filter, Simpson said, "Nothing much. Cleaning up around the house and whatnot. You have a better offer?"

"Maybe. A couple of my relatives have come to visit, and I thought you might like to meet them."

Simpson felt a chill course down his back as he listened to his friend. The statement was a key phrase Franks had distributed to the rest of HIPE only a few weeks earlier, in the event certain things transpired that required the group's attention. In truth, it was a pass code Simpson had never expected to hear, let alone use. Now keenly aware that his every word was subject to eavesdropping, he did his best to remain relaxed. "Tell me you'll have Guinness and I'll be there."

"I think I may be able to scare up a pint," Franks replied, even adding what sounded like a genuine chuckle. "Come over anytime you're ready. Be seeing you."

"Bye," Simpson said, but the other man had already ended the call. Pulling the phone receiver from his ear, he stood there, staring at it, until Hebert called to him.

"What is it, Paul?" she asked, and when he looked up he saw concern clouding her features. Returning the receiver to its cradle, Simpson cleared his throat, already trying to imagine what the afternoon had in store for them. "That was Jimmy. He or somebody he knows is harboring Grays." His mind buzzed with the first of what he knew might well turn into an endless stream of questions as the day wore on.

Jimmy better damned well have that Guinness.

"Come on, come on! Get this hunk of shit into gear!"

Gripping the Land Rover's roll bar with his right hand while trying to maintain his hold on the MAG-58 machine gun mounted to a pintle between the front seats, Staff Sergeant Angus Feder fought not to be thrown from the vehicle. Its driver, Corporal Jaxon Kelly, spun the steering wheel hard to the right, narrowly avoiding the wide trunk of a mountain ash tree that seemed to leap from the darkness. It was all Kelly could do to keep the multipurpose vehicle on the road.

"And try not to kill us both while you're at it!" Feder yelled over the sound of the Land Rover's roaring engine, ducking in time to avoid a low-hanging branch that would have taken off his head had he remained standing.

"Make up your friggin' mind!" Kelly yelled, keeping his eyes on the narrow, rough dirt road—more of a path, really—that wound its way through this section of the South Australia forest. The MPV's high-beam headlights illuminated the woods ahead, along with the dust thrown up from the dry soil comprising the road. Ahead of them, barely visible through the thick clouds of grime, Feder saw bright red lights flare up in the dark. Even though the driver of the vehicle they were chasing had chosen to run without headlights, he was still forced to stomp on his brakes to avoid his own obstacles.

Idiot.

The portable field radio clipped to his equipment harness squawked for attention, loosing a burst of static. Feder heard the voice of Sergeant Cooper Harris, a close friend and one of the soldiers posted to Checkpoint Lima, ten kilometers from here.

"Feder, this is Coop. We're closin' on your position from the north."

Nodding in satisfaction as he reached for the radio's microphone and mashed its transmit button, Feder said, "Roger that, Coop. We'll hem 'em in and go from there. Just don't go lettin' em drive that truck up your arse."

"If only to break the boredom, mate," Harris said. Feder could almost see the young, brash sergeant smiling around an ever-present wad of chewing tobacco, punctuating his reply by spitting saliva and tobacco juice with no care as to where such a vile mixture might land.

The vehicle they pursued, an older Mercedes-Benz Unimog truck of the type once used by the military but long since replaced with modern versions, had been spotted by helicopter less than thirty minutes earlier. It was seen navigating the narrow path through the forest in utter defiance of local curfews and with the obvious intent of avoiding Army checkpoints stationed at irregular intervals along the main thoroughfares. According to the helicopter pilot's report, the Unimog seemed to have been modified so that the heat signature from its engine as well as any occupants was masked from thermal imaging. The observer on the chopper had gotten lucky, spotting the truck thanks to some defect or other in that shielding that allowed some heat to bleed through.

Bastards are getting sneakier all the time.

Checkpoint runners had been on the rise in recent months, owing mostly to disruptions in imports, which in turn had caused shortages in a variety of products. Prices for everything had gone up, giving rise to theft as well as black markets and other underground barter systems. Law enforcement and military patrols were constantly on the hunt for profiteers hoarding goods and trying to run for the outback and other undeveloped regions to avoid discovery.

Running down a renegade truck stuffed with tins of processed meat or stolen pharmaceuticals was one thing, but Feder knew this likely was something different. According to the descriptions provided by police, this was the same vehicle spotted as it left Wirrabara, one of many small towns in this part of the country that was home to Chodrecai sympathizers. Recent months had seen a slow, small, yet steady increase in support for the aliens, across Australia as well as around the world. Rumors had circulated for weeks of such people giving shelter to refugee Chodrecai soldiers.

"*Angus,*" said Harris over the radio, "*you think they may be haulin' Chodes?*"

Feder grunted into his radio. "I'm not betting against it." There had been reports of locals helping shepherd Chode refugees away from cities and towns, getting them past military checkpoints and out into undeveloped areas, of which Australia had no shortage. One such report indicated the presence of Chodes in or near Wirrabara, with plans afoot by local activists to help them disappear into the South Australian forest. As for obtaining food and other supplies, official reports offered by Plysserian soldiers acting as consultants to the militaries of different countries had concluded only a limited range of foodstuffs were edible for both Chodrecai and Plysserians. Most processed foods did not agree with the aliens, but they seemed able to eat any raw or uncooked meats, vegetables, and fruit. Though it obviously was impractical to impound any produce delivery vehicle or truck supposedly hauling cattle to market, there had been some success tracking civilian vehicles observed to be carrying such goods. Several of those suspects had turned out to be sympathizers attempting to ferry supplies to Chodes they were helping to hide.

Friggin' traitors.

If this truck was carrying something other than food or supplies, then Feder knew from experience that the situation had the potential to deteriorate in rapid fashion. Of the men in his unit, he was the only one to have seen Chodes up close and was one of the few soldiers he knew who had encountered the aliens and lived to recount the tale. It had happened very early during the aliens' initial forays to Earth, with Feder and his reconnaissance unit observing the construction of a base camp and a portal generation site. The recon unit was spotted by Chode scouts and attacked, and most of Feder's companions were killed in the onslaught. Feder himself had stared down the muzzle of an alien energy weapon, but somehow managed to fire his own rifle before the alien soldier could react. He had been so close the Chode's blood spattered his own uniform, an event that now recurred in his dreams with disturbing frequency.

"C'mon, mate," Feder yelled to Kelly, crouching down behind the machine gun so as to avoid getting the shit smacked out of him by other low-hanging branches. "Move this piece of shit!" How in the name of hell had they not yet caught up with the Unimog? There was no way that beast should be able to outrun the Land Rover.

"You want me to put us into a tree?" the corporal yelled, his knuckles white on the steering wheel as he kept his eyes on the dust-clouded road ahead of them. "I can barely see past the friggin' bonnet. They must've pulled their governor or something."

That made sense, Feder conceded, grunting in mounting irritation. For even the most inept mechanic, removing the governor from a car's engine was child's play. *So why the hell do we still have them on our trucks?*

"Feder," Harris's voice said over the radio, "*they've left the road, turned right onto some kind of rabbit trail or whatever the fuck it is. They're tear-assin' through the woods. We're on 'em.*"

What the hell? The area was littered with hiking trails, service roads, and firebreaks. Maps of the region were freely available—at least, they used to be—and anyone with experience traveling the South Australian forest could do so while avoiding the major roads if they so desired. Dealing with such "shadow runners," as they were called by law enforcement and military units tasked with patrolling the forest for any signs of Chode presence, was itself almost a full-time job.

Feder saw the headlights of Harris's Land Rover first, moving at a fast clip through the trees. "There they go," he said, tapping Kelly on the shoulder and holding on as the corporal guided the MPV onto the narrow path snaking into the dark woods. The vehicle's tires caught ruts and holes in the road, bouncing both men in their seats and making Feder work that much harder to hang on. Squinting through the dust and darkness surrounding them, he searched for any sign of the fleeing truck. The forest here was not especially thick, and with the full moon visibility might be sufficient for a driver of some skill to navigate the woods and not kill himself. The Unimog's driver appeared to be such a person, but only to an extent. Once more Feder saw brake lights flare, this time close enough that he could make out the truck's silhouette among the trees.

"Gotcha, you bastard," he said, tapping Kelly on the shoulder. "Let's get him, boy." He felt himself pushed back in his seat as the corporal hit the gas, propelling the Land Rover ever faster down the winding road. Among the trees ahead of them, Feder saw brakes yet again, only this time he was sure he heard the unmistakable sound of one object colliding with another.

"That's got 'im!" Harris shouted over the radio, undisguised excitement lacing his words. *"Slimy cocksucker damn near killed a tree!"*

Feder's first thought was not that someone might have been killed in the collision. Instead, his initial concern was that there might be survivors hell-bent on evading pursuit. "Hold on, Cooper," he called into his mike. "We're almost there." He watched as the headlamps of Harris's Land Rover came to a stop in the woods, illuminating the dirty, scuffed paint on the back of the Unimog. It had indeed run headlong into a massive silk oak tree, caving in the vehicle's front end. The truck had bounced away from the tree, and as Kelly maneuvered the Land Rover closer, Feder made out an arm dangling from the driver's-side window. Only when their own MPV's lights shone upon the wrecked truck did Feder see that the arm was stained red.

Sorry, mate.

He heard voices to his right and saw Harris and his driver unloading from their vehicle, brandishing weapons as Harris gestured toward the wrecked truck. "Stay there!" Feder yelled, climbing out of his seat and moving to take up position behind the MAG-58. In front of him, Kelly retrieved his Steyr AUG A1 assault rifle and laid the weapon's barrel atop the windshield frame, aiming it at the back of the truck. Feder eyed the machine gun to verify the safety was off before he sighted down its length through the crosshair sight mounted at its far end, centering it on the rear of the truck. It had a basic Unimog cargo configuration, with a metal frame over which was draped a canvas cover. There was movement beneath the canvas, and Feder felt his pulse racing in anticipation of what might emerge from beneath the canopy.

Before he could shout a warning or instructions toward the truck, the canopy's rear flap moved aside and a pair of empty human hands emerged, waving in frantic fashion. "Wait!" a voice yelled—a young voice, possibly a woman's. "Don't shoot! I'm not armed, and neither are they!"

"Get the fuck out of there!" Harris called out. "Nice and slow."

Feder's right forefinger tightened on the MAG-58's trigger as a woman—more a girl, really—climbed over the Unimog's tailgate and lowered herself to the ground. She was dressed in khaki shorts, a dark shirt, and hiking boots, her brown hair worn in a ponytail. Though she was just a bit on the chubby side, Feder could not help thinking that her backside was rather shapely as she climbed down from the truck.

Be a damned shame to put a bullet in that.

He watched as she undid the bolts holding the tailgate closed and let it swing down, clanging open with a loud metallic bang that echoed through the forest. At Feder's direction, she stepped away from the truck, hands held over her head. Feder was close enough to see the fear in her eyes and the first tears running down her cheeks, but he did not linger on her, instead returning his full attention to the back of the truck. Thanks to the Land Rover's headlamps, Feder could now see three sets of feet inside the Unimog's cargo area. Large, gray feet.

Chodes.

"We got three of 'em!" Feder yelled, instinctively dropping down so that the bulk of his body was obstructed from view by the machine gun and the Land Rover's roll bar and windshield. He tensed, waiting for the first muzzle of a Chode pulse rifle to poke its way out from under the canvas.

"They're unarmed!" the woman yelled again, waving her arms over her head and stepping closer to the truck.

"I said stay put!" Feder barked, keeping his eyes and the barrel of the MAG-58 trained on the vehicle. A large, muscled gray arm pushed aside the canvas flap, and Feder saw the first of the Chodrecai soldiers staring back at him, its other oversized hand reaching up to shield its eyes from the glare of the Land Rover headlamps.

"You speak their language?" Feder called out to the woman, who offered an anxious nod. "Then tell them to get out of the truck and get on the ground on their knees, hands behind their heads. Do it now." He listened as the woman said something in Chode gibberish to the alien looking down at her. The Chode then dismounted the truck, simply stepping from the platform and dropping to the dirt, the sound its impact made telling Feder that this was one hefty son of a bitch.

He sensed the movement before actually seeing it. Light reflecting off a watch or bracelet, glinting as it rose from the shadows cloaking the truck's passenger side. Then the figure, a man dressed in dark clothes, emerged from the darkness, his arm raised and a dark object in his hand. That was all Feder had time to recognize before the first shot went off. One of the headlamps on Harris's Land Rover exploded, the sound of its lens shattering drowned out by another gunshot. Harris lurched backward, his weapon dropping as he reached toward his right shoulder.

"No!" the woman was yelling, her eyes wide with terror as Kelly and Feder reacted at the same instant and turned their own weapons toward the new threat. The MAG-58 bucked in Feder's hands as his finger squeezed the trigger, multiple rounds tearing into the man. He flailed in the face of the onslaught, blood erupting from numerous wounds in his torso before he collapsed in a lifeless heap to the ground. It took an extra insane moment for Feder to realize that the woman was running toward the fallen man, but he was too late to check his fire before the first of the 7.62-millimeter rounds punctured her body.

"Damn it!" he yelled, releasing the trigger and angling the machine gun away from her. "Hold your fire!" There was nothing more to be done as the woman dropped to the ground, her body partially draping over that of her companion. Her face was turned toward Feder, her eyes open yet unseeing.

Damn it damn it DAMN IT!

Tearing his gaze from her, Feder leveled the MAG-58's barrel on the first of the Chodes, all three of which remained by the truck. "*Weh otiquol atan!*" he shouted, employing one of the few Chodrecai phrases he knew—the equivalent of "Stay where you are." The aliens appeared uninterested in offering any sort of resistance, which did not alleviate Feder's all but overpowering desire to shoot them where they stood. Looking toward the other Land Rover, he called out, "Harris! You all right?"

The sergeant, cradling his Steyr in the crook of his right arm, nodded as he pressed his left hand to the socket of his right shoulder. Feder saw blood streaming between the man's fingers, and there was no mistaking his pained expression. "He popped me with that friggin' pussy cap gun."

"Sergeant Feder!" Kelly shouted, and Feder turned toward the corporal to see him aiming his rifle at yet another human passenger. This one had fared worse in the truck's collision with the tree, his left arm limply hanging at his side and blood flowing from an open gash in the side of his head. He was moving around the side of the Unimog, dragging his right foot and holding out his right hand, palm facing toward the soldiers.

"Please don't shoot!" the man wailed, his words slurred and racked with sobs. "I don't have a gun."

"Stand right there!" Feder warned, growling the words through gritted teeth. As angered as he was over the woman's death at his own hands, it was balanced by what the other man had tried to do. For the briefest of moments, the urge to kill the man bordered on the overwhelming, but he forced himself to set aside anger and other distracting emotions and concentrate on the job at hand. "Kelly, get the medi-bag and see what you can do for him." To the man he yelled, "What the fuck were you thinking? Nobody had to get hurt."

"Angus, what the bloody hell are you doing?" Harris called out, shouting the words as he stumbled forward. He raised the barrel of his Steyr and tried to aim it one-handed at the other man, who began cowering in fear.

"Stand down, Harris!" Feder barked, feeling the scene beginning to circle the drain. "He's not armed. We take him into custody."

"He's a fuckin' collaborator, Angus!" Harris shouted back, his eyes wild with disbelief. "His mate just tried to scrag me."

"I said stand down, Sergeant!" They stared at each other for several seconds before Harris finally nodded, lowering his rifle. "Get your driver to look at that wound," Feder said before turning his attention back to the new man and the Chodes, all three of which regarded him with unreadable expressions.

"Fuck the lot of you."

Feder reached for his radio, intending to call in to his superiors to report the situation and receive further instructions. He paused before keying the mike, turning to look down at where Jaxon Kelly was treating the wounded man's injuries. The other man was not so hurt that he could not meet Feder's glare, his eyes burning with something besides pain: hate.

"You killed my friends," the man said, spitting the words.

"And you'd happily have killed me and mine," Feder snapped, "so shut your fuckin' mouth."

The other man scowled at him. "It's only going to get worse, you know. There are more of us every day. You can't stop us all. We won't stop; not until the Chodrecai are free, and the Plysserians pay for what they've done."

Feder ignored him, turning his attention to the two bodies lying sprawled on the ground, the sight doing nothing except fueling the rage building in his gut. What a waste, he thought, to be forced to end two young lives like that. Is this how the end would come about? Rather than unite in the face of the gravest crisis the planet had ever known, would humans—as they had throughout the course of history—begin once again to slaughter one another over ideology? How did the Plysserians and Chodrecai fit into whatever paradigm had ruled humanity to this point?

And what would happen after that?

10

Despite the incessant activity that was a hallmark of Op04-E's Situation Center, Bruce Thompson actually felt more relaxed here than anywhere else in the Pentagon.

From where he sat at an otherwise unoccupied workstation, Thompson reclined in the station's ergonomic chair and gazed down from the top of three tiered rows. Each row was formed from a series of twelve workstations and arranged in a curve, so that every station had an unhindered view of the room's forward wall. Mounted on the wall was a set of twelve flat-screen monitors, positioned in three rows of four. Most of the time, the screens worked in concert to display a single image, that of a massive world map rendered in wondrous high-definition computer graphic simulation with the assistance of real-time telemetry supplied from dozens of satellites in high orbit above the planet. At the moment, however, more than half of the screens sported independent images, some depicting smaller maps of specific areas around the world, while others showed different news broadcasts.

With the wireless headset he wore, Thompson was able to scan through the different channels using the computer at his station, and his right index finger played across the trackball of the computer's mouse as he made a sweep of the different transmissions. With his override authority, he also could listen to the phone conversations taking place at any of the other workstations, but it was an option he had yet to employ unless specifically requested to join a call. While there might well be cause for him to eavesdrop from time to time, he preferred not to engage in such ridiculous micromanagement tactics, relying instead on his eyes, his experience, and even just his gut to tell him if someone serving under him was fucking off when they should be working.

It's not as though any of us has time for that kind of crap, anyway.

Instead, he focused on the channels corresponding to the different broadcasts on the map wall, listening to each station for a few seconds and gleaning snippets of information. One news anchor reported about the president's most recent address to the American people on the status of the war. Another screen displayed footage of a factory explosion, this one at a plant in St. Louis that had been retooled to manufacture body armor designed to Plysserian specifications and capable of withstanding most attacks from Chodrecai pulse weapons. News reports were calling this the work of the same group, Earth for Humans, that had set off an explosion at a plant near Chicago contracted to develop field rations for Plysserian soldiers fighting alongside their human counterparts. Unlike the tragedy in Chicago, which had killed five people, including one of the bombers as well as an Army colonel conducting an inspection of the plant, no deaths had so far been reported from this latest incident.

Earth for Humans.

Thompson shook his head as he considered the name, and the group it identified. It was one of dozens of activist organizations that had sprung up in recent months, most of which either disagreed with the idea of a human-Plysserian alliance for one reason or another, while others actually supported the Chodrecai. On some level, Thompson could not entirely disagree with such a viewpoint, particularly since, when one boiled away all the politics, rhetoric, jingoism, and various other distractions, the Plysserians actually were to blame for the war that had all but consumed their planet. It was because of this simple, harsh fact that diplomats around the world continued their attempts to forge a dialogue with the Chodrecai, in the hope of coming to some form of peaceful resolution. Though he fervently wished to be proven wrong, Thompson was in the camp of those who believed such efforts were futile. Too much had happened; things had gone too far. Or had they?

Not for you to decide, he reminded himself.

One of the screens displayed recorded images of a skirmish between Korean and Chodrecai forces near Seoul earlier in the day. Another offered details of looting in Bahrain as citizens there struggled to secure basic needs such as medicine and clean water.

The damned planet's falling down around our ears.

That was one of the reports that bothered Thompson even more than the disturbing and often infuriating accounts of soldiers dying in faraway lands. Despite the lack of major, large-scale conflict in recent months, the general knew that one of the war's most devastating effects had been its impact on poorer and developing countries. Assistance normally provided by more prosperous nations had been curtailed or even ended altogether, with those resources instead being channeled toward the war effort. It sickened Thompson to think of the added suffering some people were forced to endure, but the harsh reality was that if Earth did not win this war, no amount of financial or medical aid, or any other form of support, would be of any consequence to such already downtrodden people.

To say nothing of the fact that they're going to have a shitload of company.

"Bruce."

The voice was quiet, but still loud enough for Thompson to hear it with his uncovered right ear. Pulling the headset away from his other ear, the general turned in his seat and saw his second-in-command and one of his closest and most trusted friends, Brigadier General Thomas Brooks, standing near the top step of the stairs connecting the tiers of workstations.

"What's up?" Thompson asked.

Brooks nodded in the direction of the hallway over his right shoulder. "It's time, sir. Our briefing with General Grayson." A muscled, barrel-chested African-American man, Tommy Brooks still looked more than capable of playing starting fullback for the Air Force Academy's football team, as he had decades ago. Deep lines across his forehead, face, and neck suggested his real age, but any gray hair he might have sported was kept at bay thanks to Brooks's choice to shave his head bald. His Air Force uniform appeared tailored with laserlike precision to fit his commanding physique, and it was adorned with more ribbons, badges, and other accoutrements than Thompson's own.

Nodding in understanding, the general removed the headset and laid it atop the workstation's desk before rising from his chair. A last glance toward the map wall and the rows of other stations told him that nothing out of the ordinary appeared to be happening. Not that it mattered; the floor supervisor, Major Alicia Gillette, was on hand and overseeing everything currently taking place in the Situation Center. She offered Thompson a formal nod from where she stood on the steps adjacent to the first tier, receiving a status report from a civilian specialist manning one of the workstations there. The general held no doubts that Alicia could handle anything that might arise while he was being briefed.

"Okay," he said to Brooks, "let's do it." As the two men moved toward the hallway leading from the Situation Center, Thompson glanced toward his friend. "This ought to be one hell of a meeting," he said, considering who was waiting for them. "Ever regret not retiring when you had the chance?"

Without missing a beat, Brooks replied, "I've regretted not finding something else to do with my life since the first day I met you."

Thompson laughed at that, recalling the circumstances that had served to introduce the two men to each other. Also a veteran of the war in Vietnam, Brooks had not been a pilot, but rather a volunteer for one of the teams trained to enter enemy territory and rescue downed pilots before they could be captured by Vietnamese forces. After having his plane blown out of the sky by a surface-to-air missile, young Lieutenant Bruce Thompson managed to evade enemy troops for four days, long enough for an equally youthful yet strangely determined Lieutenant Tommy Brooks to lead just such a team into the thick, stifling jungle near the Laotian border. After finding Thompson, exiting the area proved easier said than done, with Brooks and his team engaging a contingent of Viet Cong soldiers in a short yet brutal firefight before managing to get themselves and their charge the hell out of there.

"You never did thank me for that, by the way," Brooks added.

"I introduced you to your first wife," Thompson retorted.

Brooks offered his friend a sidelong glance. "Yeah, and if I'd known you were going to do that, I'd have left your scrawny lily-white ass in that jungle."

The short corridor, all polished white linoleum floor tiles and equally pallid walls featuring a few framed photographs to break up its otherwise sterile confines, possessed only two doors, set into opposite walls directly across from each other. Thompson's private office lay through the door on the left and was so marked with a nameplate mounted at eye level, whereas the door on the right offered no clues as to what might be behind it. A keypad was set into the wall next to the door, with a single indicator light that glowed red. Thompson waited while Brooks entered a nine-digit access code, after which the indicator changed to a warm green glow and an audible click echoed in the narrow passageway. Reaching for the doorknob, Brooks pushed open the door and stepped aside to allow Thompson entry to the room.

Unlike the stark white corridor behind him, this room was appointed in rich cedarwood paneling, with a flat-screen television mounted on the far wall. An American flag as well as the standards for each branch of the U.S. armed forces flanked the screen, to the right of which hung a framed portrait of the current commander in chief. The room's dominant furnishing was the polished oval conference table, also constructed of cedar protected by a thick acrylic sealant. Six high-backed leather chairs were situated around the table, two of which were occupied. Sitting in the chair closest to him was Nancy Spencer, dressed in a dark blue pantsuit, her omnipresent ponytail resting along her right shoulder. She rose from her seat in deference to Thompson's arrival, her actions mimicked by the Marine general sitting at the head of the table.

Dressed in olive green trousers and jacket over a khaki shirt and tie, the general's own uniform was the epitome of perfection the Marine Corps demanded of its members. His hair, what little there was of it, was gray and shorn close to his scalp, and the tanned skin of his face was unblemished save for the single thin scar across his chin. Piercing cobalt blue eyes bored into Thompson, but the general's otherwise arresting presence was softened by the small smile he offered in greeting.

"General Thompson," said General Andrew Grayson, chairman of the Joint Chiefs of Staff, as he extended his hand.

Taking it and returning the firm handshake, Thompson clapped the other man on his shoulder. "Good to see you, Andy, though I'm sure I'm going to wish it were under better circumstances."

Grayson waved away the comment. "Well, let's just say we've been busy."

"I'll bet," Brooks said as everyone took a seat at the table. Reaching for the keypad on an interior wall near the door, he keyed another code, which locked the door and activated a series of electronic countermeasures designed to thwart any attempts at eavesdropping. To Thompson and Grayson, he said, "We're locked in, gentlemen."

Nodding in approval at his XO, Thompson leaned back in his chair and gestured toward the picture on the wall near the flat screen. "How's the president doing?"

"All things considered, pretty damned well, I think," Grayson replied, reaching with his right hand for the coffee mug sitting atop a polished ceramic coaster and emblazoned with the 4-Echo emblem. "I had my doubts about him, even before any of this mess started, but given what he's had to deal with this past year? We could've done a lot worse, that's for sure."

The current president had taken office just over a year earlier, well before the first incidents of alien activity on Earth had become known. Still, the new chief executive had inherited from his predecessor a number of issues de-

manding urgent and decisive action. A faltering economy
coupled with ongoing military actions in Iraq and Afghanistan, as well as world opinion sharply against much of the
United States' foreign policy agenda and attitudes, were
more than enough to keep any president busy until reelec-
tion, or until such time as the leader of the world's most
powerful nation simply threw in the towel and opted to flee
to Tahiti.

None of that was made any easier by the additional burden of leading the country—indeed, the entire planet, al-
beit with the assistance of other national leaders around the
world—as it faced interplanetary war. Differences and political turmoil that had embroiled the nations of Earth for
decades had to be set aside in order for humanity to stand as
one in the face of the alien threat. While the notion was a
hopeful one, reality saw to it that achieving such a goal was
not easy. Only a person possessing unique wisdom, vision,
and strength of character would be able to rise to such an
unprecedented challenge.

Was the current president that kind of person? So far as
Thompson could tell, the man seemed to be shouldering
his unique burden with aplomb, aided as he was by a tal-
ented and diverse team of civilian and military advisors, including battle-tested warriors such as the hardened Marine
now sitting before him.

"So, what brings you down to the basement?" Thompson asked.

Reaching for a silver metal briefcase positioned near his
right leg, Grayson placed it on the conference table and
spent a moment working with the dual yet independent
locks securing the case and its contents. Once it was open,
the general retrieved a quartet of red file folders, each emblazoned with a stenciled TOP SECRET label. Normally, a
lower-ranking officer acting as aide to the Marine general

would be on hand to disperse such documents to the meeting participants, but on this occasion such assistance was conspicuously absent, communicating to Thompson the secrecy surrounding the information Grayson was about to impart.

"Operation Clear Sky," he said, sliding a folder each to Thompson, Brooks, and Spencer.

Without opening her folder, Spencer asked, "Our response?"

Grayson nodded. "And then some."

Opening the folder before him, Thompson was not surprised to see only two sheets of paper. The contents were sparse, listing cold, lifeless numbers of personnel, as well as different types of military assets. By itself, the sheets resembled no more than a table of organization and equipment such as what might be generated by a military unit of any appreciable size and structure.

"The information I've provided is compartmentalized," Grayson said, obviously anticipating the question Thompson was about to ask, "offering estimates on the number of troops and levels of equipment we think will be necessary for what we're planning. What it does not contain are dates and locations, for security purposes as much as because we're still working out those aspects of the campaign."

"This is it, then," Brooks said, eyeing his own folder. "Our big push."

"It's still in the planning stages, of course," Grayson replied, "but this is the foundation."

Glancing again at his own copy of the report, Thompson was having a hard time accepting what he was seeing. "These numbers are massive, Andy. Are we really . . . ?"

"Clear Sky is going to make D-Day look like a Boy Scout jamboree," Grayson said, his voice hard. "The only way we're going to have a chance of winning this war is if we knock the Grays back on their asses, and we need to do it on *their* planet instead of ours. We've been running the numbers—every kind of computer simulation you can think of—and feel an operation of this type and scale is our best chance of putting the Grays on the defensive. After that, we turn to occupation."

"Occupation? Of an entire planet?" Spencer asked, making no attempt to hide her skepticism. "Even if it's just half, we're still . . . Jesus."

"The plan obviously calls for Plysserian assistance," Grayson countered, "both here and on their planet." He pointed to her folder. "What that doesn't tell you is that those numbers reflect the inclusion of Blue assets. We see this as a two-phased campaign, with a joint first strike designed to hit them hard and fast, followed by the longer phase of securing and establishing control of key Chodrecai targets. Transition to Plysserian command will occur during that aspect of the operation, with our units taking on a secondary role until such time as the situation is stabilized, after which they'll be brought home. Make no mistake: Without the Plysserians, this doesn't have a chance in hell of succeeding."

Leaning forward until his forearms rested atop the conference table, Thompson frowned. "How are you coordinating all of this?"

Grayson shook his head. "At the moment, we're not. Bruce, there are fewer than thirty people in the world right now who know the full scope of what this operation means to do, and it's going to stay that way as long as humanly possible." He paused, considering what he had just said, and added, "No disrespect intended toward our Blue friends, of course. Right now, unit commanders have been given specific training, staffing, and equipment procurement requirements, and ordered to integrate them into their ongoing planning and deployments. Despite how big this campaign will be, we don't have the luxury of devoting mass numbers of troops to special training for months at a time. We have no choice but to keep our forces on alert and ready to fight at a moment's notice, even while their commanders are trying to get them ready for another battle they don't even know is coming."

"What are we talking about, General?" Brooks said. "Do you even have a preliminary number of targets you're considering?"

"As of now, fourteen," Grayson replied. "Expect that number to increase."

"Fourteen?" Spencer repeated. "Coordinating something on that scale would be ludicrous."

To Thompson's surprise, the Marine general shrugged. "We don't believe that's the case, Ms. Spencer, particularly with the technology at our disposal. This is the main reason we've been pushing for the larger portal generators."

"I figured as much," Thompson said. With a wry grin, he added, "Some of the memos you boys have been sending us make more sense now." 4-Echo had fielded numerous requests from JCS relating to the research and reverse engineering of the portal generation equipment as well as other alien technology. Though he had suspected something along those lines had been in the planning stages, Thompson had to admit he was not prepared for Operation Clear Sky's potential scope, which as Grayson already had intimated would dwarf the efforts of Operation Overlord six decades earlier. More than one-hundred-fifty-thousand American, British, and Canadian troops hit the beaches of Normandy during that fateful June morning in 1944, the six-pronged assault being the vanguard of what over the next two months would swell to a force numbering more than three million. The campaign employed a coordinated offensive strategy that was the culmination of nearly two years' planning and training. More than ten thousand Allied casualties were recorded on that first day, with a comparable amount of German casualties, though to this day the actual number remained unconfirmed. How many soldiers—human, Plysserian, and Chodrecai alike—would die in those first terrifying hours as Clear Sky unfolded on the soil of a distant alien world?

"I get the secrecy, General," Brooks said, "but at some point, we're going to have to involve Plysserian military leaders on *Jontashreena*."

Grayson paused, taking a sip of coffee and then clearing his throat before replying, "We will when the time's right, but that's not now. We're a long way away from being ready for this, and given the logistics of coordinating a battle plan across two planets, the fewer people who know about this, the better off we're all going to be." He stopped, as though replaying the words he had just spoken in his mind, before shaking his head and sighing. "No matter how many times I say or even think something like that, it still sounds like some video game my grandson might play."

Thompson nodded in understanding, having been gripped by similar thoughts more than once over the past several months. Considering the information Grayson had offered and the raw numbers staring up at him from the red file folder, he could see more than one problem with the scenario currently being plotted by the Marine general and his companions at JCS.

"The portals will be the biggest issue," Thompson said, reaching up to rub the bridge of his nose. "There's no way they'll sustain an operation like this. We'll have people on the ground waiting for reinforcements, which could take as much as half an hour to deliver. For the time in between, they'll be completely on their own."

Clasping his hands and resting them atop the conference table, Grayson replied, "So were the first waves at Omaha Beach, and the other five beaches on D-Day, or any of the first groups of Marines to go ashore at any of the islands during the Pacific campaign."

"This will be different, General," Spencer said, and Thompson had to suppress a grin as he watched his trusted assistant go after the JCS chairman. "For the intervals when the portal generators are recycling and cooling down, those troops already deployed will have no support except their own asses and whatever we push through the conduits. No naval gunfire or ground-based artillery, few if any air assets. The first hours of such a campaign will likely decide how the whole damned thing will go down."

"We're working on that," Grayson said, and when several seconds passed it became obvious that the Marine was not going to elaborate. Instead, he said, "We also know that we've got a long way to go before we're ready. This operation will take a lot of coordination and effort on numerous fronts, many of which have yet to be identified. The sooner you can start making progress on the portal tech, the sooner our plans can fall into place." He tapped the folder lying before him for emphasis. "Make no mistake, people; this is our Hail Mary pass. Once we commit, there's no turning back, and the outcome of the game rests on who catches this fucking ball. So, get me something I can use, and let's get on with shoving that ball up their asses."

9:42.

Looking at the clock on the store's far wall, Brian sighed in mounting frustration. At this rate, there was no way he was going to last until six o'clock without choking the shit out of Jeff.

I'm not even supposed to be here today, he scolded himself. *Why the hell didn't I fake sick when I had the chance?*

"Come on," Jeff said from where he stood in front of the coolers along the store's back wall, wiping one door's glass front with a sponge. "You know it makes perfect sense."

Leaning on the counter next to the cash register, Brian shook his head. "Bigfoot was created by environmentalists to combat logging companies?"

"Not just one, but a whole colony of them," Jeff said as he finished with the door and moved on to the adjacent cooler. "Think about it. They get genetic scientists to create these things, drop them into places like the Pacific Northwest where the tree-huggers and the developers are always going at each other." Pausing to scratch at a stubborn stain tarnishing the glass just below eye level, he glanced over his shoulder. "Get enough people to report sightings, footprints, all that shit, then they go to the government and whine and complain that these creatures are scientific oddities that have to be protected for study. The only way to do that, of course, is to declare its natural habitats conservation areas, which means, among other things, no logging. No new housing developments or strip malls, either, which isn't such a bad thing. I mean, how many tanning salons and yoga dens and take-out Chinese joints does one planet need, anyway?"

"That's the stupidest fucking thing I've ever heard," Brian snapped, dismissing his coworker's theory with a wave. "And that's saying something, considering the shit you keep coming up with." Though Jeff had started working here less than a month ago, it had taken him substantially less time to become annoying as hell.

Before Jeff's arrival, Brian had easily handled the hectic pace of working alone—at least most of the time—at Gary's General Store, situated near the center of downtown Panguitch, Utah. However, the demand for the types of goods the store sold had skyrocketed in recent months, owing to rationing mandated by the government, and the fact that the curfews enforced by local police as well as the National Guard made traveling any great distance from Panguitch problematic at best. In the beginning, the demand had been for camping equipment and other "survivalist" supplies as people worried about being caught without power or water in the event of alien invasion. Such hysteria was short-lived, but Gary Clarkson, Brian's boss, had considered closing the store once it became common knowledge that the bizarre war with aliens from that other planet could erupt anywhere at any time. It had seemed like a logical idea, given the number of residents who had chosen to leave town and head for supposed safety in the mountains or the desert. Despite this, Clarkson backed off the idea in deference to no less than a passionate plea by the town's mayor, Tim Whitsitt. The mayor hoped to demonstrate to residents that Panguitch would persevere through the current crisis just as it had through the Great Depression, two world wars, and even the outsourcing of manufacturing jobs to factories on the other side of the planet. Whitsitt even made the point that there was probably a store like Gary's in every small town in America, doing its part to help the country through these trying times.

Yeah, but do they all have an asshole like Jeff on their payrolls? The more he thought about it, the more Brian came to believe that such was indeed the case, just as there likely was a poor schmuck like him forced to endure said asshole's antics.

The store's business, always steady dating back to its opening forty years earlier, was nothing short of brisk these days. Though the pronounced downturn in freight traffic across the country had affected the store's inventory, the town's ever-resourceful residents had stepped in to fill the void. Gardens were everywhere, from small efforts hanging from windowsills or apartment balconies to larger versions taking up entire backyards or other unused land. The tending of livestock also was on the rise, and hunting and fishing regulations had been relaxed in this and the surrounding counties. As a consequence of such activities, a barter and trade system had emerged to complement regular business, and in time Gary's shelves were filled with such items as locally and regionally grown fresh and canned fruits and vegetables, fresh meats, and even homemade tools and other useful items. The local effort did far more than simply fill in the gaps left by the decrease in regular deliveries via trucks and rail; it bloated the store to the point of bursting, making it a primary resource not just for the town but also the surrounding counties.

Naturally, the store's good fortune meant it also had its share of problems. Like other businesses around town,

Gary's had been the victim of looting and even one armed robbery. The crime problem had largely been quelled thanks to an increased police presence as well as a contingent from the Utah National Guard, but even they had been unable to discourage the occasional breaking and entering. The incidents had prompted Gary to assign a second employee to the store's late shift. Brian worked the main counter and handled most of the store's customers, while Jeff took care of stocking shelves and whatever odd jobs needed to be done, doing so while dispensing his own peculiar and oftentimes irritating viewpoint on whatever topic tickled his fancy on a given day.

The conspiracy theories had started out simple and even amusing at first, with the usual topics that Brian had already heard about, such as the JFK assassination or the moon landings being faked or some other such crap. If nothing else, the lively conversations that often ensued when Jeff revealed one of his theories helped to while away the time on slower days. Still, the fun had faded quickly as Jeff's outlandish speculations branched out to include everything from the government kidnapping innocent people they suspected of being terrorists to aliens trying to control the populace by masking hypnotic messages in the transmissions of television shows and movies over cable lines.

"Of course, their master plan isn't working as they hoped, since most people record TV shows for later viewing, and fast-forward through the commercials," Jeff proclaimed one memorable Saturday night. "That, and the government is always preempting schedules with news coverage these days. You can bet they're working on a new plan, though."

Double-checking the money in the cash register, Brian decided to play along with Jeff's latest conspiracy theory. "I thought Bigfoot was a robot created by aliens to keep hikers away from where they were hiding in the mountains or something."

Offering a disgusted frown, Jeff shook his head. "You watch too much TV, dude." Having finished cleaning the cooler doors, Jeff moved toward one of the smaller refrigeration units near the front of the store, retrieving a bottled soft drink. He twisted the cap from the soda bottle as he moved back behind the counter, pausing at the magazine racks to help himself to an issue of *Hustler*, which Brian knew the other man had flipped through numerous times already. The timely arrival of such publications had been among the first casualties to the store's rotating inventory, much to the chagrin of more than a few town residents.

"Think about it," Jeff continued. "All the stories you heard about Bigfoot in the nineteen twenties and thirties are bullshit, but there's enough there for the Sierra Club or some other group to take and use as the foundation for a massive disinformation campaign. The whole thing takes years to put together and execute. They're the ones who provide the pictures and movie footage we've seen. Remember the film that guy shot in the sixties? You know, the one with Bigfoot walking away from the camera? That was them."

Already tiring of the game, Brian rubbed his temples with his fingers. "That was a hoax, dumbass. The guy who did the makeup for the original *Planet of the Apes* movie was behind that. I read it in the paper years ago."

"Ah, you've fallen for the clever ruse, just like thousands before you," Jeff countered as he made his way behind the cashier's counter. "They put out that hoax rumor to throw people off the track of the real proof that Bigfoot is all their baby."

"Where do you get this crap?" Brian asked, lamenting the fact that—as he already had pointed out several times during the past hours—this was supposed to be his day off.

"The Internet, mostly," Jeff said without looking up from the centerfold of *Hustler*'s Honey of the Month from several months earlier. "The truth is out there, dude. It's amazing what you can find if you know where to look."

Ignoring Jeff's reply, Brian rolled his eyes as he moved from behind the counter. He needed a cigarette, he decided. Patting his pockets, he remembered that he had already smoked his last one an hour or so earlier.

Fuck.

He grabbed a pack of Marlboros from the dispenser over the cash register, making a mental note to pay for the cigarettes later as he headed for the rear of the store. "We're almost finished, so I'm gonna grab a quick smoke." The nightly curfew for businesses in Panguitch had been set at ten o'clock, with proprietors required to exit the area via a checkpoint at the north end of the main street running through the center of the small downtown district, after which time they had thirty minutes to return to their residences. Reentry was not permitted before six-thirty the following morning, after passing through the same checkpoint, and violation of the ordinances carried stiff penalties. With everyone in town feeling the need to pull together in order to get through the crisis currently gripping the country and indeed the entire world, tolerance for looting, burglary, and other crimes against property and persons was now viewed as an offense against the entire Panguitch community.

"I'll be out back if you need me," Brian called over his shoulder as he headed for the back door. Waiting for him were two garbage bags, situated in the narrow hallway and blocking his path. One of the bags had torn and allowed a vile brown liquid to leak onto the floor.

"Jeff!" he shouted back into the store, hoping against hope that some of his damn Bigfoot buddies would show up and pound him into a meatball. "Get a mop and clean this shit up, huh?"

Brian grabbed a bag with each hand as he kicked at the door and let it swing open. He stepped outside into the near darkness, leaving a nasty brown trail behind him. The store's parking lot was little more than a patch of gravel, sandwiched in the alley between two rows of buildings. At the lot's far end was a Dumpster, protected from the whims of evil garbage thieves and illegal dumpers by a perimeter of less-than-formidable chain-link fencing. Rather than unlock the fence's gate to give him access to the trash receptacle, Brian tossed first one bag and then the other over the six-foot barrier, foul dark liquid arcing across the pavement and splashing across the fence. Some of it spattered the legs of his khaki cargo pants, eliciting yet another stream of profanity.

Shaking his head in disgust, Brian reached into his pockets to extract his lighter and the recently acquired pack of cigarettes. Firing up a Marlboro, he drew the initial drag of smoke deep into his lungs, savoring the taste of the nicotine-laden tobacco as he turned to walk back to the store. Of course he knew cigarettes were bad for him and he had tried to cut down. He could honestly say that he smoked only during work these days, which he chalked up to being nothing more than a defense mechanism against beating Jeff with a baseball bat.

Pray I never quit, dickbag, Brian mused as he took another drag on the cigarette. He leaned against the brick facade of the store's back wall, trying to relax and enjoy a few precious moments of quiet and solitude. His only exertion was the effort required to bring the dwindling cigarette to his lips and flick away ash. He stared across the alley at the back door of the building opposite Gary's store and the weather-beaten poster affixed to it.

One corner of the poster had torn loose from where it was nailed to the door, and it had faded from months of sunlight beating down upon it, but it was still legible, declaring in what had once been bold red letters: HAVE YOU OBSERVED ALIEN ACTIVITY? REPORT IT IMMEDIATELY! The directive was underscored by a toll-free telephone number and a website where dutiful citizens could convey whatever they might have seen while going to and fro about their lives.

Posters like it and a handful of others, all bearing some variation of dire warning or terse instruction regarding encounters with the enemy alien soldiers, littered the town. Some of the more outlandish placards depicted outrageous caricatures of the Grays abducting women or shooting children or even crushing the very Earth itself in their massive hands. Brian's grandmother, one night over dinner, had told him that seeing the placards reminded her of the months following the United States' declaration of war against Japan and Germany. Similar posters had fueled paranoia, fear, and hatred toward America's enemies as the country's armed forces trained and readied for combat in Europe and the Pacific. In the decades following the war, such propaganda had come to be regarded in hindsight as racist hate-mongering, and Brian now forced a laugh as he considered just how easily history could repeat itself if the right circumstances were proffered.

Then there were the posters and billboards that encouraged able-bodied men and women to report to the nearest military recruiting office and do their part to assist the "war effort." At thirty-one, his parents dead and his grandmother his only remaining family member, Brian was exempt from the draft, which had been reinstated as a means of filling the ranks of America's uniformed services. With the military apparently not an option, he had explored serving in some other capacity, driven by a compulsion he could not explain to contribute in some meaningful way to the challenge the world now faced. Not surprisingly, the waiting list for applicants was long, and while he had visited a civil service human resources office and filled out numerous forms, he was still waiting to hear back from them. At the rate they and the rest of the government seemed to be moving, the war with the Chodrecai might well be over before Brian got his chance to help out.

Good thing Gary likes you, he thought as he cast a glance toward the store's open back door. *At least you've got job security.*

Resigned to his short-term fate, Brian regarded the nearly depleted cigarette in his hand, grunting at the too-quick passage of time as he dropped the butt to the pavement and ground it out beneath his shoe. Pushing off from the wall, he turned to head back to the store when the sound of something rubbing against something else caught his attention.

What the hell?

"Jeff?" he called out, glancing toward the doorway leading back into the store. Was that idiot trying to screw with him? Nothing was there, save light cast by the dim bulb hanging just inside the entrance. The parking lot offered little in the way of concealment, save for the area around the Dumpster and its fence.

As Brian regarded the fence, shadows around it started to move. Then a shadow stepped away from the Dumpster and into the dim light cast by the bulbs mounted above the doorways on either side of the parking lot, and Brian felt his body tremble in fear as he looked into the eyes of the Chodrecai soldier.

"Oh sweet Jesus."

The Gray bastard was *fucking huge*, muscled and dressed in a formfitting garment over which it wore a sort of equipment harness. It stood frozen in place, staring at him as though sizing him up and determining how much of a threat Brian presented. What the fuck was the thing doing here? What possible reason could the aliens have for even wanting to come here? Panguitch was the ass end of nowhere, possessing absolutely nothing of worth to anyone *already living* on this planet, much less anyone coming here from another world. How had it gotten here, sneaking past National Guard and police checkpoints, to say nothing of avoiding being seen by any of the town's three thousand residents? Had it been hiding behind the fence this entire time, watching him?

The very thought nearly made Brian want to piss himself, an urge that was only exacerbated as he stared into the two dark pools that were the creature's eyes. They were ovals of utter blackness threatening to absorb the surrounding light, and when it opened its mouth, Brian saw the irregular rows of jagged teeth. He was not bothered by those so much as he was by the monstrous rifle the thing carried in its massive hands. The weapon's barrel, pointing at the ground as the Gray stepped from its place of concealment, now was rising to take aim at him.

Fuck me!

Brian turned and bolted for the open door, hearing a horrific belch of power and feeling a rush of air push just past the back of his head before something punched the wall behind him. He flinched as fragments of brick and mortar peppered his back. His pulse pounding in his ears, he looked back over his shoulder and saw the Gray adjusting its aim.

That was when Brian pissed himself, even as he lunged for the doorway. This was how it was going to end? Getting blown to shit by an alien ray gun, his entrails and brains splattered over the back wall of the store, while that asshole Jeff remained safe inside? Life and fate could be heartless bitches.

He was falling over the threshold of the back door when a barrage of gunfire ripped through the alley. Curling into a ball on the dulled linoleum floor of the narrow corridor and covering his head with his arms, he still saw the glint of muzzle flashes reflecting off the walls outside. There was no way to count the number of bullets being expended, or the number of shooters, but what Brian did not hear was the gruesome burst of energy that signified the Gray's weapon firing. Instead, he heard several voices, some of them shouting what to him sounded like orders. Was it his imagination, or did he also hear grunts of pain and perhaps even fear?

Uncertain as to how long the firefight had lasted, Brian heard the rifle fire dwindle before it stopped altogether. Even with his ears still ringing, he was able to catch fragments of someone shouting over the sounds of heavy running footsteps across the parking lot's gravel. He saw figures moving past the doorway toward the Dumpster, several wearing different versions of camouflage uniforms and all of them carrying some kind of gun. The back door was swinging back and forth, and Brian saw a pattern of holes punched into its metal surface.

Then the barrel of a shotgun poked through the doorway, leveled at him.

"Jesus!" Brian shouted, raising his arms to show his hands. "Don't fucking shoot me, man!"

Darryl Coates, a friend of his and the owner of a car repair garage at the end of the street, looked at him over the shotgun's barrel. His eyes widened in recognition and he lowered the weapon, and Brian saw the look of excitement and fear on the older man's face as he stared back at him.

"Sorry, Brian," Coates said. "You okay?"

Brian nodded as he pulled himself to his feet. "Yeah, I think so." His left leg was cold and damp, and when he looked down it was to see a large stain darkening his khaki trousers, radiating downward from his crotch.

"Dude," another voice said. "You pissed yourself?" Gritting his teeth, Brian turned to regard Jeff, who was studying him with an expression mixed of equal parts fright and confusion, though there also was a hint of amusement. The other man looked once more at Brian's pants before nodding toward the door. "What's going on out there?"

"One of the things," Brian replied, now more than a little self-conscious about his damp trousers. "A fucking alien. The damned thing almost killed me."

"He was a straggler," Coates said, and when Brian looked at him this time he saw that the other man's face and hands were covered with grease and oil, bearing witness to the fact that he had dropped whatever he was doing in order to brandish his shotgun and join in the hunt for the alien. "One of the National Guard units found a group of them in the mountains outside of town. They either captured or killed most of them, but three got away, and the Guard asked us to help track them down."

For months, Coates and more than one hundred Panguitch residents had been acting as an informal militia, lending their time, effort, and weapons to act as a sort of armed "neighborhood watch" program in the event alien activity was detected anywhere in or around town. Similar groups had cropped up in cities and towns of every size across the country, helping out in situations where the military was shorthanded, freeing the professional soldiers to see to more pressing, dangerous concerns. Though precautions were taken to minimize risk, the arrangement did not preclude a civilian from occasionally coming into hostile contact with a Gray. Most of the shop owners in town served at least some time with the militia, but Brian had not volunteered, owing mostly to his strict aversion to firearms.

I think I'm going to get over that, sooner rather than later.

"Any luck?" Brian asked.

Coates nodded. "Killed one about ten miles from here, and one's still out there, somewhere." Using his left hand to reach up and wipe sweat from his forehead, Coates then gestured back into the alley. "Of course, we got this bastard, too."

"Sweet," Jeff said, stepping around Brian in order to look toward the Dumpster. "Can I see?"

Muttering vulgarities under his breath, Brian moved to stand closer to his coworker just as another man, this one dressed in a proper military uniform with the appropriate insignia, equipment, and accessories, appeared just outside the doorway. Leveling a withering stare at Brian, the soldier said, "What the hell were you doing outside? Didn't you hear the advisory to stay indoors? We've been hunting these sons of bitches for over an hour. You're lucky that thing didn't shred your ass."

Confused, Brian shook his head as he regarded the body of the slain alien, around which several other soldiers were standing, congratulating themselves on having brought down their adversary. "I never heard anything." Looking to Jeff, he asked, "Did you hear anything on the radio?"

Suddenly looking anxious, Jeff stuttered before replying, "Um, no, but that's probably because I turned off the radio a couple of hours ago, so I could watch a DVD in the back room."

"You stupid motherfucker!" It was all Brian could do to keep from throttling his coworker right then and there. Clenching his fists at his sides, Brian took a couple of calming breaths before returning his attention to the soldiers. "What the hell were they doing here in the first place?"

The soldier shrugged. "We didn't ask. Maybe it was looking for food, or a place to hide."

"Does this mean one of those tunnels, or portals, or whatever you guys call them, is around here somewhere?" Jeff asked, his expression for the first time showing genuine concern.

"Not at the location we found them," Coates replied. He said nothing else, but there was no mistaking the obvious meaning behind his words.

Brian felt tightness in his throat, which remained despite several attempts at swallowing. "Which means there could be more of those things running around."

"Looks that way, yeah." A shouted order from the far end of the alley made the soldier look in that direction and wave to someone Brian could not see. To Coates, he said, "We're moving out. Thanks for your help, sir." Turning to Brian and Jeff, he added, "I'm leaving two men here to watch the Gray's body until a team can retrieve it. In the meantime, I suggest you stay inside." Scowling at Jeff, he added, "And turn on your damned radio." With that, he turned and left, jogging across the parking lot to where his companions were convening. Watching him go, Brian could not help imagining the possibilities the soldier's remarks conjured. How many of those gray bastards were out there, perhaps on the run and looking for any kind of safe haven, with the lights of Panguitch calling out to them from the darkness?

And here I stand, Brian chastised himself, *with piss running down my leg.*

"This is some crazy shit, ain't it?" Coates asked, after the soldier had departed.

Jeff nodded. "You said it, brother."

Grunting at the understatement, Brian could only shake his head. "You want to know what the worst part about this is? I'm not even supposed to be here today."

12

Colin Laney opened his eyes, instantly awake.

Lying on his back, the first thing he saw was the web of stretched wire and springs forming the underside of the rack above him, bowed in the middle from the weight of its occupant, Recruit Alejandro Juarez. Light snoring from above him told Colin that whatever had roused him, it had not affected his bunkmate in similar fashion.

"Lucky bastard," Colin whispered, low enough that his voice did not carry and run the risk of waking the recruits sleeping around him.

In the two weeks since Platoon 3003's arrival at the barracks that was its home for the foreseeable future, Colin had yet to adjust to his surroundings enough to be able to sleep through the night. Falling asleep was easy enough, owing mostly to the mental and physical fatigue that gripped him every night as the lights in the squad bay were extinguished promptly at 9:00 P.M. — 2100, in military parlance. Despite fears and preconceptions fueled no doubt by too many movies, the drill instructors did not return in the middle of the night to harass the recruits, allowing them instead to sleep until 5:00 A.M. on most mornings. There had been exceptions, owing to some event or training exercise that required the platoon to be roused earlier in order to be somewhere before sunrise. Observing the drill instructors, Colin had come to the conclusion that the Marines adhered to a rigid schedule, the details of which the recruits knew nothing, yet the instructors seemed able to follow with pinpoint precision. That they were able to keep the fifty-plus recruits moving—overseeing them as they woke up, dressed, made their racks, and cleaned the squad bay, all in a matter of minutes—in order to have them at the mess hall for breakfast at their appointed arrival time was an act of time and personnel management to be admired and even envied by parents and civilian employers.

Still, Colin had not yet adapted to what should have become routine. He found himself waking up nearly every night, unsure as to the time since his wristwatch was secure in his footlocker and the only clock in the squad bay was at its far end, out of his line of sight. Sometimes he awakened from a dream, requiring a moment or two to recall his present location and circumstances. On other occasions, he found himself disturbed by the movements of one of the two recruits assigned to the barracks security patrol, or "fire watch" as it was called. The watches were divided into two-hour shifts, from lights out until reveille, with each recruit in the platoon pulling the duty every five or six days. Their tasks were simple: walk the floor of the squad bay, ensuring the other recruits remained in their racks, and be on the lookout for fire or some other form of disorder that might require a drill instructor's attention. One of the three instructors assigned to each platoon spent the night in the barracks, ensconced within a small office at the front of the squad bay known as the "D.I. hut." The door to the office was closed, its lights were out, and blinds were drawn across the large window overlooking the squad bay, but none of the recruits believed for an instant that the Marine inside—Sergeant Stevens on this night—would not come charging out of the room, awake, alert, and likely angry, the moment something untoward occurred.

Tonight was not a night to which Colin had been scheduled for fire watch, but it might as well have been. He now knew he was awake, and there was no way he was going back to sleep, at least not until he saw to his current problem: He needed to piss.

Damn it.

Resigning himself to the inevitable, Colin rolled out of bed, careful not to disturb his neighbors in the adjacent racks as he found the pair of shower shoes positioned beneath his cot alongside his combat boots and running shoes. Ostensibly for reasons of hygiene, recruits were forbidden to walk anywhere in the squad bay, even in the shower, in their bare feet, but the shoes were of the cheapest possible quality, spongy rubber to which had been affixed hard plastic straps to keep them on their wearer's feet. Colin hated them and the clip-clop noise they made as he walked, which he knew would sound like firecrackers going off in the otherwise dead silence enveloping the squad bay.

He stretched, working the kinks out of his lower back before reaching up to scratch his nearly bald head. His fingertips brushed across the stubble, no more than a couple of millimeters in length, and he wondered when the drill instructors would march the platoon to the barbershop to have even this pathetic excuse for hair growth removed. His first haircut, like that of every recruit in the platoon, had occurred within hours of his arrival at Parris Island and while still wearing his street clothes, the hair on his head but the first of many aspects of his former life to be surrendered to the Marine Corps.

Chicks dig bald guys, you know.

Colin walked as quietly as he could, maneuvering down the narrow passageway between the racks and the bank of

windows. As he emerged from the shadows into the open
area of the squad bay, he saw one of the recruits currently
on duty, Michael Swanson. The young African-American
man was dressed in his Marine Corps combat utility uniform along with his web equipment belt, or "war belt,"
and its two canteens of water, as well as the lightweight
silver helmet—actually a liner from an older generation
of helmet, which the Kevlar models had replaced years
ago—nicknamed a "chrome dome" by the drill instructors.
He carried a flashlight in his right hand, which was extinguished and would remain so unless something happened
to break the ·monotonous routine of walking in circles
around the barracks. Waving to Swanson, Colin pointed
toward the door leading to the head, or what Marines and
sailors for reasons surpassing understanding called a bathroom. The other man nodded in comprehension before
continuing on his circuit of the squad bay. No other communication was needed, and neither recruit wanted to risk
the slightest sound which might summon Sergeant Stevens
from the D.I. hut.

He'd dig me until dawn, Colin mused, referring to the
practice of disciplinary physical training the drill instructors loved to inflict upon hapless recruits, either individually or in groups of varying sizes up to and including the
entire platoon, for any and all reasons or infractions real or
imagined. Such "digging" often took place on the "quar-
terdeck," a small expanse of open floor near the front of
the squad bay, where recruits would be subjected to push-
ups, jumping jacks, leg lifts, or other merciless abdomi-
nal exercises. A personal favorite of Sergeant Stevens was
the "mountain climber," whereby the recruit assumed the
push-up position with arms extended, and then proceeded
to run in place while keeping the palms of his hands flat
on the floor. It was particularly unforgiving on the squad

bay's concrete floor, and it was not unusual to see puddles of sweat beneath the poor bastard selected for such punishment, which of course would have to be cleaned up upon completion of the disciplinary action. One of Stevens's habits on the nights he was alone with the platoon was to randomly select recruits for such extracurricular activities, for no other apparent reason than because it amused him. He had done so again earlier in the evening, though Colin on this occasion had escaped the sergeant's menacing eye.

So let's not fuck things up now, okay?

Colin was standing at the urinal, considering the notion of taking over fire watch from Swanson or his companion and allowing one of them to return to bed, when his attention was caught by the sounds of movement elsewhere in the head. Looking over his shoulder, he peered into the room's gloomy interior, light from outside streetlamps reflecting off the polished white ceramic tiles covering the walls. To his right was the row of toilet stalls, each stool separated by wooden partitions to offer a modicum of privacy but possessing no door. Three stalls down, Colin was able to make out the shadow of someone occupying it, and now he heard sounds he could not identify.

Shit, is somebody whacking off? Momentarily embarrassed that he might have intruded on another recruit's attempt at privacy, Colin supposed it was not out of the question; after all, the platoon was comprised of energetic young men in their sexual prime. Of course, it occurred to him at that moment that he had not even thought about such things since arriving at Parris Island. He did not believe the stories that the food the recruits ate was laced with saltpeter in a bid to forestall unwanted erections in the squad bay. Instead, Colin chalked his lack of such urges to simple fatigue and the breakneck pace of training.

Someone else, it seemed, was not about to let that stop him.

Endeavoring to keep from alerting the other, still unknown recruit to his presence, Colin stepped away from the urinal without flushing and moved toward the door when he spotted movement from the stall. A hand reached out to grab the crossbeam that sat across the entrance to the small compartment, perhaps seven feet off the floor. There was movement, most of which Colin could not see in the near-total darkness, and he almost bolted from the head to avoid being seen when he heard what he realized was the sound of crying. That, he also could understand, given the stresses and the complete culture shock to which the recruits had been subjected in just these first two weeks of training. Everything they had valued as civilians, as individuals, even as simple human beings, had been stripped away, leaving them little more than masses of soft flesh, weak muscles, and wandering, lazy minds. The drill instructors of Parris Island then used these as the ingredients for what might possibly become a basically trained Marine. The demands the men of Platoon 3003 had shouldered for the past fifteen days were just a precursor of what was to come, Colin knew, but for some of the recruits, such strain—which likely exceeded anything they had been forced to endure in their short, often undemanding lives—would prove too much to bear.

The whimpering from the stall was louder now, echoing off the tiled walls and perhaps even audible outside the head, and again Colin thought of Sergeant Stevens and the D.I. hut just across the hall. Torn by the desire to run from the room and leave the other man to his emotions and the sudden feeling that something else was about to happen, Colin found himself standing still, frozen in place by indecision.

Then something fell from the stall, and Colin flinched, stepping back and all but yelling out in surprise. At first he thought the other recruit might be trying to run away, perhaps now aware that he no longer was alone in the head. It took an extra second for Colin to realize that the pale, skinny body dressed in a dark green T-shirt and standard white cotton briefs was hanging from the stall's crossbar, and realization dawned.

"Hey!"

The other man's body was still twitching when Colin reached him, his feet dangling less than two feet from the floor. Colin could hear the sound of the wooden crossbeam groaning under the recruit's weight, and he saw something dark and thin wrapped around the man's neck and pulled taut. Without thinking, Colin grabbed the other man by his knees and lifted him up, slackening the rope or whatever it was the recruit had used to choke himself.

"Help! Somebody help me!" he yelled in as loud a voice as he could muster, the words bouncing off the walls of the head. "Get in here! I need help!" From the other side of the wall separating the stalls from the sinks, Colin heard one of the head's two doors slam open an instant before the lights came on. "Back here!" he shouted, even as the recruit he held started to buck and kick, trying to free himself from Colin's grip. "Stop it!" he shouted, maintaining his hold on the other man. Looking up, he recognized the recruit as Adam Lowenstein, a very young, very skinny kid from some small town in New Jersey. His face was flushed and his eyes were bugging out of his head, his hands and legs flailing in all directions as panic and terror at the reality of what he had just done to himself began to take hold.

"What the hell's going on?" a young, high-pitched voice asked just as Colin detected someone else's approach. It immediately was followed by "Holy fuck!" as Colin turned to see Peter Nguyen, the Vietnamese-American man who was the other recruit currently standing fire watch, staring at him in openmouthed shock.

"Help me, damn it!" Colin hissed, just as Lowenstein's right hand cuffed him across his left ear. Nguyen moved closer to help, and then there was another set of hands, Swanson's, as the other fire watch recruit reached up for whatever it was Lowenstein had tied around his neck. "Get it off him!" Other voices and sounds were coming from all around him, the rest of the platoon becoming aware of something happening in the room. All of that evaporated in response to a single barked command that Colin was certain made the walls rattle.

"Get out of my way!"

Colin held his ground, holding on to Lowenstein and watching as Swanson's fingers worked the knot in what Colin now realized were at least two laces, long and tan and intended for use on a pair of combat boots. Lowenstein had rigged the makeshift hangman's noose by doubling the laces back on themselves, and the thin material was doing an excellent job of choking the life out of the recruit. Then the knot surrendered to Swanson and Colin felt Lowenstein's body go limp in his arms. With Nguyen's help he lowered the now unconscious recruit to the cold tiled floor just as the shadow of another figure fell across them.

"What are you doing?" shouted Sergeant Stevens, but Colin did not turn to him. Whereas Nguyen snapped to attention at the sound of Stevens's voice, Colin and Swanson concentrated on removing the boot laces from around Lowenstein's neck. The recruit was coughing and sputtering, saliva streaming from his mouth and dampening the front of his T-shirt.

"Move," Stevens grunted, pushing Colin out of the way as he squatted next to Lowenstein, his hand reaching for the recruit's jaw and tilting his face to look up at him. "Are you all right?" When Lowenstein reached for the red, irritated skin on his throat and offered a weak nod, Stevens looked up and pointed at Swanson. "You. Go below to Platoon 3002 and tell Staff Sergeant Pollack to come up here—now."

"Aye, aye, sir!" Swanson replied, turning and sprinting toward the door and the stairs outside the squad bay.

Leaving Lowenstein to sit on the floor, Stevens rose to his feet and glared at Colin. He was dressed in a green T-shirt and his camouflage trousers with his belt undone. He wore no socks or shoes, and Colin realized for an insane moment that this was the first time he had seen the drill instructor without his campaign cover—the "Smokey the Bear" hat, as he and the other recruits had been warned *not* to call it. Stevens's hair was black and cropped so close to his scalp that Colin wondered why he simply did not shave it smooth.

Focus, moron.

"What happened?" Stevens asked.

Snapping to attention, Colin replied, "Sir, I was making a head call when I found Recruit Lowenstein attempting to hang himself, sir." He realized as he spoke the words that he had failed to refer to himself in the third person, as he and the rest of the platoon had been instructed on their first day in the august company of Staff Sergeant Blyzen.

For his part, the drill instructor seemed uninterested in such protocol at the moment. "You found him hanging there?"

"No, sir," Colin replied. "I was making my head call and heard him in the stall. I figured he was just doing . . . doing his thing, sir. Then he was just swinging from the beam, and I ran to lift him up."

Turning to Nguyen, Stevens asked, "You saw this?"

The recruit shook his head. "Sir, this recruit saw Recruit Laney holding Recruit Lowenstein up. Then Recruit Swanson came and helped get Lowenstein down."

With an expression of barely disguised disdain, Stevens looked down at the small, trembling recruit who still sat on the floor. Then he returned his gaze to Colin. "Have you seen him acting strange before tonight? Acting depressed, upset, anything like that?"

"Sir, no, sir," Colin replied, feeling a wave of nervousness wash over him. Was it possible the drill instructors had suspected Lowenstein or any of the others might try something like this? Lowenstein had not been a standout recruit; he had not excelled in any particular way, but neither had he failed to accomplish any task put to him and nor was he considered a burden to the rest of the platoon. To everyone around him, Colin included, the young Jewish kid from the Jersey Shore seemed to be nothing more than an average kid just doing his best to endure the situation he now faced. No doubt the drill instructors were well versed in watching for the signs of strain caused by the transition from civilian to military life, along with its constant barrage of barked orders, rushed meals, lack of privacy, and the forfeiture of anything resembling a normal life. It also stood to reason that the Marines tasked with training the new recruits would have encountered despondent or even suicidal individuals from time to time, if not here then certainly in Iraq or Afghanistan, either or both of which all three of 3003's drill instructors had seen firsthand. There likely were procedures for dealing with such situations, just as there were rules and guidelines for every other aspect of recruit training.

Pointing a thumb over his shoulder toward the door, Stevens said to Nguyen, "Get the rest of that gaggle back in their racks." Nguyen disappeared, leaving Colin alone with the sergeant and Lowenstein, and Colin noted the rare moment of calm, even appreciative demeanor as Stevens regarded him. "You did good, Laney. You probably saved his life."

Uncertain as to how to proceed, Colin merely nodded before replying, "What will happen to him now, sir?"

Rather than answering, Stevens instead released a heavy sigh as he again looked down to where Lowenstein sat rubbing his throat. The recruit's eyes were wide and he stared straight ahead, seemingly unaware of his surroundings and instead lost in the chaos of his own troubled thoughts.

Finally, the sergeant said, "Go back to your rack, Laney. I'll call you if I need you." Colin was sure he detected a hint of sadness in the other man's voice.

"Aye, aye, sir," he said, before turning and heading for the door, knowing full well that Adam Lowenstein likely would not be in his own rack when reveille sounded in a few short hours. An attempt at suicide would at least send the recruit to sick bay, where Navy corpsmen would watch over him until a doctor arrived, after which he surely would be remanded to the care of a psychiatrist. Perhaps he might even spend time with one of the Navy chaplains assigned to the recruit training battalion. Though he had no facts on which to base his judgment, Colin's gut told him the distressed recruit would not return.

Good luck, Adam, he thought as he crossed the squad bay to his rack, catching sight of the quizzical expressions on the faces of the other recruits. A few questions were tossed his way, asking him what had happened, whether someone had succeeded in killing himself, and how he had gone about it. Other recruits were hissing between gritted teeth or making other sounds in attempts to get their companions to quiet down, especially when the squad bay's front door opened and admitted Platoon 3002's senior drill instructor, Staff Sergeant Pollack, and Recruit Swanson, both of whom moved directly for the door to the head and vanished through it.

Dropping back onto his rack, Colin took in the assorted muted chatter coming from his fellow recruits, listening to their tones and detecting confusion, fear, and even contempt in one or two cases. None of that mattered to him.

Instead, Colin realized just now how tired he was.

13

"Holy Jesus."

It was the only thing Paul Simpson could think to say as he beheld the trio of Chodrecai soldiers staring back at him. He had anticipated this moment, had looked forward to it with no small measure of excitement. Now that he stood before the three aliens, the only thing he wanted to do was turn and run away, preferably without shitting himself.

"I'll be damned," whispered Amanda Hebert from where she stood next to him. She stepped closer, and without thinking Simpson held out an arm to stop her.

"Wait," he said, his eyes riveted to the "guests" currently occupying Jimmy Franks's root cellar. The Grays regarded him with expressions he could not fathom. Contrary to reports, gossip, and other bullshit that the aliens "all looked alike," Simpson was able to discern various differences between the three. One was female, at least so far as he could tell with the equipment the soldier wore. While one was taller than the others, another's physique was far more stout. The biggest differences seemed to be in the sizes and shapes of their heads, particularly the brows over their wide, dark eyes. Their uniforms were similar in design, of course, but Simpson was able to make out small markings near the neck and along the chest that appeared to denote insignia of one sort or another. It took Simpson an extra moment to realize that none of the Grays looked to be armed, just as he at first did not notice the other human standing to one side, all but obscured by the shadows cloaking most of the cellar.

"Who are you?" Simpson asked the man, trying not to let the question sound too accusatory.

The man stepped forward, dressed in faded jeans and a dark green, open-collared work shirt. His shirtsleeves were rolled up to his elbow, revealing tattoos on each forearm. Simpson recognized a few of the tattoos as those that soldiers might acquire during their travels, including one depicting the emblem of the Royal Marine Corps. His hair, completely white, was long, pulled back, and secured behind his neck in a ponytail.

"Aidan Coberly," he said, extending his right hand in greeting.

Behind Simpson, Jimmy Franks said, "It's all right, Paul. Aidan and I go all the way back to our hairless nod days at CTC. Drill leaders used to beat the both of us three or four times a day just for something to do. I trust him with my life, mate."

That was good enough for Simpson, who recalled that Franks had mentioned once or twice that he had completed instruction at the Commando Training Centre in the early 1990s. Franks rarely spoke of his service in the RMC and even less about friends he might have acquired along the way.

"Good to meet you," Simpson said, taking Coberly's proffered hand and trying not to wince in response to the other man's ironlike grip. After introducing Hebert, and with his attention returning to the trio of Grays, he asked, "Jimmy, you think this is such a good idea, bringing them here?"

Franks shrugged. "They've been here three days, and so far there's been no trouble." He reached up to smooth some of the wild hairs of the large black-and-gray mustache that nearly covered his upper lip. Other than his eyebrows, it was the sum total of hair on the man's head, and his bald scalp reflected the dim light from the single bulb hanging near the center of the cellar.

"Three days?" Hebert repeated, aghast. "Seriously?" He looked around the cellar again, realizing that, as hideouts went, there were worse places to be. With food prices on the rise and supplies far less than what they had enjoyed prior to the war, many Britons had taken to planting their own gardens to supplement their food stores. Root cellars, once either abandoned or else converted for some other use, were becoming popular again. The cellar beneath Jimmy Franks's house was spacious, and Simpson could see doorways leading to a loo as well as what looked to be a toolshed or workshop of some kind.

"No worries, mate," Coberly said. "I've got people keeping an eye out for anything screwy, but Jimmy's place here has the advantage of being out in the arse end of nowhere. We're okay for a bit, at least."

Despite their location—the windowless root cellar beneath Jimmy Franks's farmhouse on the outskirts of Hampshire—Simpson could not help looking around the room, searching for signs that their activities might be monitored. As members of HIPE, Franks and even Simpson himself were likely candidates for eavesdropping and other forms of covert surveillance, most of which likely would be undetectable by regular blokes like them. He conceded that Franks—given his long years spent in service to one government agency or another—might know what to look for and perhaps even how to counteract such measures to some degree. For all Simpson knew, the government could have twenty cameras embedded in the walls, or twenty men hiding in the cellar.

One of the Grays, the shortest of the trio, uttered something in what Simpson presumed was its native language, to his ear sounding like so much gibberish—the kind of indecipherable babbling that his neighbor's two-year-old son constantly uttered at all hours of the day or night.

"What the hell is he saying?" Simpson asked, realizing as he spoke that his own words probably sounded much the same way to the alien. To his utter surprise, Coberly turned and replied in a passable employment of the Gray's language.

"He's asking the same thing you've been asking," Coberly said after a moment. "He basically wants to know if you being here is safe. I told them that you're friends of Jimmy's, and that you want to help."

Hebert asked, "Where did you learn their language?"

By way of reply, the older man reached behind his back and extracted what to Simpson at first appeared to be a fancy dog collar. It resembled one of those gizmos that gave its wearer a mild electrical shock whenever the wayward pet crossed the boundary established by one of those fenceless perimeters that were all the rage a few years ago.

"It's a sort of translator," Coberly replied, nodding toward the Grays. "Pretty popular tools on their planet, according to these characters. I picked one up from another Gray I helped a month or so ago. It's a bit of a pisser to get used to, and gives you one hell of a headache the longer you use it, but it works, all right." He again indicated the Chodrecai with a nod as he returned the band to his back pocket. "Comes in handy for situations like these, where they don't have the time to pick up our language before we ship them off."

"How does that work, exactly?" Simpson said, perplexed. "I mean, how in God's name do you manage to pull off something like that?"

It was Franks who replied, "Well, to be honest, we're still working out the kinks. This is only the fourth time we've encountered any Grays since we started doing this."

"The first time it happened," Coberly added, "it was as much accident as anything else. A friend of mine found two of the buggers digging through her trash, looking for something to eat. She called me and a few mates for help, and when we got there they put up nary a fuss. That's where I got the headband. Those two could speak English better than the Queen herself. After keeping them hid for a couple of days, we snuck them out one night and set them off with some rations and directions to where we thought there might be some good places to hide. We've done that twice more since then."

"Where are they?" Hebert asked.

Franks shook his head. "That's not something we need to discuss now. You know, just in case." He made a show of circling the air around his head with a finger. Whether he knew or merely suspected that unwanted listeners might be overhearing their conversation, he felt the obvious need to avoid taking unnecessary chances.

"And none of the Grays you've happened across tried to shred you with one of those rifles of theirs?" Simpson asked.

Coberly shrugged. "There've been a few close calls, but it's easy to take care of business when you outnumber the tosser five to one. As for the ones we've helped, they wanted pretty much the same thing: a place to hide out until all of this blows over. They don't want to fight us, don't think it's fair to involve us in their war with the Blues." He nodded once more to the Grays. "Their names are Osibonidar, Jiqol, and Nelritap," pointing to each of them as he recited a name. "You know, in case you're curious."

Despite himself, Simpson actually offered a small wave to the trio of aliens. Realizing how stupid that gesture must have looked, he pushed ahead. "It's nice to know some-body's thinking like that," he said, feeling the first chill of the air in the cellar working beneath his clothes. "So, what do we do now?"

"Keep them here until we know the coast is clear," Franks replied. "Once we hear from our friends to the north, we'll set up a rendezvous and make a transfer."

Hebert said, "We should get the word out about this." Before anyone could say anything in protest, she held up her hand. "Hang on. I'm not suggesting we put up a bloody sign out front to let everyone know they're here, but think about the opportunity we've got. Let them tell their side of the story, talk about how they don't want to fight, they just want to live in peace, and all that."

"We could put it on the Web," Simpson added. "It damn sure beats me dressing up like a goon and reading a speech." He indicated the Grays with a gesture before pointing to Coberly. "Isn't this just the kind of thing we want people to know about? Can you think of anyone bet-ter to actually deliver our message than *them*? We let them say their piece, and you help with the translation. We'll put subtitles on the video, and distribute it the same way we've been sending out our other stuff. By the end of the day, it'll be all over the planet."

The Internet had been one of the biggest allies to activ-ist groups for nearly two decades. While other groups with more extremist views used the technology to spread hate, fear, and whatever other dumbass ideas came into their leaders' heads, HIPE and similar organizations around the globe had concentrated on more constructive messages de-signed to appeal to world leaders to seek peaceful solutions to the current crisis. Even so, the site's activities as well as those it represented were always being scrutinized by gov-ernment agents. With that in mind, the elaborate network through which videos and other messages crafted by Simpson and others reached the outside world was such that there existed no direct links to HIPE's website or—more importantly—those who maintained it.

For his part, Coberly seemed ambivalent to the notion. Looking to Franks, he asked, "What do you think, Jimmy?"

Franks nodded. "Seems like it's worth trying. We've got time to kill, anyway." Glancing toward the Grays, he added, "Besides, by the time the vids hit the Web, these blokes will be long gone."

"Yeah, but we'll still be here," Coberly countered.

"Easy fix," Franks said, before turning to Simpson and Hebert. "Simple rule: We don't let out any footage until they're gone."

His mind already racing with the possibilities afforded by this opportunity—the chance to truly spread their message of peace and understanding with the help of those affected by the current situation more than any human—almost made Simpson giddy with anticipation. This was why he had joined HIPE: the chance to make such a profound impact and perhaps even a difference.

"No worries, Jimmy," he said, smiling. "We'll take care of it."

14

Lying on his stomach and using the untamed foliage of an overgrown thicket for cover, Simon DiCarlo peered through the tactical scope's viewfinder. Fifty or so meters down a gentle embankment and sitting at the center of a wide expanse of flat, featureless land, the choice of location was ideal for a prison. As DiCarlo had observed during the previous day and their first hours of covert observation, with open land surrounding the base itself and the sloping terrain leading away from it, anyone foolish enough to attempt escape would be an easy target for pursuing guards. Only by avoiding chase long enough to scramble up one of the embankments surrounding the base and into the dense forest that lay beyond did a would-be absconder have any chance at freedom.

"One world or another," DiCarlo said, keeping his voice low, "a prison is a prison is a prison." As he had done uncounted times during the past two days, he moved the scope in order to study the compound's outer perimeter. A series of towering columns encircled the facility, between each of which stretched flexible panels of a thin metal mesh, representing the installation's most prominent security feature. The mesh itself was all but transparent; DiCarlo likened it to staring through a piece of gauze bandage.

"Sort of like an electrified fence," Michael Gutierrez had observed early the previous morning, during their first day of reconnoitering the base.

"A lot more powerful, from what we've been told," Belinda Russell had responded, explaining to the lieutenant that the energy fields coursing through the protective barriers worked on a principle similar to that of the pulse rifles with which they all were familiar. Touching such a fence would overpower a would-be escapee's—or intruder's—nervous system, disabling the individual at least long enough for security forces to arrive and take him or her into custody. Though she and DiCarlo had yet to see the effects of such a defense mechanism in action, he had wondered what might happen should a human come into contact with such a field.

A really bad day, I'm guessing.

It had taken nearly a week to make the transit to this location from the caves in which Javoquek and his unit had been hiding. Moving mostly at night, the group sought shelter before dawn each day and remained under cover so as to minimize the chances of detection by Chodrecai security forces. Unlike the terrain near many of the population centers he had seen in recent months, the land here was remarkably untouched by the war. Vegetation was lush and healthy, even if the colors were somewhat off compared to forests on Earth: more rusty reds, pale tans, and vibrant yellows and oranges rather than varying shades of green.

Earth. The single word rolled around in DiCarlo's mind. The prospect of returning to his home planet was hard not to contemplate. That he and Russell had been living on *this* world for so long was enough to make him question his hold on reality, but there was no denying these past months. It certainly had fired Russell's imagination, and she had spent many an hour scribbling furiously in the small green notebook she carried in her rucksack. An aspiring writer, she had been hunting that first elusive sale prior to her Marine reserve unit's first contact with the Plysserians and the Chodrecai in southwest Missouri. The time she and DiCarlo had spent with Kel and Javoquek's unit had sent her into overdrive. In addition to logging diary entries about their day-to-day life here, Russell also filled the book's pages with notes, rough drafts of entire short stories and chapters from what might one day be a novel. When she ran out of space in the book, Russell continued chronicling her thoughts and ideas on anything she could scrounge. When her last pen ran dry, she fashioned ink from the juice of berries Kel helped her find. Her rucksack now contained the notebook and the sheaves of parchment she had accumulated over time, her most prized possessions and a detailed account of everything she and DiCarlo had experienced during their time on *Jontashreena*.

Maybe people on Earth will get to read it all one day.

Lying next to DiCarlo near his left arm, Gutierrez was using a pair of binoculars to study the compound, which consisted of four two-story buildings, hexagonal in shape and situated near the installation's boundaries. A larger version of those structures, this one standing four stories tall, sat at the base's center, with guard stations at the corners as well as along the midpoints of each of its six walls. Though sunset had occurred nearly an hour earlier, lingering post-dusk light allowed DiCarlo to make out the shadowy figures occupying the guard shacks at the building's corners. Those along the walls appeared empty, based on observations of the past two days. That made sense, according to what Gutierrez and Javoquek had told him about the base's contingent of soldiers. At this time of evening, the compound's exterior area was all but unoccupied, the only exceptions being the four Chodrecai guards walking at different points along a narrow gravel path encircling the compound, just inside the protective fence.

"And I thought airport security was bad," said Sergeant First Class Marty Sloane from where he lay next to Gutierrez. "You can set your watch by these zombies."

DiCarlo grunted in agreement. In what had become an almost mind-numbing routine just during the past thirty or so hours, he and the others had watched each new shift of sentries take to their duties with the total lack of enthusiasm that could only be exhibited by bored, low-ranking soldiers assigned to predictable, menial duty. Four guards patrolled different areas within the compound's perimeter, their circuits never overlapping as they remained within whatever boundaries had been established for them. As a result, each guard walked alone and was unable even to pass the time in idle conversation with one of his compatriots. This at least held a modicum of logic, as a sentry engaged in distracting chatter was not operating at a full level of alertness with respect to his surroundings. However, the sentries instead appeared to concentrate on the ground in front of them, looking around only occasionally at the buildings or fence they passed. As time passed and they became more entrenched in their routine, they appeared to take even less interest in their task, and more than one guard had taken the opportunity to deviate from his patrol circuit to disappear for minutes at a time, presumably to relieve himself or indulge in a stalk of *tempra* or whatever other noxious concoction Chodrecai soldiers smoked. From the previous night's observations, DiCarlo knew the security would grow even more lax as the early predawn hours approached.

"This looks like it's going to be a piece of cake," Gutierrez whispered, pulling the binoculars from his face. "So,
why don't I like what I'm seeing?"

Keeping his voice low as he lowered the tactical scope,
DiCarlo reached up to stroke his graying, ratty beard.
"Because you're smart enough to know that some asshole
named Murphy once wrote a law telling us how things love
to turn to shit whenever we think something's going to be
easy."

"The guards know there's almost no chance of something happening without a camera or sensor picking up
on it," added Russell from where she lay to the right of Di-
Carlo. "That, and it's a sure bet nothing worth a damn ever
happens out here. This place is the ass end of nowhere.
The guards are complacent."

"All that changes once the first bullet goes off," DiCarlo
said, once more lifting the tac scope to his right eye.
Touching a control near his left index finger changed
the viewfinder's resolution to infrared and brought each
of the sentries into sharp relief, the heat from their bodies registering as yellowish-red masses walking amid a sea
of cold blue. Likewise, the energy coursing through the
compound's protective fence also was visible, registering
as a faint, warm orange glow. The scope picked up other,
smaller signatures scattered across the different buildings
as well as both sides of the fence line. Electronic surveillance, in the form of motion detectors and the Chodrecai
version of video cameras.

Though the scope was larger and bulkier than the binoculars or rifle and spotting scopes with which he was familiar, DiCarlo had come to prefer the Plysserian military
equivalent Kel had given him months earlier. The infrared
feature worked far better than the night vision goggles he
had worn on occasions too numerous to count, and, un-

like those devices, did so while retaining his field of vision's true three-dimensional perspective. He also favored the tac scope's computerized range finder, which was far more accurate than the simple crosshairs and ocular sights of the sniper scopes he had used years ago.

The downside to the infrared feature was its inability to penetrate barriers such as walls or rock, at least not from a distance. Such ability was limited to a range of somewhere in the neighborhood of fifty meters, so far as DiCarlo could tell. For him to be able to detect the presence of living beings within any of the compound's buildings, they would have to get much closer to the perimeter, by which time the energy from the fence line would almost certainly interfere with the scope's effectiveness at ground level.

Murphy, you cocksucker.

Turning his attention to the building closest to them, DiCarlo once more studied it with a critical, experienced eye, sizing up its windows, its points of entry, and their positions relative to the guard shacks on the central building. Doorways on the first level faced the fence, offering access unfettered by any of the guard stations. The immediate threat would be the sentries on foot patrol as well as any additional forces that responded to the alarm once the fence was breached.

"And we're sure that's the right building?" DiCarlo asked.

Gutierrez nodded. "So far as we can tell, it's where Wysejral's locked up each night." On their first day observing the compound, Gutierrez and his team reached that conclusion after watching the comings and goings of guards as well as a few prisoners. One older inmate, wearing ill-fitting dark gray coveralls and lacking the impressive musculature typical of soldiers and other working-class individuals, was seen being escorted from the building to the central structure early in the morning, then back again later that evening. Unlike other prisoners, this individual did not come outside for exercise at any point during the day. Using the tac scope, Kel recorded still images of the prisoner and compared them to those provided by Javoquek. The resemblance to *Laepotic* Wysejral was strong, though DiCarlo noted that the alien appeared to have lost significant weight, doubtless a consequence of reduced food rations during his incarceration.

It's him, DiCarlo mused, his eyes and his gut having told him everything he needed to know. Watching the way the Plysserian walked and how he was treated by his escort told the Marine that this was not a soldier; nor had he observed the lone, older inmate being treated the same as other, typical prisoners. No, DiCarlo decided, this individual was different from any of the prison's other occupants. Without further evidence, which DiCarlo knew would not be coming, this Plysserian was the likely target.

"What about the electronic measures they've got in place?" Russell asked, looking over her shoulder to where Kel and Sloane lay beside one another, beneath the low branches of a thick, squat bush. "Any ideas?"

The Plysserian soldier was almost hugging the ground, his large tattooed head nearly invisible amid the foliage as he rested his chin on his muscled forearms. "Most such features are directed at the entrances to the buildings and the compound itself," he answered. "The protective barrier around the perimeter is sufficient to prevent unauthorized entry or escape. There likely are gaps in the coverage of the external monitoring equipment. If this facility observes the same protocols as our regular prisons, it will go into lockdown the instant a perimeter breach is detected. Prisoners will be returned to their cells and security forces will be deployed to key defensive positions around the compound." He pointed toward the base and the large building at its center. "The observation platforms all contain mounted pulse weapons, which normally are locked to a setting designed only to subdue their targets. They are intended to quell riots or other sources of insurrection or disruption among the prison population without causing undue fatalities."

"That's damned considerate," Gutierrez said. "Of course, their stun setting is probably enough to turn one of us into a loose-meat sandwich."

The corners of Kel's thin mouth turned downward, his large dark eyes unwavering as they regarded the lieutenant. "I do not understand the reference, but if you are inferring that the weapons are lethal to humans, it would seem likely."

Russell said, "What about some kind of electronic jamming, like what we were able to do against their weapons?"

"We don't have anything like that," Sloane replied. "Also, the Grays found a way around that trick a couple of months ago. They've got some kind of shielding in place on their equipment now that blocks radio transmissions or whatever it was you managed to do to them."

DiCarlo said, "So you're thinking we blow the fence?" Even then, he knew that was but the first obstacle. Once through the barrier, they would be outnumbered and outgunned. How much support could the prison call in, once an attack started? How long would it take for such backup to arrive?

"Sloane and I have enough stuff on us to start the ball rolling," Gutierrez said. "But it won't be enough, not if their soldiers have any kind of training." He extracted a ruggedized, military-issue cellular phone from a pouch on his equipment harness, and it took DiCarlo an extra moment to remember what the lieutenant had said about using such devices in concert with the beacon he and Sloane had brought with them as a means of sending messages back to Earth.

"The cavalry?" Russell asked, also remembering the briefing.

Gutierrez nodded as he began tapping out a text message. "Relax, and leave everything to me and mine. You're gonna love this."

15

Am I being punished?

It was not the first time *Esat* Vrinoq had asked himself
that question since arriving for duty at the Ichiltral Detention Facility. Indeed, it was not even the first time Vrinoq
had posed the query since beginning his duty shift on this
night. Like countless other sentries before him, Vrinoq
hoped that the monotonous routine might be broken by
anything, perhaps even a prisoner attempting escape. He
personally did not require that level of excitement, happy
instead merely to encounter a detainee outside after curfew. That alone would dispel a few moments' boredom
as he returned such a hapless prisoner to his cell, but not
before inflicting a few painful reminders pertaining to the
futility of disobedience.

Vrinoq sighed in frustration as he passed the waste receptacle located near the rear entrance to Housing Block
3, the landmark he had chosen on this evening to act as
the starting point for each new circuit he walked. The compound was divided into quadrants, with sentries assigned
to each quadrant and given the responsibility of monitoring all activity, personnel, and materiel within that area.
Vrinoq and his fellow *fonsata* had endured interminable
briefings on this subject prior to the low-ranking soldiers
undertaking their duties. Their unforgiving instructor, *Zoli-*

tum Dekrad, had stressed that variation of a sentry's patrol pattern was vital, in order to prevent one's activities from becoming predictable. Familiarity and complacency bred laziness in the guard and opportunity for those waiting to take advantage of such situations. Vrinoq agreed with the *zolitum*'s viewpoint, if not the conviction with which such information was imparted.

Still, Vrinoq did as he was told, making a point to alter his movements through the compound with each circuit. He made a game out of devising new paths in, around, and through his assigned quadrant while ensuring that no area received greater or lesser attention. There were a few detainees about whom Vrinoq knew little or nothing, but he found it difficult to believe that any of them were worth the expense to feed, clothe, shelter, and guard. With the war that had raged since before he was born having expanded to include *another planet*, surely there were better uses for the soldiers of this world.

No one seems interested in your opinion.

When knowledge of the other planet became public, along with the technology developed by the Plysserians that had made it possible to bridge the two worlds, Chodrecai military leaders had scrambled to assemble personnel and materials on an unprecedented scale in order to stage a large-scale assault. Vrinoq somehow managed to be overlooked while other *fonsata* from his section were reassigned to other units destined to serve as part of the invasion force. Surely even he, a lowly *esat*, possessed the rudimentary skills necessary to march into battle with thousands of his fellow soldiers?

Perhaps one day, I will find out, but not today.

Vrinoq's route brought him back to the gravel path ringing the compound's outer boundary, just inside the mesh barrier that served to contain not only the prison's irksome population but also himself. Feeling the small stones shifting beneath his feet, he reached down and retrieved one. He held it up so as to examine its features, noting the sharp edges and smooth sides, which came as a courtesy of the working parties tasked with pulverizing larger stones into these smaller ones for purposes of filling gaps in the path. Even such menial work, Vrinoq decided, had to be more interesting than the duty he now faced. How pathetic was that?

"*Esat.*"

Looking up at the sound of the voice calling out his rank, Vrinoq turned to see one of his superiors, *Kret* Brolakelneta, walking toward him. Second in command to Dekrad and responsible for much of the sentries' training, Brolakelneta lacked the *zolitum*'s near-obsessive approach to instruction and discipline. This did not mean he did not take his responsibilities seriously, but he did seem to approach them from more of a realistic standpoint than Dekrad. He was a large, imposing soldier, the badges and other accoutrements on his formal dress uniform gleaming in the compound's harsh artificial lighting. A large pistol rested in a black holster along his right hip. It took Vrinoq a moment to remember the ceremony that had been scheduled for earlier in the evening, and to which he had not been invited. Someone was retiring, or had died, or had been decorated for their valor; Vrinoq could not recall.

He began walking toward Brolakelneta. "Yes, *Kret?*" he asked, straightening his posture as he closed the distance.

"What are you doing?" his superior asked, nodding toward the stone Vrinoq still carried in his hand.

Embarrassed, Vrinoq dropped the stone, hearing it strike others as it fell to the ground. The sound seemed only to punctuate the awkwardness he now felt. "I was only . . . that is, I simply was . . ."

Holding up one massive hand, Brolakelneta shook his head. "An explanation is not required. Tell me, *Esat*, do you feel that activities such as that are conducive to carrying out your assigned responsibilities?"

Unlike *Zolitum* Dekrad, the *kret* possessed a talent for rebuking subordinates without rancor. His tone of voice and the way he phrased his queries were all that was needed to convey his point. Appropriately chastened, Vrinoq shook his head and struggled to maintain eye contact with his superior.

"No, *Kret*. It is not my intention to shirk my duty. I allowed myself to be distracted only for a moment, and for that, I apologize."

Brolakelneta nodded. "I have observed you for some time, *Esat*. I know that you are not satisfied being here, and would prefer to be assigned to a unit where your contributions would be more beneficial to our ongoing war efforts. Such desire is to be commended; several of your fellow *fonsata* are quite content to while away their time here, safe and far from battle. I find that interesting, considering the attention they give to their duties, whereas you carry out every task given to you without complaint, and it is a rare occasion when someone is able to find fault with your work."

The unexpected compliment caught Vrinoq off guard. He had no idea what to say, and therefore remained quiet, choosing the option that carried with it the least possibility of making a fool of himself.

"Given your performance and conduct since your arrival here," Brolakelneta continued, "it would be a shame for such a complimentary service record to be tarnished by a single act of inattention or sloppiness. Would you not agree?" Again, his words cut through Vrinoq with the ease of a finely honed blade, and it required physical effort not to fidget or wither beneath his superior's unwavering gaze.

"It would, *Kret*," he replied, humbled as he struggled to maintain his bearing. "It will not happen again."

For the first time, Brolakelneta smiled. "I am certain it will not. Good evening, *Esat* Vrinoq," he said, before turning in the direction of the building that served as a barracks for the soldiers and civilian guards assigned to the detention facility.

He took only a few steps before a flash of harsh, intense light illuminated a section of the compound ahead of him, followed an instant later by the muffled report of a small explosion blasting through a section of the prison's outer security perimeter.

"What in the name of—" Brolakelneta was unable to finish the question before another explosion rumbled across the courtyard, this time from the opposite side of the compound. Successive blasts quickly followed, each one at a different location around the security barrier. Now alarms were sounding, their shrill sirens adding to the din washing over the grounds.

Vrinoq shouted, "We are under attack!" even as he pulled his pulse rifle from his shoulder and checked its power level. He heard shouts of warning, confusion, and fear from different areas of the compound as shadowy figures emerged from buildings—soldiers rousted from their beds and answering the alarms with little more than the rifles they carried.

"Come with me," said Brolakelneta, clapping Vrinoq on the shoulder as he set off across the open courtyard, brandishing his pistol and moving with a speed and grace that belied his muscled frame. Vrinoq followed, cradling his rifle in the crook of his left arm. Ahead of them, he saw the new breach in the security barrier, noted the crackling of energy as the containment field suffered the rupture. Glancing toward other sections of the wall, he noted similar damage.

"It is a coordinated assault," Brolakelneta said, dropping to one knee and aiming his pistol at the breach. Vrinoq did the same with his rifle, but saw nothing or no one attempting to come through the hole.

An attack? Here? To Vrinoq it made no sense. There was nothing here of any real military value. An attempted breakout seemed the only logical explanation, but for what purpose? So far as he knew, even the prisoners themselves were little more than the flotsam of society, castoffs to be forgotten. Might there be among the population someone who was worth the effort of staging such an assault?

Hearing the sounds of voices and running footsteps growing closer, Vrinoq turned to see five other *fonsata* coming toward him. All of them appeared to have been roused from sleep, most wearing little more than undergarments but all of them carrying their weapons. Their attention was focused on the barrier breach as one of them, also holding the rank of *esat*, gestured to his companions.

"Spread out," he said, directing the others' movements until the group had assumed a semicircular line with all rifles aimed at the hole.

Nodding in approval, Brolakelneta said, "Follow me," before indicating with his free hand for everyone to move forward. The *kret* led the way, both arms extended and cradling his pistol as he searched for threats that did not materialize. Vrinoq fell in behind him and the other *fonsata* followed as Brolakelneta stepped closer to the breach, hugging one edge of the newly created hole. As he passed through the opening, Vrinoq noted the distinct lack of the familiar hum that signified energy coursing through the barrier. Now outside the wall, the only thing waiting for them was the expanse of open ground surrounding the prison. Looking up and down the length of this section of wall, Vrinoq saw other soldiers emerging from similar breaches, mimicking his actions and searching for an enemy that had not yet chosen to show itself.

Turning back toward the hole, Vrinoq shook his head in confusion. "I do not understand," he said, just before catching sight of a pair of dark objects positioned on the ground near the wall, one on each side of the breach.

"Get back from the wall!" Brolakelneta shouted, having also seen the strange objects. He frantically gestured for the *fonsata* to move away from the barrier and whatever had been placed there.

Then it was too late.

16

Gutierrez waited ninety seconds after activating the beacon and transmitting portal coordinates back to Earth before triggering the first detonation.

"Showtime," he said, his voice low as his thumb depressed a button on the multifunction wireless remote transmitter. The result was immediate, a quick flash of light and a sharp snap heralding the initial explosion.

Lying in the grass less then thirty meters from the detention facility's security perimeter—beyond the farthest limit of the illumination from the compound's exterior lighting—DiCarlo flinched in response to the blast, seeing smoke rising from the newly created hole in the perimeter wall on the compound's far side. Gutiérrez nodded to Sergeant Sloane, and without further communication the pair began transmitting the detonation codes for other explosives the two soldiers had planted. One after another, the dozen improvised devices detonated, tearing new holes in the wall.

"Baby go boom," Sloane said, making no effort to hide his satisfied smile.

A few seconds' worth of destruction was the end result of more than four hours' work on the part of Gutierrez and Sloane, who with painstaking care had maneuvered across the open ground separating the prison from the team's concealed vantage point. With Kel directing their movements so as to keep them from tripping any of the compound's surveillance and security measures, the two men had crawled across the exposed terrain. Their progress had been measured in inches rather than feet as they used the minimal cover offered by tall grass and the occasional boulder, as well as those few artificial structures—freestanding buildings that looked to be unused guard shacks, squat boxes that Kel identified as power junction relays, waste disposal receptacles—that presented themselves. Setting the IEDs had also been a slow, meticulous task, owing to the careful deployment worked out by Gutierrez, Sloane, and DiCarlo with Kel's assistance in order to achieve maximum effect. Placement of the explosives was critical if Gutierrez's plan for dealing with the prison's numerically superior military presence was to have any chance of success.

Lying on the soft, cold ground next to DiCarlo, Russell nodded in the direction of the prison. "Here we go."

Using the tactical scope, DiCarlo watched as doors to the various buildings opened, disgorging dozens of Chodrecai in various states of disheveled undress. From this distance it was easy to make out shouts of alarm and uncertainty as soldiers scrambled to react to the chaos unfolding around them. Though he could decipher only some of the actual words, DiCarlo still understood the implicit meaning in a few of the voices as someone in the compound tried to take charge of the tumultuous situation. If the guards had any sort of training, it would take only seconds for someone to reassert some level of control before deploying the soldiers in some manner of defensive posture.

At least, that's what DiCarlo hoped would happen.

His heart doing its level best to punch through his chest, he looked to Gutierrez. "How much longer before the portal opens?"

The lieutenant glanced at the luminescent dial of his wristwatch. "If my math's right, between four and eight more minutes. It takes the computer guys a bit of time to reconcile our coordinates into something the portal generators use to establish a conduit." Noting the skeptical look on DiCarlo's face, Gutierrez added, "Don't look at me. I suck at math. That's why I blow shit up for a living."

"Look," Sloane said, pointing toward the compound. "They're going for it."

No one said anything else, watching in silence as the scene played out before them. Chodrecai soldiers were converging on the different breaches in the security perimeter. DiCarlo counted at least twenty-five Grays, each of them armed either with pulse rifles or smaller pistol versions of the deadly weapons.

"That's not all of them," Russell remarked, "but I suppose that was too much to hope for."

DiCarlo grunted in reply. He considered luring as many as half of the prison's security contingent to the wall a win. It would be up to Gutierrez and the ace up his sleeve to deal with any stragglers.

Seconds seemed to drag into eternity as the team watched Grays scramble toward the barrier and the twelve ruptures inflicted upon it. A few of the holes were overlooked in favor of those in other locations. That action made DiCarlo wonder if those openings had appeared near areas of the installation that were deemed more sensitive. Those near the main entrance, for example, seemed to be attracting much attention, whereas the breach Gutierrez had chosen for entering the facility in search of *Laepotic* Wysejral appeared to be ignored by all but a pair of soldiers.

Through the scope, DiCarlo was able to make out the Grays' matching expressions of fright and anxiety.

"It is likely the remaining guards are seeing to the prisoners," said Kel, lying prone in the grass next to Sloane. "Lockdown procedures would almost certainly be in effect by now."

DiCarlo nodded. "It's as good as it's going to get," he said. He looked to Gutierrez. "Blow the rest and let's get this show on the fucking road."

"Now you're talking my language," the lieutenant replied, nodding to Sloane before holding up the remote and punching a new string of numbers into its keypad and thumbing the device's transmit button.

Once again the effect was quick in coming, only this time the detonations were louder, bigger, and far more powerful. The ground rumbled beneath DiCarlo, the dull, low reverberations coursing across his body as the IEDs detonated, doing much more than simply inflicting damage upon the prison's defenses. This set of charges, placed in proximity to the first group, was designed to cause casualties as well as confusion. It did so with devastating efficiency, thanks in no small part to the fact that the Chodrecai soldiers played right into the ruse. Bodies were ripped apart and thrown in all directions and others seemed to disappear, vaporized by the force of the different explosions. The successive concussions were enough to buckle at least two small structures situated next to the larger barracks buildings. Though windows here were not constructed of glass but rather a less fragile transparent material, the name of which DiCarlo could not pronounce, the force of the blasts was still sufficient to shatter numerous portholes in each of the major buildings. For a fleeting moment, DiCarlo felt for the prisoners locked within the detention blocks, powerless to do anything except huddle on the floor of their cells as the small windows that offered meager sunlight exploded inward on them, showering them with shrapnel.

"Okay, that's it," Gutierrez hissed through gritted teeth, pushing himself to his feet. "Sloane, blow the power boxes."

The sergeant nodded as his thumb pressed his remote's transmit key, generating half a dozen new, smaller explosions around the outside of the prison. The positions of the power junction stations were a fortunate happenstance, though DiCarlo certainly understood the logic of such planning. Such vital infrastructure components were susceptible to sabotage, but in a prison the likely candidates for such action normally were the inmates. Potential points of vulnerability often were positioned beyond the reach of the prisoner population.

Didn't count on us, though. Did ya?

With the press of a single button, Marty Sloane plunged the entire prison into darkness. Lights across the compound extinguished in unison, along with the motors of venting and air-conditioning and circulation equipment. The alarms ceased as well, their silenced wails now replaced by the unfettered cries of agony and terror emitted by the numerous victims of Gutierrez and Sloane's handiwork.

"Automatic backups will engage," Kel reminded the rest of the team, reinforcing what he earlier had conveyed when discussing the plan for infiltration. "Power will be directed to the most critical areas first, namely detention control, the infirmary, and the communications section."

DiCarlo already could see the faint flicker of renewed artificial lighting beginning to emerge from the shadows now enveloping the entire compound. He also saw more than a few shadowy, indistinct figures moving about, most of them running toward one of the buildings. Bedlam gripped the prison for the moment, but he knew that moment was fading. "Let's go," he said, anxious to get on with the business at hand.

Nodding, Gutierrez looked to Kel before raising his chin toward the prison. "You wanted to lead the way."

Without any sort of acknowledgment, the muscled Blue soldier set off at a trot across the open ground, heading for the nearby breach in the security barrier, with the rest of the team falling in behind him. Kel stopped at the breach, looking for signs of danger before stepping through and moving to his left to clear the opening. DiCarlo was next, moving to his right and keeping the now inoperative barrier to his back. With the main exterior lighting out and their dark clothing, they were all but invisible against the barrier's mesh panels. Lifting his pulse rifle, he peered down the length of its barrel as he swung the weapon from left to right, looking for any signs of Chodrecai soldiers. He saw a few, moving about in the feeble emergency illumination between other buildings, but none were in proximity to their target, nor did they seem to be moving toward the interlopers. For the moment, at least, their entrance appeared to have gone unnoticed.

Don't jinx it, dumbass.

Russell stepped through the breach and moved to stand next to DiCarlo, her own rifle pulled into her shoulder and ready to fire. Gutierrez had followed Kel, leaving Sergeant Sloane outside the perimeter to act as backup. DiCarlo's eyes had adjusted to the darkness well enough for him to see some of the results of the explosives set by Gutierrez and Sloane. Body parts, fragments of skin and bone, shredded clothing, and equipment littered the ground. The odor of fresh offal assaulted his nostrils and he forced himself to breathe through his mouth.

Glancing over at Russell, he saw that she was making a physical effort to avert her eyes, but the expression on her face indicated that the scene before her threatened to over-whelm her. He regretted that she had to see such things, just as he bemoaned the cold fact that there was nothing he could do to relieve her discomfort. At best, DiCarlo could sympathize with what she must be feeling.

It had been a very long time since he had seen carnage on such a scale. His first weeks in Vietnam had been a cruel enough teacher on that front; at the time he had been gripped by the same emotional turmoil he knew Russell must now be feeling. Even the horrific effects of the count-less roadside IEDs on American troops in Iraq and Afghani-stan, or even the damage inflicted upon human tissue by Chodrecai pulse rifles set to full strength, seemed to pale in comparison to what he now witnessed. Long ago DiCarlo had learned to disassociate himself from feelings of remorse or sadness when looking upon such scenes, compartmental-izing the disturbing imagery and convincing himself that what he beheld were not living beings but simply targets. Such justification, brutal though it might be, had likely pro-tected him from the unrelenting grip of depression or per-haps even madness.

Pushing away the troubling thoughts, DiCarlo turned his attention to where Gutierrez and Kel still stood with their backs to the barrier. He exchanged hand signals with the lieutenant, gesturing for them to move on the target building. Nodding to DiCarlo in agreement, Gutierrez stepped away from the wall, shadowing Kel's movements as the Blue warrior began his advance.

"No matter what happens, you stick with me," DiCarlo whispered to Russell. "Understand?" There was no way to predict what they would encounter once inside the build-ing, and he was taking no chances with Russell's safety.

She nodded, reaching out to pat his right arm before the pair moved to follow Gutierrez. Though the young

Marine reservist had seen her fair share of combat since initial contact with the aliens all those months ago back in Missouri, DiCarlo still tended to watch out for her. Russell had proven herself more than capable of holding her own in even the most stressful of situations. If not for her, DiCarlo likely would have died after being wounded during the battle to thwart the invasion of Washington, D.C. Despite all of that, as well as years of training and simple day-to-day interactions with women Marines, he knew that in some ways he was a hopeless, sexist relic of a bygone age. He was doomed to hold doors open for ladies, stand when they approached him at a dinner table, and protect them should he find himself in combat alongside them. That went double for the woman with whom he had fallen in love.

Stop it, he chided himself. *Keep your mind on your fucking job.*

Kel was the first one to the doorway leading into the target building, cautiously moving through the entrance with his pulse rifle leading the way. Gutierrez was right behind him, with DiCarlo motioning for Russell to follow the lieutenant. DiCarlo saw faint glows of subdued illumination coming from several of the narrow windows running the length of the barracks. Backup power, or at least some sort of temporary substitute, was up and running.

Now inside, DiCarlo saw that they had entered a corridor that seemed to run the length of the building, just as Kel had described in his portion of the team's pre-mission briefing. A few doors were visible on either side of the passageway, some standing open but most of which were closed. While the hallway itself was almost dark, DiCarlo noted the dim light coming from an area near the center of the building where the corridor expanded, possibly a foyer or receiving area for the barracks' main entrance. Figures were moving about in that part of the floor, the feeble illumination casting their shadows upon the walls.

Gesturing for the team to follow, Kel pressed forward, the muzzle of his pulse rifle trained on the hallway ahead of him. He paused at each open doorway, pointing his weapon into the different rooms. Satisfied that a room was empty, he continued to advance, repeating the exercise at every door.

Where the hell is everybody? Perhaps whatever guards or other military personnel remained in this barracks were on the lower, basement levels, seeing to the security of any prisoners as Kel had described. Still, DiCarlo figured there had to be at least one sentry manning a station somewhere, if for no other reason than to field any communications to and from the building.

Kel paused at one open door, inspecting the room beyond. DiCarlo watched the Blue soldier's body jerk in reaction to something and felt his own muscles tense in anticipation. His finger tightened on his pulse rifle's firing stud, sure Kel would shoot at whatever target he had found.

Instead, the Plysserian merely turned to face DiCarlo and the others.

"There is something you need to see."

The way the words were spoken, the haunting look that seemed to fill Kel's large, dark eyes, chilled DiCarlo. "What is it?" When the Blue soldier said nothing but instead turned and took up a defensive posture with his attention turned back toward the corridor, DiCarlo felt himself drawn to the door. He motioned for Russell to stay behind him as he and Gutierrez converged on the room, their expressions of uncertainty mirroring each other. Gutierrez got to the door first and peered inside, his reaction as rapid as it was alarming.

"Oh, my holy God."

The room resembled an operating theater, at least in the most general sense. Tools and other devices, which DiCarlo instinctively identified as surgical instruments, were scattered across tables and even on the floor. A Chodrecai computer workstation sat atop a high table along the room's far wall, its bulky keyboard interface nearly too large to accommodate human hands. None of that truly registered, as DiCarlo's attention was drawn to the table at the room's center, and the remains of the human male lying upon it.

"What the fuck . . . ?" The words trailed away as DiCarlo stared at the horrific image before him. The man—at least, he was certain it had once been a man—was arranged in spread-eagle fashion, the body seemingly small and fragile as it lay across the wide, long table, which obviously had been constructed with Chodrecai or even Plysserian physiology in mind. The body's torso had been cut open from throat to crotch and the skin and muscle tissue pulled back to reveal the skeleton and internal organs. Blood was everywhere, covering the table and dripping onto the earth-colored tile floor. A section of the sternum and rib cage had been removed, and DiCarlo saw that at least one lung as well as the heart were missing. The arms and legs were present, but the hands and feet were nowhere to be seen. The top of the skull also had been removed, though from this angle DiCarlo could not tell with any certainty if the man's brain was intact or missing.

A sharp intake of breath from behind him made DiCarlo turn to see Russell staring into the room, her left hand clapped over her mouth and her eyes wide as she took in the grisly scene. "What did they do to him?" she asked, her voice barely a whisper. "An autopsy?"

DiCarlo shook his head, his gut telling him that this was something else. The way the body was splayed in such an obscene fashion across the table—like a child's forgotten biology class project—seemed to imply more than a simple postmortem examination. Besides, why would a Chodrecai doctor bother with an autopsy of a dead human?

An examination, but not an autopsy.

"Holy Christ," DiCarlo whispered, his eyes locked on the hapless victim now lying before him. His mind raged with the same questions: What unrelenting hell had this poor son of a bitch been put through, and how long had he lived while it played out?

"We've got to go," Gutierrez said, his tone cold.

Forcing himself to look away from the table, DiCarlo said, "He can't be the only one."

"Probably not," Gutierrez replied, his expression pained.

Frowning, DiCarlo regarded the lieutenant. "You knew about this shit?" he asked, seeing the distant look in the other man's eyes.

"We heard rumors," Gutierrez said, "here and there, from Blue soldiers helping us, or from Gray soldiers captured and questioned." He grimaced, shaking his head.

Looking over his shoulder, Kel said, "It is not unreasonable. Humans represent unparalleled research opportunities for the scientists of my world. They would want to explore the various anatomical differences as well as any possible similarities. Military leaders would of course be interested in understanding the potential of the human body's numerous vulnerabilities."

"To develop weapons and tactics to use against us," Russell said.

Kel nodded. "That is correct."

Glancing at his watch, Gutierrez said, "We're on borrowed time, people."

"We have to find out how many others are here," Di-Carlo said, his jaw clenching. There was no way they could leave behind any other human prisoners.

If Gutierrez was going to argue, he seemed to think better of it. "We'll look, but we have to find Wysejral." He turned to head away from the room but just as quickly stopped, his left hand moving to the comm unit in his left ear. Then he looked back at DiCarlo, a thin smile on his face.

"The portal's open."

17

Chief Warrant Officer Charles Roland had flown nearly every helicopter in the United States Army's arsenal, along with several of those belonging to other countries' military forces. He had experienced every kind of weather condition to which a helicopter could be subjected, safely or otherwise. His aircraft had been shot at, shot down, and even blown up around him, at the hands of human as well as alien enemies.

Even with all of that behind him, along with the accompanying medals and scars, and though he likely would never say as much out loud, Chuck Roland was still pretty fucking scared.

"Here we go," he said, forcing his right hand to relax around the joystick as he guided the MH-60L Black Hawk helicopter toward the swirling mass of energy looming ahead of him. Morning sunlight filtered through the chopper's windshield as he directed his eyes over the instrumentation panels arrayed above and below the canopy, paying particular attention to the altimeter and the attitude indicator. Everything was where it was supposed to be, but that did little to ease Roland's anxiety.

"Nice and easy," said his copilot, CWO Osvaldo Garcia, from where he sat in the cockpit's right-hand seat. Roland glanced at his partner and saw the Latino man attempting a sly grin. "The life you save could be mine, you know."

Despite the tension permeating the Black Hawk's cramped cockpit, Roland allowed himself a small chuckle. An accomplished pilot in his own right, with thousands of hours at the controls of various helicopters—a sizable percentage of those while engaged in combat operations—Garcia, "Oz" or "Ozzy" to his friends, always had possessed a knack for saying the right thing at just the right time. His humor and general good nature usually were more than sufficient to put those around him at ease, regardless of the situation they faced. Nothing seemed to faze the man, who had earned a reputation for broadcasting smart-ass comments over his chopper's P.A. system even while taking fire from insurgents in Iraq. A video clip of one such incident had been making its way around the Internet for years, with Garcia's voice clearly audible over the sounds of gunfire as he chastised his attackers for their inability to hit their target even as he flew over their heads. Garcia himself had never commented on such incidents, shrugging and offering only a dismissive wave whenever the subject was broached.

So far as Roland was concerned, as long as Garcia continued to fly in the manner that had earned him a Distinguished Flying Cross, among other decorations, he could say whatever the hell he wanted.

Feeling his pulse beginning to race as the swirling vortex of energy now filled the Black Hawk's window, Roland lowered his helmet's tinted visor, reducing the intensity of the barely controlled chaos that was the portal. He felt a tingle on his skin, and a buzzing in his ears that he thought might be feedback from the speakers in his oversized pilot's helmet. "Altitude five meters," he said.

"Okay," Garcia replied, "even I'll admit that's kind of low." He grunted into his helmet microphone, a sound that to Roland's ears sounded like a car backfiring.

What the fuck are we doing here?

Roland had practiced this set of maneuvers numerous times with the aid of computer simulation. Still, the insanity of what they were about to attempt remained at the forefront of his mind. As a pilot with the Army's elite 160th Special Operations Aviation Regiment (Airborne), Roland had taken his share of dangerous missions. It was expected of the Night Stalkers, as the members of the 160th were known, dating back to the unit's inception in 1981 and its first combat action two years later during the U.S. invasion of Grenada. In Roland's opinion, everything the unit had experienced or accomplished since that time paled in comparison to what he, Ozzy Garcia, and other Night Stalkers had now been asked to do.

"Coming right to one five eight," Roland said, eyeing the console's horizontal situation indicator—or compass, as normal people might call it. Alignment with the portal was critical, he knew, having practiced the insertion maneuver as part of several crash course simulations held during the past few days in preparation for this moment. He recalled the briefing that had preceded those training exercises, in which he and Garcia had been informed of their role in what was described as a search-and-rescue operation for a Plysserian scientist on *Jontashreena*.

I'm flying to another planet, Roland's mind had screamed at him countless times since then, *and it's taking less time than a weekend hop to Vegas.*

It was a scenario for which the 160th had been preparing for months, since being notified by the Pentagon of plans to begin conducting more overt missions to the alien world. Many of the "big thinkers" in government and the military believed this to be the only way to keep the war between the Plysserians and the Chodrecai from spilling over to Earth more than it already had. Many in the rank and file, Roland included, were certain such thinking meant an eventual counteroffensive of some sort, and while there had been more than a few rumblings on that front in recent months, nothing official had been said or reported. There was little use in speculating about such things, Roland decided; when the time came, he would be told what to do and where to go.

Five hours after receiving such notification, Roland sat at the controls of his Black Hawk, one of three making the transit to *Jontashreena*. Lieutenant Michael Gutierrez, the agent from the Pentagon who had provided the 160th with its original briefings, was on the alien planet and had transmitted a status report back to Earth that he had located the Plysserian scientist. A subsequent message contained coordinates for plotting the endpoint of a portal and a call for immediate air support to be pushed through the conduit. Roland did not think of himself as an uneducated man, but he did not pretend to understand the process by which the portals were created or how they could be aimed at a particular location. So long as the engineers and computer wonks told him it worked, that was good enough for him.

Roland called into his microphone, "Guardians Two and Three, this is Guardian One. Everybody ready to play?"

"Roger that, Guardian One," came the voice of CWO Teddy Vanderbilt, piloting the Black Hawk that would follow Roland's through the portal.

"That's affirmative," added the pilot of the third chopper, CWO Faran Robau.

The tingling sensation playing across Roland's skin was now almost uncomfortable, and the low buzz in his ears had risen to a piercing whine. He and the others had been told to expect this during the simulations, and Roland had tried to imagine it while going through the flight exercises, but, as always when it came to combat operations, training took you only so far. "Hold on to your nutsack, Oz."

"Like I need another excuse to do that," Garcia quipped. Adopting a more serious tone, he added, "Orientation looks good, straight down the middle."

Roland nodded, trying not to hold his breath. The approach angle being off by as little as twelve inches in any direction would bring the Black Hawk's chopper blades into contact with the edges of the portal, and that would be all the lady wrote.

One of the drawbacks of the original portals that had brought the aliens to Earth was their size. They were too small to allow larger vehicles and equipment to pass through. This limitation may well have saved the planet from being overrun soon after the Chodrecai's arrival, as it required the breaking down of such materiel into components small enough to make the transit to Earth, after which it had to be reassembled. The Grays had overcome that shortcoming, at least in a manner sufficient to support the attacks they had launched months ago against Washington, Beijing, and Moscow. Such technology had not been seen since the failed offensive, fueling much speculation among military and government leaders that the Chodrecai might have expended their best hope for an invasion of Earth.

I'm not betting on it.

In the months since that campaign, human and Blue engineers had worked on expanding the original portal technology, increasing the size of the conduits as well as the length of time they could remain active. Both propositions required tremendous amounts of energy, a prospect Roland easily could believe. So far, the prototype portal generator developed by the research teams had passed all the trials put to it, with large test objects such as decommissioned tanks and helicopters being sent through the conduit to the other side with no ill effects. This was to be the first test sending through manned vehicles.

Lucky us.

"Portal threshold in five seconds," Garcia called out, counting down to one before punctuating his report with "Now."

The Black Hawk groaned as it crossed the threshold, the reverberations playing across its hull translating to the joystick and collective in Roland's hands. Everything inside the chopper's cramped cockpit seemed as though it might rattle loose from whatever was holding it in place. Roland ignored the hellstorm of multicolored energy roiling just beyond the windshield, his attention focused on the console's attitude indicator and compass. Instinct and training took over now, and he held the helicopter steady even as he pushed the craft forward through the conduit.

"I should've called in sick," Garcia shouted over the cacophony of the chopper's chorus of bangs, rattles, groans, and other protests.

As quickly as it had started, the vibrations ceased and the frenzied tempest enveloping them was gone, replaced by near total darkness.

"Holy shit," Roland said, gripping the joystick tighter as the Black Hawk stopped trying to buck him from his seat. It seemed silly not to have thought about it before, but Roland had not considered that it might be nighttime here on *Jontashreena* at the same time that it was daylight at the other end of the portal on Earth. *Duh, moron.*

Without being asked, Garcia reached for a control to dim the cockpit's internal illumination and the console backlighting, but did not engage any of the chopper's external lighting. Nodding in appreciation to his copilot, Roland called out, "Guardians Two and Three, sound off."

"Guardian Two here," replied Vanderbilt. *"Who turned out the lights?"*

"Guardian Three. We're here, Chuck," said Robau.

Roland released a sigh. "Well, looks like the hard part's over." He knew they still had to go back through again, assuming they survived the next few minutes. For now, he and his team had made it, and now flew over the surface of an alien world.

"I've got some lights to our three o'clock," Garcia said, hooking a thumb over his right shoulder. "Must be the prison, or whatever it is."

Roland nodded. From what he could see beyond the canopy, the terrain was not all that different from some areas of North America: flat, grassy plains occasionally interrupted by rocky bluffs and the occasional stand of trees and other vegetation. He knew this would be the case, based on information gleaned from Plysserian soldiers, but Roland supposed now that he had been expecting more.

Maybe all alien planets really do look like southern California. Or Canada.

With practiced ease, Roland banked the chopper until the installation was centered in the windshield. The compound consisted of five large buildings and a host of smaller structures encircled by a wall of some sort. As for the wall, it had sustained heavy explosives damage. Small fires smoldered at the points of detonation, and even from this distance Roland could see bodies strewn across the complex grounds. What little lighting the facility possessed was weak and scattered, barely enough to silhouette the buildings.

"It looks like downtown Detroit after the Red Wings win the Cup," Garcia said, before pointing toward the compound. "I'm seeing runners on the ground. They know we're here."

"Stand by on the guns," Roland said before calling into his mike, "Guardians, switch to primary tac frequency." When Garcia gave him a thumbs-up sign, Roland continued, "Sidewinder, this is Guardian One. We are in the neighborhood, and the locals are getting ready to send the welcome wagon."

There was a momentary pause before the voice of Lieutenant Michael Gutierrez responded, *"Guardian One, this is Sidewinder. Acknowledge your sitrep. Be advised we are still shopping. Maintain defensive posture. There may be noncombatants on the ground, so engage only verified threats. We're inside the building at eight o'clock relative to your approach vector from the portal, so stand by for extraction. Copy that?"*

"Roger that, Sidewinder," Roland replied, not particularly happy with the lieutenant's report. Coming abreast of the compound, Roland looked through his side window and saw a Chodrecai soldier on the ground, taking aim at the chopper with his rifle—one of those monstrous energy weapons the alien soldiers carried. Knowing how the rifles treated human flesh and not wanting to see what they might do to the belly of his chopper, he guided the Black Hawk away from the compound, climbing for altitude.

"Guardian Three here," said the voice of Robau in his helmet. *"We're taking fire, Chuck."*

"You are authorized to neutralize any threats," Roland ordered, before turning his attention back to Gutierrez. "Sidewinder, do you have an ETA for extraction?" They were here, now, and there was no hiding their presence. All they could do was engage any targets on the ground and do their best to keep the outside situation under some semblance of control, blanketing the area with suppressive fire and hop-

ing everyone kept their heads down when it was time for
Roland to fly into the compound to retrieve Gutierrez and
his charges. The plan the lieutenant had proffered in his last
situation report hinged on hitting the prison hard enough to
disrupt the small force assigned there, followed by a quick
insertion to locate the Plysserian scientist *Laepotic* Wysejral. The three Black Hawks Gutierrez had requested would
provide extraction and air support to get him, his team, and
the scientist back to the portal. So far, the first part of the
plan appeared to have gone off without a hitch, but now the
clock was ticking. How long would it take before survivors
on the ground rallied?

   Not long enough.

18

His left hand to his ear as he listened to the transmission from the leader of the newly arrived trio of Black Hawks, Gutierrez did not see the Chodrecai soldier step into view, his pulse rifle aimed at the lieutenant. DiCarlo did.

"Get down!" DiCarlo yelled, shouldering the other man behind the curve of the nearby wall as the blast from the Gray's weapon sliced through the space where Gutierrez's head had been and into the wall itself. DiCarlo grunted in momentary pain as flecks of hot shrapnel peppered his face and neck and bounced off his protective vest.

Another burst of energy filled the corridor as Russell aimed her pulse rifle around the bend, firing without bothering to aim. She repeated the action before pulling back and flattening herself against the wall.

"I think there's two of them," she said, her breaths rapid and shallow.

DiCarlo patted Gutierrez on the shoulder. "You okay?"

The lieutenant nodded. "Yeah. Thanks." Gesturing toward his ear, he added, "Choppers are here. They'll be covering our asses once we get out of here, assuming we can find this bastard."

"I'm all for that," DiCarlo said. Gutierrez's plan to place the beacon in the open field away from the prison and activate it remotely had been an inspired bit of thinking. Even considering how long it might take engineers on the other end to interpret the information Gutierrez had sent and complete the calculations necessary to establish the portal at this end of the conduit, the lieutenant had timed the execution of that portion of his plan with near perfection.

One less thing to fuck up, I suppose, DiCarlo mused, edging forward to get a better look down the corridor. Shadows flickered in the subdued lighting, and he heard voices even though he could not make out the words. "What are they doing?"

Behind him, Kel replied, "I believe they are calling for assistance."

"Bullshit," Gutierrez said, pulling open the breach on the grenade launcher attached to the underside of his M4 assault rifle. Satisfied with the round already loaded, the lieutenant pushed away from the wall and sidestepped around the bend in the corridor, giving himself a clean shot. "Fire in the hole!" he shouted, giving DiCarlo and Russell just enough time to cover their ears before pulling the grenade launcher's trigger.

Light flooded the corridor as the high-explosive round detonated, the explosion all but deafening in the confined space. DiCarlo felt the wall behind him shudder. Smoke rolled down the passageway, and he could hear something falling to the floor somewhere ahead of them. Not waiting for the smoke to clear, Gutierrez stepped forward, ejecting the spent grenade shell and inserting another one into the launcher.

"Let's go," DiCarlo said, his ears still ringing as he tapped Russell on her arm and gestured for her to follow him. Calling back over his shoulder to her and Kel, he said, "No idea if that guard got out a call for help, but count on backup trying to get down here. Kel, watch our backs." When he glanced again over his shoulder, he noted how the Blue soldier's eyes narrowed, his expression one of confusion. "Make sure they don't come in behind us."

Kel's massive head nodded. "Understood."

Ahead of them, Gutierrez was sifting through what remained of the corridor where the grenade had gone off. Two Chodrecai soldiers lay amid chunks of wall and ceiling, a cloud of dust hanging over the entire scene. The grenade had done its job with lethal efficiency, catching both Grays in its kill radius. Thick, dark blood ran from numerous wounds in both bodies, coating the floor and walls around them.

"Fuckers got off light," Gutierrez said, shaking his head in disgust as he beheld the bodies. The lieutenant had been simmering at a near boil after the discovery of two more human corpses subjected to dissection. The condition of the bodies prevented anything beyond basic gender identification—one man and one woman. While the man appeared to be of Asian descent and the woman Middle Eastern, there was no way to be sure. No clothing or personal effects had been found for any of the victims, and their missing hands prevented taking crude fingerprints in the hope of getting that information back to Earth for possible identification.

Tapping one of the soldiers' fallen pulse rifles, DiCarlo looked to Gutierrez. "You sure you don't want to trade up?"

It was the second time he had asked the lieutenant that question. Despite the limited effectiveness of the still-experimental Teflon-tipped 5.56-millimeter ammunition fired by his M4 carbine, Gutierrez had elected to hold on to his rifle rather than shoulder it in favor of one of the Gray weapons.

This time, he answered, "I never did get the feel for those things when I played with a few at the Pentagon." He held up the M4. "So, I brought extra ammo." Pausing, he stepped closer to one of the fallen Chodrecai and reached to retrieve the soldier's sidearm. "These, however, weren't as plentiful at our R and D center." Kneeling beside the dead Gray, Gutierrez unfastened the pistol's holster from the soldier's equipment belt, and with some fussing found a way to attach it to his own harness. Satisfied with his handiwork, he rose to his feet, nodding toward the pulse rifle in DiCarlo's hands. "I'm still trusting you to bring the heavy artillery when we need it."

"No problem," DiCarlo said.

"Do you think they got a call out?" Russell asked, keeping her attention on the corridor behind and ahead of them as she searched for signs of other Grays who might be coming from elsewhere in the building.

"I wouldn't bet against it," Gutierrez said, reaching up to adjust his radio's lip mike. "Guardian One, this is Sidewinder. Be advised there may be reinforcements converging on our position." There was a pause while he waited for a response from the Black Hawk pilot in his earpiece, then he nodded. "Roger that." For DiCarlo and Russell's benefit, he said, "They'll try to keep the worst of them off our backs."

Nodding, DiCarlo reached up to wipe sweat from his forehead. "That's great, but it doesn't count out anyone still left in this building. Also, we don't know who else in this place is calling for backup from some other location." The image in his head, with the three Black Hawks facing off against whatever attack aircraft might respond to a summons from the prison, did not sit well with him. "Let's find this guy and get the hell out of town."

Standing near Gutierrez, Kel regarded the portable data device he had purloined from the guard station on the building's main floor. The Blue soldier held up the device for the others to see its animated two-dimensional schematic of the building. "If I am reading this correctly, *Laepotic* Wysejral is toward the far end of this passageway." He gestured down the corridor, past the devastation Gutierrez's grenade had wrought.

"Assuming that gizmo's right," Gutierrez said. "I mean, they're only as smart as the idiot programming it or loading data to it, right?"

DiCarlo grunted. "As long as it's not running Windows, we should be okay."

Without another word, Gutierrez began moving once again up the hallway, leading the way with the muzzle of his M4. DiCarlo indicated for Russell to follow the lieutenant, and he proceeded after her, leaving Kel to bring up the rear.

The doors, like everything else, were bigger than what DiCarlo was used to seeing, just as the corridors themselves were wide and tall, in keeping with the generally larger physiology of this world's native inhabitants. His eyes checking every door they passed, he was relieved to see that this part of the building at least seemed to match the description provided by the Chodrecai guard Kel had overpowered on the main level.

The Gray had resisted Kel's attempts to question him about the location of *Laepotic* Wysejral, but had relented when the Blue soldier found the data device and consulted it, finding all the information the team needed to get to the incarcerated Plysserian scientist. Fearing that his usefulness was at an end and that he would be executed, the guard became quite forthcoming with respect to the building's lower levels. He even had volunteered the information that no prisoners usually were housed here, but instead the building was devoted to administration and other personnel support functions. The sole exception was Wysejral himself, billeted on the lowest level and kept in proximity to the

computer and engineering lab that had been established
for his use while he worked on improving the portal generation technology he had helped to create.

Rendering the guard unconscious instead of killing him
was a tactical risk, DiCarlo knew, but there was no way he
could kill even an enemy soldier in cold blood. Gutierrez at first had protested the idea, but relented almost as
quickly. As for the information the guard had provided, Di-
Carlo had not believed a word of it, but so far everything
was on the money.

Murphy's got a law for this kind of thing, too.

At the front of the column, Gutierrez came to a three-
point intersection in the corridor and paused, taking care to
look around the corner as he searched for threats. Glancing
over his shoulder, he nodded to the rest of the team and
made a gesture indicating the passageway was clear. Di-
Carlo stepped around Russell, moving into the intersection
and keeping his pulse rifle aimed down the other hallway
as he covered Russell's crossing. Using the wall as cover, he
rested the barrel of his weapon against the smooth surface,
sighting down its length. Unlike the main thoroughfare
they currently traversed, the intersecting corridor was only
partially lit, one overhead light fixture blinking erratically,
casting the entire passageway into frenzied shadows. Ignoring the light, DiCarlo concentrated on the shadows themselves as Kel maneuvered behind him. Once the Blue was
clear, DiCarlo glanced back the way they had come before
giving the other corridor one final look.

One of the shadows moved independently of the others.

DiCarlo fired without a second thought, the rifle bucking
as it belched energy. The shot struck something in the middle of the passageway and then DiCarlo saw an indistinct
figure stagger from the force of the blast. It stumbled forward, another Chodrecai solder clutching his own weapon.

The Gray fired, and DiCarlo flinched even though the shot was badly aimed, hitting the ceiling well away from him. He fired again, this time hearing the grunt of pain as the blast struck the Gray in the chest. The soldier sagged to his knees, dropping his rifle before falling limp to the floor.

"Any others?" Russell said, crouching next to him and aiming her own rifle down the corridor. DiCarlo saw Kel out of the corner of his eye, moving around him again and into the open, training his weapon on the fallen Gray.

Shaking his head, DiCarlo squinted to see past the flickering light. "Not that I can see. Then again, I barely saw that one." With a grunt of irritation, he took aim at the fixture and fired, the energy pulse ripping the unit from its ceiling mount and sending it crashing to the floor. That section of the corridor was plunged into near darkness, but at least now DiCarlo could see past it and confirm that the rest of the passageway appeared empty. Leaning against the nearby wall, he released an irritated sigh. "You know, I really am getting entirely too old for this shit."

The hallway rumbled with the echoes of M4 fire, and DiCarlo turned to see Gutierrez firing at something around the next bend in the corridor. Muzzle flashes from his rifle lit up that section of corridor as the lieutenant poured it on, stepping forward and keeping his finger on the weapon's trigger. With Kel and Russell following him, DiCarlo sprinted toward Gutierrez as he moved beyond the turn in the corridor. DiCarlo got there in time to see the lieutenant standing over the body of yet another Chodrecai, this one dressed differently from the guards they had encountered to this point.

"He's dead," Gutierrez said, poking the Gray with his rifle's muzzle before ejecting a spent magazine from the weapon and inserting a fresh clip from one of the pouches on his equipment harness.

DiCarlo indicated the dead soldier with his own rifle. "His uniform insignia indicates he was a *nomirtra*, a low-ranking officer." Looking to Kel, he asked, "What do you think?"

The Blue nodded. "He likely was a supervisor to the *fonsata* assigned to this building."

"Guys."

They turned to see Russell standing at a nearby door that now gaped open. Before DiCarlo could ask how she had managed to unlock the door, Russell pointed to the large keypad set into the wall, which showed a blinking blue light. "It was unlocked. Look at what's inside."

Stepping to the door, DiCarlo moved so that he could see into the room, and a rush of relief swept over him as he beheld the room's only occupant.

Laepotic Wysejral.

"I'll be go to hell," DiCarlo said, shaking his head in disbelief as he recognized the aged Plysserian from the photographs Gutierrez had provided. The alien stood amid half a dozen pieces of stout, complicated-looking machinery, which DiCarlo took to be computer peripherals of one sort or another. A table and a *tilopwat*—the backless chair of the type preferred by Plysserians and Chodrecai alike—sat in one corner, covered with stacks of reference materials and multicolored hexagons: portable computer data storage media similar to compact discs or DVDs. As for the Plysserian himself, he regarded them with wide, black eyes, his mottled, wrinkled gray skin featuring none of the blue tattoos sported by many Plysserian warriors. Stoop-shouldered and standing with the support of a gnarled wooden cane, Wysejral appeared ready to keel over at any moment.

"That's him, all right," Gutierrez said.

When the aged scientist spoke, DiCarlo could not understand a damned word the Blue was saying.

"He does not know your languages," Kel offered, stepping into the room and offering a formal bow to Wysejral. When he spoke to the elder Plysserian, it was in a series of sounds, grunts, and clicks that DiCarlo only half understood. He was able to pick out the scientist's name, and a few words explaining why they were here, to which Wysejral nodded before responding to Kel in his native tongue.

How the fuck have I been here six months and not learned to speak the language?

"Ask him about his work," Gutierrez said, waving toward the computer towers. "Is this everything, or have they taken some of it elsewhere?"

Kel relayed the query to Wysejral, who nodded before responding. "He says he has prepared numerous reports, schematics, and computer simulations while he has been held here, most of which were taken for review by parties unknown to him."

"Shit," Gutierrez said. "That's just the way it goes, then." Shaking his head, he shrugged off his rucksack and dropped to one knee. "Tell him to gather up as much of his work as he can carry." As he spoke, he set his rifle down on the floor next to his right foot and began rummaging in the pack. "Reports, computer discs, or whatever you call them, everything that'll fit in here or in his pockets." From the pack, he extracted three preset C-4 charges of the type he and Sloane earlier had used to blow the holes in the perimeter wall.

"That's a lot of bang," DiCarlo said, eyeing the charges.

Gutierrez nodded. "That's the idea."

19

"Prairie Dog, this is Sidewinder. We've got the package. I'm rigging up some parting gifts, then we're heading for the roof. Do you copy?"

Lying prone on the cold, damp ground, concealed from view by the tall grass and darkness as well as the sniper's ghillie suit he wore, Sergeant First Class Marty Sloane did not move even the slightest bit as he answered the voice in his ear. "Copy that, Sidewinder," he said, his reply barely a whisper. "Be advised that you've got Grays on the ground." Through the scope of his M40A3 sniper rifle, Sloane watched as six—no, seven—Chodrecai soldiers scurried about in his line of sight. A few were pointing at different breaches in the prison's mesh security perimeter, while two others attempted to douse one of the small fires burning on the grass near one hole. One Gray in particular had Sloane's attention; he was dressed differently from his companions and moved about the area with an air of authority the others lacked. Sloane decided he must be an officer or at least a senior member of the prison's staff. As the Gray pointed at the other soldiers and directed their movements, taking charge of the situation, the sergeant decided he would be the first one to go once the shooting started.

For the most part, the hasty plan he and Lieutenant Gutierrez had devised, along with the able assistance of

Sergeant Major DiCarlo and the Plysserian soldier, Kel, had worked well enough. Though Sloane did not believe the explosives they had planted had inflicted as many casualties as would have been preferable to mask the lieutenant's infiltration, little in the way of organized resistance had been offered to this point. Those soldiers not killed or seriously injured in the chain reaction blasts were still reacting to the hectic situation with little or no oversight. Only now was any semblance of order and discipline being restored. Of course, now they also were responding to the new threat offered by the sudden appearance of the three Black Hawk helicopters flying through the night sky around the prison.

Suck on that, you sons o' bitches.

"Sidewinder, this is Guardian One," said the lead Black Hawk's pilot, his voice small and tinny coming through Sloane's earpiece. *"Be aware that we have six minutes thirty-eight seconds until the door slams shut."*

Gutierrez responded, *"Roger that, Guardian One. We're moving now. Unless we encounter resistance, we should be on the roof in three minutes. If we're not there in five, you're ordered to bail."*

Though he did not take his eye from the sniper scope, Sloane still heard in the distance the distinctive churning of chopper blades as the trio of Black Hawks maintained their defensive posture, awaiting instructions from Gutierrez to commence extraction procedures. The sergeant's attention instead focused on the courtyard itself, watching those few visible soldiers who appeared to have escaped the initial diversionary attacks without injury. There had to be at least a few others inside the other buildings, he reasoned. Perhaps they were dealing with containing the prison population? Sloane also knew that someone somewhere down there was calling for reinforcements. How long would it take for that backup to arrive? Ten minutes? Less? It was not something the sergeant wanted to test.

New movement from one of the closer buildings caught his attention, and Sloane moved the sniper rifle just enough to sight in on two Gray soldiers emerging from a doorway, each holding one end of what to his practiced eye looked like a larger version of the pulse rifles the soldiers carried.

"Uh oh," he said, his muscles tensing as his right forefinger started to stroke the rifle's trigger guard almost without his conscious thought.

Maneuvering to an open piece of ground away from the building, the two Grays lowered the large piece of equipment to the soil, extending a built-in tripod from its underside. Now there was no mistaking the object for anything other than a weapon.

"Guardian One, Prairie Dog," he whispered into his lip mike. "The Grays are starting to set up some heavy ordnance. You want me to take them?"

"*Negative, Prairie Dog,*" responded the lead pilot. "*Maintain your cover. We've got this.*"

It took less than twenty seconds for the Black Hawk to make good on its pilot's promise. Looking away from the scope, Sloane watched as the helicopter banked toward the prison, its engines whining as it accelerated. Its two companions mimicked the maneuver, though they maintained a distance behind and to either side of their leader. Then a pair of Hellfire missiles shot forth from the pods mounted beneath the chopper's wings, sending contrails of thick white smoke streaking across open space. A pair of orange-white fireballs erupted one atop the other in the prison courtyard, obliterating the pair of Gray soldiers and their weapon emplacement.

"*Scratch two bad guys,*" said the voice of Guardian One as the helicopters arced away. Over the sound of their blades Sloane could hear the reports of pulse rifles fired in-effectually at the departing craft.

His attention away from his scope, the sergeant turned his head to see the feverish yet contained flare of energy sitting alone on the vast expanse of open ground to his left. The portal's vibrant maelstrom had impressed him from the first time he had seen a conduit in action, and despite the jaded, matter-of-fact outlook with which he tended to view everything around him, he had been enthralled with the pure wonder and imagination it must have required to cre-ate something as marvelous as a means of connecting two worlds. It was a pity that an achievement of that magnitude had been born out of military necessity, rather than the drive merely to learn something new—something more. Of course, Sloane knew from history and experience that tech-nological advancement often arrived via such means.

Though he viewed himself as a simple soldier, he had spent much time trying to broaden his perspective with re-spect to the world around him. He had begun with straight-forward attempts to understand the different enemies his government sent him to fight. He read their religious texts and their literature as well as whatever material might pro-vide insight into their culture, beliefs, and attitudes, not only toward outsiders but themselves, as well. Over the years, as maturity and wisdom came with hard-won expe-rience, Sloane's quest for knowledge had expanded to a rigorous course of night study at local community colleges wherever his military assignments stationed him.

While he had answered the call to duty and would con-tinue to do so, such actions did not prohibit Sloane from wishing for a time when people of his chosen profession were no longer needed, and that the resources and effort directed to the art of war might one day be utilized for a grander, more benevolent purpose. Should they survive the

crisis they now faced, would Earth and its people see this
conflict as motivation to finally travel the path toward creating a better world and life for everyone, regardless of political, racial, religious, or socioeconomic differences?

"*Guardian One, this is Sidewinder,*" Gutierrez's voice
snapped in Sloane's ear, pushing through the distracting
thoughts and bringing his focus back to the matters at hand.
"*We're ready to hit the roof. Come and get us.*"

"*Copy that, Sidewinder,*" replied the Black Hawk pilot.
"*We're inbound. ETA twenty seconds.*"

*Wax philosophical on your own time, dickbag. Back to
work,* Sloane mused, chastising himself and returning his
attention to his rifle. The prison's courtyard once more
revealed itself to him through the green tinge of the rifle
scope's viewfinder, the bodies of visible Chodrecai soldiers showing up as lighter green, almost white silhouettes.
Somewhere to his right, he heard the pitch of helicopter
engines change as the Black Hawks adjusted their trajectories, and once more those Grays on the ground were reacting to their approach.

This time, rather than simply playing escort to the
lead chopper, the other two Black Hawks opened fire,
the air filling with the sounds of machine gun fire as well
as launching rockets. Hot orange tracer fire stitched the
ground inside the wall, ripping up dirt and grass and tearing into the smaller structures scattered around the compound. Gutierrez had given strict instructions to avoid
other barrack buildings unless fired upon from those locations, for fear of injuring unarmed prisoners or other noncombatants.

Centering the crosshairs of his scope on the one Chodrecai who still seemed to be acting in some form of leadership capacity, Sloane took a deep breath as his finger
caressed the M40's trigger. At his present distance of less

than one hundred meters, any bullet he might fire would punch clean through his target, even one as tough as the muscled physique of the alien warrior. The Gray was waving at the helicopters and gesturing to the soldiers around him, no doubt directing them to fire. Though Sloane had never seen the effects of a pulse rifle on anything as big as a Black Hawk, he had heard reports of other skirmishes where such weapons had been effective at damaging or even incapacitating vehicles and smaller aircraft. This was not the time to be taking any chances.

Releasing most of the breath he held, Sloane pulled the trigger.

The Teflon round launched a sizable portion of the Gray's head into the air, spattering the ground around the soldier's body with whatever passed for their blood, bone, and brain tissue. The Gray sagged in a disjointed heap to the ground, his death having an immediate effect on those soldiers nearest to him, with one backpedaling away from the body and searching for whoever or whatever had fired the killing shot. Another simply stood motionless, the barrel of his weapon drooping as he regarded his dead superior. Cycling the rifle, Sloane repeated the breathing and sighting exercise on that soldier, the scope's crosshairs coming to rest in the middle of the Gray's face. Then the Chodrecai turned and ran, tossing aside his rifle and scampering away, with his companion following after him.

Sloane let them go.

Instead, he turned his attention to the Black Hawks, two of which were orbiting the prison and raining down streams of machine-gun fire. The barrage was enough to cause most of the Grays on the ground to dive for cover, or remain in whatever places of concealment they had managed to find. The third helicopter was diving for the nearest building, its pilot leveling the chopper's descent as he brought the craft to a hover less than five meters above the structure, from which he gently lowered the Black Hawk toward the roof.

That motherfucker can fly.

Glancing at his watch, Sloane figured they had just a little more than two minutes before the portal shut down.

It was going to be close.

Looking out the left side window, Chuck Roland held the joystick with only the fingertips of his right hand, easing the Black Hawk to a landing but unwilling to let the helicopter come to rest atop the building's roof. There was no way to know if the structure could withstand the chopper's weight, and he was in no mood to gamble.

"Okay, we're here," he said, ignoring his racing heart and trying to take comfort in the smooth vibrations of the helicopter. "Let's pack 'em in, Ozzy."

"Roger that," Garcia replied, disengaging his pilot's harness and working his way out of his seat to assist with getting the extraction team on board. Roland glanced over his shoulder and saw Staff Sergeant Derek Attico already crouched in the partially open doorway, his hands swiveling the door-mounted M60 machine gun into position. Extracting the M9 pistol from the holster under his left arm, Garcia tapped Roland on his helmet before pushing open the door and taking up a protected position opposite Attico.

There was movement outside the door, and Roland tensed until he saw that the approaching figures—three of them, anyway—were human. Gutierrez was easy enough to identify, but the bedraggled man and woman accompanying him were another matter. The man's hair was long, pulled back into a ponytail, and his gray beard looked to have last been trimmed with a dull butter knife. Both he and the dark-skinned woman wore remnants of what might once have been military uniforms, though they also sported clothing and equipment that looked more appropriate for the massive Plysserian soldier accompanying them. As for the Blue, he all but carried another alien, this one much older and frail looking, along with a satchel of some sort slung over one bulging shoulder. Roland was sure he should know these other people, but the demands of the current situation did not allow him time to ponder their identities.

"*Guardian One, this is Prairie Dog,*" came the voice of Sergeant Sloane in his ear. The sniper was still in position somewhere outside the prison. "*Do you have them?*"

"That's affirmative," Roland replied. "They're at the door. Start heading for the portal. We'll grab you en route."

"*Prairie Dog is hauling ass,*" the sergeant replied.

Reaching the helicopter first, Gutierrez put his back to the Black Hawk, covering the others as they ran to the open doorway. The other man helped the woman aboard before climbing in after her, then turned and held out a hand to the Blue soldier and with Garcia's help assisted him in getting the elderly Plysserian into the chopper. Even though the Black Hawk was designed to carry up to ten fully loaded combat troops, the helicopter still shifted to the right as the Blues got aboard.

Roland reached out to pat the console before him. *Don't get moody on me now, baby.*

Just behind his right shoulder, the other man donned a headset, adjusting the microphone so that it rested in front of his mouth before tapping Roland on the shoulder. "Sergeant Major Simon DiCarlo, sir," he said, offering a smile. "Nice of you to give us a ride."

Of course, Roland thought. *I should've known.* DiCarlo and Sergeant Russell, the two Marines who had ended up transported here months ago after their unit had engaged the Grays in Missouri. There was no mistaking the relief in the other man's eyes. How long had they been here? Even a tour in Iraq or Afghanistan at least offered the possibility of one day returning home. What must life have been like here, wondering if rescue would ever come?

Checking to see that everyone was aboard, Roland offered a quick salute to the Marine before returning his attention to his flight controls. "You can thank me later, Sergeant Major, assuming we don't fuck this up on the final play." Looking to Gutierrez, he asked, "You ready?"

Hunkered near the door and wearing a headset, the lieutenant nodded, holding up what Roland recognized as a remote detonator transmitter. "Yeah."

"Do it," Roland said, pulling up on the collective and tilting the joystick to his left, banking away from the building. As he did so, he felt a rumble coursing through the body of the helicopter at the same moment he caught sight of hellish fire belching from the windows of the building below him. The charges Gutierrez had set—after first determining that the building housed no prisoners—worked as advertised, the first step toward destroying the work *Laepotic* Wysejral had conducted and amassed during his internment here.

"*Guardian Three to Guardian One,*" said the voice of Faran Robau. "*Firing on primary target.*"

"*Guardian Two,*" added Teddy Vanderbilt. "*Firing.*"

The Black Hawk's angle of departure was such that Roland was able to see the streaks of smoke following after the eight missiles that slammed into the side of the building. Explosions ripped through the exterior walls, expelling metal and other debris through shattered windows and newly created ruptures. Then that entire side of the building began to collapse in on itself, the wall disappearing in an expanding cloud of dust and smoke that billowed out in all directions. Roland cast one final look at the scene of destruction before angling the Black Hawk away from the prison and out over the open ground.

Hope they have good insurance.

"Guardian One, this is Guardian Three," said Robau over the channel. *"We have Prairie Dog on board."*

"Roger that, Three," Roland replied, relieved to hear the news. "Head for the portal."

"We're taking fire!" Vanderbilt's voice was loud enough that it almost dissolved to static, making Roland wince. *"Repeat: We're taking fire. We need—"*

There was no time to say or even think anything before a bright orange flash erupted somewhere to Roland's right. Jerking his head in that direction, he peered through the chopper's still-open door in time to see one of the Black Hawks vanish in a ball of fire, its forward momentum fading as gravity seized what remained of the helicopter and pulled it inexorably to the ground.

"God damn it!' Roland said, his hands instinctively guiding the chopper into a dive designed to shake possible targeting by an enemy.

Robau's voice echoed in his ears, his words tinged by shock. *"Guardian Two is down! I repeat: Guardian Two is down!"*

His hands gripping the controls tight enough that he could feel his pulse in his fingertips, Roland adjusted his flight path and headed toward the ground. Accelerating this close to the hard deck was a risk—no, it was fucking suicidal—but it beat taking a rocket or energy bolt up the ass. "Damn it! Ozzy, can you see anything?"

Hanging on to a support strap near the door, Garcia replied, "Negative. They're gone, Chuck."

Damn it all to fucking hell. Fuck! They were so close, so damned close. Teddy Vanderbilt had been his roommate at flight school. He had been Teddy's best man, and was the godfather of his only son.

Fighting back tears, Roland forced his attention back to the matter at hand as the portal loomed once more in the windshield. Eyeing the controls before him, Roland risked another look over his shoulder at the aged Plysserian sitting on the floor of the Black Hawk's passenger compartment. The alien seemed to register his scrutiny, his large, dark eyes gazing at Roland. What information did this Blue have? What made him so valuable that they'd gone to so much trouble and risk in order to retrieve him? Was his knowledge enough to justify having to tell Teddy Vanderbilt's wife she was now a widow?

"I hope you're worth it," Roland said, feeling the now familiar tingle on his skin as he turned his attention back to his controls seconds before the helicopter entered the portal.

The Gathering Storm

20

Sitting less than twenty feet from *Zolitar* Teqotev, Colin Laney flinched at the bright white flash and the whine of energy that howled from the weapon an instant before it bucked in the Plysserian soldier's hands. His eyes registered movement from the oversized rifle's muzzle, something like an invisible fist pushing through the air ahead of it. Crossing the expanse of open sand before Teqotev, it slammed into the man-sized, pale gray dummy positioned fifty feet in front of where the Blue stood. The target exploded from the waist up, disappearing in a wash of pale shrapnel that rained down upon the ground and the grassy berm at the firing range's far end.

Occupying a set of bleachers, each of them sitting as directed by their drill instructors, with backs straight, feet together, and hands resting on their knees, the recruits of Platoon 3003 nevertheless were unable to refrain from reacting to what they had just seen. Though Colin said nothing, several of his companions gasped, and there were more than a few muttered curses in response to the weapons demonstration.

It was but the latest occurrence of the platoon's "typical" Marine recruit training as augmented with instruction by a Plysserian soldier. In the weeks since training began, 3003 and its sister platoons had undertaken extensive courses in a variety of topics pertaining to their alien allies as well as that of their enemy. Classes on Marine Corps history, customs and courtesies, and other related matters had been infused with similar information from both the Plysserian and Chodrecai perspectives, including a sweeping overview of the aliens' conflict on *Jontashreena*, which had eventually spilled over to Earth.

"Sweet fucking Jesus almighty," breathed Carl Gibbons, the recruit sitting next to Colin, his words barely audible even as he drew out the first and last words in what Colin figured was just the way people talked in Gibbons's hometown of Macon, Georgia. Though he dared not turn his head, Colin still saw the other man shift in his seat. Unlike Colin, Gibbons was a draftee, and had made no secret of his desire to be anywhere but where life and fate had chosen to place him. "Did you see that fucking thing? What the fuck does it do to a human?"

"At ease," growled Staff Sergeant Blyzen as he stalked back and forth in front of the platoon. Though he was dressed like the young men in his charge, Blyzen's combat utility uniform was immaculately tailored to fit his lean, muscled frame. The sleeves of his blouse were rolled to a point just above his elbows, the folds precise and wrinkle-free. The cuffs of his trousers fell just below the tops of his brown suede combat boots, and the polished black leather belt he wore around his waist—a symbol of his status as the platoon's senior drill instructor—along with its gold buckle, gleamed in the morning sun. The brim of his campaign cover shaded his face, but did not dim his piercing gaze as he scanned the recruits. "Keep it up, ladies, and you'll be digging holes to China." He glared at the platoon for an extra few seconds, as though daring any of the recruits to test him, then turned back to Teqotev and nodded. "Continue."

Still standing at the firing line and holding the rifle, the Plysserian soldier pressed a control on the weapon's stock before stepping closer to the assemblage of recruits. Extending his arms so that the platoon could get an unobstructed view of the rifle, he said, "This is a *Bretloqa*-class pulse rifle, a standard-issue weapon for Plysserian military units." Colin was impressed by the Blue soldier's command of English, the alien speaking with perfect diction and cadence, his large, black, seemingly bottomless eyes moving to study each of the recruits as he spoke. "Instead of firing projectiles, this rifle generates an energy sphere of a size approximate to that of the human skull. Rather than cause grotesque wounds, this weapon is primarily intended to attack a target's central nervous system."

Moving his right hand, Teqotev indicated a crimson jewel-like button set into the rifle's stock, just above the handgrip. "The intensity level is variable, based on this selector control. It can be set so as to render your target unconscious, and upward through increasing power levels to a point capable of inflicting physical harm on internal organs and, yes, even death."

The Blue turned from the bleachers and pointed to the target he had just destroyed. "It is also important to remember that these weapons were designed with my species as the intended targets. Our physiology is much different from that of humans, not simply in size and general appearance, but also in the operation of our internal organs as well as our more robust nature. Your military is currently employing engineers to develop projectiles usable by your weapons against my species. Still, much of your small-arms weaponry remains ineffectual, at least not without applying concentrated firepower or aiming for vulnerable areas, such as our eyes, throat, groin, and so on." Once more, he held up the pulse rifle. "In contrast, human physiology has proven to be most susceptible when confronted by weapons such as these, even when fired at mid-range intensity."

Thanks to the wonders of modern-day news coverage, Colin had witnessed the frightening effects of the alien weaponry on humans. Such carnage had been depicted via journalists and their camera operators embedded with military units around the world, or local reporters covering what at the time had been alarmingly frequent encounters with Grays. That the news outlets saw fit to broadcast such brazen, raw images at any time of the day or night was something to which Colin had not become accustomed. He wondered about the long-term effects of these ongoing barrages of disturbing imagery, and how they already were stirring uncontrolled hostility in a populace tired and terrified by the constant specter of war in their very backyard. It was having tangible effects in some quarters, he knew, with people becoming so desensitized to the notion of such brutality that they decided that personal survival and victory over the Grays justified the abandonment of anything resembling civility or mercy toward the aliens—or even their fellow humans, for that matter. Such behavior had been widely reported for months, with people gunning down neighbors or store clerks or whoever might stand in their way as they secured food, medicine, ammunition, and whatever else they deemed important.

If the Grays were smart, they'd just sit back and wait for us to destroy each other, then waltz in and pick up the leftovers.

"In order to provide human military forces with at least some measure of tactical equality," Teqotev continued, "Plysserian military engineers and weapons specialists are working with human counterparts to replicate our weaponry for your use, in a form better suited to your smaller physiology." He did not say "weaker" or "inferior," but Colin thought he detected that sentiment in the Blue's words. At first he considered resenting such an implication, but the simple fact was that, unspoken or not, the observation indeed was true.

Teqotev asked, "Are there any questions at this point?"

A single hand, belonging to Recruit Juarez, a young man from the Bronx, rose into the air. At Teqotev's prompting, the man stood at attention and proceeded as the recruits had been instructed when asking a question. "Sir, Recruit Juarez has a question about something the instructor said. What did the instructor mean by his species, sir? Aren't Plysserians and Cho . . . the other guys . . . different species?"

"Of course not," Teqotev replied, his voice offering no hint that he found the question inappropriate. "Plysserians and Chodrecai are the same, just as your different ethnic subgroups belong to the human species. It is our ideology that separates us, rather than our physiology. In that regard, both our planets have much in common."

Returning to the topic at hand, Teqotev said, "While the Chodrecai employ weaponry similar to the *Bretloqa*, their versions of the rifle are not as advanced as ours. The basic functionality is largely similar, though theirs do not possess the same variety of intensity settings. In practice, this makes their weaponry more dangerous to humans, as given the choice between simply stunning an opponent and eliminating them, most Chodrecai *fonsata* operating without supervision will choose the latter option." It took Colin an extra second to recall the alien word from the list he and his fellow recruits had received as part of their reference materials, or "knowledge," as it was called by the drill instructors. *Fonsata* was actually a Chodrecai word, as Colin remembered from his nightly study, meaning a low-ranking soldier.

Infantry. Grunts, like us.

"Another element the Chodrecai lack is any meaningful defense against such weaponry," Teqotev continued. Stepping to his right, the Plysserian pointed to another target, standing parallel to its ill-fated companion at the other end of the firing range. Unlike its predecessor, this target was outfitted with what at first glance appeared to be body armor of the type designed to shield its wearer's entire torso, from neck to crotch. "My people already wear a form of protective equipment that guards against Chodrecai pulse weapons, though of course exposed areas of the body remain vulnerable. The vest you see on the target has been engineered based on our armor, but again, tailored to better suit human physiques."

His hand again moving across the buttons on his rifle's stock, Teqotev turned toward the target, raised the weapon to his shoulder, and took aim. Though he was ready for it this time, Colin still cringed a bit when the Blue soldier fired the weapon. Again there was the bright muzzle flash and the sensation of something roiling through the air as it screamed toward the target, followed by the sound of something striking the dummy. Positioned atop a single steel rod sticking up from the sand, the target rocked backward in response to the violent assault, and Colin was certain he registered the displacement of the protective vest as it absorbed the impact. Then the dummy returned to its upright position, trembling as the last effects of the attack faded.

"Ow," Gibbons said, his voice barely a whisper.

"Make no mistake," Teqotev said as he laid the rifle atop the waist-high table that marked the firing point, "a direct hit at that intensity on any exposed part of your body, such as your head, will be fatal, and in the fashion I earlier demonstrated. Work continues on developing protective headwear, but even that will still leave some risk to the wearer."

"In other words," Staff Sergeant Blyzen said as he regarded the assembled platoon with his hands on his hips, "your best bet is to put down your enemy before he can get a bead on you. Understand?"

"Sir, yes, sir!" shouted Colin, joined in unison by his fellow recruits.

Rolling his eyes in exaggerated disgust, the drill instructor countered, "Why are you whispering? You afraid to wake the neighbors? *Understand?*"

"*Sir, yes, sir!*"

Without moving his head, Colin detected new movement in his peripheral vision to either side of the bleachers. Teams of Marines and Plysserian soldiers were taking positions at each of the firing range's fourteen stations. Every team had with them a *Bretloqa* pulse rifle. At the far end of the range, two other Marines were replacing the target Teqotev had destroyed during his earlier demonstration. All of the targets wore the specially engineered vests.

"Eyeballs," Blyzen ordered.

"Snap, sir!" replied Colin and the other recruits.

The drill instructor provided terse instructions for the platoon to fall in on the firing points, and after the command to move was given, Colin found himself first in line at the sixth station, standing at attention before an African-American Marine corporal wearing combat utilities and a tan desert pith helmet that designated him as a weapons range instructor. The Marine's Plysserian counterpart towered over both men, his black one-piece uniform stretched across his broad chest and shoulders while leaving bare his thick, tattooed arms.

"What's your name, Recruit?" asked the corporal, whose name tag read "Sutherland." When he spoke, it was in a calm, controlled, almost paternal voice.

"Sir, this recruit's name is Recruit Laney, sir," Colin replied.

Sutherland nodded. "Okay, Laney, here's how this is gonna work," he said, his right hand resting on the stock of the pulse rifle lying atop the wooden table. "This thing is heavier than the M16 you're used to, and it's got a kick that'll knock you on your ass if you don't pay attention and hold it right. When you pick it up, you pull it tight into your shoulder and then you lean into it. Understand?"

"Sir, yes, sir!" Laney responded, shouting out of force of habit.

"And stop screaming at me," the corporal replied. "I can hear you." He pointed to a set of ear protection lying to the left of the rifle. "Pick those up and put them on your grape."

Doing as instructed, Colin next lifted the pulse rifle as directed by Sutherland. It was not as heavy as he was expecting, though it definitely outweighed the M16s he and his fellow recruits had been carrying during close-order drill exercises.

"The blue button near your thumb is the safety," said the Plysserian soldier, pointing with one huge hand to where Colin's wrapped around the handgrip. "It is currently engaged. Press it to disengage it."

A knot forming in his stomach, Colin moved his thumb over the control, feeling its curved surface as it rose from the side of the weapon. Pressing it produced an audible click, followed by a noticeable reverberation from within the rifle itself.

"Relax," Sutherland said. "That's the power cell coming online. It's radioactive, but it won't kill you. Doesn't mean I'd hold it next to my nutsack or anything, if I were you." The levity was a welcome change from the normal demeanor of the drill instructors, who to Colin's knowledge had yet to utter anything resembling a joke. More serious now, the corporal indicated for Colin to assume a firing stance. With his help, Colin maneuvered the rifle into position, pulling it back into his shoulder socket and leaning forward as instructed. He held that stance until the recruits at the other thirteen stations readied themselves, waiting as ordered for the command to fire.

From somewhere behind them, another voice called out through a loudspeaker, "Ready on the right? Ready on the left? All ready on the firing line. Shooters, you may commence firing at your instructor's command."

"Fire," Sutherland ordered.

His right forefinger moving to the firing stud at the front of the rifle's handgrip, Colin pressed it without hesitation, and the results were immediate. Even with the hearing protection the muzzle blast was jarring, and despite his preparation the weapon still punched him in the shoulder, but to his surprise its muzzle did not buck upward or out of his other hand. In front of him, he saw everything above the neck of his target's vest vanish in a small cloud of white debris expanding outward to litter the ground behind it.

Sweet.

"An excellent shot," said the Plysserian soldier, nodding his massive head in approval.

"Damned right it was," Sutherland said, clapping Colin on the shoulder. "Right in his piehole. Shit, you're a natural."

Stealing glances at the other targets, Colin saw that fewer than half had even been hit. Some had suffered damage to an extremity, but only three others had fallen victim to a hcad shot.

"Okay, you're done," Sutherland said, as orders were shouted for the recruits on the firing line to secure their weapons and stand by to replace any targets for the next round of shooters.

As he followed his instructions and ran to a cargo bin containing a selection of dummies, Colin could not shake the image of the damage he had inflicted on his unmoving, unarmed target, and wondered when he might be facing a real enemy, one made of flesh and blood and quite capable of shooting back at him.

21

Bruce Thompson considered himself a reasonably intelligent man. With two bachelor's degrees and one master's, he had spent a sizable portion of his adult life learning and opening his mind to all manner of new ideas and perspectives. His military career and the experiences he had gained in both peace and war also had contributed to his ongoing education. He was self-assured to the point that he could hold up his end of conversations with politicians, scholars, even his fourteen-year-old granddaughter, who had announced her intentions to join the Air Force one day and become a pilot, all as a precursor to being the first woman to walk on Mars.

Despite all of that, when Thompson was in the company of the people with whom he now shared his conference room, he felt like an idiot.

"Good morning," he said, walking the length of the room toward his chair at the far end of the polished conference table. He affected a polite smile as he took his seat and placed his coffee mug on the table, turning to face the over-sized plasma flat-screen display mounted against the wall to his left. "Rather, good evening."

On the screen, the image of an attractive American woman and a serious-looking Indian man stared out at him from their own conference room, buried somewhere in a basement level of a top secret research facility in Chennai, India. The facility belonged to a U.S.-based civilian contractor with offices around the world, a simple, cold reality of a global economy and the monetary savings to be had by outsourcing American jobs to overseas locations. "Best-shoring" was one of the more recent terms Thompson had heard to describe the practice. While he had no love for it, the Department of Defense, when procuring goods and services from outside vendors, more often than not was required to award contracts to the company offering the lowest bid. So long as the U.S. government kept to that policy, it was inevitable that the DoD would deal with contractors who employed outsourcing or best-shoring or whatever they wanted to call it.

"*Good morning, General,*" Professor Melloy replied. Along with her companion, Professor Ravishankar Subupathy, Melloy currently led one of the research groups tasked with replicating and improving upon the portal generation technology, working with Plysserian scientists and engineers. Below the pair, a bright red band stretched across the bottom of the screen, with the caption SECURE COMMLINK ENABLED scrawled in yellow block letters. Thompson knew that a similar message accompanied his image on their screen in India; if such was not the case for either party involved in the teleconference, the connection would immediately be severed.

As for Melloy, Thompson recalled from her personnel file that she was in her mid-forties but looked ten years younger. Deep-red, shoulder-length hair framed a tanned, angular face. The professor wore no makeup, not even lipstick, and in Thompson's opinion required none of those things. He recalled also from her file that Melloy was married to an engineer working for NASA somewhere in California, and that she had volunteered for the assignment in

Chennai because of the unprecedented opportunity the position offered.

Thompson glanced at his watch, checking the time and performing the conversion to Chennai local time in his head before saying, "It's coming up on twenty-one hundred in your neck of the woods, so I can assume you've got something you didn't want to wait for a secure courier to get to me."

Sitting next to Melloy, Professor Subupathy replied, "*Indeed we do, General. We continue to make progress with expanding portal size as well as the duration that the resulting conduit can remain active. Our biggest hurdle is still maintaining stability. As you know, operating a portal requires tremendous amounts of power.*" As he talked, he waved his hands about him in rather animated fashion. It was almost amusing, Thompson decided.

"*We're talking on par with the power grid for a small city, General,*" Subupathy continued. "*Tapping into existing plants is not feasible, for security reasons if nothing else, which is why we were forced to build our own.*"

"*But that doesn't help with the feedback issue,*" Melloy said. "*The energies harnessed by a conduit when it's in operation are staggering. Keeping it contained requires a series of stabilization enablers, which we've constructed according to specifications provided by our Plysserian friends working alongside us.*" She paused, sighing. "*That said, we still face the problem of overheating power transfer coils, which require cooling after being in operation for a prolonged period.*"

"I'm aware of all this, Professor," Thompson said, reaching for his coffee. "According to the latest field tests, you were able to keep a portal measuring twenty meters in diameter in operation for nearly nine minutes." The test had come under fire, with the portal utilized as a vital component of the rescue operation that had successfully retrieved the Plysserian scientist Wyscjral, along with those two Marines who had spent months living, working, and fighting alongside Plysserian allies on the alien world.

Melloy nodded. *"Yes, but we were just barely able to keep it open long enough for those rescue choppers to return from* Jontashreena. *One more minute and the portal would've collapsed, possibly with the Black Hawks still in transit."* Her expression turned to one of worry. *"No one's been able to tell us what happens when something like that occurs, but I can assure you, General, that I have no plans to be traversing one of those conduits when it decides to shut down."*

"So why are we talking?" Thompson asked. "Have you been able to improve the performance of your test generator?"

"To a degree, yes," Subupathy replied. *"Our current tests have resulted in the creation of a portal opening spanning thirty-eight point six meters. The conduit remained stable for nearly six minutes before we were forced to power down and avoid overheating. Analysis of the power transfer coils by* Laepotic Wysejral *and other Plysserian engineers has provided us with avenues to explore with respect to improving that performance."*

Six minutes. Thompson rolled the number around in his mind, trying it on for size. It did not sound like an impressive period of time, but a lot could happen in six minutes, particularly with respect to the movement of people and equipment into combat. "How long does it take for the power coils to cool enough that you can reengage the generators and reactivate the portal?"

On the screen, Melloy's expression faltered. *"That's still a problem, General. Our most recent tests resulted in the coils requiring at least twenty-seven minutes to cool sufficiently."*

Thompson shook his head, unhappy with that bit of news. "Twenty-seven minutes is an eternity in combat, Professor, particularly if you're already in a landing zone and waiting for reinforcements while you're getting the shit kicked out of you by a numerically superior enemy force. What happens if you deactivate the portals before you're forced to? Instead of waiting to see how long it stays open, what about setting a predetermined limit? Let's say three minutes."

Subupathy said, *"We've already tried scenarios like that, General. As you're probably thinking, limiting the time of operation does mitigate some of the heat sink requirements, but only marginally. A few minutes at most."*

"That's a start," Thompson said. "A few minutes might make the difference between securing a beachhead or getting our asses punted right off that planet. Now talk to me about the beacons. They've been field-tested, and Lieutenant Gutierrez has already used one in a combat situation. Was that a fluke, or are they reliable?"

"So far," Subupathy answered, *"the beacons have performed flawlessly. The time required to complete calculations for locking in a portal endpoint has been reduced tenfold. The tests we've conducted with reestablishing a conduit forced to shut down—for overheating or any of a number of unforeseen circumstances—also have proven successful."* Holding up an object Thompson recognized as one of the prototype beacons still being tested, the professor continued, *"Our research department currently is working on a way for a beacon to transmit real-time telemetry back through a conduit, and allow computers on the far end to continuously update the calculations necessary to maintain a stable conduit with fixed endpoints."*

Thompson did not even try to wrap his head around that concept. From previous briefings, he knew that the process of determining the probable location of a portal opening at the conduit's endpoint and then maintaining that corridor relied on computations so complex that dedicated super-computers were required to perform the calculations. Even the orbits of the two planets, as well as their relative positions in space, factored into the Byzantine equations.

"If you try to give me details," Thompson said, "my brain will likely explode." He paused to take another sip of his coffee before adding, "I swear, I don't understand how the Plysserians could possibly have stumbled across this by accident. Even the idea of teleporting from place to place on a single planet boggles the mind, let alone crossing between two worlds."

"The prevailing theory around here," Melloy replied, *"is that the conduits create a 'fold,' warping space in such a way that the two planets can be joined. It is believed that understanding this possibility may offer more informed insight as to calculating and maintaining conduits."*

Having heard that theory before, Thompson remained as skeptical now as he did then. "How far have we come that even I don't bat an eye whenever somebody says something like that to me?" He waved away the question before either professor could attempt offering an answer. "I don't care about any of this right now. Have your teams continue to work on improving that generator efficiency. We need to cut that recycle time in half, at least."

He figured Melloy would not take those instructions well, and the professor did not disappoint. *"Half?"* she repeated, her eyes wide. *"General, that may not be feasible, at least not with the equipment we have at our disposal."*

"Find a way," Thompson said. He knew that simply telling his colleagues the reasons behind such a blunt request would be more than sufficient for them to rise to the challenge and search for any means of meeting his demands. But it also would violate a dozen rules and regulations pertaining to operational security and the need to protect sensitive information. The stakes simply were too high, particularly now, to risk having the information he possessed—

fragmented and compartmentalized as it was even for him—reach the wrong people, human or alien.

Despite his lack of clarification, Melloy and Subupathy both seemed to understand at least some of what Thompson had left unspoken. *"How soon?"* she asked, her eyes seeming to communicate her comprehension.

"Consider this your thirty-day notice," Thompson replied. In truth, he did not know for sure whether that was the true target for which the JCS was shooting. General Grayson and his fellow Joint Chiefs had not been *that* forthcoming with the information they had chosen to share with him, but enough hints had been dropped and innuendo offered that he felt comfortable working with the number he had provided.

To their credit, neither of the professors looked the least bit surprised to hear his answer. *"We'll do our best, General,"* Melloy said, nodding with new conviction.

Thompson nodded. "I just hope your best is good enough."

22

For the first time in recent cycles—more than she cared to count—First *Dekritonpa* Vahelridol Praziq was hopeful. After generations of conflict that had all but consumed this world and now threatened the well-being of another, might peace finally be at hand?

Standing before the large window that formed the back wall of her expansive office, Praziq took in the spectacular, unfettered view of Aedrindy, the sprawling city that had served as capital of the Territorial Confederation since the seventeen individual Chodrecai nations came together more than one hundred generations earlier. The once thriving metropolis was but a shadow of its former self.

Most of the visible activity on the streets and thoroughfares was due to military units, either moving to assigned duty stations or checking vehicles, and people making their way to homes, places of employment, or whatever other destinations called for them to be in the city. Many buildings were vacant and dark, while others stood damaged or had collapsed due to the stresses of repeated bombing raids and other attacks. Even the capitol building that housed Praziq's offices as well as those of most of the First City's elected officials had sustained some damage during previous skirmishes, but the structure was constructed to withstand far more punishment than it had yet received. Gazing out at the once proud city, Praziq longed for a time when all repairs and rebuilding might be complete and Aedrindy resumed its place as one of the most active, vibrant cities on the entire planet.

Will that happen in my lifetime? There were days, like today, when Praziq was certain that never would be the case.

Turning from the window, she regarded *Jenterant* Lnai Mrotoque, the commander of the confederation's military forces, one of her most trusted advisors and — as unlikely as it might have seemed upon her first taking office — one of her closest friends.

"Tell me what happened, Lnai," she said, knowing that Mrotoque would provide her with frank, direct answers, no matter how unpleasant they might be. His blunt honesty, a refreshing change from the calculated reticence that seemed to imbue far too many of her interactions with other politicians and even other military officers, was but one of the traits she valued in him as a friend and confidant.

As always, Mrotoque did not disappoint. "The facility where *Laepotic* Wysejral was being held was attacked. Reports on the scene indicate a small force, comprised of Plysserians and humans."

"Humans?" Praziq was surprised to hear that. "I have read and heard the same rumors you have, of isolated sightings of humans living and working with Plysserian military units. I simply dismissed them."

"It would seem to be true," Mrotoque replied. As Praziq listened with growing interest, the *jenterant* described in clinical detail how the combined strike team penetrated the prison compound's perimeter, located Wysejral, and, with the assistance of flying warcraft from the humans' planet that arrived through a portal, made off with the renowned scientist and disappeared back through the conduit.

"Wysejral's research area was destroyed," Mrotoque continued, "along with the data and notes he had accumulated, though you can be sure he took copies with him. Thankfully, the actual prototype portal generation equipment is located in a different area of the facility, so it was spared when the building containing Wysejral's laboratory and quarters was destroyed."

"And the people we had working with him?" Praziq asked. "Will they be able to carry on without Wysejral's guidance?"

Mrotoque shook his head. "Though they retain some of their own notes and data, as well as several computer simulations on which to draw, I do not believe they will be able to match his knowledge and experience."

"No one could," Praziq replied. "There are three, perhaps four other scientists of his ability on the entire planet." She knew that Wysejral was part of the original team that had developed the wondrous portal generation technology, learning only upon his capture that he had been one of two individuals to present the idea to the Plysserian government. His companion had died cycles ago, before being able to see and enjoy the fruits of her imagination and labor. "How great is the setback to our efforts now that Wysejral is gone?"

"It is difficult to say, *Dekritonpa*," the *jenterant* replied. "He had only just begun to outline testing for his prototype of the enhanced portal generator. Full-scale testing was not to begin for some time. While construction of the prototype was nearly completed, there will be much effort expended on installing and adjusting various components. There is also the energy concern, which the current team leader has brought to my attention at least three times since learning of Wysejral's . . . departure."

Turning back to the window, Praziq clasped her hands behind her back as she once more looked to the streets of

Aedrindy. She found no solace in the activity taking place far below. "How were they able to find him? I thought the facility was secure, and secret."

"We have known for some time that we have security issues," Mrotoque said. "Our own intelligence reports tell us that some of the information gathered by covert agents and even our own people has made its way to the Plysserian leadership. Some of that information was relayed to parties on Earth, presumably military leaders located there, as well as the leaders of their human allies."

Her attention still focused on the city before her, Praziq said, "We have discussed before that the humans might be planning some sort of counteroffensive, likely with Plysserian aid."

"Indeed we have, *Dekritonpa*," Mrotoque replied. "However, we have so far been unable to learn anything beyond hearsay."

Praziq nodded, understanding. Mrotoque had briefed her on such matters more than once, admitting his frustration at the seeming inability of Chodrecai agents or informants to learn anything of substance with regard to this supposed human battle plan. "Any such campaign requires that they come here," she said, "just as we attempted to move assets to Earth. They likely will attempt to avoid our mistakes. Based just on that presumption, it is obvious why they came after Wysejral, even with the risks involved in such a venture. They must think him key to helping them assist in the creation of more efficient portal technology, or enhancing whatever technology they already possess. So, are the humans merely desperate, or have their plans progressed to a point that Wysejral's assistance moves them that much closer to being able to launch their attack?"

Grunting in mild irritation, Mrotoque said, "It is not a scenario I would dismiss."

Images of humans, Plysserians, and Chodrecai battling on the streets below flashed in Praziq's mind. How large might such a battle be? Any campaign the humans might be planning to mount would take many thousands of troops and related support materiel. Did they possess sufficient resources for what would have to be a mammoth undertaking? How large would an assault force need to be, given the depleted conditions facing many Chodrecai cities?

"I know that look," Mrotoque said after a moment. "You are troubled."

Praziq let slip a mild, humorless laugh. "Your gift for understatement is as sharp as always, my friend." Reaching to her bald head, she ran a hand over her scalp. "When I took office, I wanted what each of my predecessors sought. Ending the war has been the driving force behind every *dekritonpa*'s administration since before I was born. Despite our most noble of intentions, we have failed in that regard. We and the Plysserians have failed all the people who currently live under the oppressive shroud of prolonged conflict, and we have failed those who came before us: those who managed to live in peace despite their differences. Now our war threatens to engulf another world, damning its inhabitants just as it has forsaken us. The question we face is whether to stand by and allow that to happen." She turned from the window, her gaze meeting that of Mrotoque's. "I cannot."

"You propose surrender?" the *jenterant* asked, his expression one of skepticism.

"If that is what is required to ensure some possibility of a future for my people," Praziq replied, "is that not my responsibility as their leader?"

Stepping forward, Mrotoque held out his hand. "You know that I stand at your side without reservation, *Dekritonpa*, but we are not the wronged party here. The Plysserians attacked us. Yes, it's possible, perhaps even probable, that we would have initiated actions against them given time and the proper circumstances, but the simple fact is that we did not. You cannot expect the populace to accept the notion of surrendering to those who wronged us."

"You have another option?" Praziq asked.

Mrotoque nodded. "Surrender may not be necessary. The humans, despite their apparent penchant for inflicting violence against one another, do not seem eager to endure the hardships that surely will come from a prolonged war with us. Their world has been embroiled in various conflicts since the dawn of their civilization, including several under way before we found them. My instincts tell me they would welcome the opportunity to avoid entering yet another war, especially if the potential exists for all parties to benefit."

Praziq said, "Given my initial reluctance to attack the humans' planet, I am more than agreeable to pursuing a peaceful solution. However, will they be willing to help us with reconstruction? Our technology is advanced in many areas compared to theirs, so we have that to offer, but will they be able to put aside any lingering bitterness once peace is declared?"

"While I would hope so," Mrotoque replied, "there are many, both in the military and within your own administration, who feel otherwise."

"Then we simply will have to convince them," Praziq said, a sense of conviction and determination beginning to wash over her.

DiCarlo regarded himself in the full-length mirror on the outside of the door leading to the waiting room's small bathroom. After so many months, the reflection staring back at him still seemed almost that of a stranger.

Despite the weight he had lost, feverish last-minute tailoring had seen to it that the green service uniform he now wore fit him to perfection. The beard was gone, of course, and his long, stringy hair was gone, replaced with a haircut well within Marine grooming standards. Indeed, he noted that his hairline had even receded a bit. There were new lines around his eyes, and his cheeks were sunken slightly.

As with any of his previous long-term deployments, the return from *Jontashreena* had come with its share of adjustments. Sleeping on a regular bed, eating ordinary meals at consistent times, being able to take a shower, these and so many other mundane things taken for granted during the course of a normal life were to be relished. Though he had seen the Plysserian equivalent of news and entertainment broadcasts, it could not compare to sitting in a comfortable recliner and watching a baseball game while drinking the first of several ice-cold beers and enjoying the third or fourth slice of take-out pizza.

And the cigars. Thank God for the cigars.

"I didn't know hash marks could go that far up your arm."

Turning from the mirror, DiCarlo saw Russell smiling as she stood in the waiting room's doorway. Looking down at his arms, he regarded the collection of service stripes— "hash marks," as they often were called—adorning the lower half of his sleeves. Each stripe represented four years of service, and DiCarlo wore eight such stripes. What the stripes did not convey were the five years he had spent, after Vietnam and his first enlistment, drifting aimlessly at his uncle's car repair garage. Bored with civilian life, he had returned to the service. That was an eternity ago, and the hash marks reminded him that under other circumstances, he would be overdue for mandatory retirement.

Funny how life can get in the way of things like that.

Like him, Russell was dressed in the "Alpha" service uniform, with green skirt and matching blouse over a khaki shirt. His eyes caught the new blue, white, and red ribbon sitting atop the other decorations above her left breast. Nodding toward it, he smiled. "I know it's politically incorrect, chauvinist, and totally Neanderthal to say this, but even after two or three wars, seeing that on a woman still looks weird to me. But since I'm being a pig here, I'll also say that it looks good on you."

Russell chuckled. "Well, for what it's worth, it feels weird to be wearing it." She made a show of rolling her eyes in mock surprise. "I mean, when I enlisted, they said I'd never get dirty, let alone get shot at. I think my recruiter lied to me."

"Welcome to the club," DiCarlo replied. "We had hats made, and everything."

The president of the United States himself had pinned the Silver Star decorations to their uniforms at a special ceremony held at the White House and broadcast to all the major news outlets. Shaking their hands, the president complimented them both for their service, their sacrifice, and the incredible actions they had undertaken while on *Jontashreena*. The ceremony itself was a formal affair, but not two minutes after its conclusion, the president had asked them both to sit with him in the Oval Office and spare no details about their time on the alien planet. All of that was captured for the newscasts and other programs, as well.

The public relations wonks responsible for setting up the whole thing told DiCarlo and Russell that seeing two heroes who had actually been to *Jontashreena* and fought alongside humanity's Plysserian allies was vital to the morale of the American people and their continued support of the military at this critical time. DiCarlo had been around long enough not to buy that line of bullshit, but in the interests of "national harmony," or whatever it was the PR people were trying to engender, he opted to remain silent.

That was their first visit to the White House, with this morning's visit the second. Unlike that first occasion, there were no cameras or reporters here today. By all accounts, this visit appeared to have been scheduled in total secrecy.

"Did you hear about Lieutenant Gutierrez?" Russell asked. "He and Sergeant Sloane took a team back to *Jontashreena*, to join Javoquek's group."

"Heard about that this morning," DiCarlo replied. He approved of the decision, which really was just the latest in an ongoing effort to place human teams on the alien planet. Soldiers were embedded with Plysserian military units, while civilian and military science and engineering specialists had been sent as envoys to their government, working alongside their Blue counterparts while pursuing much of the same technological research and development currently under way here on Earth. "It's good to have people there, helping our friends." On-site research and intelligence gathering was but one important facet, but Di-Carlo knew that the greater value in having human teams on *Jontashreena* was that their presence was a tangible representation of their partnership with the Plysserians. Living, working, and—yes—fighting alongside their allies on both planets could only serve to strengthen that bond.

"Do you have any idea why we're back here?" Russell asked.

DiCarlo shook his head. "Debriefing, maybe? That's all I can figure. Why else would they want us? What I don't get is why everything's on the hush-hush."

Neither DiCarlo nor Russell said anything else for a few moments, before Russell, sighing as she fidgeted with the green "bucket cover" that was her chosen headwear for the day, said, "Listen," and DiCarlo noticed the uncertainty crossing her features. "There's something I've been wanting to talk about, but there just hasn't been time." Her eyes met his. "Now that we're back, I'm wondering what's next. You know, for us."

It was a valid question, DiCarlo conceded, one to which he had given much thought since their return to Earth. While fraternization among the enlisted ranks was not strictly prohibited, DiCarlo's position of leadership over Russell when her reserve unit was activated for their training assignments still made him her direct superior, despite the bizarre circumstances that had defined their lives these past several months. Were they to be assigned to the same unit in the coming days or weeks, their personal relationship would almost certainly become an issue, if not for each other, then for senior leadership in their chain of command. The differences not only in their ranks but also their ages would likely be cause for much gossip once knowledge of their relationship became known.

Fuck it. Fuck them. Fuck everybody.

"For now," DiCarlo said, "we roll with it, and see what happens. We'll deal with any problems if they come up." He stepped closer, taking her hand in his. "But I'm not going to waste a lot of time worrying about things that might not happen. Christ knows, none of us may have time for that sort of thing before long. You know?"

Russell nodded. "Yeah, I know." She kissed him, quickly and lightly on the mouth. "I love you, old man."

With one finger, DiCarlo caressed her cheek. "I love you too, kid."

There was a knock on the door a moment before it opened to admit a young Navy lieutenant dressed in a service dress blue uniform. His bleach-blond hair and blue eyes reminded DiCarlo of surfers or volleyball players at Huntington Beach in California, though the lieutenant appeared considerably younger than those men had been.

Everybody looks young to you.

"Sergeant Major DiCarlo. Sergeant Russell," the lieutenant said, nodding to them. "I'm Lieutenant Pearson. If you'll follow me, the Joint Chiefs are waiting."

Wait. What?

"The who?" DiCarlo asked. Then, remembering that Pearson outranked him despite his resemblance to the kid who used to deliver his newspapers, he added, "Begging your pardon, Lieutenant, but do you by chance have any idea why we're here? Nobody's told us a thing, let alone what the JCS would want with us."

Pearson shook his head. "I'm afraid I'm not at liberty to say anything, either, Sergeant Major. However, rest assured that General Grayson wouldn't have called for you if he didn't think it was important."

There was no disputing that, DiCarlo knew. A general could summon him to take his order for McDonald's, and it would be important so far as the man—or woman—with stars on the collar was concerned. Nodding, he attempted a small smile. "Well, when you put it that way . . . Lead on, Lieutenant."

Because he expected to be led to the White House Situation Room now that he knew with whom he and Russell would be meeting, DiCarlo was disappointed when Pearson instead directed them into what appeared to be a normal conference room. While the standard government-issue polished wood conference table and leather chairs were unremarkable, the occupants of six of those chairs were anything but boring or mundane. In addition to the Joint Chiefs of Staff, he saw two Plysserians, dressed in their usual black formfitting uniforms bearing insignia identifying them as *tilortrel*—officers—standing along the far wall. Everyone in the room was looking at DiCarlo and Russell as they entered the room, and the man at the head of the table, a Marine general DiCarlo recognized as Andrew Grayson, the JCS chairman, rose from his seat and moved around the table toward them. Acting on reflex, DiCarlo stepped into the room and adopted a position of attention, with Russell mimicking his movements.

"Good morning, General," he said as Grayson approached. "Sergeant Major DiCarlo and Sergeant Russell, reporting as ordered."

Extending his hand to DiCarlo, Grayson said, "At ease, Sergeant Major. Thank you for coming on such short notice. Welcome back, by the way. I'm sorry I didn't have a chance to meet with you before now, but I'm sure you can appreciate that things have been a bit hectic around here for quite some time."

"I've heard something about it, General," DiCarlo said, unable to resist the small joke. Grayson took it in the spirit in which it was intended, smiling as he shook Russell's hand before indicating empty chairs at the table.

Taking one of the proffered seats, DiCarlo nodded formal greetings to each of the flag officers sitting at the table. In addition to General Grayson and his vice chairman, Admiral Danilo Herrera, the JCS comprised highest ranking officers from each of the four service branches. Exchanging glances with Russell, DiCarlo could not help the errant thought that chose that moment to cross his mind.

There are constellations with fewer stars than are in this fucking room right now.

"You're both no doubt wondering what a bunch of old farts hiding in the White House basement want with you two, but I hope you can understand just how unique you both are. The knowledge, skills, and experience you acquired living and working on *Jontashreena* is worth its weight in gold. We want to tap in to that expertise."

"An offensive," Russell said from where she sat to Di-Carlo's left, blurting out the words. Realizing she had spoken out of turn, she cleared her throat and sat up straighter in her chair. "Begging your pardon, General. I didn't mean to . . ."

Grayson waved away the rest of her apology. "No worries, Sergeant. I wouldn't have called you here if I didn't want you to speak your mind. Besides, you're allowed to get away with that shit if you're right. We are indeed planning an offensive." Tapping his finger on the table, he turned and nodded to Admiral Herrera.

"Everything you're about to hear is classified at the highest levels of secrecy," said the vice chairman. "At present, there are only a handful of people in the world who possess all of the information we're about to give you. Our hope is to keep things that way until the last possible moment. If the Grays find out what we're doing before we're ready to launch, then that'll be all she wrote."

"What are we doing?" DiCarlo asked, leaning forward in his chair.

"Operation Clear Sky," Herrera replied. He glanced at Grayson before continuing, "I don't know if we'd go so far as to call it an outright invasion, but it's about as close as you can get to being one and still be able to call it something else. For the past couple of months, we've consulted with top military officials from around the world, quietly obtaining information on manpower, equipment, and so on. Our information's been augmented with comparable data provided to us by a network of Plysserian advisors, engineers, informants, spies, whatever you want to call them."

DiCarlo nodded, realizing what it was he was hearing. "D-Day," he said, more to himself than anyone else, "and Omaha Beach is on another planet."

"The Normandy invasion is probably the most accurate analogy," Herrera continued, "but the logistics of this campaign will be much different. Still we are talking about a massive, multipronged campaign, focusing on several primary targets along with a host of secondary attack points. The general idea is to hit them hard in a lot of places at the same time."

"Like the Grays did to us?" Russell asked.

The admiral shook his head. "Not exactly. We think the big flaw in the Gray attacks against Russia, China, and us was that they tried to hit us directly via the portals. If they'd used them instead to pre-position assets at various key locations, they could have launched conventional attacks on the target cities and likely overwhelmed the forces we would've been able to deploy to those areas."

"So we're going to transfer troops and equipment to staging areas on *Jontashreena*," DiCarlo said. "A massive buildup, like we did in the first Gulf War." After Iraq's annexation of the small, oil-rich country of Kuwait in August of 1990, the United States, along with more than thirty other countries, deployed more than half a million troops to the deserts of Saudi Arabia in the months that followed.

"Exactly," Grayson replied. "Only this time we'd prefer to keep as much as possible off CNN."

DiCarlo snorted. "That'll be some trick." The age of twenty-four-hour news reporting on television and the Internet saw to it that very little escaped public notice. Would Operation Overlord have unfolded with the same degree of success if required to do so under the watchful eye of a global audience receiving real-time updates from embedded journalists?

"Secrecy is paramount if we have any hope of pulling this off," Herrera said, "as are the target selections we're considering. They have satellite imagery and other advanced surveillance and reconnaissance assets just as we do, a lot of it far superior to anything we've got. Some of that is under Plysserian control, but the Chodrecai still have quite a bit of their own. The key to our plan is hitting softer targets first, which in turn will deny command-and-control capability to the larger concentrations of ground and air forces. It's hoped that such action will have the effect of throwing their chain of command into disarray and afford our forces opportunities to advance with the least possible resistance."

"The portals are the key," added General Phillip Exley, Chief of Staff of the Air Force, resting his elbows atop the conference table. "With them, we can position troops and materiel far enough away from designated targets to hopefully avoid discovery, yet close enough that they can move on those targets in short order once the operation is under way."

Herrera said, "The portals are also the major hurdle. Without them, and the means to keep them open long enough to get troops and equipment through, we don't stand a chance."

"What about communication?" DiCarlo asked, frowning as he tried to wrap his mind around all of the variables relating to an operation of this size. "How are you getting intel from the other side?"

"A network of spies and informants," Grayson said. "We have several Plysserian agents working with us, both here and on *Jontashreena*. Using captured portal points, they've been able to relay information on Gray troop levels, movements, and planning." He paused, shrugging. "We also know they're spying on us. More often than not, their efforts fail—just as some of ours do—but so far, our best intel shows us they're not anticipating our attack. At least, they don't seem to be planning for anything like what we're trying to put together."

"We've heard rumblings about trying to get Gray leaders to the negotiating table," Russell said, "to try and work something out." Once more aware of the attention offered her as she regarded Grayson, she cleared her throat before asking, "Is that still an option, General?"

Grayson shrugged. "Diplomatic overtures continue, but so far there's been no progress, nor even acknowledgment of the messages sent by various governments. Still, it's not our job to worry about those things. Our concern is what the president will have us do when it's apparent the Grays will never answer our calls."

24

Paul Simpson nearly broke his neck scrambling down the stairs, the echo of Jimmy Franks's booming voice bouncing off the narrow passage to the root cellar.

"Where's everybody hidin' at?" yelled Franks, from somewhere below him.

Cursing the lack of a handrail on the steep wooden stairs, Simpson regained his footing and continued his descent. At the last instant he remembered to duck his head and avoid smacking into the railroad tie serving as a crossbeam for the doorjamb at the bottom of the stairwell. As always, the air down here was cooler than upstairs, and Simpson felt a slight dampness. He wished he had thought to grab one of his fleece jackets before answering Franks's summons.

"What the hell is the bloody emergency?" Simpson called out, looking about the cellar before his eyes fell on the open doorway to Franks's workshop. Peering into the other room, Simpson saw that Franks, along with Carl Hosey and the three Chodrecai soldiers, Osibonidar, Jiqol, and Nelritap, all were standing inside, crowding around one of the worktables positioned along the cellar's far wall.

Pointing to the Grays, Simpson asked Franks, "Any word from Coberly?" The last thing he had heard before retiring for bed the previous evening was that Aidan Coberly, Franks's longtime friend from their joint service in the military, had left in the hope of making contact with other HIPE members to aid in the transfer of the three Chodrecai to a safer, more isolated location. From there, they would commence their search for a quiet, unoccupied northern corner of the country in which to wait out the war.

Franks shook his head. "Nothing. After the last transfer went bad, our contacts have gotten more careful. Getting them to come out of hiding is proving to be a giant pain in the balls."

The first attempt at handing off the Grays to friends of Coberly's had been called off when it became known that British military patrols of the surrounding region were on the upswing, with troops closely monitoring all vehicle traffic and even searching homes and other buildings in the vicinity. So far, no one had come knocking on Franks's door, but Simpson had to wonder how long their good fortune might last.

"So what's going on?" he asked as he stepped closer to where the group was gathered around Hosey, who sat at the table before his laptop computer. The younger man had brought the device with him, a military-issue version with a rugged outer shell designed to protect the unit while it was used in field operations. In addition to its power cord, a thick silver cable ran from the back of the device, which Simpson had at first taken to be a simple Internet modem cable. That assumption had died a quick death once Hosey took it upon himself to explain in no uncertain terms that this was no "ordinary" computer. Where he had obtained the equipment was anybody's guess, and Hosey had so far chosen not to answer such questions. It was quite apparent, though, that the lad was impressed not only with the equipment but also himself and his ability to acquire and employ it.

Condescending tosser.

"Carl's found something," Franks said upon noting Simpson's arrival, and nodded toward the computer. "Seems the military's up to some interesting games."

Such statements made Simpson's gut twitch, just as it did every time Hosey used the laptop to monitor various military and government websites. That the young computer wizard seemed to have no problem—technical or moral— accessing several sites that were supposed to be unreachable by civilians, using nothing more than standard Internet navigation software and techniques, did nothing for Simpson's anxiety. He imagined what it would be like to stand before a judge and answer to the charge of illegally entering a restricted military computer network. He did not know for certain, but he was reasonably sure that the penalty for such crimes had to involve at least a protracted stay in prison.

"What are they doing?" Simpson asked, regretting the question even as he spoke the words.

Instead of Franks, it was Hosey who answered. Without turning from the laptop, he pointed to the device's screen. "There are a lot of troops and equipment being moved around to various bases and other locations around the country." On the screen, Simpson recognized a map of the United Kingdom, and superimposed on the image were seven blinking red circles. When the man said nothing else after several seconds, Simpson cast a disparaging look toward Franks.

"Yeah? And? It's not like they don't do that every bloody day, right?"

For the first time, Hosey looked away from the computer and directed a scathing glare at Simpson. "This is different." With a thumb, he indicated the map on the screen. "I built that map after tracing through a couple weeks' worth of e-mails and other message traffic, a lot of it classified. While moving men and equipment around is no big deal, particularly these days, there's something else going on here. The seven dots you see represent some of the smaller, less active bases around the country. A couple of them are so small they barely rate being called bases at all—just a handful of buildings surrounded by fences. Communications stations, fuel and ammo depots, radar stations, that sort of thing, though rumor has it a couple of them were used for top-secret R and D projects at one time or another."

Simpson heard footsteps on the stairs outside the room, and he turned to see Amanda Hebert descending from the house's main level. Her hair was still damp from the shower she had been taking when Franks first called for everyone, and the look on her face was one of curiosity.

"What's up?" she asked as she stepped into the room. Seeing Hosey at the computer again, her expression turned to one of concern. "Is he hacking into military networks again? He's going to get us all arrested or shot."

"It's not hacking if you already have a way in," Hosey said, releasing an exaggerated sigh.

Franks added, "I was assigned to some of the security applications they still use, back in my contractor days. Don't know anyone worth a damn who worked on that thing and didn't put at least one back door into the system. You just have to know where to look."

"And it doesn't hurt to have friends still working on the inside," Simpson said.

Hosey nodded. "Damned right." Returning his attention to the computer, he continued, "As I was saying, the bases where all the activity is taking place aren't normally sites for this kind of thing. Makes you wonder what they might be doing there, yes?" Without waiting for an answer, he added, "So I went digging into some of the local utility company computer systems. Interesting stuff I found. It seems that power usage is up at those locations, and I mean way beyond anything they would normally be doing there."

"That doesn't mean anything," Hebert said, shaking her head. Simpson glanced at her, and saw that she was standing with her arms crossed, and that she appeared to be slightly hunched over, as though fighting off a chill brought on by coolness in the cellar.

Sighing again, Hosey now looked perturbed, and he held up his hands as though waiting for a neck to be inserted between them so that he might choke it. "You could turn on every light, every piece of machinery, every damned thing hooked into any power outlet at those bases, and you wouldn't come close to the power usage going on there. There's something else: The usage isn't constant. It spikes, six or seven times during overnight hours, with the times varying from base to base, of course. The level of power consumption during the spikes is pretty consistent from base to base, too." When no one said anything, the man rolled his eyes, a gesture that made Simpson want to punch him in the throat.

"All right, Hosey," Simpson said, allowing his growing annoyance to show. "Life's too short to be standing here listening to you run your suck hole. You're the one with all the bloody answers, so spit them out, already."

Hosey looked like he was going to respond to that, but Franks interjected, "He's right. Get the fuck on with it."

Chastened by the rebuke, Hosey turned to the laptop, presenting his back to the rest of the group, but he never had the chance to say anything. Instead, the answer came from behind them.

"Portals."

Turning at the sound of the deep, rumbling voice, Simpson's eyes widened as he beheld the three Chodrecai, who to this point had stood in silence. "Come again, mate?" Simpson asked Osibonidar, the leader of the trio.

The alien replied, "It seems logical to conclude that

your military is constructing portal generators at the identi-fied locations."

"Why would they want to do that?" Hebert asked, frown-ing. "Don't they already control a handful of sites captured from the Chodrecai?"

Nodding, Hosey said, "My best guess? They need to cre-ate additional locations so they can move larger numbers of troops and equipment."

"Wait," Simpson replied, holding up a hand. "Are you saying our boys are planning some kind of attack on the other planet?"

Franks grunted. "Sooner or later, we knew they would have to take the fight there. Of course, it only really makes sense if you figure our troops won't be doing that sort of thing all by their lonesome."

Realization clicked, and Simpson felt his jaw go slack. "You think this is part of some larger plan? What, with the Americans?"

"For starters," Hosey said, "along with whoever else has the resources to build the kind of equipment needed to generate a portal. Fucking right, that's what I think."

Osibonidar added, "That also is a logical conclusion. Initiating a counteroffensive is a sound military tactic, par-ticularly given the current situation of our respective forces and your people's propensity for taking aggressive action when you feel threatened."

"What, and they're so stupid that they left tracks all the way to their front door for you to find?" Hebert asked. "That doesn't make any sense."

Hosey replied, "It does if you realize that most of the sys-tems I've had to crack to pull all of this together aren't even on the public Internet." Turning toward Hebert, he hooked a thumb over his shoulder toward the laptop. "What I've shown you here is the result of two nights' digging around in hundreds of different directories on dozens of different machines scattered around the country. I'm not some punk kid downloading illegal music or skin flicks, lady, so quit looking down your fucking nose at me like that. I know exactly what the bloody hell I'm doing."

"Ease off, boy," Franks said, planting a massive hand on the younger man's shoulder. "Mind your manners in my house, or I'll put my boot so far up your arse you'll taste leather and cow shit." He looked to Simpson and Hebert. "What he lacks in civility, he makes up for in skill. He knows what he's talking about."

His gaze locked with Hosey's while the two men attempted to stare down each other, Simpson said, "Okay, so what do we do with this information? We can't just go blabbing about it to anyone who'll listen."

"Sure we can," Hosey countered. "Abso-fucking-lutely. We're supposed to be about peace and equality for everyone affected by this war, right? Telling people about this attack is one way to get people to listen to us." He pointed toward the three Grays. "Just think: Put them on a vid, talking about what we've found. Pure gold."

"We'd be shot as traitors," Hebert said.

"She's right," Franks added. "It's one thing to march in protest or post shit on the Internet. It's another thing entirely to leak classified intel that might endanger troops readying for combat. I got no love for the war, but I'm not about to sell out brothers in arms to make our voices heard." Before Hosey could respond, he held up one pudgy finger and pointed it at the other man's face. "Not a fucking chance, boy."

Holding up his hands in a gesture of surrender, Hosey said, "Okay, okay, but what about keeping things vague? Same message, but with no particulars? Warn people that we don't want the war escalating to the point that our troops must go to the other planet to fight. There has to be a peaceful solution, and so on." He again indicated the Grays. "They're stuck here with us. Let's use them, for Christ's sake."

"There is another alternative," Osibonidar said, and Simpson turned to regard him as the Gray stepped forward.

It required almost no effort on Osibonidar's part to snap the human's neck.

Loosing his grip and allowing the now-dead human to fall to the floor, Osibonidar turned at the sound of the female releasing a cry of terror. That was all she was able to do before Nelritap reached her, grasping the front of her head in one massive hand and jerking her violently off her feet. Osibonidar heard the sound of brittle bones snapping, and the female's body went limp in Nelritap's hand.

"God damn it!" the older human male yelled, his voice echoing off the subterranean chamber's walls and low ceiling. At least, that was what Osibonidar believed him to have said; his grasp of the local human language was still incomplete, despite the several days spent working with the other human and the translator bands they each had worn. As for the human before him, Osibonidar saw him reaching for something out of his line of sight, and deduced it was a weapon of some sort. Jiqol already was moving toward the human, his expression communicating his intent.

"Do not kill them," Osibonidar ordered, his voice loud enough to stop Nelritap from moving against the other human, who had raised his hands in a gesture Osibonidar understood to mean he was offering no resistance or presenting any threat. As for his companion, he had brandished what Osibonidar recognized as a small projectile weapon, one that Jiqol removed from the human's possession with no difficulty before rendering it useless and tossing it to the floor at his feet. Both humans regarded them with wide eyes, an all but universal indication of fear. This was good, Osibonidar decided; it would make them compliant.

"Why did you do that?" the older human asked, holding his hands away from his body and making no further attempts to retrieve a weapon or some other illicit item.

"They were of no further use," Osibonidar replied. "You and your companion, on the other hand, still retain some value." After remaining idle for the past several cycles and wondering if he had made a tactical error by allowing himself and his companions to be taken into custody by these humans, Osibonidar was relieved to see that his patience had been rewarded with this opportunity. Given that members of the group had a propensity to dress themselves like soldiers while utilizing weapons and equipment that he had come to recognize as that employed by human military forces, Osibonidar at first believed he had succeeded in being taken by such a unit. Only after they were brought here and with the assistance of the human Coberly, who spoke to him with the use of a translator band, did Osibonidar realize how he had misjudged his "captors." They wanted to help him, and other Chodrecai!

He had listened to the humans talking, learning their language with the assistance of the translator bands and coming to understand the goals they pursued. He and his companions even participated in their prerecorded communications, calling on their government to seek peace with the Chodrecai. The humans had seemed misguided, he thought; pursuing their goals through no direct action seemed a waste of time and resources.

At first, the humans' temporary inability to move them from this serviceable hiding place felt to Osibonidar like a dangerous delay. He almost gave the order to kill them so that he and the others could continue with their attempts to seek some isolated region in this part of the humans' world and await rescue by a Chodrecai military unit. It was only fortunate happenstance that a few of the humans had apparent access to information that Osibonidar would think unobtainable by nonmilitary personnel. This caused him to change his plan, deciding instead to watch and see what he and his companions might learn.

The equipment used by these humans, like most of their technology, was very much inferior to comparable devices from Osibonidar's world. Despite such limitations, he had learned from observing these two humans during the past several cycles that they were well versed in its operation and its ability to interface with other machines like it. Now that they had actually provided some information of potential use to Osibonidar's superiors, it was time to change the dynamics of the situation and move forward on a more constructive course. Whereas he could have tasked Jiqol, the most technically proficient of his group, with attempting to understand and operate the device, directing the humans to provide what he sought seemed a more prudent use of time and resources.

In their native language, Nelritap asked, "Even if they are able to provide anything of value, what are we to do with that knowledge? We do not even know the location of any of our forces."

Indicating the primitive equipment with a nod of his head, Osibonidar answered, "No, but I am certain information on that subject can be found via this conduit." They had at least some time, he decided. The human, Coberly, likely would return in short order, but like these other humans he presented no threat. No, Osibonidar decided; despite the cost in time and personal safety, which he knew would grow the longer they stayed here, this was an opportunity to be exploited.

25

"General Thompson to the Situation Center, please. General Thompson, please report to the Situation Center."

The summons came at the same time the alert Klaxon began sounding throughout the Op04-E bunker. Thompson was moving even before the man on the intercom finished his initial call for him, pushing open the door leading from his office to the division's operations control room. As was his habit, the general glanced at the map wall, noting that all twelve screens were active and displaying different images. Most of them depicted what looked to be news anchors. Some sat at whatever amalgam of wood and plastic their station's paltry productions could afford, while others occupied desks designed to emulate the control consoles of futuristic command centers.

"What is it?" he asked, stopping at the stairs connecting the top tier to its two companions.

Standing on the main floor near the map wall, Nancy Spencer looked up from the conversation she was having with General Tommy Brooks and pointed toward the array of screens. "The reports just started, but it's already all over the place." She turned to one of the military technicians manning a workstation on the first tier. "Put up screen four and replay their footage from the beginning."

"Yes, ma'am," replied the young Air Force staff sergeant—Leisner, if Thompson remembered correctly—his fingers stabbing at his keyboard. In response to his instructions, the image displayed on the fourth screen of the uppermost row of monitors quickly enlarged to fill the entire map wall. The broadcast was that of an older man that Thompson recognized as the lead anchor for the evening news program on one of the broadcast networks. The bags under the anchor's eyes were even more pronounced than they had been in recent months, and Thompson realized the man's hair, which once had been black with a peppering of gray, had now gone completely white.

When the hell did that happen? Thompson dismissed the irrelevant question as he descended the stairs toward the main floor.

"Starting the replay now," Leisner said, tapping another key.

On the screen, the frozen image of the news anchor began speaking in the calm, composed voice that had informed and comforted viewing audiences for the better part of two decades. *"Good afternoon. This is Charles Ivy, coming to you live from our studios in New York, to bring you a stunning new development in the ongoing conflict with the Chodrecai people. Just moments ago, a portal—a gateway from Jontashreena, the home planet of the Chodrecai and the Plysserians—opened on the National Mall in Washington, D.C. You no doubt recall that the Mall was the site of a massive battle fought six months ago between the Chodrecai and U.S. military forces, with the assistance of Canadian and British troops."*

"The fucking Mall?" Thompson said, aghast. "Again? Do we have units moving on its position?" It was all he could do to tear his eyes from the screen, conscious of his breathing beginning to accelerate as tension gripped him. The Grays could not possibly be launching another attack now, could they? Nothing, no intelligence report, no rumor filtered to 4-Echo, supported such a notion. How could they have been so terribly wrong? "Where is it?"

"Between the Washington Monument and the World War II memorial," replied Brooks, who had moved from the main floor to another workstation on the first tier and was peering over the shoulder of the Navy lieutenant sitting there. "Spotters on-site say there's no sign of aggressive action, but we've got two F-22s on the way there now, along with a squadron being scrambled from Dover. We've also got a ground unit being repositioned from the far end of the Mall."

"Get me Gardner and that Plysserian advisor of his," Thompson ordered. Glancing at personnel occupying other workstations, he asked, "Do we have video?"

"Local news crews are already broadcasting on-site," Spencer replied from where she now sat at another console, waving toward the screen. "We've got it on other feeds, but he's getting ready to cut to that now."

"We're going to go live now to our Washington, D.C., affiliate," Ivy continued, *"WDCT, and their field reporter, Ron Hanagan, who is on the Mall with a camera crew broadcasting live video of the portal and the lone Chodrecai who has emerged from it. Ron, what can you tell us?"*

The image on the screen shifted from the anchor to an exterior location and another man standing on the grass of the Mall, dressed in a red knit sports shirt with the logo of a local D.C. television station. He was somewhere in his mid- to late forties, Thompson guessed, with brown hair liberally brushed with gray and matching beard. The caption on the screen read, BREAKING NEWS: ALIENS RETURN TO D.C., along with Hanagan's name. Behind the reporter, Thompson could see the roiling, swirling circle of energy that could only be a portal, in front of which stood a lone figure, a Chodrecai.

"The alien came alone through the portal," Hanagan said. *"So far, there's nothing to indicate that anyone or anything accompanied him. It's also worth noting that this Chodrecai is not dressed in anything resembling the uniforms or equipment we've seen their soldiers wear."*

The Gray was dressed in flowing multicolored robes that covered it from head to foot. Only the alien's massive hands were visible, clasped as they were before its body. It carried no weapons or equipment that Thompson could see, save for a large silver device worn around its neck. "What is that thing he's got on?"

"It is a voice amplifier, General," replied a deep, rumbling voice behind him, and Thompson turned to see Makoquolax and Corporal Bradley Gardner standing at the top of the stairs near the entrance to the Situation Center. Gardner was dressed in the dark green trousers and jacket of a Marine daily service uniform, with khaki dress shirt and tie, whereas his companion wore the typical black all-purpose, formfitting garment of a Plysserian soldier.

"You're sure about that?" Thompson nodded, splitting his attention between his own people and the journalist on the screen, who continued to describe the unfolding scene.

Makoquolax nodded. "It is a common device, often used by politicians and other public figures when addressing large audiences. His clothing represents the vestments of a political official, specifically one serving in a high and trusted advisory position in the Chodrecai government."

"You get all that from his wardrobe?" Gardner asked. "Maybe we need to dress up our politicians the same way."

Thompson's first instinct was to reprimand the corporal for his lapse in bearing, but he opted against that action. *Not the kid's fault he's right.*

Movement on the screen again caught his attention, and he watched as, behind the Chodrecai, the portal faded and broke apart, dissolving into nothingness and leaving the alien standing alone on the green-brown grass of the Mall. The Washington Monument and part of the Smithsonian National Museum of American History were visible behind him, both structures still displaying evident damage from the battle fought here months earlier. The image shifted again as Hanagan moved into the frame, holding his left hand to his ear.

"*Ron,*" the voice of Charles Ivy said, "*we're getting reports now of similar activity taking place in Moscow and Beijing, the other two sites that Chodrecai forces attacked six months ago as part of that massive multifront offensive. You've been following and reporting on battles between our military and the aliens for months: Does this sound like coincidence to you?*"

Hanagan shook his head. "*Not a chance, Charles. Whatever's happening here, I think we're about to find out that the choice of arrival points for these Grays, whoever they are, is intentional.*"

"*People of Earth.*"

The voice, calm and composed, drowned out those of Ivy and Hanagan on the screen. Hanagan stepped out of the picture just as the camera zoomed in on the Chodrecai, though Thompson knew that police on the scene likely prevented the news crew from getting too close. As for the alien, he had not moved so much as a step since emerging from the portal.

"*People of Earth,*" the Gray repeated, "*my name is Trela Dren. I serve as counsel to Vahelridol Praziq, First Dekritonpa of the Chodrecai Territorial Confederation. Dekritonpa Praziq occupies a seat in our government similar to the presidents and prime ministers of your various nations, and has sent me to you on this day with a message of importance to all your peoples. She requests an audience, not only with*" *the heads of the Plysserian governments but also the leaders of your world, to discuss the cessation of hostilities between our peoples and the opportunities to be enjoyed by moving forward together, in peace."*

"Holy shit," Thompson said, feeling his jaw go slack.

"The same message is being delivered in Moscow and Beijing," Brooks said, indicating a pair of computer monitors at the workstation he stood behind, each of which displayed an image eerily similar to that on the map wall. Thompson recognized the towering spires of the buildings surrounding Red Square in Moscow, their metal facades reflecting the fading late-afternoon sunlight of a time zone eight hours ahead of Washington, D.C. In Beijing, Tiananmen was bathed in the harsh glare of spotlights, owing to the fact that the Chodrecai representative had arrived in the Chinese capital well before dawn.

"Are they surrendering?" Spencer asked, frowning. "It doesn't really sound like it, does it?"

"I suspect the language has been deliberately chosen so as to avoid reflecting a position of weakness," Makoquolax replied. "However, given what we know of their current military strength, they may well have decided this was a wiser course than continuing the fight."

"Well, they've got my attention," Thompson said.

"*Dekritonpa Praziq has instructed me,*" Trela Dren continued, "*along with my fellow emissaries dispatched to other locations around your planet, to wait here for a reply, along with any instructions or concerns your leaders would communicate to her. She wishes it known that she would enjoy the opportunity to travel here, to your world—on your terms—in order to conduct these discussions, and is hopeful of their positive outcome.*"

"There we go," Brooks said. "That sounds like surrender to me."

"Not really," Thompson countered, shaking his head. "They've had a setback, but they're not *that* weak. They could keep dragging this out for months or even years if they wanted to." Was it possible that the feelings of remorse about the unfortunate and unanticipated involvement of Earth in their war had finally overcome the Chodrecai leadership, just as similar regret had been expressed by their Plysserian counterparts?

Several moments passed before Thompson realized the alien envoy was saying nothing else, nor was he moving or offering any other hints at interaction. On the screen, the image of the Chodrecai shrank in order to reveal a close-up of Charles Ivy, still sitting at his news desk in New York.

"You've just heard the remarkable message delivered by a Chodrecai official," Ivy said, *"expressing the desire for peace talks on behalf of his government's leaders. To call this a staggering development would be a criminal understatement. We're still receiving information from correspondents around the world, but I'm being told that in addition to Moscow and Beijing, similar messengers have arrived in capital cities around the world. Tehran, London, Seoul, and Tel Aviv are confirmed, with others being verified as we speak. Things are moving pretty fast at the moment, and I hope you'll bear with us as we try to bring you as much information as quickly as possible."*

"Where else are we going to go?" Gardner asked. Thompson turned to the Marine just as he looked to his Plysserian companion. "What do you think, Max?"

Taking a moment as though considering his reply, Makoquolax finally said, "I find it . . . interesting, and encouraging."

Thompson nodded. "That's a damned good way to put it."

26

For the first time in more cycles than she could count, First *Dekritonpa* Vahelridol Praziq was hopeful.

"Despite their initial and quite understandable misgivings," she said, looking up as the doors to her private office opened to admit *Jenterant* Lnai Mrotoque, "Earth's leaders have agreed to meet."

Mrotoque nodded. "I have seen the reports," he said as he moved to stand before her large desk. "I will admit to being surprised at the swiftness of the responses. I would have expected more skepticism."

"Your years of military service have colored your perceptions, my friend," Praziq said.

"Only in the sense that I am less an idealist than I was when I was much younger. Still, the reports, if they are accurate, are cause for much celebration."

Praziq smiled. "I do not believe we are ready for that just yet, but I will agree there is much here about which we should be optimistic." Holding up the portable information reader given to her by one of her aides, she extended the large oval-shaped device to Mrotoque. "Every envoy we sent to Earth returned with similar messages from human leaders. They desire to meet with us. Given a choice, they want to talk, not fight."

"Talking is always good, *Dekritonpa*," Mrotoque replied as he accepted the reader from her, "particularly when one is also preparing to fight." Before she could respond to that, the *jenterant* held up his free hand. "I did not say that is what the humans are doing, but it is a possibility of which we need to remain aware, no matter how this other scenario moves forward."

Scowling at him, Praziq said, "Scenario? We're talking about ending the war, Lnai, something you and I both thought unlikely until the moment I sent those messengers to Earth. You cannot tell me you are not uplifted by this news."

"I am a soldier, *Dekritonpa*. My duty and my oath require that I be ready for war while simultaneously hoping you need never call upon me. I look forward to the day that I and those like me no longer have a function in our society."

Praziq smiled. "You are wise, my friend, and for that I shall always value your counsel and your friendship." Walking back to the large, curved desk positioned so that she sat with her back to the window, the First *Dekritonpa* eyed the suite of compact display monitors built into the desk's surface. Each one was tuned to a different information feed, and all were updated constantly, affording her real-time status reports from her various aides and other appointed officials as well as civilian and military news organizations. One screen was reserved for personal correspondence, most of which remained neglected as she concentrated on the demands of her office.

"I do not expect military training or readiness operations to be compromised, in keeping with your well-intentioned paranoia," she said, smiling once more to communicate that she was teasing Mrotoque. "However, all combat operations are to cease immediately. No reconnaissance missions, no scouting parties, no hostile action of any sort are to be initiated from this point without my authorization. Engagements in the interests of self-defense remain valid, of course, but nothing beyond that." As one of the stipulations for the peace talks, she had proposed a unilateral cease-fire. Similar arrangements, she was told, were being put into place by the humans on Earth and Plysserian units both there and here on *Jontashreena*. It was understood that small numbers of forces from all sides and located on either planet might not be aware of this development. Still, all leaders had pledged to see that word of the forthcoming peace summit was spread in the hope of reaching even those soldiers and units operating without benefit of contact with higher authority.

Seeing Mrotoque's thoughtful expression, Praziq asked, "What is it, Lnai? You still appear troubled."

The *jenterant* paused, cocking his head as though listening for indications that their conversation might be overheard. Then, returning his attention to her, he asked, "*Dekritonpa*, may I speak freely?"

Praziq frowned, suddenly concerned. "Always. You know that." Though Mrotoque consistently practiced and respected all forms of protocol when interacting with and addressing her as well as other civilian leaders in the presence of others, he had long ago earned the privilege of conducting himself in a relaxed manner when meeting with her in private. That he now felt the need to observe such formalities in this setting troubled her.

"You know that there are those who would wish these talks to fail," he said after a moment, stepping closer and lowering his voice, "or even for them not to occur at all. To them and many more like them, Earth represents a means of regaining the prosperity we have lost, and they are unconcerned for the plight of the humans, or the Plysserians, or anyone else who does not share their view."

Nodding, Praziq replied, "Such individuals have always existed, Lnai. Even before the war began, there were those calling for us to launch preemptive strikes against our enemies, to wage war on their land before they could come to ours." She paused, glancing at her desk. "Remember, it was that mind-set, and the actions our nations took in the service of such beliefs, that eventually brought the war to us."

Unlike her predecessors, Vahelridol Praziq had not believed in many of the policies and actions of previous leadership administrations. Prior to the war, military power often had been used as a means of enforcing the expansion of Chodrecai territory and interests. It had gone that way for generations, until only the Plysserian Union, itself a loose conglomeration of dozens of smaller nations who had chosen on their own to join together under a banner of cooperative spirit, stood ready to oppose the Chodrecai Confederation and its efforts to influence smaller states around the world. A fundamental difference of belief in the government's role with respect to its citizens lay at the heart of nearly every disagreement between the Plysserian and Chodrecai governments. The Chodrecai valued the time-honored traditions of the citizenry serving the needs of the community over the individual. Personal rights and freedoms were secondary concerns when measured against the needs of society as a whole, and some form of public service was expected of nearly every able-bodied person. These values seemingly were not shared by Plysserian citizens.

Appointed as an advisor to the previous First *Dekritonpa*, Praziq was one of a growing number of people who believed the Plysserian and Chodrecai societies were more alike than dissimilar—that there was room for negotiation and compromise, if only one side could be convinced to listen and respect the position of the other. With the war in full swing at the time she accepted her appointment, Praziq held no illusions of such progressive opinions—let alone actions—ever being given a chance to succeed. Instead, she concentrated on her duties, providing honest counsel to senior leadership while taking whatever opportunities presented themselves to offer minority, even dissenting opinions on issues of the day. It did not take long for members of the leadership as well as the media to begin associating her name and those of like-minded individuals with a progressive, optimistic outlook that at times was diametrically opposed to the political message being disseminated by senior governmental leadership. Though at first Praziq feared her public notice might attract unwanted attention in the halls of power in Aedrindy, the First *Dekritonpa* made no secret of the fact that he appreciated her counsel and valued the opinions of all who served him, even if they did not always agree on one topic or another.

Then the First *Dekritonpa* died.

Though public elections were suspended in the face of the ongoing war with the Plysserians, Praziq unexpectedly found her name being bandied about as a possible successor. Other senior advisors supported this uncommon decision, and even the Second *Dekritonpa*, instead of assuming the duties of First as law demanded, stepped down from his office. To this day, Praziq remembered with utmost clarity the heartfelt speech the Second had given, citing the needs of the people as the paramount concern, that he knew the time had come for a change from the status quo, and that Praziq personified that change. A special election was held, and Praziq in short order found herself occupying the office of First *Dekritonpa*.

"Come, Lnai," she said, eyeing him. "What is your real concern?"

Mrotoque replied, "You are not naïve. Surely you understand that the views you espouse, while popular with a war-weary populace, remain quietly contested by those who see your ideas of reform and progress as the beginning of the end for everything they value about Chodrecai society?"

"Some of the things that define Chodrecai society are outdated and counterproductive to the collective good," Praziq countered. "If the Plysserians or even the humans can teach us anything, it is that pluralism and the rights of the individual over the state are not notions to be marginalized or dismissed." Indeed, she had spent many sleepless nights considering just what they as a people might learn from these humans. Observation and interviews— interrogation, some might call it—revealed a civilization constructed of numerous cultures, beliefs, and values. Some of their tenets seemed completely at odds with one another, and yet the humans had managed, barely, to avoid casting themselves into the abyss of unrelenting global war. Were the similarities and shared trials enough to compensate for conflicting ideals? Or had the humans simply not reached that point of no return, as had the people of *Jontashreena*? This of course begged another question: Might working together with those of this planet help the people of Earth avoid such a fate? Surely, that potential was worth exploring, even as the two worlds worked together to forge a better future.

You always were an idealist.

Holding up a hand, Mrotoque said, "Take care with your words, *Dekritonpa*. Until such time as the Plysserians and the humans demonstrate that they are earnest in their desire to put the war behind us, there will always be skeptics. Most will simply stand by and voice their discontent, whereas others will be motivated to other, more drastic action."

It was a troubling statement, to be sure. Praziq studied her friend's face, looking for some hint of clarification, but none came. "What are you saying, Lnai?"

"What I always say, *Dekritonpa*," Mrotoque replied. "Proceed with caution."

The *jenterant* turned and exited the office, leaving Praziq alone with her thoughts. Though she remained excited at the possibility of peace and mutual cooperation and the potential to rebuild two—no, three—societies so affected by war, the words of her sage, trusted advisor continued to ring in her ears.

With luck, my friend, I will prove you wrong.

"Mister President, you look tired. Should we call it a night and reconvene in the morning?"

Glancing at his wristwatch, a gift his wife had presented to him on Inauguration Day—now a dimly remembered occasion that seemed to have taken place a century ago— Leonard Harrington, president of the United States, was more than a little irritated to discover that the time it displayed was the same as on the clock standing in the corner of the Oval Office.

2:27. A.M. *Very* A.M.

"I used to stay awake for three days straight, cramming for finals," Harrington replied, offering a wry grin to Jennifer Black, his chief of staff, as he reached up to massage his temples. Grit rubbed his eyes and his mouth was dry and pasty, sure signs of fatigue and of too much coffee consumed during the past however many hours he had spent here with his inner circle of advisors and confidants.

"You don't want me to remind you just how many years ago that was, do you, sir?" Black asked, making a show of consulting her BlackBerry.

Sitting on one of the two couches that faced each other across a low-rise coffee table, General Andrew Grayson said, "Mister President, my staff and I have enough to keep us busy for the next few hours, if you'd like to take a break."

The president shook his head, scratching his throat above his loosened tie and open shirt collar and trying not to dwell on the fact that the general's uniform—jacket still buttoned and tie knotted in place—looked as crisp and smart as it had when Harrington first met with him more than eighteen hours earlier. How in the name of hell did Marines always manage to pull that off?

"We'll all take a break, once we're done here." It was not his habit—at least so far as circumstances and practicality allowed—to require his staff to work overtime if he himself was not also present. Black had argued with him more than once that in his case he was really never "off the clock," but Harrington had learned early in his professional career to lead by example. Yes, his staff was more than capable of seeing to the numerous details pertaining to the United States' role in what was now shaping up to be nothing less than a global peace summit long enough for him to take a nap, but what message would that send? No, Harrington decided. If his people worked through the night, then he would, as well. They could all sleep when they were dead.

Though let's not try to get too excited about that *notion.*

Rising from the marginally comfortable parlor chair—one of two situated between the couches and his desk—Harrington allowed himself the luxury of stretching the weary muscles at the small of his back. It was not until he felt his right hand tapping the shirt pocket over his left breast that he realized he was searching for a cigarette. Fifteen years after breaking the habit, his body still itched for the occasional fix. Finding the pocket empty, the president moved around his desk to where he had draped his suit jacket over the chair there, reaching for the gum he kept in one of the interior pockets. "Jennifer, you're going to get carpal tunnel if you keep that up," he said to Black, watching his chief of staff tap the keys of her BlackBerry at a furious pace. "Any updates?"

Without looking up from the handheld device, Black replied, "Taiwan has sent word that they're in. We're expecting confirmation from Kenya and Singapore within the hour." She paused, stifling a yawn before reaching for the coffee cup on the small table next to her chair. "Once we hear from Pyongyang, that will make it unanimous." A petite woman, she seemed ready to shrink inside the jade pantsuit she wore, her long, bright red hair pulled into a ponytail that rested on her right shoulder. The long hours were beginning to take their toll on her, too. Dark circles were visible beneath her eyes, contrasting sharply with her fair skin.

Harrington shook his head as he folded a piece of gum in half and put it in his mouth. "A hundred ninety-one of a hundred ninety-two member states, and the lone holdout surprises no one." He pointed to Black. "And you wanted to take bets." Sighing, he asked, "Do we have any idea when they might deign to give us an answer? Any answer?"

"The North Korean ambassador assures us we'll have a detailed response by morning," Black said. Frowning, she added, "Morning as in 'when sane people finally get out of bed' morning, sir."

"So noted," Harrington said, leaning against the front of the desk and folding his arms. "Have we heard back from the secretary general on the venue?"

Seated across from General Grayson, Gisela Ribiero, the current secretary of state, answered, "Enough members have voiced dissent that he's considering holding the summit in Geneva." Shrugging, she added, "I have to say, Mister President, I think that works in our favor." A matronly woman who would celebrate her sixty-fifth birthday later in the year, Ribiero spoke with a thick Brazilian accent that gave her words a soothing, lyrical quality.

"I know, I know," Harrington said. "We need to play nice." Several U.N. members, including more than a few for whom relations with the United States had been less than cordial in recent years, naturally had taken every opportunity to point the finger of blame for the world's current plight squarely at Washington, D.C. After all, it was American military forces that had so quickly allied themselves with the Plysserians, embroiling themselves and—by extension—the entire planet in a conflict about which they knew nothing. In the opinion of more than one rival nation, the "arrogance of the West," which had continued unabated even after the aliens' arrival, might well spell doom for human civilization. "I just wish that, for once, some of these little pissant whack jobs could put aside the dick-measuring contests long enough to realize we've got real problems to deal with, instead of using every little thing as an excuse to toss shit over the wall at us."

The rhetoric was having an effect, in that several countries had expressed misgivings about their leaders attending the summit if it was to be held at the U.N. General Assembly Hall in New York. Considering the crisis facing every human regardless of political, cultural, or religious beliefs, it troubled Harrington that anyone could still be devoting so much time and energy to petty differences that had no bearing on how the Chodrecai would treat them should Earth lose this war.

"Troubled" is what you say in speeches and at press conferences, the president corrected himself. *What you really mean is that it pisses you off.*

"If going to Geneva means getting some folks off the fence, then that's what we do," he said. "I'll call the secretary general to smooth things over, but if somebody could find a way to put me in the room with some of these irritating little tin-pot pricks and a baseball bat, I'd consider it a personal favor."

Grayson laughed. "We'll see what we can do about arranging those meetings, Mister President."

All joking aside, it was a topic to which Harrington had given much thought in the months since the aliens' arrival. His administration had been in place little more than six months at that point. His plate had been filled with all manner of other issues—ongoing military operations in Iraq and Afghanistan, a stumbling economy, surging energy prices, and health care, to name just the big-ticket items—when this was added to the mix. Given the widespread nature of the conflict and its potential impact on the entire world, the people and governments of many nations had joined together, setting aside their own squabbles in order to face this new threat. Whether such solidarity would continue if and when the current conflict ended was impossible to predict, but Harrington liked to think something positive and lasting might emerge from the trials every human now faced.

"Okay," he said, crossing the office to where a steward moments ago had placed a tray with a fresh pot of coffee. "We do this in Geneva. The U.N. says they need at least two weeks to prepare the venue. Security alone will be a nightmare."

"U.N. peacekeeping forces will be on hand," General Grayson replied. "Crowd control, perimeter security, physical security of the buildings, that sort of thing."

Black added, "Secret Service is already prepping an advance team to start their preliminary sweeps. Even with all of that, you know it's going to be a circus."

"The lady has a gift for understatement," Harrington said, sipping his coffee and relishing the taste of the thick, rich blend. "A hundred ninety-two world leaders and their respective entourages, media, other VIPs, and who the hell knows who else? Yeah, it'll be one for the books, all right."

Grayson said, "Geneva won't allow military units from individual countries to deploy inside Swiss borders, and airspace will be clear for a ten-mile radius."

"I'm still going to want the *Eisenhower* and *Truman* carrier groups deployed there," Harrington replied. "We might not be able to have boots on the ground, but I want to shove planes up their asses if something happens." The order had come at the recommendation of Grayson and the other Joint Chiefs, both of whom outlined in stark detail what he already had been considering from the moment the peace summit was proposed.

"What about this portal-scattering whatchamahoozit the Blues have proposed?" Harrington asked. "Does it work?"

Seated farthest from him, in front of the fireplace set into the Oval Office's front wall, Nathan Schmidt, the secretary of Homeland Security, replied, "The Plysserian scientists working on this with our people have a prototype, Mister President, but it's nowhere near the size and power needed to defeat a full-size portal. There's no way a functioning model can be ready for Geneva." He paused, drawing a deep breath before adding, "I have to say, I'm not at all comfortable with you placing yourself in such a vulnerable position."

"Is there such a thing as an invulnerable position anymore, Nathan?" Harrington asked, taking another drink from his coffee mug. "With those portals, there's nowhere on Earth they can't get to, given enough time. Besides, it's not as though we'd be protected from any kind of conventional attack, either." He waved away the comment. "It doesn't matter. We can't not go. This will be a defining moment in the history of this planet, and I don't plan to watch it from a TV in my office or the bunker or wherever the Secret Service would have me hide."

Since entering the conflict with the Chodrecai as allies of the Plysserians, the president had resisted all efforts by the Treasury Department to relocate him from the White House to an undisclosed, secure location. Refusing to leave the White House even in the face of the massive Gray attack on Washington six months earlier, he had agreed to move to the underground bunker at the behest of his protection detail. He had remained visible to the American people throughout the crisis and its tumultuous effects — curfews, resource shortages, the countless disruptions and sacrifices he had asked the country to endure as it readied for yet another war. Even if he were not the leader of the most powerful, most influential nation on the planet, he could not in good conscience refuse to be on hand as the leaders of two worlds united in peace.

Looking to Black, he asked, "Jennifer, how's the speech for Tuesday night coming?"

The chief of staff replied, "You'll have a draft by the end of the day, sir."

Harrington nodded in approval. "Good. It's important that we make clear to the American people what we're after before the summit convenes. There's going to be a lot of ground to cover in the coming months — a lot of animosity and fear to overcome."

"It's going to be a tough pill to swallow," Ribiero replied. "Sending resources to their planet to help with rebuilding efforts; having them help us out." She shrugged. "Of course, there's some excitement about this, as well. Private-sector energy, for example. They're champing at the bit to send exploratory teams there, drooling at the idea of the kinds of minerals and whatever else they might find. The trade opportunities alone are mind-boggling. We could be talking about the creation of entirely new sectors of industry. The potential for technological advancement is staggering."

"It's immigration I'm worried about," Schmidt countered. "We have enough problems in that area, but now we're talking about who knows how many Plysserians and even Chodrecai wanting to relocate to Earth. It could take years to sort out all of that."

"We'll find a way," Harrington said, his tone sharp enough to sever the remainder of the conversation. "If there's one thing this country does well, even if it takes a little time to get its head out of its ass, it's that it adapts, particularly in the face of adversity. I don't see this as being any different. Will it be hard? Yes, but then again, nothing worth doing is easy." Looking at Ribiero, he continued, "You emigrated here with your parents from Brazil, and the lawn-mowing business your father started in his garage when you were fifteen is now one of the largest commercial and residential landscaping companies in the country. Your father went from cutting your neighbors' yards so you could eat one decent meal a day to owning a house on fifty acres of land in Colorado, and that's after he donated the other fifty acres so a children's cancer treatment center could be built. Who's to say a few Plysserian immigrants won't come here, start new lives, and then have a positive impact on the world around them?"

Setting the coffee mug down on his desk, the president continued, "Yes, it'll be difficult, just as moving forward after the Second World War was a challenge, but that effort produced the greatest era of prosperity this country has ever known. For all we know, we're on the cusp of something even larger here and now. The American people always find a way to adapt and to thrive, and they'll do it again. All they need is the chance, and the right leaders to guide them along the way." He paused, contemplating the taupe carpet before him and the seal of the president emblazoned upon it.

Despite urban legends and rumors to the contrary, the head of the eagle that dominated the seal had yet to turn so that it faced the bundle of arrows held in its left talon, as opposed to its right and the olive branch it clasped. Stories had circulated for years that the subtle change—the eagle facing the arrows—was supposed to be a reminder that the United States was at war, as though such a prompt might actually be necessary for the person currently represented by that seal. Instead, the eagle faced the olive branch as it always had, and in this case Harrington hoped that might serve as a positive sign of good things to come.

"Besides," he said after a moment, "we can discuss this until my replacement shows up, but it comes down to this: Faced with everything we're talking about—along with whatever we haven't even thought of yet—or the alternative, do we really have a choice?" As he expected, there were no responses to his query, and he nodded in satisfaction. "There you go, then. Okay, enough navel-gazing. Let's get back to work."

27

The charge went off less than six feet from Colin Laney's head, the muffled explosion like a hammer against his skull as water and mud rained down on him.

"God *damn* it!" he hissed through gritted teeth, his ears still ringing from the blast as he lifted his head from the mud. More mud, grass, and barbed wire lay before him. Ahead and to his right was a parapet of sandbags surrounding a wooden boxlike structure rising two or three feet out of the ground. The explosion had come from there, a charge designed more to make a lot of noise than inflict any actual damage. Still, it was cordoned off within a circle of thick ropes passed through holes drilled into wooden posts, with the recruits instructed not to approach it or others like it.

To his left and right, Colin could make out the shadowy figures of other team members crawling on their bellies, forging their own paths through the obstacles around them. Machine-gun fire sliced the night air over their heads with bright streaks of orange from tracer rounds mixed in with the live ammunition. The drill instructors had repeatedly told the recruits not to stand up anywhere on this part of the course, to avoid the risk of being hit by live fire. Intellectually, Colin was certain that if he simply followed the orders he had been given, proceeding with the knowledge that the drill instructors were not seeking to inflict intentional harm upon their recruits, he was in no real danger.

That did not stop him from wanting to piss himself.

"Keep moving! Keep moving!" a voice shouted from somewhere ahead of him, and Colin looked up to see Sergeant Stevens pacing back and forth across a patch of dirt at the course's far end. His face all but cloaked in darkness by the brim of his campaign cover, the drill instructor was very animated, shouting and pointing at other recruits who were farther along the course, maneuvering their way beneath strands of barbed wire.

Ignoring the chill running down his entire body from his damp, cold, dirty clothes and equipment, Colin reached out with his left hand and dug his fingers into the soft mud, using that tentative grip as purchase as he dug in with his boots and pushed himself forward. Every movement seemed to drain more energy from his already spent body, deprived as it was by a merciless combination of fatigue, hunger, and prolonged exertion. Around his other hand was wrapped the sling of his M16. The rifle, like him, coated in dirt and grime. It now seemed to weigh fifty pounds, rather than eight or nine. As he dragged the weapon with him, moonlight glinted off the dull, hard rubber blade of the training bayonet fixed to its barrel.

Jesus. How long has it been since I slept? Since I ate? Twelve, possibly sixteen hours, Colin figured. It felt like years.

The infiltration course had started simply enough. Colin and nineteen other recruits advanced through a line of trees at a drill instructor's direction, brandishing their M16 rifles with fixed bayonets and wearing Kevlar helmets—some of them decorated by their wearers, Colin included, with small branches from bushes stuck into the slits of the protective headgear's cloth camouflage cover. The course—

which, like nearly every aspect of training, was enhanced by the participation of Plysserian soldiers—was the latest hurdle in a grueling string of events and obstacles known as the Crucible. For the past forty-plus hours, the challenge had done its level best to include everything instilled into Platoon 3003 during the previous six weeks. The test was designed to push the recruits to their limit and beyond, challenging them to apply the skills and knowledge they had learned. Sleep and meals were minimal, further taxing stressed, exhausted bodies as the recruits faced test after test, learning as they progressed inch by agonizing inch that individuals were destined to fail, whereas teamwork would lead the way to triumph.

Maneuvering in the near darkness using stealth, cover, and concealment, Colin and the recruits to his left and right communicated via hand and arm signals as they advanced through this first leg of the course. It was a clear, cloudless night, and with almost no artificial light in the immediate vicinity, the stars were brilliant in the evening sky and the moon offered sufficient illumination for Colin and his team to negotiate the small stretch of forest, mindful of trip wires and other booby traps, as they had been taught by their instructors. Ahead and to either side, gunfire seemed very close, rolling through the woods and evoking goose pimples across his skin.

It was not until the team found their first real obstacle— a wooden wall perhaps seven feet tall, blocking their path and requiring them to climb over in order to proceed— that the real fun began.

"Stay in your lanes!" a drill instructor shouted from somewhere just beyond the course's outer boundary, using a megaphone to be heard over the sounds of weapons fire and the occasional explosion. Some of the noise was artificial, coming from speakers positioned in trees, sandbag embankments, or fake rocks, while a lot more of it was generated by actual machine guns in fixed mounts firing off rounds every few seconds. Colin made short work of the wall, rolling over the top edge and dropping easily to the sand below, waiting in a crouch for the rest of his group to do the same so they could continue their advance as a team.

The next part of the course would be the hardest, a lesson the recruits had learned hours earlier while navigating it in daylight. At least then it was easier to see the obstacles that lay ahead, whereas now trees and other structures lining the course cast much of the ground before him in shadow. Colin fought through fatigue to remember the course's general layout, which he had tried to study while waiting for the rest of his platoon after he completed the daytime training evolution. The open patch of sand, mud, and water forming this part of the course was probably fifty yards in length. Narrow, winding paths crossed the broken terrain, carved by recruits who had already negotiated the course. While watching members of his platoon crawling through muck earlier in the day, Colin had smiled as he recalled his grandfather's descriptions of similar drills and exercises he had undertaken as a recruit decades ago.

Another charge exploded, this one behind him, and though he flinched, Colin resisted the urge to curl up into a fetal ball as a rapid succession of three small blasts rumbled across the field. Movement to his left made him look in that direction in time to see a large target rise from behind a pile of sandbags. It was little more than a silhouette, an oversized caricature of a Chodrecai warrior, with huge, angry black eyes and a gaping maw filled with sharp, jagged teeth. No sooner did the target come into view than it was obliterated by a blast of energy from a pulse rifle wielded by a Plysserian soldier. The Blue, positioned inside the confines of a protected bunker, was moving the muzzle of the massive weapon back and forth from left to right, searching for other targets of opportunity and adding to the general chaos enveloping the course.

Grandpa sure as fuck didn't have to deal with that. Colin knew the training he was receiving had changed considerably from his grandfather's day, and even from that undertaken as early as two years ago, based on correspondence the two had shared since the younger man's arrival at Parris Island. Staff Sergeant Blyzen had even told his recruits as much during one of the senior drill instructor's frequent "school circles" held in the platoon's squad bay after the evening meal but before lights-out. In addition to the compressed training cycle—seven weeks, as opposed to what once had been fourteen—the curriculum now was more heavily weighted toward combat-related subjects, which began much earlier in program than they had previously. Then there were the obvious differences brought about by the inclusion in the training of Plysserian soldiers, who brought with them information and experience in the areas of weapons and tactics, and knowledge of the aliens' planet and people. Colin had found that part of the training fascinating, along with the opportunity it presented to learn about beings and civilizations from another world and to work alongside its representatives.

A subdued *whump* echoed from somewhere ahead of him, and Colin caught sight of a white streak arcing into the air. The flare climbed several hundred feet before erupting into a ball of brilliant white light, casting pale illumination across the entire course as it began drifting to the ground, suspended by a miniature parachute. As he had been taught by Staff Sergeant Medina, Colin shut his right eye—his shooting eye, to preserve from the abrupt brightness whatever natural night vision he might still retain—as he took advantage of the flare to study the ground ahead of him. He was almost there, facing a final series of barbed-wire obstacles strung at knee level across an expansive puddle of muddy water. Quick glances to either side revealed that other recruits were slightly ahead and behind him, making their own progress through the field.

"What are you waiting for?" a voice shouted as the flare faded, and Colin saw Sergeant Sykes, the lanky, perpetually pissed-off drill instructor from Platoon 3001, standing outside the course's rightmost boundary, a megaphone hiding most of his face and his free hand pointing in Colin's direction. "They don't deliver pizza out there, boy! Get it in gear!"

Colin pushed himself along the damp sand, mindful to hug the ground as he crested a small rise before scurrying back into a small depression. The sand was everywhere, in his mouth and running down the sleeves of his uniform blouse. He resisted the urge to wipe his eyes, knowing it would just make the gritty feeling there worse. Another target popped up, less than five feet from where he lay, and an instant later it was destroyed by the Plysserian manning its pulse rifle. Turning his head away from the blast, Colin noticed a speaker poking out from a half-rotted sandbag, projecting sounds of helicopters and offering the illusion that such craft were swooping low over a battlefield, offering fire support or looking for a safe spot to land.

"Move your asses!" another voice bellowed from somewhere to Colin's left. It sounded like Staff Sergeant Medina, who likely would stomp across the field regardless of any threats from machine guns to get in a recruit's face if he thought it was necessary.

When his left hand touched water, Colin looked up to see the forward edge of the massive puddle and the first strands of barbed wire. To his right, another recruit, Joshua Wolfe, was almost close enough to touch as he prepared to negotiate the wire in his own lane. The two young men exchanged expressions that communicated the same unspoken thought.

Well, this is gonna suck.

Crawling as close as he could to the puddle without actually entering it, Colin steeled himself for what he knew was coming as he rolled onto his back. He rested his M16 atop his chest so that the handle of the bayonet rested on the forward lip of his helmet before using his legs to push himself a few more inches along the ground. The brown ankle-deep water was cold, eliciting a gasp from him as it seeped into his uniform. No small amount of mud was working its way past his collar and down his neck and back, but Colin tried to ignore it, tilting his head to locate the first barbed-wire strand. Finding a handhold between two knots of the twisted steel cable, he used it for leverage as he dug in with his boots and propelled himself forward while using the M16 to keep the wire from snagging on his uniform, his helmet, or even just the skin of his hands. Muddy water sloshed the side of his face and Colin tasted sludge. Focusing on moving, he reached past his head for the next wire strand, pulling himself another foot ahead.

"Shit! I'm fucking stuck!"

The voice was Wolfe's. Colin recognized the drawl that characterized his Alabama roots. Colin looked over to see that the other recruit had elected to move through the obstacle on his belly and had become snagged on at least two strands of wire, the barbs of which were embedded in the fabric of his uniform blouse. Flailing in the muddy water, Wolfe was trying to reach back to free himself, which only worsened his problem, as his left arm also snagged on the wire. He kicked his legs, which did nothing except send splashes of sludge in all directions, some of it landing on Colin.

"Calm down, dude!" Colin hissed as another flare burst in the sky overhead, the new illumination showing him that he had almost cleared the obstacle. Dragging himself out of the puddle, he rolled back onto his stomach and wormed his way over to Wolfe's lane, cradling his M16 in the crooks of his arms, until he was alongside the other man. "Hold still," Colin said, reaching out with his right hand to pull at the wire ensnaring Wolfe's arm. The recruit yelped in momentary pain when the metal barbs dragged across his skin, but said nothing else as Colin reached for the other wires, detaching the man's clothing from it. Pushing himself back the way he had come, Colin nodded to Wolfe. "Okay, you're free."

The other recruit sighed in relief. "Thanks, Laney," he offered as he followed Colin out of the obstacle.

Within seconds, both men were free, and Colin dug deep for the strength needed to belly-crawl the final twenty yards. His hands found purchase at the edge of the raised dirt path encompassing the field and he pulled himself to his feet, knowing he had cleared the most dangerous part of the course. Wolfe was on his heels, and both recruits glanced around to get their bearings. On his flanks, Colin saw other recruits either emerging from the field or gathering themselves for the next part of the course. Billy Rickert, the wiseass from Minnesota who had worked for a bookstore or music store or some such thing before receiving his draft notice, had dragged himself from the muck and now propped himself up on hands and knees, gasping for breath and looking as though he might at any second collapse to the ground. His respite was longer than Colin expected—at least three seconds—before Sergeant Stevens was on him, the drill instructor crouching down and aiming one long index finger at the recruit's face.

"What are doing, Rickert? You ain't done yet! Get your nasty body off my frickin' infiltration course!"

In the early days of training, the drill instructors' deranged, spittle-laden rants, uttered at the slightest provocation any time of the day or night, had sounded odd when delivered with modified words to replace various obscenities. It had not taken long for that strange feeling to evaporate, as the lack of actual vulgarities did little to diminish the constant, merciless barking that characterized most of the Marines' interaction with the platoon. Sergeant Stevens in particular was a gifted practitioner in this regard, as Colin had learned on that very first day of training and on uncounted occasions thereafter.

Within moments, the rest of the twenty-man team was on the path, and the recruit in the middle of the line who had been designated the leader, Daniel Abraham, gave the signal for the group to advance. Staying abreast of one another, the recruits scurried across the path toward the grassy area on its far side. Colin ran holding his M16 with both hands in front of his body with the muzzle pointed upward to his left—"port arms," as he had learned weeks ago. It took only a few seconds for the team to converge on the next part of the course, where moonlight illuminated a row of ten dummies, canvas silhouettes stuffed with sand and suspended by ropes from a metal frame painted olive green. Each of the mannequins was oversized and gray, its head painted to resemble a Chodrecai soldier's. White paint on each of the dummies indicated areas of the body where the aliens were vulnerable to direct attack—head, neck, groin, under the arms. Standing to either side of the metal frame were two drill instructors.

"Any day," growled one of the other Marines, waving with his right hand for the recruits to advance. "Attack!"

One of the first to get to the obstacle, Colin drew a deep

breath and loosed his best primal war cry as he charged the nearest dummy, stepping into position as he had learned during repeated close-combat training. He lunged forward, extending his arms and stabbing the fake Gray with his fixed bayonet. Pulling back the weapon and uttering another primal yell, Colin stepped closer, swinging the butt of his rifle into the mannequin's groin. The final motion of the three-point attack was a downward slash of the training bayonet's deliberately dulled edge across the target's throat.

"That's what I'm talkin' about!" the other drill instructor shouted. Pointing to Colin's helmet, he added, "That is motivated! You make me want to sign up for the infantry all over again. Move it out!"

"Sir, yes, sir!" Colin yelled, running from the bayonet station even as the drill instructor returned his attention to recruits attacking other dummies. Glancing to his right, Colin saw two other recruits running with him, Danny Elliot and Matthew Worthington. Elliot, a redneck from somewhere in Tennessee, and Worthington, a lanky man from Baltimore who supposedly had a history with street gangs in that city, had made an unlikely pairing early on, but had forged a friendship during the weeks of enforced proximity and the atmosphere of teamwork that pervaded almost every waking moment of a recruit's training. Worthington was smarter than he let on, excelling at nearly every written test the platoon had undergone, and taking to the physical aspects of the training regimen with undisguised zeal.

The three of them ran across the expanse of open ground toward what Colin knew was the final station on the course. A waist-high wall of sandbags had been erected here, atop which sat ten Plysserian pulse rifles. Three Blue soldiers and two drill instructors waited at the station, the aliens watching in silence as the Marines directed the recruits with hand gestures and no small amount of yelling toward the rifles.

"Get on them weapons," snarled one of the instructors, whom Colin now recognized as Staff Sergeant Blyzen. "We ain't got all night."

Propping his M16 against the sandbag parapet, Colin settled in behind one of the pulse rifles. He pulled the stock of the heavy weapon to his shoulder and leaned into it, just as he had done weeks earlier during the familiarization fire exercises and later at the rifle range when he had fired for qualification. His prowess with the alien weapon had been commended by his instructors, the praise all the more noteworthy given that, prior to attending boot camp, Colin had never so much as held a firearm.

The targets for this part of the exercise were different from those at which he had fired during previous training exercises, laid out at varying distances from where he stood. As before, they approximated the general size and shape of a charging Chodrecai soldier, only these were simple cutouts, constructed from material similar to that used in the protective armored vests worn by Plysserian forces. When Colin fired this time, the rifle's energy pulse struck the target in the head, knocking it backward until it fell from view. Not stopping to admire his handiwork, he instead took aim at another target, this one ten yards farther away, and fired. The energy pulse slammed into the silhouette's torso and pushed it out of sight. In the near darkness, sighting in on the third and last of his targets was something of a challenge, but Colin was able to make out enough of the cutout to get a clear sight picture, and his third shot was also a hit.

"Out-fricking-standing, Laney!" Blyzen said as Colin secured the pulse rifle and returned it to where he had found it lying atop the sandbags. When he turned to face his senior drill instructor, he saw that a wide smile had broken through the Marine's normally reserved demeanor. "Piece of cake, ain't it?"

"Sir, yes, sir!" Colin shouted as he brought himself to attention.

"You're cold, wet, and tired, and you hurt like a son of a bitch, don't you?"

"Sir, yes, sir!"

Blyzen smiled again. "But that don't matter because you're alive, right? You don't need no frickin' sleep, do you? You don't need no hot chow. You'd rather kill more aliens, right?"

"Sir, yes, sir!" Colin yelled, feeling new energy coursing through his weary body as he pulled himself to attention and returned his rifle to the port arms position. Somehow, his rifle no longer felt so much like a lead weight.

Stepping closer, Blyzen lowered his voice as he asked, "You made it this far, but you know what that means, right?"

Uncertain as to how the answer had come to him, Colin was still confident that he knew what to say. "It's still not the real thing, sir."

Blyzen nodded in approval, and Colin was sure he noted a hint of sadness in the other man's eyes. "You're damned right." There was a pause before the senior drill instructor nodded with his head for Colin to continue the course. "Now carry the hell on."

"Aye, aye, sir!" Colin shouted in response, the pain of the past minutes' exertion seeming to fall away in the face of the unexpected praise as he turned and ran the final fifty yards to the end of the course.

The Crucible would soon be over, he knew. After that, the Marine Corps waited, and with it, the war. Or did it? Despite the controlled, insulated bubble in which their drill instructors kept the recruits in their charge, word already was circulating about the arrival of the Chodrecai emissaries and the message of peace they had brought. Did this mean that peace might truly be on the horizon, and sooner rather than later?

Colin could not think about that. For now, his focus had to be on his training. As his drill instructors had warned him and the other recruits, militaries might pray for peace, but they always did so while preparing for war.

28

"I think I'm going to throw up."

Standing next to Makoquolax, Bradley Gardner tried not to appear nervous as he looked out from the stage at the front of the Assembly Hall to the gathering of dignitaries and other guests. None of the vast chamber's twelve hundred seats was empty, and dozens more people stood along the walls on the main floor as well as the balconies. Hundreds of hushed conversations were taking place, generating a low rumble that filled the air.

Without moving so much as his eyes to look at his friend, Makoquolax asked, "Are you ill?"

Gardner tried not to look panicked as he shook his head and hissed through gritted teeth, "I'm scared shitless." The neck of his Marine dress uniform felt even tighter than normal, the formfitting blouse seemingly squeezing him like a vise.

"If I understand your idioms and quirks of language correctly," the Plysserian replied, keeping his voice low, "being free of your body's natural waste products would seem to be a good thing."

Despite his anxiety, Gardner almost laughed at the remark, all the more because of his friend's sincerity. "I'm nervous about being up here. We're standing in front of the most powerful people in the world, Max." Before him, the leaders or duly appointed representatives of the United Nations' 192 member countries awaited what had come to be regarded as the most significant meeting of this august body since its inception.

So what the hell am I doing here?

It was a question that Gardner had continued to ask himself, even though he had been provided the answer by no less a personage than General Bruce Thompson himself. Being among the first humans to interact with the aliens—Plysserians, in his case, with Max's help—and the first known to have communicated with them, Gardner had, according to Thompson, secured himself a prominent place in history. It was a notion to which Gardner was still becoming accustomed, and he was uncertain as to how to view himself or his role in what had transpired since the aliens' arrival nearly a year earlier. However, others seemed quite comfortable with the situation, including Thompson, who had informed Gardner that President Harrington himself had requested the Marine's presence in Geneva, to act as translator for First *Dekritonpa* Vahelridol Praziq when the Chodrecai leader addressed the U.N. General Assembly.

Gardner had nearly vomited upon hearing that, as well.

Arriving here on this day had taken weeks of planning. During that time, encounters with Chodrecai on Earth fortunately had been limited to small skirmishes with pockets of soldiers operating independently and without benefit of communication with higher authority. Such groups had no knowledge of their leader's desire to meet with her human counterparts to discuss the cessation of hostilities. With the assistance of Gray soldiers and civilians who had joined the joint human-Plysserian cause, several confrontations had been defused without incident. Even with that effort, there still were reports of firefights and other actions involving

Grays, but from what Gardner had been told or learned on his own, such incidents seemed to be decreasing.

Could it all soon be over? Really?

The suppressed murmurs of countless conversations quieted, drawing Gardner's attention to the assemblage of world leaders. Once more he took in the panorama sweeping away from the stage, the gentle slope of rows and rows of seats—groups of eight positioned before polished wooden tables arranged in a manner that reminded Gardner of the pews found in large cathedrals—that climbed in tiers toward the back of the chamber. Given what everyone hoped was to happen here today, he could not imagine a more fitting venue than the Palais des Nations, the seat of cooperative spirit, multilateral diplomacy, and global peace for more than seventy years, dating back to the time of the U.N.'s predecessor organization, the League of Nations.

Shifting his eyes across the first few seats, Gardner caught sight of President Harrington, and seated in the aisle next to him in an oversized chair provided for the purpose was Nhiraplo Baezom Ghaas, Chancellor of the Union of Plysserian Allied States. His attire consisted of a formfitting stark white single-piece garment, over which he wore a long maroon jacket with a high collar. The patterns of several tattoos visible on the Plysserian's head and neck, many of them faded with age, told Gardner that Ghaas had once been a soldier. A pronounced brow partially obscured his wide black eyes, and the edges of his mouth were turned downward, giving the Blue a dour expression.

That is one mean-looking son of a bitch.

Trying to calm himself, Gardner took to playing a mental game of trying to see how many of the dignitaries he could pick out. He recognized more faces than he was able to name, and the exercise did little to ease his discomfort at standing before such a distinguished audience.

"Ladies and gentlemen, your attention, please," a female voice said in English, sounding through the chamber's audio system. It was followed immediately by other voices, repeating the salutation in various other languages. "*The Secretary General.*"

Movement to his left caught his attention, but Gardner remembered at the last instant not to jerk his head to look in that direction. Instead he stood even straighter, locking his body into a position of attention as Suresh Daryapurkar, a stoop-shouldered, gray-haired man with dark skin walked with a cane toward the podium situated at center stage. His arrival was greeted by enthusiastic applause as everyone in the chamber rose to their feet. Upon reaching the podium, he waited a moment before raising his free hand toward the audience. The applause faded in response, and Daryapurkar waited another few moments as everyone reseated him- or herself. From his vantage point, Gardner could see that many of the leaders, delegates, and other audience members reached for headsets that allowed them to hear the secretary general's remarks in one of the languages recognized in the Assembly Hall.

"Good day to you all," he said, his voice amplified by the sound system. Waiting for the translations with what Gardner suspected was practiced ease, Daryapurkar continued in a measured cadence, "Thank you for being here on this momentous day. Never before in the history of our world have we encountered the challenges we now face, not as countries or societies at odds with one another, but as one people united in common purpose." His attention focused on Daryapurkar, it took Gardner an extra moment to realize that the secretary general—by all accounts and despite his age, a gifted and charismatic public speaker—was presenting his speech without the aid of a teleprompter or even a script or note cards on the podium. Though Gardner was unable to explain the feeling even to himself, something about the simple gesture, offered as it was on this day, just seemed appropriate and genuine.

According to the biographical information Gardner had obtained from the Internet, Daryapurkar had been born in India and, after attending university in England, had remained at Oxford to teach political science. He had written nine books on various topics relating to international diplomacy, their shared central theme being the need for greater cooperation between the industrialized nations in their efforts to aid developing countries. He had served on the U.N. Security Council for five years before being nominated for the position of secretary general.

Daryapurkar's first two years in that office had been focused on enhancing the organization's relevance in the face of rapidly changing political, ideological, and even environmental landscapes. He had worked earnestly to erase many of the stigmas surrounding the U.N. with respect to its role—or lack of presence, real or perceived—when it came to matters of global import, and while he had his critics, the international response to his work to this point had largely been positive. Following the arrival of the aliens, Daryapurkar's had been one of the louder voices calling for peaceful resolution of the conflict, seeking some measure of understanding and cooperation should the two worlds be able to set aside their differences and together move forward. Upon hearing the news of First *Dekritonpa* Praziq's desire to address Earth's leaders and propose that very notion, Daryapurkar had been the first to champion her cause, insisting that the meeting be held here in Geneva.

If the world had more people like him, Gardner thought, *we'd all be a hell of a lot better off.*

"After months of conflict and an uncertain future before us," Daryapurkar continued, "we have arrived at a turning point in the history of two worlds. What remains to be seen is if that history will be shared, and if so, to what end. We are assembled here today because we seek the answers to those questions, but we also are presented with a unique opportunity. It is my sincere hope that we leave here with a mandate for peace with our former enemy, as well as a united outlook on how we move forward, not as individual countries, but as one people. Such mutual respect and support will allow us to repair the damage to both our worlds even as we forge lasting friendships, not only with our newfound friends from *Jontashreena*, but also with one another."

More applause greeted the remarks, and even from where he stood Gardner could see the small smile of satisfaction gracing Daryapurkar's aged features. The elderly man seemed to stand just a bit straighter as he took in the reaction to his words, and he nodded with conviction as he gazed out across the assembly.

"With that, I present to you the leader of the Chodrecai Territorial Confederation, First *Dekritonpa* Vahelridol Praziq."

The response to the Gray leader's introduction was more restrained than that for Daryapurkar, but still impressive. Everyone in the audience stood once more, and the applause was not quite so loud and raucous this time. When the secretary general turned to his right, Gardner could not help turning his head to look just as two figures emerged from offstage. Both looked to be Chodrecai, at least with respect to their lack of tattoos and other markings on their bodies. The first Chodrecai, a female, was tall and slender, her head narrow, and her skin smooth. She wore a multicolored garment that resembled a robe, which fell almost to the floor and covered her feet so that when she walked she appeared to float. The garment was not secured at her waist but instead flowed around and behind her as she crossed the stage. Her companion was a male Chodrecai that Gardner recognized as Trela Dren, the advisor to Praziq who also had acted as one of her envoys to Earth. He was the one who had traveled via portal from *Jontashreena* to Washington, D.C., to deliver her message and request. He was smaller than the Gray soldiers Gardner had encountered. Instead of the usual formfitting uniform that might have denoted him as a member of the military, the Gray instead wore a stark, dark-green one-piece garment that covered him from neck to mid-calf. The leggings of the garment were tucked into high black boots. He carried a slim case that resembled a portfolio, which Gardner assumed carried whatever passed for a clipboard or personal computer or whatever else Praziq would utilize when delivering her remarks to the assembly.

Reaching the podium, Praziq and Dren stopped before Daryapurkar, who offered what Gardner knew from briefings was a practiced series of gestures with both hands. The sequence re-created a silent greeting from the region of *Jontashreena* where Praziq had lived for most of her life prior to entering public service. His efforts must have been satisfactory, for Praziq's reaction was to offer her best attempt at a smile, as she reached out and took Daryapurkar's hands in her own. They seemed to exchange a few brief words, which surprised Gardner, as he had been told the Gray leader was not versed in any Earth languages. Of course, it made sense that she would endeavor to learn at least some of Daryapurkar's native tongue as part of her preparations for greeting him.

Greasing the wheels, and all that.

Daryapurkar moved aside, allowing Praziq to take her place before the podium. As he had practiced earlier, Gardner stepped forward, swallowing the massive lump in his throat as he marched in taut military manner to stand to the left of the Gray leader. Praziq turned and nodded to him, smiling as he extended his left hand and proffered one of the two translator bands he carried. The First *Dekritonpa*'s expression changed to one of understanding and she took the band, reaching up to place it upon her head. Gardner mimicked her actions, feeling the device resize itself so that each of its twelve nodes rested comfortably around the widest part of his head. After so many months of working alongside Plysserians like Max and those few Chodrecai who had been captured or had surrendered and expressed their support for humans, wearing the band was almost second nature to him. Even the headaches he had experienced during his first weeks working with the wondrous device had ceased to be a problem. His proven ability with the device as well as his command of various Blue and Gray dialects had made him one of the military's leading translators, and a valuable asset to General Thompson and his team at the Pentagon.

From where he stood to her right, Dren reached forward and laid the item he carried atop the podium's slanted surface and touched it, activating an embedded display screen that contained lines of indecipherable text. Even with the progress he had made understanding Chodrecai patois, many of the written languages still escaped him. He ignored that as a transparent lens descended from the translator band to rest before his eyes. Looking to Praziq, Gardner nodded that he was ready to proceed.

Here goes nothing.

"Leaders of Earth, and Chancellor Ghaas," she began, allowing Gardner a moment to comprehend and translate her words into the microphone he wore attached to his uniform blouse, "I bring you greetings from the Chodrecai people of *Jontashreena*. If you will forgive the momentary indulgence, I would like to think that I address you, not simply as the leader of the Chodrecai Territorial Confederation, but as a citizen of my world." The initial response to her greeting seemed to resonate with the audience, as Gardner was able to hear various murmurs. In the front row of the chamber's center section, President Harrington nodded in what seemed to be approval, or at least acceptance. To his left, Chancellor Ghaas's expression remained fixed.

"Allow me to be the first of the Chodrecai people to offer a formal apology to the citizens of your world for involving you in the conflict that has embroiled my planet for generations. It does not matter who came here first, or who allied with whom for whatever reason; the simple fact is that it is our war, not yours. It is a failure of my leadership that I did not act to prevent your being pulled into our affairs." Praziq paused again, allowing the translation to carry forward to the audience, and once more Gardner saw the reactions from the assembly. Their attention was without exception focused on the Gray leader, hanging on her every word. So far, she seemed to be saying everything he expected they wanted to hear.

"Early on," she continued, "when so little was known about you, we saw your planet as a salvation, a way of somehow repairing or perhaps even escaping the devastation we had inflicted upon our own world. As a people, the Chodrecai learn from an early age that citizens are expected to contribute to the larger society, to give of themselves so that everyone can attain larger, greater goals. Resources are utilized in the furthering of such goals. Earth was seen as a new means of achieving those ends.

"As time has passed, I have been able to reflect on those earlier decisions, made in the heat of battle and, yes, even desperation. I now see how horribly wrong we were. I hope you will believe me when I tell you that there are vast segments of our population, Chodrecai and Plysserian alike, who grieve with you for the losses you have suffered as a consequence of our coming to your planet. Given all that has happened between our two peoples since our arrival here, I know that it is inappropriate to ask your forgiveness. Instead, I would ask for your empathy as you consider that we were motivated not by malice but simply by a desire to survive. I certainly believe that the people of Earth were driven to act for similar, understandable reasons, and anyone with good conscience cannot take issue with their actions." Gardner sensed that she had not intended to pause at this point, but she was interrupted by applause, louder even than when she had first entered the Assembly Hall. Turning to him, Praziq offered her version of a smile before returning her attention to the audience.

"If we can agree on these points, then it seems we have the basic foundation upon which to build something even greater: a pledge to cease hostilities and instead focus our efforts on establishing a lasting relationship between us. It would be a bond forged from the mistakes we all have made, and the promise that the life we choose to live from this time forward will be one of peace and mutual benefit. As a gesture of my commitment to this process, I am prepared to order the immediate cessation of all military operations under my authority. I request only that this action be commensurate with similar actions on the part of Plysserian as well as human units, be they on Earth or *Jontashreena*." She stopped, taking a moment to look out over the assembly, and nodded as though to herself before adding, "I understand that there is a human turn of phrase to describe a proposal such as mine: 'too good to be true.' I comprehend the meaning of those words, and I hope I can alleviate such concerns through voice and deed. My leadership council is ready to issue those instructions upon hearing from me, and it is my sincere hope that I can offer that guidance before leaving you today."

I'll be goddamned. The words echoed in Gardner's skull, almost drowning out the cacophony of imagery and energy being translated into his mind via the translator band. Though he had expected Praziq to offer some form of surrender, he had not counted on her apparent willingness to call off everything with the alien equivalent of a simple phone call home. He was not alone in his reaction, judging by the responses emanating from the assembly floor. Leaders and dignitaries were turning to each other, talking and gesturing with barely restrained frenzy.

All things considered, Gardner could not see this as anything other than a best-case scenario. Despite the time that had passed since the war's beginning and regardless of what had happened since, the Chodrecai by all rights held a legitimate claim to being the victims of aggressive action on the part of the Plysserian government. Though their ideology might have differed from their enemy at one time, it was not sufficient cause to start a war, was it? Further, it seemed to Gardner from listening to Praziq that the First *Dekritonpa* believed some facets of Chodrecai culture and society might well have outlived their usefulness, not only for themselves, but also with respect to any long-term relationship with the Plysserians and, yes, even humans.

One can only hope.

Praziq seemed as though she intended to continue speaking, but halted when Secretary General Daryapurkar stepped forward again, placing his free hand on Gardner's arm and motioning for the younger man to step aside. He gestured toward the podium and the microphone positioned there, and Praziq nodded in understanding before moving to allow him access. Without taking his gaze from her, Daryapurkar leaned toward the microphone.

"First *Dekritonpa* Praziq," he said, glancing to Gardner and gesturing for him to translate for the Chodrecai leader's benefit, "as you might imagine, with so many different governments represented here today, an immediate response to your request presents a challenge. However, I believe I can speak for the assembly when I say we welcome you and the proposal you bring to our people, and it is my hope that we can act quickly to bring about the peace we all seek."

Thunderous applause erupted across the Assembly Hall, with every audience member—Chancellor Ghaas included—coming once more to their feet. Shouts of joy and hope added to the mix, and Gardner was certain he could feel the excitement wash over him like waves on a beach. The ovation went uninterrupted for more than a minute, continuing as Daryapurkar and Praziq once more exchanged gestures and held hands. Behind the First *Dekritonpa*, Trela Dren reached for the device containing Praziq's speech before stepping away from the podium. He said nothing even as his long, thick fingers played across the device's display surface, and Gardner almost turned away but stopped when the Gray looked up from the unit, an odd expression clouding his alien features. His wide, dark eyes met Gardner's, and when he spoke, Gardner heard the regret in the Chodrecai's voice.

"For my people."

Oh, damn. Oh, God damn!

Instinct pushed Gardner across the stage toward Dren, who stood motionless. Gardner did not know what to expect, his eyes searching for some sign of a weapon or a threatening move on the part of the Gray, but there was nothing. Only the alien's expression and the words ringing in Gardner's ears offered any hint that something might be amiss. Gardner reached him just as Praziq and Daryapurkar turned in response to his movements, their faces also masks of confusion.

"Young man," Daryapurkar said, "what are you—?"

Anything else the secretary general might have said was lost as a hum of energy, increasing with every second, began to drown out the voices of perplexed audience members. Light flickered in the air above the floor of the Assembly Hall, and Gardner turned to see a writhing ball of light appear from nowhere, growing and stretching. A maelstrom of colors danced and tangled with one another as the ball elongated.

"A portal!"

Gardner turned at the sound of the deep voice, seeing Max lumbering across the stage toward him. "Evacuate the hall!" Max shouted before his arms closed around First *Dekritonpa* Praziq in a bid to pull her to safety.

"What is going on?" the Gray leader asked, her expression tight with confusion and even what Gardner recognized as fear.

In front of them, everyone in the hall was fighting to move away from where the portal opening was continuing to expand. Unlike other portals he had seen, this one floated in midair rather than resting at or near the ground. His mind filling with visions of Gray soldiers pouring through the conduit and inflicting unchecked carnage upon the assemblage of delegates, Gardner reached without thinking for Daryapurkar. "Sir, you need to come with us!"

Then the howl of energy faded as the portal settled into what Gardner took to be its final form, an opening perhaps three meters across, hanging in the air several meters above the heads of those on the floor. Across the hall, guards and other agents for various leaders emerged from numerous doors along the walls, running past and sometimes over other attendees in their quest to reach whoever they were assigned to protect. President Harrington's Secret Service detail had already closed around him, forming a perimeter even as they began moving him toward the nearest exit.

"What is it?" Daryapurkar asked, even as he allowed himself to be pulled by Max away from the podium and toward the exit at the left side of the stage.

Still held by Max, Praziq looked to Dren. "Trela, what did you do?" Her words were laced with desperate pleading, matching her anguished expression. For his part, Dren said nothing, standing still, his features calm and composed. Gardner felt frustration and helplessness beginning to grip him as he regarded the Gray, and if he thought he could do so without breaking every bone in his hand, he would have punched the alien in the face.

Movement from the portal caught his eye, and Gardner turned to see a metallic blue sphere emerge from the conduit, light from the hall as well as the portal itself reflecting off its smooth, unmarked surface.

His gaze also locked on the sphere, the Chodrecai's answer was as enigmatic as his earlier statement. "I did what was necessary."

29

Lnai Mrotoque emerged from the transport lift, pushing past the slowly opening door and into the expansive hallway leading to his headquarters building's command center. He cursed the door's slow cycle, then realized the stupidity of his reaction.

Focus on the real problem, Lnai. Whatever that might be.

The emergency message had arrived as he worked in his private chambers, his attention mired in the endless stream of situation and readiness reports filtered up to him by his subordinate commanders. Details were sparse, but the message did contain one salient point that sent tremors of fear through Mrotoque's body.

Unauthorized portal activation.

Despite several moments spent trying to reach the commander of the installation where the transgression was alleged to have occurred, Mrotoque had yet to speak to anyone in authority there. That in itself was alarming, but considering it had been the same location from which First *Dekritonpa* Praziq had departed for Earth, something told Mrotoque this latest news was not nearly so ominous as whatever he would learn in the coming moments.

As he drew closer to the command center, his heavy boots echoing off the hall's polished floor, the pair of *fonsata* standing with regal bearing to either side of the entrance's heavy reinforced door rendered the appropriate gesture of respect. Then one of the guards reached for a control panel set into the wall behind him, and Mrotoque again had to wait as the pressure seal disengaged with a hiss of escaping air, allowing the door to cycle open.

"What has happened?" he asked, realizing as he stepped through the doorway that despite being all but devoid of personnel, the command center was awash in activity. Behind him, the door closed and its pressure lock engaged once again, sealing the room from unauthorized access. Mrotoque turned his attention to the array of active holographic displays above several of the room's workstations, broadcasting a variety of computer text and images. News broadcasts—both military and civilian—were evident, but it was the series of displays hanging over the room's central briefing table that demanded his attention. There, he recognized the text and format of standard ordnance reports, of the sort used by installation commanders responsible for the storage and security of mass-casualty weapons. Standing at the table, *Malirtra* Curpen and *Nomirtra* Farrelon—the room's sole occupants—turned at the sound of Mrotoque's voice. When they began to salute him, he waved away the attempt at protocol.

"We are still learning the details, *Jenterant*," Farrelon replied, and Mrotoque noted the uncertainty in the younger officer's voice. "It appears there has been an unsanctioned deployment of a *Koratrel* weapon."

A sense of dread gripped Mrotoque as he comprehended the possible meanings in the *nomirtra*'s words. *Koratrel*-class explosives were among the largest, most powerful ordnance in the Chodrecai military arsenal. Though it was not a thermonuclear device, it was still classified as a mass-casualty weapon due to its sheer destructive power. The Plysserians had similar explosives, and no less than two models that surpassed even the *Koratrel*s, but such weapons had not been employed for nearly a generation, by mutual agreement. On more than one occasion, Mrotoque had marveled at the diplomats for both sides and their ability to agree on which weapons would be used to fight the war, all while seemingly being unable to bring the conflict to a close.

"Where?" he asked, already knowing the answer.

Curpen's expression was response enough, though the *malirtra* still replied, "Earth. The site of the peace gathering. We are still receiving reports from those members of First *Dekritonpa* Praziq's envoy team, who, rather than accompanying her, stayed with human and Plysserian diplomats at a separate site. Initial indications are that the entire complex playing host to the gathering was destroyed."

"How is that possible?" Mrotoque asked, pushing the words past his lips. Staring down at the briefing table, he ignored the status reports and other images on display. He had last spoken to Praziq just prior to her departure for Earth, wishing her well and telling her that he sincerely hoped the proposal she took with her would be well received by the Plysserians and humans. Nothing less than the very survival of the Chodrecai people, as well as the Plysserians, depended on the progress she made on this day.

Feeling his massive hands tightening into fists, Mrotoque forced them to his sides, lest he give in to the impulse to pound them on the table before him. "On whose authority was the weapon deployed?" He all but shouted the question. "Such weapons can only be used on the First *Dekritonpa*'s order."

Farrelon answered, "That information is not yet known to us, *Jenterant*." As he spoke, Mrotoque noted how the younger officer shifted his stance, as though he were uncomfortable. That seemed appropriate, the *jenterant* decided, considering how completely his subordinate seemed to be failing at his duties at the moment.

"Not yet known to us?" Mrotoque moved around the table to get a better look at the status displays. "Are you trying to tell me that someone circumvented every protocol we have for the release of such weapons?" It was a staggering notion, and one that even had been considered, long before the peace gathering or even the war itself. The devastating power inherent in devices like *Kolatrel* explosives required that they be handled with multiple independent layers of security and approvals. This included a frequently changing set of cipher keys, which literally had to be transmitted to the device selected for deployment by the final authority with respect to its use. Rather than any member of the military, that power rested with the First *Dekritonpa*, who had been on Earth and now, apparently, was a victim of the very weapon only she or—in the event of her inability to carry out her duties—her Second *Dekritonpa* should have been able to activate.

Wait.

Mrotoque's stomach lurched as he contemplated the scenario his mind now presented him. "Where is the Second *Dekritonpa*? Is he in his office?" By law, Hodijera Lyrotuw, who had served at Praziq's side since his election to the post of secondary leader to the Chodrecai people, was required to remain in the official residence whenever the First *Dekritonpa*'s duties took her out of the capital city. While he had been a firm supporter of engaging the humans once it became apparent that they would ally themselves with the Plysserians, and had expressed doubt at the viability of meeting to discuss a possible truce, his every word and deed had been focused on supporting the First *Dekritonpa*'s political agenda.

Could all of that have been a lie? Did Hodijera Lyrotuw

really possess the ability to maintain such a convincing pretense? Had he so completely disagreed with Praziq's stance on the war and on pursuing peace with the humans and the Plysserians that he was motivated to seize power? If so, how long had he simply bided his time, waiting for an opportunity to put into motion his own schemes, and what would be the price for his actions?

"Upgrade the security posture around all government and military facilities," Mrotoque said, moving around the table to the bank of control consoles embedded there. "I want immediate status reports from all installation and forward unit commanders. Place the protection details for the Second *Dekritonpa* and the remaining leadership councillors on full alert."

"That will not be necessary, *Jenterant*."

Mrotoque flinched at the sound of a sidearm firing, its harsh burst of energy echoing in the sealed room. Jerking his head toward the report, he was in time to see Curpen slumping across the table, his body disrupting the holographic imagery displayed over its surface. The young officer remained there for a moment before the weight of his body pulled him to the floor in a disjointed, unmoving heap.

"What are you doing?" Mrotoque shouted, ceasing his movements as he turned to look at the muzzle of the weapon Farrelon held, the sidearm appearing like a toy in the *nomirtra*'s hand.

"I apologize for this, *Jenterant*," Farrelon said, neither his eyes nor the weapon moving at all as he regarded Mrotoque. "It is an unfortunate sequence of events, but it is necessary."

Of course. The unspoken statement taunted him from within the depths of his mind. "It is Lyrotuw," he said, his voice almost a whisper. The Second *Dekritonpa* naturally would require assistance, at all levels of civilian and military leadership. How far did his influence reach?

"First *Dekritonpa* Lyrotuw has a vision for our people," Farrelon said, "one which does not include subservience to our enemies, most especially the humans. The very thought of heeding the whims of such a woefully inferior species should sicken anyone who is loyal to our way of life."

Despite the weapon pointed at his face, Mrotoque seethed with growing fury. "How dare you refer to that traitor by an unearned title? Do you realize what he has done? He has condemned us to yet more war, rather than the peace our rightful leader sought." The peace summit obviously was a failure, as would be any further notion of pursuing diplomatic solutions. In addition to the Plysserian chancellor, leaders from every major nation-state on Earth had been in attendance at the gathering. If all of them had been lost, their various governments would at this moment be taking steps to ensure continuity of their leadership. They would be motivated by fear in the face of the appalling attack upon them, and many of those newly appointed leaders would want to seek vengeance. "How can the Plysserians or the humans possibly trust an enemy willing to assassinate its own leader in the name of protecting . . . what, exactly? Our national or cultural heritage? He may well have doomed us all."

"He predicted you would say such things," Farrelon countered, eyeing him along the sidearm's length. "That is unfortunate."

From this distance, Mrotoque could see the younger officer's finger tighten on the sidearm's trigger.

"DiCarlo was right," said Lieutenant Michael Gutierrez as he sipped *gangrel* from the oversized mug. The harsh liquid's aftertaste still made the inside of his mouth feel like he had just ingested battery acid, but it was tolerable. "You do start to get used to this stuff after a while."

"If you can live long enough to get past the hole it's probably eating in your stomach lining, you should be good to go," replied Sergeant First Class Marty Sloane. The men sat on a low-rise bench fashioned from pieces of scrap wood found in the remnants of the abandoned industrial complex where Javoquek and his unit currently made camp. Sloane regarded the dark, steaming contents of his own mug, which he had brewed soon after rising for the day. "This stuff tastes like it was filtered through a linebacker's jockstrap. Makes me actually miss the coffee we used to make in Afghanistan, and you don't *want* to know how we made *that*." He held up the mug in mock salute. "Here's looking up your doctor's address."

Gutierrez smiled as the sergeant took a hearty drink from the cup, then grimaced as he swallowed. "I suppose we could break down and use the real coffee we brought with us." During their first visit here and the mission to retrieve the Plysserian scientist *Laepotic* Wysejral, the time spent with Javoquek's people as well as Sergeant Major DiCarlo and Sergeant Russell had been a learning experience. When Gutierrez was offered the assignment of leading a small reconnaissance team to *Jontashreena* for extended operations with Javoquek's unit, he made certain to apply those lessons. That included the foresight to pack along various essential equipment with a small yet treasured selection of "comfort items." While he was not a smoker and only drank on social occasions, the thought of prolonged periods without coffee was too terrible to contemplate. The small packets of coffee contained in standard military rations were fine in a pinch, but nothing beat the Colombian blend he preferred and that he procured from a small grocery store on the street corner near his apartment.

The shop owner was surprised when Gutierrez arrived late one evening and purchased the entire stock of the coffee, with only the explanation that he was being deployed and would not be back for some time.

Shaking his head at the suggestion, Sloane replied, "We should save the good stuff for special occasions. After all, we might be here awhile." To emphasize his point, he reached into his uniform jacket's left breast pocket and extracted a small circular container that Gutierrez recognized as the packaging for the sergeant's favorite chewing tobacco. "Just like I'm nursing this stuff. I don't know what I'm going to do when my stash runs out."

"You could always quit," the lieutenant said, eyeing Sloane with a wry grin.

Sloane frowned. "Now, that's just plain crazy talk, sir. I already gave up cigarettes, and I don't remember the last time I had a decent shot of bourbon, and since being here means I've elected for celibacy, the least I can do is enjoy a good chew now and then."

"Well, if the choices are you being celibate or you not chewing," Gutierrez replied, "go ahead and feel free to stuff that whole can in your mouth."

"Roger that, Lieutenant," Sloane said, chuckling as he rose from the bench and turned to his daily task of inspecting his weapons and equipment. It was a habit he practiced whenever he was deployed. Gutierrez had served with the sergeant in both Iraq and Afghanistan, had pinned on the stripes for his last two promotions and the two Bronze Stars he wore on his dress uniforms, and long ago had come to respect the man's near fanaticism when it came to preparedness.

Be it the maintenance of weapons and equipment, training, or planning for battle itself, Marty Sloane gave no quarter when it came to being ready to fight. When in command of subordinates, either within the safe, ordered confines of a base or the chaotic, ever-changing haze that was a forward area in harm's way, he accepted few excuses for any failure, and none resulting from negligence, complacency, or laziness. In his mind, a combat unit's inherent responsibility was to be ready for war at a moment's notice, and anything threatening that goal was an obstacle to be avoided or overcome at any cost. His attitude was contagious, filtering down through the ranks to the unit's lowest-ranking soldier, and it was a mind-set that was vital to the survival of such a unit once the shooting started. Because of that, Gutierrez had learned early on to shut the hell up and let the man do his job. The results spoke for themselves: While their units in Iraq and Afghanistan had sustained casualties, none of those could be blamed on the failure of a soldier to follow instructions, or on the training he had received, or on the breakdown of that trooper's weapons or gear.

"Lieutenant Gutierrez," a voice called to him from the doorway of the small room where he and Sloane shared sleeping quarters, and Gutierrez turned to see *Malitul* Javoquek regarding him. Though he was still learning to read Plysserian and Chodrecai facial expressions, the lieutenant was able to note that the Blue officer looked almost stricken.

"What is it, Javoquek?" he asked, moving toward the doorway. "Is something wrong?"

The Blue nodded. "Very much so. There has been an attack on Earth, at the site of the peace summit. The structure where the meeting was being held has been destroyed, along with much of the immediate surrounding area, killing everyone inside that perimeter."

"Jesus fucking Christ," Sloane said, denial embracing every word. "Are you shitting me? How?"

Javoquek lowered his head, casting his eyes toward the floor. "A mass-casualty weapon was employed. In addition to our chancellor, your president and leaders and other dignitaries from the various members of your United Nations number among the dead."

Reeling from the blunt statement, Gutierrez allowed himself to sink down to his makeshift cot. "Dear God," he whispered, feeling moisture at the corners of his eyes even as his breath came in fluttering, rapid gasps. "How did it happen?"

"We are receiving only sporadic reports, of course," Javoquek replied, "and there is much that is still not known. However, it is my understanding that there has been a disruption within the Chodrecai government, and that the attack was carried out by a rogue group."

Gutierrez shook his head in disbelief. "They staged a coup?"

Pausing as though verifying he understood the meaning of the word, Javoquek said, "We do not know. Hodijera Lyrotuw has long been a proponent of continuing the war with us, and according to our reports was one of the most vocal detractors of the First *Dekritonpa*'s proposal to seek peace both with us as well as Earth. While the Chodrecai supreme military commander was a supporter of hers, there are many high-ranking *tilortrel* who disagreed with that stance. However, no evidence has been found to implicate any of those officials."

"If they ordered the murder of their own leader," Sloane said, "they're probably not going to want that to get out."

Javoquek replied, "Regardless, many Chodrecai believe that neither my people nor yours can be trusted to negotiate in good faith for peace."

"Well, it sure as hell's not going to happen now," Gutierrez snapped. "The fucking trust issue just got ass-raped." When Javoquek regarded him with a quizzical expression, the lieutenant waved away the statement. Rising from the cot, he tried to pace but found his efforts thwarted by the too-small room cluttered with his and Sloane's equipment.

"What about the Chodrecai people? Surely, they can't all be buying into this."

"Lyrotuw has always been a leader capable of galvanizing a populace," Javoquek said. "It was one of the reasons First *Dekritonpa* Praziq wanted him in her administration. Now he is using that trust to tell the people that he renounces what happened; that Praziq's stance still was a threat to the security of the Chodrecai people; that she lacked vision to lead them during this time of crisis. Military and civilian officials are being removed from office and branded as traitors. Some of those individuals have been murdered."

Frowning, Gutierrez reached up to rub his forehead, closing his eyes and trying not to imagine the United Nations General Assembly evaporating in a cloud of molten ash. "You can't tell me the people would stand by and allow this guy to just take over if there was any hint he might've killed his predecessor and anyone who supported her. We know there are Chodrecai who side with us, so where the hell are they?"

"They exist," Javoquek said, "but they are outnumbered by those who will follow where Lyrotuw leads, because they fear that their way of life will be lost if any accord is reached with your people or mine. Still, Praziq held enough support, among the civilian populace as well as the military, that there is bound to be all manner or disruptions and unrest. If it comes to light that Lyrotuw was behind this, there may well be a revolution across the Chodrecai Confederation."

"And here we sit," Sloane added, "stuck in the middle of the whole mess."

Ignoring the sergeant, Gutierrez instead asked, "What do we do now?"

"For now, my orders are to remain here," Javoquek replied, "but I have been tasked with gathering as much information as possible regarding the current state of Chodrecai military units in this region. My superiors believe that there may be instances of field commanders who choose to disobey the orders they receive due to their loyalty to Praziq. These units may well surrender to Plysserian forces, or even turn on other units who have pledged allegiance to Lyrotuw."

"Fuckin' A," Sloane said, nodding. "Where do we send the memo?"

"Our people definitely can help with the recon," Gutierrez said. It would be useful to provide a human perspective of the situation here, he decided, particularly if what he suspected might happen actually came to pass. "Is this intel getting sent back to Earth?" Though he said nothing aloud, he could not help the thought echoing in his mind. If the situation among the Chodrecai populace, and especially its military, was anything like Javoquek described, then the tragedy that had taken place on Earth might also have provided an unparalleled opportunity for the Plysserians and their human allies to seize the offensive once and for all.

Javoquek nodded, regarding Gutierrez as though reading his mind. "Indeed. The new chancellor has already made public statements asserting the continued alliance between our peoples, and his belief that this appalling attack on both our worlds has made our bond all the stronger." For the first time, he attempted what passed for a smile on a Plysserian's face. "It seems we will enjoy one another's company for the foreseeable future."

"Wonderful," Gutierez said. *And something tells me this planet's getting ready to have all the humans it can handle.*

30

"We're coming to you live from the White House, where Vice President Martina Valenti is about to take the oath of office, which will make her the next president of the United States, and the first woman ever to occupy that office. Of course, the historic nature of this day is overshadowed by the events that have conspired to elevate her to that august position."

Everyone in Op04-E's Situation Center stood or sat in silence, watching the map wall as its four center screens, which had been configured to display a single image, broadcast the lined, weathered face of the veteran news anchor. When the anchor spoke, Bruce Thompson heard the slight break in the older man's voice. His eyes were puffy, indicating the emotional strain he likely was under as he struggled to conduct himself with the bearing and dignity that had been his hallmark for nearly a generation.

"It's been almost fifty years since a U.S. president has died while in office," the anchor continued, "the last being John Fitzgerald Kennedy in November of nineteen sixty-three. On that occasion, our nation mourned, as did our allies. Today, every man, woman, and child grieves together as scenes like the one about to unfold in the Oval Office take place in capital cities around the world."

The man was not exaggerating, as Thompson could see merely by shifting his eyes to take in the imagery from other screens on the map wall. Along with the death of the Plysserian chancellor, Nhiraplo Ghaas, every member of the United Nations, 192 member states, had lost at least one primary leader. In some cases, delegates or surrogates had been sent to Geneva, but even those had been high-ranking individuals within a particular government. In addition to President Harrington, the United States had lost the secretaries of state and defense, along with ten senators and sixteen members of the House of Representatives. All of the support personnel sent to accompany those officials also numbered among the victims. Add to that the loss of all those in attendance who carried out the same functions for each of the U.N.'s member states, and the tragedy was fast becoming a nightmare scenario unimagined even by the most inspired writers of political or techno-thriller fiction.

"We've got a NEST team on-site," said Nancy Spencer from behind Thompson, approaching where he sat at an unoccupied workstation on the Situation Center's top tier. As Thompson turned to face her, he saw that Spencer's eyes were red and puffy, a sign that she had been crying but had pulled it together in order to continue her work. "They're not reporting any radiation, at least nothing we're familiar with. According to Plysserian commanders who've had a chance to review the video footage, they're certain the device was a conventional explosive—their version of a MOAB."

Sighing, Thompson shook his head. He never had been a fan of the unseemly nickname, "Mother of All Bombs," given to the GBU-43/B Massive Ordnance Air Blast explosive, but he could appreciate the image it evoked. The bomb, normally dropped from a C-130 or similar cargo aircraft, was capable of devastating everything within a 140-

meter radius. According to on-site accounts from Geneva, the device detonated inside the Assembly Hall had leveled everything within a 325-meter radius, which included a sizable portion of the Palais des Nations and its surrounding grounds.

"Small favors, I suppose," Thompson said, with no trace of humor or irony in his voice. "At least we don't have to seal off Switzerland inside plastic and duct tape." Despite the caustic remarks, he still was relieved to hear the news. Units from the military's Nuclear Emergency Support Team, tasked with managing the containment of any area affected by nuclear contamination, whether by explosion or accident, had been augmented with Plysserian personnel and equipment in recent months. In the early days of the conflict, many leaders—the late President Harrington among them—had feared the Chodrecai might simply begin sending their versions of nuclear weapons through the portals to Earth.

Thompson reached for the cup of coffee situated near where his right hand rested atop the workstation desk. He brought the mug to his lips and took a sip, recoiling with a frown at the taste of the cold, acrid liquid. How long had it been sitting there unattended? Grunting in disgust, he returned the cup to the desk and pushed it away, working his tongue around the inside of his mouth in a vain attempt to lessen the foul taste. *Is it too early to switch to scotch?* He turned his attention back to Spencer, who was staring past him at the map wall. When she noticed him looking, she pointed toward the screens. "They're administering the oath."

Thompson swiveled his chair around so that he could watch the proceedings. The image on the map wall's center screens was the one captured by a single camera positioned before the president's desk in the Oval Office. Vice President Martina Valenti, her auburn hair cut in a short, feminine style that left her neck exposed, wore a conservative gray skirt with matching jacket over a cream silk blouse. She looked tired, Thompson thought. No, he decided, that was not it. Watching her facial expressions as she stood in front of the desk, holding up her right hand while placing her left on a Bible held by the Chief Justice of the United States Supreme Court, Thompson could see that that Valenti was exerting enormous effort to maintain her bearing, to appear presidential, even regal, as the Chief Justice administered the oath of office.

"How did she find out?" Thompson asked.

"Same as the rest of us," Spencer said, moving to take a seat at the adjacent workstation to the general's left. "She was watching the assembly in her office. Secret Service had her in the bunker about fifteen seconds after the bomb went off. She spent the next half hour kicking and screaming to get out of there until the official word came down that there were no survivors in Geneva." The initial assessment, offered minutes after the explosion, had relayed the same information, but it was not until military jets from the United States and several other countries flew over the site that confirmations began to come in. While it was possible that a few survivors might still be found in the rubble at the outer edges of the blast zone, it was universally understood that there would be none in what had been the Assembly Hall and now simply was "Ground Zero" or "the point of detonation."

Watching as Valenti repeated the oath at the direction of the Chief Justice, Thompson wondered what must be going through the woman's mind at this moment. Though she had worked with President Harrington during the past months to offer steadfast leadership to the American people in the face of the alien crisis, the shock of suddenly being thrust into her predecessor's role under such catastrophic circumstances had to be taking a toll on her. In addition to the demands now placed upon her shoulders, she also was faced with communicating and working with leaders around the world forced into the same precarious position she now occupied. Some nations would be better prepared than others to handle the transition of power and responsibility to a designated successor, but what about those governments that lacked such arrangements? Would they prove to be allies, hindrances, or even enemies in the days to come?

That's her job, Thompson reminded himself with no small amount of bitterness. *You've got your own problems to worry about right now.* Indeed, one of the first orders received from the vice president, issued even as she waited for the chief justice to arrive in the Oval Office, had been for Op04-E and the Joint Chiefs to accelerate the planning for Operation Clear Sky. It was a bold directive, and one that Thompson knew could not have been easy for Valenti to give, considering her well-known position on wanting to pursue peace with the Chodrecai. She had been one of the most vocal proponents for the summit in Geneva. Was she feeling betrayed by what had happened, and reacting now out of some base need for retaliation? No, the general decided. So far as he knew, Martina Valenti had never made a rash decision in her entire political career. Doubtless she had received security briefings in the aftermath of the tragedy and, based on the information provided to her by General Andrew Grayson and his people, now was issuing orders intended to keep things moving in as orderly a manner as possible despite the chaos now gripping the entire world.

It'll be like juggling cotton balls in a hurricane.

Lumbering footsteps from behind him made Thompson turn in his seat, and he looked up to see the bulky, muscled physique of a Plysserian soldier standing at the door leading from the Situation Center's top deck. For an instant, the general thought he was looking at Makoquolax, the Blue soldier who, with Marine corporal Brad Gardner, had become such a valuable consultant in the months since the aliens' arrival. That feeling was just as quickly replaced by a momentary pang of sorrow as he realized that both Gardner and Max had been at the General Assembly by request of President Harrington, in effect making the duo 4-Echo's contribution to the sacrifices made in Geneva on this day.

Damn.

"Yes?" Thompson prompted as his eyes met the Blue's. He realized now that he recognized the alien as one of the Plysserian military advisors attached to Op04-E. While the alien's name escaped Thompson, the insignia on his tight-fitting uniform designated the Plysserian as a *malitul*—at least, that's what Thompson thought it sounded like—a mid-level officer somewhat equivalent to a captain or major, as it had been explained to him. "I'm sorry," he said, genuinely apologetic. "I can't remember your name."

"*Malitul* Ojaletyrolid, General," the Blue replied, unfazed by Thompson's statement. "Some of your people have taken to calling me 'Ojo' for the sake of simplicity." In his oversized left hand, Ojaletyrolid held what the general recognized as the Plysserian version of a personal digital assistant or even limited-function laptop computer. "We have been receiving a number of intelligence updates from various operatives deployed to *Jontashreena*."

Thompson had been expecting that. Receiving such information had become far simpler in recent weeks following the deployment of recall beacons to field agents on the alien planet. The beacons, designed originally to help with the quick location of a conduit endpoint for a portal generated on Earth and bound for *Jontashreena*, also worked quite well with respect to sending burst messages through miniature, less power-intensive versions of the astonishing interplanetary channels.

"What have you got?" Spencer asked, extending her hand for the portable data display Ojo carried.

Passing the device to her, the Blue replied, "The attack on our leaders appears to have been ordered by members of the Chodrecai government acting on their own agenda."

"I got that much from watching their leader getting blown up along with ours," Thompson snapped, immediately regretting the tone of the remark. Pausing, he forced himself to draw what he hoped was a calming breath before continuing, "I apologize. That was uncalled-for. Are you saying their government has been overthrown?"

Ojo shook his head. "Not in the strictest sense. Subordinate leaders within First *Dekritonpa* Praziq's advisory council, working with military leaders loyal to them rather than to her, appear to have orchestrated a transition of power. The Second *Dekritonpa* has assumed the mantle of leadership, and has ordered the removal of several advisors as well as their highest-ranking military leader and several of his subordinate commanders. Like Praziq, these individuals supported peace initiatives with your people as well as mine."

"They were killed because they wanted to end the war?" Spencer asked, frowning as she looked up from the data display. "You can't tell me the Chodrecai civilian populace will stand for that. How do the ones responsible for this expect to explain what's happened?"

"Chodrecai civilian news outlets have been under government control since the earliest days of the war," Ojo replied. "According to our informants, the deaths will be explained as having taken place during the incident here."

Leaning forward in his chair until his elbows rested on his knees, Thompson reached with both hands to rub his temples. "Jesus," he breathed. "What are they after with this? They can't possibly want to keep fighting. That's just insane."

"I do not believe it is simply a desire for the war to continue," Ojo said. "Based on what we know of those responsible, they fervently disagreed with First *Dekritonpa* Praziq's peace proposal because they feared it would not ultimately be beneficial to Chodrecai society. There is much concern that such an arrangement with my people and yours would result in them being subservient to us, their cultural identity and personal freedoms curtailed or removed as a consequence of lingering distrust and even hatred."

Spencer shook her head. "That's ridiculous."

"But not unprecedented," Thompson countered. "History's full of examples. I suppose you can't blame them for feeling that way, not after all this time. On the other hand, that doesn't make our lives any easier."

Ojo replied, "Indeed. For those now in power, and the many who apparently support them, the only way the war can end is with a Chodrecai victory and Earth in their control."

"They can come and get us," Thompson said, allowing the first hints of his anger at what had transpired in Geneva to push through his usual composed demeanor. He had managed to maintain his composure throughout the morning as more information and images came out of Geneva, but watching newscasts and reactions from around the world during the past few hours had eaten at him. With a single strike, an entire civilization had been attacked, all the worse because the assault had come from an enemy who chose to hide its aggression behind the cloak of peace. The people of Earth, who throughout history had waged war upon one another for the feeblest of reasons, seemed now to be crying out with a single pain-shattered voice. Did they seek justice or vengeance?

Does it matter?

Pushing himself back in his chair, he considered what Ojo had told him. "Assuming this is all true and that they're operating mostly by keeping the Chodrecai people uninformed as to the details of their little coup, they can't have universal support. There are already splinter groups working to help us; somebody somewhere is going to figure out the truth behind what's happened. Won't that increase support for ending the war peacefully?"

The Plysserian officer replied, "That would seem likely. Though many senior government and military leaders loyal to First *Dekritonpa* Praziq have been removed, there remain any number of lower-ranking officials who also pledged to support her."

Spencer added, "The sudden shift in power would certainly cause at least some disruption." She turned in her chair, looking to Thompson. "Think about it. They're going to spend time and resources figuring out who's on their side and who isn't. That's going to have an effect on readiness and organization, which you know they'll be worried about because they can't believe we're not working on how to strike back at them. There are bound to be groups and factions loyal to Praziq that are keeping their heads down, waiting for the right moment to take some kind of retaliatory action. Hell, for all we know, there might be plans to rebel in the event of something like this."

"I don't know if I'd go that far," Thompson said, frowning, "but the notion that whoever's now in power played their cards too early has some merit. They chose to make their move in conjunction with the peace summit, no doubt for the dramatic impact it would have, there and here. What if they've underestimated the fallout from what they've done?"

"Exactly," Spencer replied. She said nothing else, but Thompson could tell from her expression that she was employing discretion in the presence of Ojo and because even here, in the allegedly secure confines of the Situation Center, unwanted ears might be listening. Still, he knew what she was thinking.

Striking back at the Grays. They might never get a better chance.

"*General Thompson,*" a voice called through the bunker's intercom system. "*You have a secure call from the president. General Thompson, incoming secure call from the president.*"

"That didn't take long," he said, glancing over his shoulder to the map wall, which had been reconfigured now that President Valenti's ceremony was concluded. If she had given a speech, he had missed it, though he doubted she had wasted time on such formalities. Instead, she seemed determined to jump into the chaos of her new role with both feet.

Sounds like a good plan to me.

Nodding toward Ojo, he looked to Spencer. "At least now, we'll have something interesting to talk about."

31

Every muscle, every bone, every last skin cell in Colin Laney's body hurt.

The straps of his pack bit into his shoulders. Every square millimeter of the bottoms of his feet felt as though he were walking across molten lead, and he was certain he had walked right out of his skin down there. His uniform was heavy with his own sweat, clinging and rubbing and binding and pinching him in places not seen by anyone since his mother had changed his last diaper a lifetime ago. His armpits were raw, his crotch itched, and the weight of his gear pushed him into a perpetual stoop. Perspiration ran down the sides of his face, burning his eyes and stinging the corners of his mouth.

Colin tried to ignore all of that.

Instead, he kept his eyes on the pack of the man in front of him, listening to the rhythm of the different pairs of feet around him as Second Platoon, along with the three other platoons that constituted Kilo Company, marched along the narrow paved trail. Somewhere behind him and over his left shoulder, someone was shouting marching cadences, and most of the Marines around him were responding in kind. It took Colin an extra second to realize that he also was chiming in; he had simply blocked the singing out of his mind. How long had *that* been going on?

"Fuck," hissed Private Joshua Wolfe, one of the other graduates of Platoon 3003 and now one of Colin's closest friends. "Are we there yet?"

Reaching for the runner's watch he had removed from his wrist and secured to a ring on his equipment harness, Colin checked the time. Kilo Company had begun their fifteen-kilometer forced march at 0500, just before daybreak on what was fast becoming another hot, humid day in North Carolina.

"Just after zero nine hundred," he said, keeping his voice low so as to avoid the wrath of the instructors. "I think we're almost there."

Wolfe grunted, trying to shift his pack to a more comfortable position on his shoulders. He nodded toward one of the Plysserian soldiers marching alongside them. "Look at that shit. He's not even breathing hard."

Glancing at the alien soldier, Colin nodded. "Yeah, he's making us look bad." Like the Marines around him, the Blue carried a pack on his wide, muscled back, along with body armor and a pulse rifle. Second Platoon currently boasted forty-four members, of which thirteen were Plysserians. Though it was understood by everyone that the Blue soldiers surpassed their Marine counterparts in almost every measure of physical fitness and strength, their presence here carried a larger purpose. Plysserians had been integrated into the training unit as a means of fostering camaraderie between humans and aliens who in short order likely would be working and fighting in close proximity. They also facilitated the Marines' efforts to familiarize themselves with both Plysserian and Chodrecai weapons and tactics. For their part, the Blues did their best not to seem superior to their human companions as they bested them in the training's array of physical challenges. Still, more than one Plysserian soldier had commented on the abilities demonstrated by several of the Marines—Colin included—when it came to marksmanship with the alien weapons, as well as their ability to adapt to the fluid, chaotic situations thrown at the platoons during training.

Ignoring his own discomfort, which seemed heightened by the fact that the Blues in the platoon seemed to be exhibiting no outward signs of exertion, Colin glanced once more at his watch. According to the day's calendar of events, the march would take until 0930, but Colin guessed they were ahead of schedule. Endless stands of pine trees and scrub brush had given way to the first hints of what passed for much of the "civilization" at Camp Geiger, a satellite base attached to the much larger and better-known Camp Lejeune, the Marine Corps installation occupying 630 square kilometers of North Carolina real estate.

Instructors had bounced the young Marines from their racks at 0330, in much the same manner Colin's drill instructors had done every morning at Parris Island. After nearly three weeks of intensive combat skills training within the immersive environment of the Marine Corps School of Infantry, the men of Kilo Company—and the women, five in Second Platoon and twenty-eight in the company— were about to employ everything they had learned to this point while undertaking a sixty-hour "battle skills exercise." As Colin's instructors had described it, the exercise would make "the Crucible" he and his fellow recruits had completed at boot camp seem like a family vacation in comparison. Getting past the coming training evolution essentially signified completing the course. Upon graduation, those Marines who did not hold infantry-related assignments would be sent to other installations for further training in their designated occupational field—communications, supply, motor transport, computers, or one of numerous others—whereas Colin and others like him would continue with advanced combat training.

Though he had aced every test and vocational aptitude battery put before him and qualified for any job the Marine Corps had to offer, Colin had chosen to be a "grunt," the backbone of the Corps, around which all other activities and priorities were centered. To hear anyone in the infantry say it, there were two types of Marines: grunts, and everyone else. Everyone else was a "pogue," an oxygen thief, a REMF—rear-echelon motherfucker. In truth, many grunts respected the work performed by Marines in noncombat roles, because it was understood that if those jobs were not done, grunts did not get paid, did not eat, and were not provided with the ammo and explosives they needed to blow shit up and kill bad guys. Colin understood this, even if he chose to give good-natured shit to those friends of his in the platoon who soon would be administration clerks, radio operators, mechanics, or whatever.

Of course, in the days following the attack in Geneva, more than a few of the Marines in Colin's platoon had met with instructors and officers, requesting reassignment to a combat arms field. Anger and betrayal fueled much of that change of heart, just as the terrorist attacks of September 11, 2001, had motivated many young men and women to enlist in the military, answering a call to duty many of them could not explain yet still understood with a raw, visceral intensity. The explosion that had obliterated the U.N. assembly had taken with it one of the last lingering hopes for finding any sort of peaceful resolution to war with the Chodrecai. Now the news coming from the aliens' home planet was that the Grays' leadership castes were in disarray, falling victim to civil unrest as the Chodrecai population disagreed on how to deal with the humans. While many called for peace, others viewed Earth as salvation from their own war-ravaged planet and were willing to take it at any cost.

Such sentiments existed here, as well. With many governments still reeling from the loss of their own leaders, many people around the world were crying for the conflict to be halted before it could escalate to consume both civilizations. Others, angered over the attack, which had occurred under a flag of truce at a gathering of peace, wanted vengeance in the form of humanity's full military might brought to bear against the Chodrecai and anyone on Earth who supported them. Perhaps the leaders of both worlds eventually would work through their own inner turmoil and find a way to unite in peace, but Colin was not counting on it.

"Company!" a voice shouted from somewhere near the front of the column.

"Platoon," called out Sergeant Grant, one of Second Platoon's instructors.

"Attention!" the voice at the front finished, and all the Marines in the Kilo Company immediately fell into step with one another, marching with whatever vestige of bearing still remained within their weary bodies. Colin heard groans of discomfort coming from several of the Marines around him, while the Plysserians in the platoon remained conspicuously silent as they fought to match their longer strides to the measured pace required to keep the Marines in step and in line with one another.

A moment later the command was given for the company to halt, after which the Marines faced to their left. Colin and his companions watched as Kilo Company's commanding officer, Captain Harriman, exchanged a few brief, inaudible comments with First Sergeant Morehouse, the company's senior enlisted Marine. Both men still wore their packs, helmets, and body armor, just like the troops they led, having been at the front of the column for the entire fifteen kilometers. Morehouse saluted Harriman before the captain turned and walked off, at which time the first sergeant turned to face the assembled Marines.

"First, Third, and Fourth Platoons," he called out, every word delivered in clipped, precise cadence, "when you receive the command to fall out, you will fall out to the field behind you, eat chow, and take water. Corpsmen will be on hand to treat any foot issues or other ailments. Second Platoon, you will drop your gear in place, keeping your weapon and one canteen, and form a school circle on my position. *Fall out!*"

"What the fuck?" Wolfe said, making no effort to hide his surprise. "What did we do now?"

Colin did not answer as he loosened the straps on his backpack and let it slide from his shoulders. The removal of the weight from his back and neck felt sublime. Wolfe had raised a valid point. Had Second Platoon committed some as yet unknown infraction? While the field rations—MREs, or Meals Ready to Eat—that formed a large portion of their diet at SOI these past weeks in no way resembled fine cuisine, the simple fact was that Kilo Company had not eaten breakfast prior to the start of the march, and now Colin was hungry. Even the packet of cold tuna waiting for him in his pack sounded good right about now.

Okay, let's not get carried away.

"Any day, people," Morehouse snapped, his gravelly voice reminiscent of Colin's drill instructors.

The men and women of Second Platoon moved into position around the first sergeant, and as he dropped to the grass and folded his legs in front of him so that he could rest his M16 rifle in his lap, Colin caught sight of a new arrival. An older Marine, his face tanned and lined, was approaching them, dressed in service green trousers and a khaki shirt bearing the rank insignia of a sergeant major. The midmorning sunlight glinted off polished black shoes as well as the gold or silver accessories attached to several of the numerous ribbons he wore above his left breast pocket.

"Any idea who that is?" Wolfe said, taking a seat to Colin's right.

Colin shook his head. "Beats me." This was not Sergeant Major Pineda, the Marine combat training battalion's senior enlisted member, so who was it, and what was his interest in Second Platoon?

Shut up and listen, and you just might learn something.

As though reading his mind or—more likely—impatient with the Marines' progress, First Sergeant Morehouse said, "All right, ass in the grass, mouths shut, eyes on me." He waited a few moments as the last stragglers sat down. The Plysserian members of the platoon, as had become customary, stood at the rear of the group, their large legs not conducive to sitting cross-legged for any length of time. Morehouse began to pace back and forth before the assemblage, eyeing the Marines and their Blue counterparts as he talked.

"You know from watching the news that things are heating up. You've probably heard rumors of a big push being planned to the alien planet. There's no sense in playing dumb about it; I think we all know what's going to happen, and that it's going to happen sooner rather than later. That's why you've been doing what countless Marines before you have done: training for war, to be ready to answer the call to go and fight wherever our leaders send us. That's what Marines do. That's what we've always done, and it's what you will soon be doing."

A chorus of war cries—"Oo-rah!" and other variants—erupted from the platoon. Morehouse tolerated it for a moment before waving the young Marines to silence. He then gestured toward the sergeant major, who to this point had stood quietly to one side, hands clasped behind his back as he watched the proceedings.

"This is Sergeant Major DiCarlo. If that name rings a bell inside any of your skulls, it's because he's the one who was trapped along with another Marine on the alien planet. For months, he worked, lived, and fought with Blue soldiers just like the ones you've been training alongside. He's been dealing with politicians and bureaucrats for weeks since he got back." Morehouse aimed a long finger at the Marines. "But he's flown down here today to talk to *you*, so you will give him your undivided attention." Turning to the new arrival, he offered a formal nod. "Sergeant Major."

DiCarlo stepped forward, shaking Morehouse's hand before stepping in front of the platoon. "Good morning, Marines," he began, a small smile curling the edges of his mouth. "It's been a long time since I've had the opportunity to say that, and I never get tired of saying it." Another round of motivated whoops and war cries answered him, and the sergeant major's smile grew wider.

"You've spent the past few months of your life learning to be Marines, and training for war. First Sergeant Morehouse is right: When Marines aren't fighting a war, they're getting ready to fight the next one. It's not a pretty thought, but neither is war itself. Only those who've actually seen combat can really comprehend the desire to never have to do so again. They can understand that only by training and preparing for war do you have any real chance of succeeding—and surviving—when you're sent to fight. There used to be a bumper sticker that Marine recruiters handed out. It said, 'Nobody likes to fight, but somebody has to know how.' That's you, Marines."

He paused, looking at the faces staring back at him, and Colin was certain he saw fatigue and resignation in the older Marine's eyes. This was a man who had seen a lot of action in his time. The array of ribbons on his chest bore testimony to his participation in conflicts from Vietnam to the Persian Gulf and who knew how many places in between. The topmost decorations, a Silver Star, a Bronze Star, and a Purple Heart—the last two featuring attachments indicating multiple awards—told Colin that Sergeant Major DiCarlo had been far more than a simple "participant."

"I can see on most of your faces that you're wondering why I'm here," DiCarlo continued after a moment. "It's because of what you've been doing since you arrived here. Kilo Company is one of several joint human-Plysserian combat units being trained at bases around the world. There are only twelve such units in the U.S. military. They're small, mobile, and they've been designed with particular missions in mind. Your unit, Second Platoon, has scored some of the highest ratings when it comes to joint tactics and exercises. The Marines have adapted to Plysserian weaponry and equipment with remarkable results." As he spoke, his eyes fell on Colin, who now felt uncomfortable for reasons he could not identify.

"The training you've received, beginning with boot camp, has been accelerated. You were some of the first participants to undertake such training, and the skills you've learned will soon be put to the test. Why am I here?" DiCarlo paused, clearing his throat. "I simply wanted to meet you, here, and before you undertook your final training. I wanted to meet the Marines I'm going to war with."

There were no cries of jubilation or bravado this time. Instead, the Marines of Second Platoon merely exchanged looks of uncertainty.

"Your unit is among the best when it comes to the joint training you've completed," DiCarlo said. "Your ability to work together, human and Plysserian alike, is a unique bond, and yet it's not at all unlike the bond that has always united fighting men. We're going to put that to the test, Marines, because we, and other units like ours, will form the tip of the spear as we take the battle to the aliens' home planet."

Several gasps and murmurs filtered from the platoon. DiCarlo said nothing to stifle the reactions, instead watching the Marines in silence until the responses died down. This was it, Colin realized. Earth was going to strike back. He saw several tentative hands rise into the air, their owners doing their best to swallow whatever lumps had formed in their throats, but DiCarlo waved for the hands to be lowered.

"Save your questions," he said, "for now, at least. There's nothing specific I can tell you at this point, anyway. You'll find out what you need to know soon enough. For now, concentrate on your training, and the men and women around you. The rest will take care of itself." He nodded once more to the assembled group. "Carry on, Marines. I'll see you soon."

No one said anything as DiCarlo turned and left, and even First Sergeant Morehouse did not move right away to usher the platoon off to whatever was next on the training schedule. Perhaps he felt, as Colin did, that a moment of reflection was in order.

They were going to war.

I'm going to war.

J-Day
Operation Clear Sky

32

Standing at the window of his office and looking down at the Situation Center, Bruce Thompson sensed the tension gripping his people.

Here we go. Again.

It was not all that long ago that he had stood in this very spot, fidgeting as minutes seemed to drag into eternity while waiting for battles in Washington, Beijing, and Moscow to begin. As he had on that occasion, he now watched as the men and women under his command went about their duties in like fashion and with comparable focus. They occupied various workstations along the room's three tiers, or moved back and forth across the center as they performed some task or errand. Final preparations here were nearly complete; all that remained was to receive status reports from commanders on the ground at the different launch sites, indicating their readiness to proceed. No matter how hard he tried, Thompson was unable to keep his eyes from moving to one of the banks of digital clocks positioned above the map wall.

"The calm before the storm," he said, to no one in particular.

From behind him, he heard General Andrew Grayson say, "I've always hated this part." Thompson turned from the window and saw the JCS chairman regarding him from where he sat in one of the two chairs in front of Thompson's desk. In his right hand, the general held a stout, octagonal glass filled to the halfway point with single malt scotch from the Op04-E director's private supply. The bottle rested atop the desk, next to another glass that Thompson had filled, then ignored.

Turning from the window, Thompson offered a somber nod. "Waiting sucks, doesn't it? I always just wanted to get on with it."

The period just before battle was one Thompson dreaded. Time slowed, seconds stretched, the world fell away, and all that remained was the warrior, his weapons, and the thoughts of what lay ahead. It was at these moments that a soldier's imagination was his worst enemy, his mind conjuring visions of all the horrors war brought with it. Thoughts like that had troubled Thompson before each mission he had undertaken as a young, supposedly unflappable combat pilot. Being shot down and captured by an enemy force was only the start; it was what might happen afterward that always had unnerved him in the hours leading up to receiving the "go order."

"I was scared shitless the night before we hit the ground in Desert Storm," Grayson said, taking a drink. "It was my first real combat mission. I just missed Vietnam, and I always seemed to be assigned to the wrong unit whenever they sent Marines somewhere like Grenada or Beirut. For the first Gulf War, it's not like it is now. Most of the younger Marines—even the grunts—had never seen combat to that point. I had a first sergeant in my unit who was in Vietnam and who had helped dig his buddies out of the embassy in Beirut, but that was it. The rest of us were rookies." He shook his head, smiling as though recalling an amusing memory. "Thank God for that salty son of a bitch. If not for him, I'd probably have shot my own damn foot off that first night."

Thompson nodded as he moved around his desk and all but fell into his high-backed leather chair. "Well, I suppose if there's anything good to be taken from having fought two or three wars over the past few years, it's that we have more vets on the ground. They'll be there for the new guys." He had read the reports with details pertaining to recruitment and training over the past several months. Though the ranks of the American armed forces were filled with veterans of one conflict or another, there still were a staggering number of troops who had joined only within the last six months. It was the same in countries around the world, the global military buildup on a scale not seen since the 1940s. Though conscription accounted for a significant percentage of the new recruits, that count was dwarfed by the number of volunteers, particularly in the United States. As they had for every previous conflict, the sons and daughters of America had answered the call to arms, determined to do their part in allegiance not simply to their country, but to their planet. The catastrophe in Geneva had spurred even greater activism in people around the world seeking to join their nation's military, to the point that services were turning away hopeful candidates.

Will there be anyone to write books about the men and women going into battle today? It was not the first time Thompson had posed the question, though he had yet to ask it of anyone other than himself. Would future generations see fit to immortalize the events about to unfold in literature or film? How many memorials would be erected in order to pay tribute to the price exacted on this day? Those who fought the Second World War—along with those who had lived through the hardships of that time without ever seeing combat or even serving in the military—had come to be known as the Greatest Generation. What title would be given to the people living through the current crisis?

Hell, will there even be anyone left to give a damn?

"The president called me about an hour ago," Grayson said. "Wishing us all luck, that sort of thing." The general shook his head. "Hell of a way to settle into a new job." In the weeks since her swearing-in ceremony, President Valenti had been at the center of a whirlwind of activity as countries around the world struggled to recover from the loss of multiple leaders, all while directing what likely would be the largest military operation in the history of human civilization. "You think the top brass was feeling like this the night before D-Day?" Grayson asked, reaching for the scotch bottle. "I'm not talking about what they said they were doing in all those interviews and books and movies and all that crap. Seriously, what do you think they were really doing that night?" He poured himself another scotch.

Thompson sighed, holding up his glass. "I'd hope they were feeling as uneasy as I am right now. I know I should've tried to catch a nap or something, but how in the name of hell do you sleep the night before you send thousands of people into harm's way? Christ, I'm not even the one making that call, and look at me: I couldn't fall asleep if you shot me with a tranquilizer gun."

After months of planning, training, and covert deployment of troops and materiel—spurred on in recent weeks as the world continued to recover from the loss of so many prominent leaders in Geneva—this was the day that likely would determine the course of human history. Plysserian forces both here and on the aliens' homeworld also were readying themselves to carry out their role in the largest military operation Thompson had seen outside of a history book.

J-Day.

He, along with Grayson and the other generals who would oversee the campaign from Op04-E's secure Situation Center, already had received a heartfelt message from the president, thanking them for their efforts to this point. Later, once combat operations had commenced and enough forces had been deployed to their designated landing zones and the first situation reports began to filter back from *Jontashreena*, the president would address the American people and indeed the entire world. Unlike the D-Day invasion, Operation Clear Sky would benefit from the latest in twenty-first-century human communications technology as well as that of their Plysserian counterparts, and even captured and exploited Chodrecai materiel. Coordination of the battle would be on a scale unimagined by anyone on that crisp June morning in 1944, with countries around the world engaged in simultaneous operations that would—if all went to plan—startle and overwhelm beleaguered yet still formidable Chodrecai forces. While Operation Overlord had benefited from months of preparation and capitalized on a regimen of training and resource allocation in place since the earliest days of America's involvement in World War II, this campaign had come together in much less time and would be utilizing the military units of far more nations than had participated in D-Day.

Operational security had been paramount, with every precaution taken to prevent information about the campaign preparations from leaking. Multiple versions of the invasion plan had been created, each one denoting sites on *Jontashreena* that would serve as portal endpoints. The different plans were coded, creating a signature in the event any of them were leaked. Fewer than ten people in the entire world knew which of the plans was the correct one. Ground commanders would receive their final mission briefing materials at the last possible moment before deployment, their training and assignments broad enough that adapting to whatever their orders outlined would—in theory, at least—be simple. In many cases, conventional forces were being deployed to secure footholds on the alien planet, from which they would push outward in bids to seize or destroy key military and government targets as well as vital points of infrastructure.

If secrecy had been the watchword during the planning stages, then audacity was to be the maxim once the operation commenced. Countries who once viewed each other as enemies had united in cooperative spirit in order to fight their common foe. While Thompson knew that political and cultural ideologies were so ingrained as to prevent an easy truce from taking hold, differences had—for the time being, at least—been set aside in order to deal with that larger threat. Perhaps the old schisms would return, but that likely was a problem for a day that was weeks or months in the future, if not longer.

And that's only if we win.

"I wish I was going," Grayson said, pausing to sip his drink. "I've never been one for sitting in the rear. I know it goes with this job, but that doesn't make it any easier."

Thompson nodded. "I hear you. One morning, the flight surgeon grounded me because I had the flu. The fucking flu, in 'Nam, of all places. It made me sick to my stomach to watch buddies of mine heading off to their planes while I had orders to stay in my bunk. I was about to sneak out the back door and head to the flight line, but the doc had probably seen that a few times. He was waiting for me in the hallway." He smiled as he recalled the memory. "Threatened me with hourly enemas if I didn't go back to bed."

"Normally you have to pay extra for that kind of thing," Grayson replied, one of the few occasions the general had allowed himself a moment of levity in all the time Thompson had known the man. Shaking his head, Grayson regarded his half-empty glass for a moment before finishing its contents in a single swallow. He grimaced as the scotch burned its way down his throat, and then glanced at his watch. "I guess it's time to find out whether the past six months have been a waste."

According to the plan drawn up by military and civilian strategists working with JCS as well as Thompson's team at Op04-E, the initial stages of the campaign relied on information gathered on-site by reconnaissance teams sent through portals to target locations across Chodrecai-controlled regions of *Jontashreena*. With the guidance of Plysserian military officers, twenty-six locations had been selected, some of which were chosen not as points of attack but instead in the hope of drawing Gray forces to those landing zones and away from actual targets. The target locations, which had been selected for legitimate strategic value, ranged in importance from civilian and military command-and-control centers to energy oversight and transfer points to what Plysserian tacticians identified as key transportation hubs.

Working in their favor was the notable lack of Chodrecai air- or spaceborne reconnaissance assets. Though both sides had at one time employed numerous orbiting satellites for communications and for weather research and prediction, as well as a vast array of military operations including covert surveillance, many of those satellites had been destroyed at the war's outset. As a consequence, there were enormous gaps in coverage, which either side had used to maximum effect as the war continued. Moving assets into positions on *Jontashreena* without attracting too much attention would not be the major obstacle. It was what likely would occur once those assets engaged Chodrecai resistance that bothered Thompson.

Even with reduced numbers and depleted resources, the Chodrecai still posed enough of a threat that engaging them head-on was not a desirable course of action. The Grays still possessed sufficient numbers of attack aircraft as well as large-scale armaments and indirect fire assets—their version of artillery, which like the rest of their weaponry was more advanced than anything on Earth. While the inclusion of comparable Plysserian troops and materiel would help to mitigate those factors, the simple fact was that engaging the Grays on their home soil posed a significant risk to human forces making the transit to the alien planet.

To that end, Grayson and his people had elected for a campaign of misdirection and rapid deployment and maneuver with respect to human forces traveling via portals to *Jontashreena*. Smaller, more mobile teams would be dispatched first to verify a landing zone's viability. If a site was determined to be usable and—more important—reasonably free of enemy resistance, full-scale landing operations would begin. For those areas where a landing was deemed inadvisable, alternate sites had already been selected. Plysserian scientists working with some of the brightest human minds Earth could offer were at this moment continuing to update the calculations necessary to generate a conduit to connect the two planets at the desired location.

"Don't worry," Grayson said, rising from his chair and buttoning the front of his green uniform jacket, "even if the advance teams send back a thumbs-up, there're still a lot of things that can go wrong once the shooting starts. You know that old saying: No battle plan has ever survived initial contact with the enemy."

"Tell me about it." Thompson nodded, reaching up to rub his temples. "It's not the first wave of troops going through that worries me; it's the ones who are supposed to follow them for backup. If this doesn't work, those first groups will be about six kinds of fucked."

As a means of countering the limitations of the portal generators developed by human engineers with Plysserian assistance, Grayson and his team had come up with the notion of alternating portal launch points to the same landing zone. Once the first portal generator assigned to send troops to a given endpoint had to shut down in order to cool its power systems, a second origination site would come online, establishing its own conduit to the same destination and allowing the passage of reinforcements for the first groups. This step would be repeated one more time, further augmenting forces already on the ground at the landing site. This action would be mirrored at sites around the world, involving the military might of dozens of nations. The theory was that by the time the third wave had completed its deployment, the original set of portal generators would be ready for use, starting the cycle again and repeating it for as long as necessary to move all of the troops, vehicles, and equipment through the conduits. Intervals had been built into the timetable to allow for delays in getting portals back online, and included contingencies in the event a landing zone was cut off from any portal.

Yeah, Thompson mused. *It's called "dig in and pray."*

His ponderings were interrupted by the sound of the intercom system flaring to life. *"General Thompson, General Grayson, your presence is requested in the Situation Center."*

Pausing out of habit before the mirror on the door to his private bathroom to check that his uniform and its accessories were in place, Thompson turned to Grayson. "Here we go."

Grayson nodded, his expression grim. "God help us all."

33

As the back hatch of the *Lotral* transport craft cycled open and the wind brought him his initial whiff of predawn air on *Jontashreena*, Staff Sergeant Angus Feder's first thought was that the place smelled like the unwashed ass of a well-traveled prostitute.

"Dear Jesus!" he said, bringing up his hand to cover his nose as the craft settled into its landing pattern. "What the hell is that supposed to be?"

From behind him, he heard the voice of *Zolitar* Niila-jun, one of the Plysserian soldiers attached to Feder's unit. "Chemical waste," the alien called out, shouting to be heard above the *Lotral's* engines. "It is a by-product of the manufacturing process for the power cells that are this facility's primary export."

Feder heard a disgusted grunt, and turned to see Sergeant Cooper Harris regarding the Plysserian soldier with an expression of disdain. "They didn't say nothin' about toxic waste," Harris said. Shaking his head, he reached up to rub his right shoulder, which still caused him pain from the bullet he had taken weeks earlier. "We're invading an alien planet, storming one of their factories, and along the way we'll eat seventeen kinds of shit from God knows how many Chodes they've got hiding in there, and if we manage to survive all o' that, we'll get cancer from whatever noxious fart gas we're breathing on the way in. Fuckin' lovely."

Nodding toward Harris's shoulder as the other man continued to rub it, Feder offered a wry smile. "You could've stayed home, you know, in the rear with the rug rats and the cripples and the cowards."

"What, and leave you swingin' in the wind, lost as a newborn pup crying for Mommy's tit to suck on?" Harris affected a mock expression of disappointment. "You know you wouldn't last five minutes here without me." Making a show of taking a deep breath, he reached for his crotch and patted himself there. "I'm just sorry I didn't have a chance to let my boys blow ballast before we left, seein' as how the damned things'll shrivel up and fall off from whatever crap I'm taking in right now."

"Your hand on the rag again?" Feder asked, laughing without waiting for his friend's response. Glancing over his shoulder, he saw Niilajun studying them, his expression unreadable. "What's the matter, Niles?" he asked, employing the nickname bestowed upon the Plysserian soldier a few weeks earlier by Corporal Jaxon Kelly.

"I know that you and Sergeant Harris, as well as many of the humans I have encountered, have a propensity for engaging in inappropriate humor," the alien said, "but I question its value prior to our entering battle."

Grinning, Harris said, "This guy has 'em lining up at the clubs, don't he?"

The exchange again made Feder laugh. To Niles, he said, "No worries, mate. Just a little harmless yabbering to pass the time before we step off. Helps take your mind off the shitstorm we know's comin'."

Truth be told, Feder was ready to get on with the mission. After being cooped up for nearly a week in the temporary barracks provided for them by the Plysserian unit with which his detachment was partnering for this first phase of operations, he was getting edgy. The more time they waited, he figured, the more time the Chodes had to sniff out what was going on and prepare themselves to repel the coming assault.

"Stand by!" shouted a new voice, this one belonging to Lieutenant Michael Schuster. He was standing next to the now open rear hatch, holding a support grip with his left hand while his right arm cradled his Steyr A99, the Australian Army's equivalent to the M470 rifle developed with Plysserian assistance by the Americans. As platoon leader, Schuster's would be the first boots to hit the ground when the time came to disembark the transport. Feder considered the man a solid officer, who had seen action against the Chodes in Australia as well as in support of other countries' actions against the alien enemy in different locations around the South Pacific in recent months. Still, he was not the most congenial type when it came to playing cards or having a beer with the troops at the end of a long training day. That honor belonged to Lieutenant Matthew Bartus, a good friend and one hell of a soldier, who had been one of the first Australian casualties of the Chodrecai soon after their arrival on Earth.

Sure wish you were here with us now, mate.

Holding himself steady with another of the handgrips as the transport tilted forward, Feder looked over his shoulder and counted heads. All of the platoon's forty-five members were standing, either holding themselves steady by gripping support straps or else busying themselves with final checks of their weapons and gear. Intermingled with the platoon were the other members of Niles's contingent of Plysserian soldiers. The *Lotral*'s passenger complement was one of dozens currently engaged in the assault operation. Still others were waiting for the signal to begin their own approaches as other transports off-loaded their troops and cleared the area. Feder felt his stomach lurch as the ship slowed its speed and banked to his left. He peered through the open hatch, watching the ground below him spin as the transport spun into position for landing. Even without the benefit of running lights in the predawn darkness, he still was able to make out patches of grass and other vegetation scattered among broad swaths of dirt and rock, with several craters also visible.

During the past several days, this entire area had been subjected to near-continuous bombardment by fighter and bomber craft as well as indirect fire from fixed and mobile assets positioned kilometers away in several different directions. The attacks had focused on the area surrounding the plant, rather than the installation itself, which had been selected as a primary target for seizure due to the enormous amounts of ammunition and other materiel it produced for Chodrecai military forces. It was one of five such facilities scattered across Chode territory, and according to the information Feder's unit had been given during their mission briefing, the plant originally had belonged to the Plysserians, falling into Chode hands years earlier. The facility was monstrous, consisting of several buildings and storage warehouses spread across what amounted to more than five square kilometers, occupying more land than the small town of Bullfinch in Western Australia where Feder had spent most of his childhood. Its value to the Chodes was immeasurable, but it could not simply be destroyed, as the Plysserians wanted it back. It and sites like it around the world, once retooled for civilian use, would serve as a vital component in any rebuilding efforts once the war was concluded.

Of course, the bloody Chodes know that, too, which is why they'll be defending this place with every swinging dick they can find.

"We're taking fire!" Schuster called out, an instant before the entire *Lotral* shuddered around Feder. He felt the shock in the soles of his boots and transmitted through the handgrip he held, and the bulkheads around him groaned in protest as something struck the transport's outer hull. The ship reverberated again in rhythmic fashion as its own weapons were fired, and when Feder placed his hand against the smooth wall he could almost feel the power being unleashed as the transport fought back at the attempts to shoot it from the sky.

"I guess this means we're not going to surprise them?" Harris said, smiling like a maniac and reaching for a support hold as the transport angled to the right, the deck plates shifting beneath the soldier's feet.

Behind Feder, Corporal Jaxon Kelly replied, "Now it's getting exciting."

Aerial reconnaissance conducted by Plysserian pilots had confirmed the presence of hundreds of Chodes forming a defensive perimeter around the installation, along with field artillery—mobile pulse cannons and other, larger field armaments—to supplement their manpower. Though indirect fire assets had not yet been found, no one with a functioning brain cell was ruling out the presence of such weapons. The days of bombardment had been effective in mitigating the size of the defense force, and intel reports showed no significant air support at this location, as the Chodes were redirecting most of those assets to other areas in response to the multiple attacks being carried out by human and Plysserian forces. None of that mattered to the situation faced by Feder and his fellow soldiers: an enemy who was dug in and waiting.

So let's go get 'em.

He now heard the faint sounds of weapons fire beyond the confines of the transport and the howl of its engines.

Dropping to one knee, Feder was able to see dozens of Plysserian *Lisum* attack craft, far ahead of where the transports were landing. They swirled about the sky, spinning and diving as they unleashed their weapons at various targets on the ground. It was still dark enough that he could not make out anything resembling troops or weapons emplacements on the ground, though there was no mistaking the now familiar flashes of pulse rifles blinking across the uneven terrain. The farther the transport descended, the better his view of the landscape ahead of him, and now Feder could make out shadows and other shapes set out in somewhat regular fashion across the terrain. Anything out in the open like that would have received no small amount of pounding from the aerial phase of the assault, but there was only one way to be sure how many of those positions might still be occupied by troops or larger weapons.

Gotta go knocking on doors. In addition to foot soldiers like Feder and his platoon, the operation was supported by dozens of ground assault vehicles, the Plysserian equivalent to tanks and other components of a mechanized infantry. On the ground below him, Feder could make out the dark shadows of *Jenitrival* armored assault vehicles, each mounted with a quartet of heavy pulse cannons. Feder had heard that model of battle wagon referred to by other soldiers as an "octopus," due to its cannons' ability to fire at simultaneous, independent targets in different directions.

A howl of energy and the sensation of air being pushed out of the way rattled the inside of the transport's passenger compartment, and Feder flinched as something wet splashed across his face. There was a heavy thump as Lieutenant Schuster's helmet, along with whatever remained of his head, slammed into the bulkhead even as his body fell limp against the man behind him. That soldier screamed in horror as he was swathed in blood, and he frantically kicked the blood-soaked helmet as he fought to move away from the open hatch.

"Fuck me!" Feder said, hunkering down and trying to fuse with the nearby bulkhead as the transport fell the final few meters to the ground. More shots were coming now, some of them screaming overhead while others slammed into the ship's hull. "Get the hell out!" he shouted over his shoulder. "Move your fuckin' arses, boys!"

Holding his Steyr across this body, Feder leaped through the open hatch, his boots sinking a few centimeters into the soft earth and absorbing the impact of the jump. He fought for balance and pushed himself forward, running from the transport and hearing the sounds of the other soldiers following his lead.

"Spread out!" shouted Cooper Harris, and Feder looked in the direction of the sergeant's voice to see his friend directing the movements of the rest of the platoon, getting them away from the transport and onto the ground in search of whatever cover they could find.

To either side of his unit, Feder saw dozens—no, hundreds—of shadowy figures moving across the broken terrain, soldiers disembarking from other transports and making their initial push forward. Now he saw the familiar, horseshoe-shaped profiles of Chode attack fighters—only a dozen or so but still enough to cause problems—trying to engage the Plysserian craft. The air screamed with the sounds of pulse weapon fire, and he was able to make out dozens of energy flashes along the ground far ahead of him, showing him the Chode positions. Behind them, he saw the lights and silhouettes of the buildings comprising the processing plant, their illumination making visible the ghostly outlines of larger weapons placements. Many of the pulse cannons' oversized muzzles pointed skyward as they attempted to engage the landing transports as well as the supporting attack craft, while others aimed across the landscape, searching out smaller, softer targets.

All around him, Feder heard shouted orders and cries of fear and frustration. He tried to ignore them, just as he fought to block out the horrific sight of the enemy weapons finding their first targets. Less than fifty meters to his right, an unknown soldier's legs were vaporized, the rest of his body falling to the ground. The new body armor and helmets, developed with Plysserian assistance, were effective enough against Chode small arms fire, but the larger weapons were another matter.

"We're gonna get sliced to shit out there!" Harris yelled, his eyes wide with terror. Feder's own body trembled as he fought to channel his own fear into the energy needed to push ahead. Looking up, he saw several *Lisum* fighters sweeping in low, their pulse cannons flaring in rapid succession, the weapons chewing into the ground and throwing dirt and rock into the air, along with what Feder hoped were a few Chode asses.

"Keep moving!" Feder yelled, taking charge of the platoon in the absence of Lieutenant Schuster. He repeated the order, using his free hand to gesture for the rest of his soldiers to follow him. Slowly, handfuls of centimeters at a time, Feder began the agonizing process of crawling toward their objective.

34

If there was one thing Wu Ailiang did not like about flying the Plysserian *Lisum* fighter, it was that the attack craft conveyed almost no sense of motion. A pilot with the People's Liberation Army Air Force for almost all of his adult life, he had long ago become accustomed to the pull of gravity and inertial forces on his body while at the controls of an airplane. The faster the plane was moving, the more difficult and intense the maneuvers through which the craft was put, the more alive Wu felt. In contrast, learning to fly the alien ship, while a fascinating, exhilarating experience in its own right, was lacking something. There was no arguing the *Lisum*'s superior speed and performance, or its instantaneous response to his every command. His single complaint—if it honestly could be called that—was that the fighter's advanced inertial damping technology, while certainly useful in allowing him to put the craft through maneuvers that would have been impossible for most human-manufactured aircraft, removed all but the most fleeting sensations of movement. He supposed that was an advantage, with the dampers having all but removed the risk of blacking out during high-speed turns and other aerial acrobatics.

Still, as his hands caressed the once alien controls, which he now understood and operated as extensions of his own body, Wu wished he could feel himself *moving*. He had lost a lot of that awareness after making the transition from fighter jets to slower, less maneuverable bombers, but now he felt as though he were sitting inside a simulator. Only the passage of the clouds in the sky and the ground below indicated that the *Lisum* was doing anything except sitting idle. Without those visual cues, Wu might well be tempted to lean back in his pilot's chair and sleep.

Any such notions retreated in the face of the incoming weapons fire, which the *Lisum*'s onboard threat assessment and response systems registered much faster than even Wu's reflexes could manage. The fighter banked to his right, angling toward the ground far below and accelerating. Keeping his eyes not on the forward windscreen but instead on the cockpit's broad, sloping console, he scanned the rows of multicolored indicators and controls set into the black, smooth surface. Though he was sure he had felt the craft lurch in response to at least one impact from incoming fire, the ship's inertial damping systems were functioning normally, and none of the console's monitors or other readouts were registering any damage.

"They know we're here," said his copilot, Meng Jun Sen, as he pointed to the computer display situated at the center of the console. The screen provided a 360-degree representation of the area around the attack craft. An array of cameras and other sensors installed across the fighter's outer hull provided all manner of telemetry regarding the *Lisum*'s current position relative to other craft or threats. On the screen, multiple pale dots were shown inbound from its outer edges toward the center, where the *Lisum* was denoted by a blinking magenta dot.

"It looks that way," Wu replied, now happy that the ship's computer was capable of identifying and reacting to the inbound weapons fire, leaving him free to fly the craft—with the computer's help, of course—and Meng to oversee the weapons. They had learned during their compressed training evolutions that the *Lisum* attack craft were capable of addressing threats from the air or the ground, without pilot intervention. It was a feature for which Wu at first could see no practical application. What if the computer initiated evasive maneuvers and the decision resulted in the ship being directed into a field of fire while attempting to elude the first hazard? He could not believe that any seasoned pilot of any worth would stand by and leave such responsibilities to a machine, reducing the person in the seat—and in the line of fire—to nothing more than a passenger.

His skepticism was somewhat eased during training, when he observed the onboard computer reacting to multiple, simultaneous threats at speeds far greater than any human—or Plysserian—pilot could achieve. There were a few simulations in which the systems had been overwhelmed by having to deal with too many problems at once, but those scenarios had been engineered as tests to measure the software's maximum capabilities, rather than generating a situation likely to be faced by pilots and their ships.

Meng said, "I'm not picking up any other traffic on the radar, or whatever the Plysserians call it." He pointed to the screen. "Must be the mountain placements they warned us about."

Nodding, Wu replied, "Long-range weapons. We're probably in their range by now." In addition to the information regarding their target, an electromagnetic telemetry collection and dissemination facility—the aliens' equivalent to a radar tracking station—pre-mission briefing materials had included information about the Chodrecai equivalent to land-based antiaircraft weaponry, which used radar guidance systems to home in on targets. According to the file he had read, such weapons could lock onto a craft over distances exceeding one hundred kilometers. According to the *Lisum* onboard computer's navigational database, a mountain range perhaps thirty kilometers beyond the target site was believed to be home to a cadre of fixed weapon stations, acting as a defensive line for anything that might pose a threat to the installation now on Wu's targeting screen.

"It's only going to get worse as we get closer," Wu said. "Engage targeting protocols."

Meng nodded. "Acknowledged," he said, reaching for the laptop computer that had been installed on the console to take the place of the original controls, which remained out of their reach in the oversized compartment. When he keyed instructions in to the computer, several of the other consoles blinked, their displays wavering for a moment before returning to normal. The reaction made Wu wince, and he shook his head at the latest of the numerous little "glitches" that plagued the efforts of human and Plysserian technicians to link components for use by human pilots, such as interfacing their helmets with the comm system. Other changes permeated the cockpit—for example, the original pilot seats had been replaced with seats designed for physiques decidedly smaller than those of Plysserian pilots. Many of the controls set into the console were original equipment, though the uppermost rows of switches and displays were out of reach for most humans. The functionality of those components had either been rerouted to portable monitors and other equipment attached to the console, or else deactivated after being deemed nonessential.

"I guess this is it," Meng said, turning to look at Wu. Meng's features were impassive, and even though Wu saw the anxiety in his copilot's eyes, he still sensed the man's resolve to carry out his duties. The radar tracking station that was their primary target, one of more than three dozen scattered across the continent, served as a vital link in the Chodrecai military's electronic intelligence-gathering apparatus. Though several of the stations had been damaged or destroyed over the years by Plysserian forces, replacement facilities had been erected, and defense of the installations had been increased. Though the majority of the stations had been targeted as part of the multifaceted campaign devised by military leaders from nearly every country on Earth, Wu knew that not all of those actions would be successful. Chodrecai defenses would at least be sufficient to thwart some of the attacks, so every victory during this phase of the massive operation was critical.

We cannot fail.

It had been a long journey for him to arrive at the forefront of the immense battle currently unfolding across this planet, which was so different and yet so similar to his own. While fighting the Chodrecai in service to the Chinese people had been his reality for months, he never believed he would find himself in this situation and on this day, as part of a multinational coalition seeking to attack the alien threat to Earth at its very core.

Faced with more ships than pilots qualified to fly them, Plysserian leaders had turned to human military commanders for assistance. Given the stakes, there was no shortage of pilots from around the world volunteering for the chance to fly aircraft built on another planet. Wu Ailiang had been among those volunteers, anxious for a chance to make a worthwhile contribution to the war effort. As a result, he had all but learned how to fly all over again, but the time and energy he expended during training was more than worth it. He knew that eventually the new skills he was acquiring would allow him to make some measure of recompense for the disaster that had resulted from his first encounter with the Chodrecai nearly a year earlier.

With the Chinese army engaging the alien invaders across the country, the order had been issued to attempt sending a nuclear weapon through a portal to the alien planet, in a desperate bid to force the Chodrecai forces to check their advance. Wu, along with his fellow pilot and longtime friend, Bai Peitan, had drawn the unwelcome assignment. Wu himself was the one to arm and fire the missile that carried the bomb to its target. Instead of entering the portal and making the transit to *Jontashreena*, the missile instead came into contact with the conduit itself. What no one could possibly have foreseen was the horrific effect of the resulting detonation. The violent disruption of the tremendous energies harnessed and manipulated to create the portal had resulted in devastation unparalleled in human history. The blast radius covered nearly five hundred kilometers, killing tens of thousands of people and inflicting an indelible wound onto Chinese soil.

Not a day passed that Wu didn't think of that tragedy or his role in the destruction that had been unleashed. His superior officers and no less than three different psychologists all had done their best to reassure him and Bai that they were not at fault, but months passed before Wu was able to accept their counsel. Bai, on the other hand, could not forgive himself, and within weeks of the incident was found dead in his quarters—a gun in his hand, a bullet in his head, and a bloodstained note on his lap.

Angered as much at his friend as he was at his own inability to identify any warning signs, Wu refused to exonerate himself for his failure to act on Bai's behalf, adding to the guilt he carried from the failed mission. Instead, he channeled his anger and despair into constructive energy, focusing on his duties and pledging that those lost on that day would not simply be the first Chinese victims of the Chodrccai.

A telltale indicator tone sounded from the console, and Wu looked to the display readouts before him, confirming what the alert signal was telling him. "Targeting sensors are online," he said, forcing his hand not to adjust the control that would override the *Lisum*'s threat recognition and response systems. Ignoring the impulse to take total command of the craft, he instead allowed the ship's computer to perform its share of the workload as his hands moved to the maneuvering controls. In response to his commands, the ship banked back to the left and angled its nose downward, shedding altitude while increasing airspeed.

"Arm weapons," he ordered. "Stand by to fire."

Reaching for the targeting controls, Meng nodded. "Weapons armed."

The threat detection system chose that moment to go insane.

"What is that?" Wu asked, hearing the alarm in his own voice. He swallowed, forcing down the emotion and directing himself to concentrate on the tasks at hand.

Meng pointed to the display monitor. "We're being targeted from multiple locations." His head bobbed back and forth as he gathered information from different readouts, displays, and indicators. "The mountains ahead of us, and points on the ground behind us as well as between us and the tracking station."

"What?" Wu asked, his brow furrowing in confusion. "There was nothing in the intelligence reports about those ground sites."

There was no time to discuss the discrepancy before the *Lisum*'s onboard systems took over, directing the craft into a dive that sent it hurtling downward. Even with inertial damping in operation, as he looked through the windscreen at the ground rushing up to meet him, Wu still felt the need to push himself back into his chair.

"It's an ambush!" Wu shouted.

"How could they know we were coming?" Meng asked, his voice now an octave higher than it had been a moment earlier.

Wu had no answer for his friend's question, and for the moment he did not care. What now mattered was adapting to this unexpected turn of events and continuing with the mission.

"We're not abandoning the objective?" Meng asked.

"Negative," Wu responded. "Get a fix on the target and prepare to fire."

His hands sliding across the maneuvering controls, Wu looked up from the console and through the windscreen in time to see the tracking station come into view. A sprawling grid of metal beams lay at an angle in the side of a low hill studded with all manner of protrusions, which Wu took to be transmitters and receivers, perhaps batteries or other power storage components and possibly even weapons of some sort. Wu had no desire to test that theory. A squat structure stood at the center of the vast grid, unmistakably the station's control facility and the focal point of this operation.

"Target locked," Meng said. Wu did not acknowledge the report, concentrating instead on maneuvering the *Lisum* into firing position. The ground was now quite visible through the windscreen, close enough that he could make out patterns in the overgrown vegetation. He also saw lights coming from the tracking station, as well as the obvious signatures of Chodrecai pulse weapons aimed at him.

A shrill alarm sounded in the cockpit, and Wu's eyes turned to the display monitor in time to see more pale dots than he could easily count converging on the cursor at the screen's center.

"They're blanketing us!" Meng shouted.

Wu's stomach lurched as he felt the entire craft shudder around him. A disjointed chorus of thumps and thuds sounded from somewhere outside, and when the ship turned to evade other incoming fire, Wu realized that his body was responding to the change in direction.

"Inertial dampers are out," Meng said. When another alarm filled the cramped cockpit, he pointed toward the console. "We're losing maneuvering control."

Wu did not need that report, realizing that the controls beneath his fingers were not responding to his touch with the same crisp efficiency to which he had grown accustomed. Each attempt to make a course correction was met by silent protest from the console, alert indicators flashing a harsh crimson.

Then the *Lisum* rocked again, and this time half of the console's lights and readouts went dark.

"Firing control is out!" Meng reported, his hands moving across the console in an attempt to compensate for the damaged systems.

Then something punched through the windscreen, and the copilot's head and upper torso disappeared in a blast of red wash that splashed the entire cockpit. Wu blinked away the mist that sprayed across his eyes, and when he wiped at his face his hand came away coated in streaks of dark red. He looked toward Meng and saw that what remained of the copilot's body still twitched and spasmed in its seat, blood flooding the deck beneath its feet. Wu only barely forced back the urge to vomit. It took every scrap of self-control he still possessed to keep his hands on the console, continuing to guide the *Lisum* on its attack course.

He felt the ship tremble again as it absorbed the brunt of another assault. Scanning the rows of blinking indicators before him told Wu everything he feared. Systems across the board were giving up, he realized, feeling the sluggishness in the maneuvering controls. Through the windscreen, the tracking station was growing larger with each passing second even as the ship continued to be pounded by incoming enemy fire. The ship was doing its best to avoid the worst of the attacks, but it was not enough. For a moment, Wu wondered if the computer would simply give up before the craft itself was destroyed. How much time did he have left? Seconds?

Fighting against the ship's constant buffeting as it bore the brunt of the multiple attacks, Wu reached to the console and without a moment's hesitation disengaged the threat response system. Applying more thrust, he pushed the wounded craft ever faster. Every strike against the hull was channeled through the instruments and up through the deck to his body, but he ignored all of that. It took two tries with the maneuvering controls, but then the ship's nose angled downward once more. Outside, the tracking station all but filled the window.

This won't set things right, Peitan, but it's all I have to give.

For the fourth time, Belinda Russell checked the placement of the AN/PED-1 LLDR—Lightweight Laser Designator Rangefinder—verifying that the squat tripod on which the unit sat was stable. Next, she inspected its two components, the target locator and laser designator modules, ensuring that they were operating correctly. Despite heavy cloud cover, the light from *Jontashreena*'s three moons was still sufficient for her to examine the unit without using her flashlight. Not that it mattered, as she was certain she could perform the checks with her eyes closed, thanks to the two weeks' worth of extensive training she had received. With its embedded software and straightforward user interface, operating the LLDR was as simple as navigating the menus on her digital video recorder or portable music player back home.

Too bad this thing doesn't have pay-per-view.

Feeling eyes on her, Russell looked up from where she knelt behind the LLDR, catching sight of the five Marines chosen by Simon DiCarlo to be his team for this initial phase of the operation. All of them were lying prone in the tall orange-brown grass, their dark uniforms and painted faces helping to break up their outlines among the vegetation and the shadows. Lying a few feet from her was DiCarlo himself, situated beneath the low-hanging branches of a large tree. Most of his face was cloaked in shadow thanks to the wide-brimmed boonie hat he wore, with the cloud-obscured moonlight reflected in his eyes and making them appear as two disembodied orbs in the dark.

"What?" she whispered. Then, realizing why he was watching her, she smiled, shaking her head. "Yeah, I know. It's fine, so leave it alone?"

DiCarlo nodded, returning the smile. "You know me too well."

"Well, for what it's worth," Russell countered as she once more looked through the LLDR's thermal sight, "I'm not touching anything. Just deciding if I've got the best target or not."

Peering through the sight provided her with an unfettered view of the installation a mile away from and slightly above her current position. Once more she counted fourteen structures, all of them resembling warehouses with rounded bulkheads at either end, and each one tethered to at least two of the other buildings with what appeared to be a slapdash collection of pipes and connecting walkways. Most of the buildings bore signage of varying sizes and colors, most of which were lost in the haze of the LLDR's viewfinder. Series of lights were mounted atop each structure, with more lining the compound's perimeter, each beam picked up by the targeting sight as a ghostly halo.

It was not the buildings that drew her attention so much as the massive craft hovering over one of the structures.

"God damn, that's a big ship," said Lance Corporal Colin Laney from where he lay in the grass next to the tripod, holding a pair of night-vision goggles to his face.

Russell nodded in agreement. Like most of the Plysserian and Chodrecai aircraft she had seen, the immense tanker craft employed a series of eight vectored thrust engine ports in order to suspend the ship above the ground, or in this case the fueling depot. While she had always ascribed a sort of beauty to the different combat craft she had encountered, Russell could not do the same for the ungainly tanker, which most definitely was designed with function taking precedence over form. A squat rectangle with a recessed windscreen formed the head of the ship and housed the cockpit, according to the information she had been given. It in turn was attached to an unseemly web of metal support struts and crossbeams, along the outside of which were positioned the eight downward-facing engine ports. Inside this structure were collected four octagonal modules. As had been explained to Russell and her team, these units stored fuel, and each could be disconnected from the tanker's support structure and delivered to separate destinations. A pair of larger, blunt engine ports emerged from the hull at the ship's far end. Even from this distance, the low, constant drone of its engines still reached her.

"Big enough," she said, keeping her voice low for the sake of noise discipline, on the off chance that their talking might draw the attention of an alert guard or someone else wandering around. Though the team had swept the area with night-vision goggles and the LLDR's thermal sight had revealed no unwanted parties in the vicinity, Russell knew that now was not the time to be taking chances. Peering through the LLDR's viewfinder, she saw that the tanker was still connected to the structure below it by a trio of thick connector conduits, which swayed from side to side as a consequence of being beneath the ship's engine wash. She estimated the length of the tanker as somewhere in the neighborhood of five hundred meters. From this distance, targeting the craft would—in theory, at least—be child's play.

Looking away from the tripod setup, Russell noticed Laney looking up at her. Even through the haphazard patterns of green, brown, and black paint covering his face, she still saw the quizzical expression clouding his features. "Something on your mind, Marine?"

Laney blinked several times as though startled, turning away as he shook his head. "Sorry, Sergeant. I didn't mean anything. I was just . . . I mean, I . . ."

"You didn't expect to be fighting alongside a woman, did you?"

Reacting as though slapped, Laney again shook his head, this time in such rapid fashion that Russell feared it might separate from his neck. "No, not that. I mean, there were a few women in my platoon back at MCT, and we knew there'd be more once we got to our units. I guess I just expected all the women to be newbies, like me, but hell, you've got more time fighting the Grays here on their planet than anyone. Except for Sergeant Major DiCarlo, maybe."

"Actually," Russell replied, smiling, "I've got him beat, too. Remind me to tell you the story of how I hauled his ass out of the fire."

DiCarlo released a heavy mock sigh. "I'm never living that down, am I?"

"Not a chance," Russell replied, her grin widening.

In truth, she considered Laney's reaction to her presence here fairly tame, at least compared to other remarks she had heard in the weeks since her return to Earth and the start of training for this operation. American military doctrine had only recently begun shifting to include women serving in combat arms roles. Even before the aliens had come, that paradigm had evolved to some extent, owing in large part to the conflicts in Iraq and Afghanistan, where every service member faced some risk of encountering enemy action on any given day. Now that humans faced an enemy that literally could appear anywhere, the concept of "front-line troops" had become all but obsolete. Every service member, regardless of job skill or specialization, needed to be able to employ ground combat skills with the same efficiency as any infantry foot soldier. The Marine Corps had been a practitioner of this philosophy since its inception, and the harsh reality of the current conflict only served to motivate the other American services along with their counterparts around the world to follow suit.

None of that had stopped DiCarlo from broaching the subject, though he did so only once, at the start of their predeployment training. He at first expressed his concerns for her well-being, given what they likely would face as the counteroffensive operation on *Jontashreena* unfolded and expanded. Russell had received no opportunity to voice her opinion, and instead had watched with no small amount of amusement as DiCarlo talked himself back from his own position, realizing that she and other women service members would soon be marching into battle alongside their male compatriots. If that was going to happen, then he wanted her with him. They had already worked, lived, and fought alongside each other long enough that they had forged a bond as much from fire as from the love that also had brought them together. She could not envision returning to *Jontashreena* without DiCarlo, and he had expressed similar feelings.

"I know it breaks every rule in the book," he had said one evening, "but I don't give a shit. What are they going to do? Send me to Leavenworth? Fuck 'em."

Clearing her throat, Russell looked down to make sure that her M470 rifle—one of the first generation of human-engineered pulse weapons based on Plysserian technology—had not fallen to the ground from where she had positioned it atop her backpack. Though not as powerful as the Plysserian technology that had spawned it and requiring more frequent replacement of its internal power cell, the M470 was still more effective against alien physiology than the standard small-arms weaponry employed by most human militaries. At least, that was what she had been told by the armorer who issued her the rifle. Though the weapons had been subjected to extensive testing, they had yet to see action under actual combat conditions.

Nothing like being a guinea pig.

Next to Russell, Laney was once again studying the compound through his goggles. "I don't see anybody outside. You think they pull people in during fueling ops?"

She shrugged. "Makes sense, I suppose. Of course, if anything went wrong and a ship like that took a header, I don't see how being inside one of those buildings makes you any safer." Though she currently saw no signs of life, her earlier studies of the compound had revealed the presence of at least eight figures, walking the area in patterns that told her they were sentries. The entire installation was surrounded by a barrier not unlike the one she remembered from the prison from which they had liberated the Plysserian scientist *Laepotic* Wysejral.

"Well, we'll consider this an object lesson for them," DiCarlo said. Glancing at Russell, he asked, "You have a clean sight picture?"

"Yes," she replied. "As good as I can get from this angle, anyway."

DiCarlo chuckled. "You don't have to be that close." He pointed toward the fueling depot. "They're going to do all the hard work for us."

Russell recalled what she and the team had been told during their very rushed pre-mission briefing, which had come mere moments after they had learned that Operation Clear Sky was on and had received their initial objectives for the opening hours of the massive counteroffensive.

DiCarlo had said something similar to the officer providing the briefing, though that version had included a few
choice profanities, which had extracted some laughs from
the otherwise tense group. It somehow was calming to hear
him once again offer the same assurances. He always had
a knack for saying just the right thing to put her at ease. It
was one of the traits that made him an effective leader, and
it was one of the qualities she admired in him as her friend
and lover.

I guess I'll keep him.

Russell's ears picked up a faint buzzing sound somewhere close, and she turned to see Lance Corporal Geoffrey
Thorne reaching for the military-issue cellular phone—
encased in a rugged shock- and water-resistant shell—lying
next to his right elbow. The phone's digital display was illuminated, emitting a soft red glow. The African-American
Marine's hand was so large it almost swallowed the unit
when he picked it up, and he studied its readout before
looking first to Russell and then to DiCarlo, his expression
one of anticipation.

"It's the beacon, Sergeant Major," Thorne said. "They're
on the way."

Rolling slowly to a sitting position while still keeping
himself under cover, DiCarlo replied, "Now we're talking."
Reaching for the radio clipped to his equipment harness,
he keyed his microphone. "Kel, this is DiCarlo. Did you
get the beacon signal?"

The Plysserian's voice echoed in Russell's own radio earpiece. *"Yes, DiCarlo. We are designating the target now."*

DiCarlo nodded. "Same here. Stand by." To his own
team, he said, "Look sharp, boys and girls. Time for the
kickoff."

Time to see if this crazy-assed plan works, Russell
mused, retaking her position behind the LLDR and peer-

ing through its sight. Once more the image of the tanker hovering over the fuel depot dominated the image, and she grunted in satisfaction as her left hand reached for the controls on the unit's laser designator module. Now when she studied the ship, the rangefinder's status indicated that it had acquired the target, selecting a spot on the bulkhead of the ship's center fuel tank. With the selection now locked in, the LLDR was sending continuous pulses of laser energy, which were in turn bouncing off the target and into the sky, waiting for the incoming missiles to detect them.

That was it; she had done her part. Elsewhere, she knew that the other half of DiCarlo's team, led by Kel, was performing the same action, acquiring a target on one of the depot's central storage facilities. All that was now required by either team was to maintain their targets, wait, and watch the show. The rest would be handled by the pair of missiles that—theoretically—were coming closer with every passing second.

The plan seemed simple enough: Use portals to deliver from Earth to *Jontashreena* a battery of missiles augmented by Plysserian technology to enhance their onboard navigation and target acquisition systems. For DiCarlo's team, two AGM-123B missiles had been deployed, fired from two U.S. Navy F/A-18 Hornet fighter jets into a portal generated at a top-secret installation aboard the Marine base at Camp Pendleton, California. Laser-guided bombs and missiles were a proven technology, with different models in use for decades. The only question here was their use in conjunction with the portals, given that the size of the ordnance limited the ways in which they could be deployed through the conduits. To that end, missile guidance systems had been improved with the assistance of Plysserian engineers, incorporating a navigational sensor that would keep a projectile on a steady course during the 2.9-second interval spent in transit through the conduit between worlds. After making it to their assigned locations on the other side, the missiles would lock onto targets with the assistance of teams like DiCarlo's, already on the ground and in position to provide laser guidance for the final transit to the point of impact. The missiles had been further enhanced so as to make them easier to guide with the ground-based LLDRs, such as the one Russell currently operated. All that remained to be seen was whether the cloudy sky would have any effect on the targeting process.

Something, an alien sound, caught Russell's attention. Could she already be hearing the missiles approaching? She glanced at her wristwatch, which she had synchronized during her pre-mission briefing. Whereas it was a little less than three hours before the dawn of another 32.7-hour day on *Jontashreena*—as measured on Earth—her watch's luminescent dial read 1433, 2:33 P.M. Eastern Standard Time. According to the briefing they had received, H hour for Operation Clear Sky was commencing more or less right on schedule.

"Incoming," Laney said, the young Marine having rolled onto his side and angled his night-vision goggles so that he could search for signs of the inbound missiles. "Time to impact is forty seconds." While Russell heard excitement in his voice, she did not detect fear. Laney had comported himself almost like a seasoned veteran from the moment DiCarlo had taken charge of his unit. According to the sergeant major, Laney's scores during boot camp and combat training were well above average, and he had adapted quickly to Plysserian weapons and equipment. He also had earned a reputation as an innovative problem solver as well as a natural leader. Those were just some of the reasons DiCarlo had selected him and a handful of standouts from Laney's MCT platoon to accompany him, and why Laney himself had received a meritorious promotion from private first class to lance corporal and assignment as Russell's partner during their predeployment training. He had displayed tremendous proficiency with the LLDR equipment, not just in using it but also in disassembling and even repairing it should the need arise. Given his enthusiasm, Russell almost felt guilty about not letting him operate the unit while she took over spotting duties.

Sorry, kid, she mused, unable to resist the mischievous thought, *but I need something to write about someday*.

Now the sound of the approaching missiles was unmistakable, even though Russell knew she would not yet be able to see them. If all was proceeding according to plan, the weapons were traveling along a low trajectory, which hopefully would prevent them from being detected by Chodrecai sensor tech. The pre-mission briefing reports had indicated no such equipment or security measures at this location, but commanders tended not to rely on such reports once the shooting started. Still, the fuel depot, which was considered a military target, had been selected deliberately—along with nearly two dozen other locations—for this first phase of Operation Clear Sky as part of a larger strategy designed to inflict chaos upon the Chodrecai military leadership.

The intention here was simple destruction, rather than seizing or holding such locations, with no discernible pattern to be found among the chosen targets, which were scattered throughout Gray territory. Chodrecai forces would, in theory, react to the apparently random attacks taking place all around them, and enough confusion and miscommunication would be sown to delay any meaningful response to other phases of the campaign. It was those stages upon which Clear Sky truly depended, with both human and Plysserian forces moving en masse against numerous other strategically vital Chodrecai targets. Once footholds were established, the process would be repeated and expanded, making use of the portal technology to transfer ever more personnel and equipment from Earth to supplement Plysserian assets already on the move toward their assigned objectives.

"Impact in ten seconds," Laney said, keeping his voice low.

Thorne said, "I see them." He pointed with his left hand and Russell turned in that direction, now able to make out a pair of nearly invisible arrowlike shapes slicing through the night air. They had been traveling with one in front of and to the right of the other, but now Russell could see them beginning to pull away from one another, pursuing independent trajectories toward their designated targets. Returning her attention to the LLDR, she verified that she still had a lock on the tanker as Laney began counting down from five.

He reached zero, and a heartbeat later Russell saw the first missile strike the side of the ship, and she pulled her eyes from the rangefinder's sight as the middle of the craft erupted in a monstrous ball of flame. Staring over the top of the unit, she watched as the entire depot was bathed in the harsh orange light of fire as the explosion expanded, obliterating the center fuel pod before tearing into its companions. Then the second missile struck the fuel storage facility immediately behind the tanker. By the time the sounds of the detonations reached her ears, the building's forward wall was already tumbling inward, releasing more fire and roiling dark smoke into the night sky. The structure's ceiling buckled, and flames were visibly piercing various joints and connections along the conduit connecting the building to its neighbors.

"Holy shit," Thorne said, and all of them watched as the tanker, still hovering above its fuel transfer hub, shuddered and collapsed in on itself even as its engines exploded and what remained of the craft fell toward the ground. Striking the roof of the storage facility only accelerated that structure's demise, adding to the hellish maelstrom enveloping the entire depot.

"Anybody bring any marshmallows?" DiCarlo said, now holding the stub of an unlit cigar to his lips. Russell knew he would not light it, not while they were in a tactical situation, but chewing on the thing seemed to relax him.

A miniature sun flared where the depot once had stood. Secondary explosions were ripping through the rest of the buildings, fire consuming everything as a massive plume of thick, black smoke rose into the sky, forming a menacing cloud that threatened to block out the weak illumination of *Jontashreena*'s three moons. Were similar attacks currently under way across Chodrecai-occupied territory meeting with such success?

"That's going to attract some attention," Laney said, securing his night-vision goggles into the carrying case he wore strapped to his equipment harness.

With the cigar now stuck between his teeth, DiCarlo nodded. "Sounds like a good time for us to haul ass out of here." Reaching up to key his mike, he said, "Kel, this is DiCarlo. You ready to get moving?"

"DiCarlo," replied Kel's voice in her ear, *"we are preparing our equipment for transport, and will be ready to meet you at the designated coordinates."*

The sergeant major said, "Roger that. We'll see you at Rally Point Alpha. Go silent until we meet up."

"Acknowledged," Kel said, before there was a snap in Russell's ear, signifying that the Blue soldier had deactivated his radio. The plan called for minimal use of radio communications, even though it was unlikely Chodrecai detection equipment would pick up the human technol-

ogy's comparatively weaker signals. DiCarlo found that ironic, considering the havoc radio communications had wrought on alien weaponry during the early days of the Chodrecai incursion to Earth. The Grays had solved that problem, and perhaps they also had found a way to lock onto the Earth forces' communications. Maintaining radio silence was yet another concession to planning for the unexpected, and the long-accepted axiom that no battle plan in the history of organized warfare had ever survived initial contact with the enemy.

No sense taking any chances.

"Okay, people," DiCarlo said, donning his backpack and lifting his M470 so that it rested in the crook of his right elbow. "Time to get gone. We've got places to go, people to meet, and other shit to blow up. Ooh-rah, and all that."

As she and Laney turned to the task of disassembling the LLDR and as Thorne and the rest of the team gathered their own gear, Russell's attention was drawn back to the burning, destroyed depot and the realization that they now had moved past the point of no return. She and thousands of able-bodied men and women like her were now making the journey here, engaging the denizens of this planet in a bid to safeguard the world from which she had come. Had the soldiers storming the beaches of Normandy or Japanese-held islands in the Pacific nearly seven decades earlier experienced similar thoughts? Did they, like her, wonder if they would ever again see home? What would that home be like if and when she was able to return?

Her eyes turned to DiCarlo, and she saw him staring at her, a knowing expression clouding his weathered features, and he nodded once to her. Did he sense her feelings?

"Yeah," he said. "I know."

36

Energy screamed past Corporal Patrick Freeman's head the instant he threw himself to the ground, the impact against the dry, packed dirt driving the air from his lungs as he scrambled for cover. Behind him, he heard Private Joseph Steverson mimicking his movements. Both men rolled into the shallow hole that was the firing position they had only just finished securing. Freeman heard the reports of other pulse rifles firing, and something slamming into the reinforced composite shielding from which the firing position had been constructed. Not for the first time, he gave silent thanks for the alien material, which, like the vests worn by most Plysserian soldiers, offered protection from Chodrecai pulse weapons.

The two men's scrambling kicked up a cloud of dust in their wake. Freeman coughed at the abrupt assault on his lungs, reaching to push back the brim of his helmet as he peered above the lip of the protected firing position and took stock of his surroundings.

"Freebie, you okay?" a voice echoed in his right ear, filtered through the small earbud of his tactical radio. It belonged to his sergeant, Daniel Balsam. If the deployment plan had not been screwed too badly, Freeman figured that the other man should be ahead of him and somewhere to his right.

Fat fucking chance of that happening.

Verifying that Steverson was uninjured, Freeman hacked up more dust, then wiped his lips with his left sleeve before adjusting the microphone near his mouth. "Yeah, we're fine. Wanker nearly popped my cherry with that shot." A month away from celebrating his tenth year of service with the British Army, including combat tours in Iraq and Afghanistan and multiple engagements against the Chodrecai over the past year, Freeman had never so much as broken a nail in a firefight. Now these gray bastards were threatening to fuck up his percentage. "What the hell are they doing here? I thought this area was supposed to be secure, for fuck's sake."

"*I got the same briefing you did, mate,*" Balsam replied, and Freeman heard the irritation in the sergeant's voice.

"*Clear the bloody channel!*" shouted the terse voice of Lieutenant Alan Porter, the platoon commander. "*Return fire!*"

Ignoring the sounds of weapons fire—human and alien—filling the air over his head, Freeman turned to his left and scanned the uneven, broken terrain. His ability to differentiate the shadows in the predawn darkness was aided by the light from the last of *Jontashreena*'s three moons hanging low on the horizon behind him. He saw movement in the vicinity of where the rest of his squad should be. To either side he saw dozens of other troopers, most of them hugging the ground or peering out from their own shielded firing positions or from behind the scattered vehicles and stacks of cargo crates that were all the cover to be had in this part of the forest glade. A few bodies—rather, what remained of those bodies—lay scattered along the ground around the firebase, victims of the attack's opening salvos.

"Third Squad," he said into his lip mike. "Everybody okay?" He listened as the other team members reported in. So far, he had suffered no losses.

Not for lack of trying. Bloody intel pricks. According to everything they had been told prior to deploying, this area—an isolated meadow in the middle of unoccupied territory—was free of Chodrecai activity. The glade was large enough not only to accommodate the portal itself but also to act as a staging area for troops and equipment arriving from Earth. Those assets and personnel would in turn be directed to other rally points, from which they would board Plysserian transport craft for further movement to one of four Clear Sky target objectives identified in this region. Freeman's company had been given the assignment of securing the area and continuing the process of hardening it for use as a landing support site, strengthening defenses already constructed by Plysserian soldiers as well as setting up areas to store supplies and other materiel that would soon begin transiting from different points on Earth.

In contrast, it was one of the easier missions to which Freeman and his unit had been assigned since the aliens' arrival on Earth. During those first weeks, after it became known that the Chodrecai, either by design or accident, had established a significant presence in the United Kingdom, British military units were dispatched across the country in pursuit of the alien "invaders." Freeman himself saw battle against the Grays seven times in as many weeks. Numerous casualties were suffered during those initial engagements, mostly owing to the Chodrecai's superior weaponry, which offset their smaller numbers and lack of larger vehicles or equipment.

When the truth behind the conflict between the Plysserians and Chodrecai became common-knowledge, there were widespread calls for British forces to stand down, to find some means of establishing peaceful dialogue with the aliens. Much of that sentiment was lost more than a year ago, after the Chodrecai elected to launch their major offensive against Earth. When that effort failed, Freeman had wondered how long it might take for leaders around the world to decide the time was right for hitting back.

We waited too bloody long. News of the attack in Geneva reached Freeman and the rest of the company while they were in the field conducting training with a Plysserian unit. Emotions ran high that day, particularly with the loss of the queen, who had journeyed with the prime minister to the peace conference. Freeman knew of no soldier who was not itching to offer payback for the egregious assault on the realm and the rest of the world.

Now he and his fellow troopers were here, on the alien planet, preparing to do exactly that. While this was not glamorous duty, Freeman knew it was a necessary preliminary step for allowing British troops to transit safely from Earth. To that end, Plysserian troops and engineers had already been on-site for several days, laying the groundwork for the firebase's basic structure, and were in the process of erecting a perimeter protective barrier, which would add another layer of security. Anticipation and even excitement were palpable throughout the compound as preparations continued.

Freeman and the rest of his company were on-site less than two hours when the shooting started.

He ducked at the sound of renewed weapons fire, and he caught sight of muzzle flashes—pinpoints of light at this distance—scattered along the ridgeline. "Third Squad, they're in the hills to the north, about a hundred fifty meters. Knock the piss out of them." Laying the barrel of his American-made M470 rifle atop the fighting hole's parapet, Freeman used the weapon's thermal sight and took aim at what looked to be a Gray hiding among the rocks. His right forefinger mashed the weapon's firing stud and the pulse rifle belched energy, the weapon's recoil driving its stock into Freeman's right shoulder. Unlike the Plysserian rifles on which it had been modeled, the M470 emitted a visible pulse, a pale-blue halo surrounding the bolt of energy as it howled across the open space between him and the ridgeline. Freeman was able to track the shot until it slammed into a large boulder, behind which he was sure a Gray crouched undercover. The pulse slammed into the rock, chewing into the smooth stone and sending shrapnel in several directions. He repeated the exercise twice more, and on the third shot he was rewarded by the sight of a hulking form scrambling away from the rocks and across the open terrain, his body a glowing blur in Freeman's thermal sight as the Gray soldier doubtless sought new cover. Another shriek of energy from his right made him wince just as he saw the projectile from Steverson's rifle slicing the near darkness, striking the exposed Chodrecai in the back and slamming the soldier to the ground. Steverson fired again, his second shot striking the Gray's head.

"Nice shooting, nod," Freeman said, unable to resist grinning. "Good to see they're still teaching you fuzznuts something worthwhile in basic." From behind him, Freeman heard the distinctive sound of a conventional Minimi machine gun, followed seconds later by a harsh stream of orange tracer fire slicing through the gray-black sky on its way to the nearby ridgeline. Larger crew-served weapons of that sort, unlike many small arms carried by foot soldiers, had proven effective against the aliens from the first encounters with them a year ago. Right now, the rapid, taut rhythm of the machine gun's stream of fire was music to Freeman's ears.

Ahead of him, he saw the first faint glow of sunrise peeking over the hills on the horizon, a thin orange-pink band stretching across the sky. The outlines of trees and rock formations set into the sides of the low, sloping ridgeline were growing more distinct. While the natural terrain provided ample cover in the hills surrounding the glade, Freeman detected no signs of any artificial constructs. There were no sounds of vehicles or other heavy equipment. However many they were, they did not seem to be anything more than foot soldiers.

And what if there's a shitload of them? And what if they call friends? By his count, fewer than a hundred men were now on the ground here, not counting the dozen or so Plys-serian soldiers already on-site when Freeman's company began arriving through the portal. The vast majority of the troops who eventually would be deployed from this location were still on Earth, waiting for the signal that the firebase was secure and ready to begin its landing support operations.

"They were waiting for us," Steverson said, hissing the words between gritted teeth and flinching as another bolt of energy ripped through the air somewhere over the younger man's right shoulder. "Sons of bitches were waiting in the hills for us to hang our asses out here." He spoke without looking away from the ridgeline, his right cheek resting against the stock of his M470 as he searched for another target.

Freeman shook his head. "No way. We had teams con-duct a sweep of the area, and there was nothing. The Blues checked it out when they first got there, and they didn't find anything, either. I don't think they were waiting for us, but they knew we were here, unless you want to believe they just stumbled across our hairy asses all by accident." The likely explanation, Freeman knew, was that the activity of the Blue soldiers in this area over the past several days somehow had attracted unwanted attention. Had their pres-ence been discovered by a Gray unit patrolling the area, or had the firebase been seen from the air as part of some high-altitude reconnaissance? Freeman knew the Chodrecai still possessed some satellites from which they could conduct orbital surveillance, but this area had been chosen because it allegedly fell outside the tracks of the few remaining satellites still in Gray control. In Freeman's mind, that was sufficient to explain the size and relatively poor execution of the attack they now faced.

Maybe we should thank bleeding Christ for small favors.

Firing again, Steverson said, "Why the hell are we just sitting here?" He glanced over his shoulder. "And why aren't they sending more troops through the bloody portal?"

"Still takes time to recalculate new coordinates when they shift starting points, remember?" Freeman replied, glancing at his wristwatch. It had been less than five minutes since the portal's deactivation, and he guessed it would be another two or three minutes until it reappeared, this time generated by the second of three transfer sites on Earth. Even with the overlap between the multiple starting points, that lag was still the main drawback to the otherwise wondrous alien technology, and it was this shortcoming that had necessitated the planning of staging areas like this as part of Operation Clear Sky's multifaceted attack plan.

Nice plan, that. For the next few minutes, Freeman and his mates were still on their own.

"Bugger me stupid," Steverson said, and now Freeman could hear the first hints of fear in the younger man's voice. To his credit, the private was keeping his attention focused forward, aiming his weapon and firing with discipline. He might be rattled, Freeman guessed, but Steverson was—for the moment, anyway—holding up.

The rate of fire from the ridgeline was tapering off, Freeman realized, and the sun had risen enough that a gray pall was cast over the entire area. He caught sight of figures moving between the rocks and trees, using whatever cover they could find to advance toward the firebase.

"They're moving on us," Freeman said into his radio mike as he watched some of the alien soldiers on the move, "trying to get to the flanks." He quit counting when he reached twenty, figuring there had to be more he could not see through the scattered clumps of trees and rocks. Indeed, he was hoping the Grays would continue to come closer, for they would soon run out of places to hide. The Plysserian soldiers who had established this landing area had done an exceptional job of clearing trees and other natural obstacles from a hundred-meter perimeter around the firebase. If they had not done so, or had made the perimeter smaller, the Grays might well have been able to maneuver close enough to slaughter a sizable number of the company before anyone knew what was happening.

A high-pitched whine pierced the air overhead, and Freeman looked up in time to see the dark silhouettes of five Plysserian *Lisum* attack craft rocketing past, close enough to the ground that he was sure he felt the rush of air displaced by the fighters' passing. The five ships were gone almost as quickly as they had appeared, disappearing over the ridgeline.

"Where the hell are they going?" Steverson asked. Freeman was about to guess aloud when the voice of Lieutenant Porter rang once more in his ear.

"Listen up, people. Our Blue friends are tracking inbound enemy air assets. Somebody knows we're here, boys and girls. Keep your heads down."

As if to emphasize the lieutenant's words, another *Lisum* roared past, this one flying slower and even lower than its predecessors. Much to Freeman's delight, the attack craft began strafing the trees at the base of the ridgeline, its weapons chewing into the ground and vegetation.

"Now we're talking," he said, taking aim at another lumbering figure moving between two distant trees. His shot was wide of the mark, but he had no time to dwell on the miss before the trees were shredded by the *Lisum*'s weapons. The ship swept in low, firing strings of pulse energy as it banked to its right before climbing again into the sky, already maneuvering for another pass.

"I think they're breaking ranks," Steverson said, his right eye all but mashed against his rifle's thermal sight. "I can see a few of them heading back for the tree line."

Peering through his own scope, Freeman counted four shapes, blobs of yellow-white in the thermal sight, moving away from the firebase and back toward the denser clumps of trees and rocks. Above them, the *Lisum* was allowing no quarter, showering the area with pulse weapon fire that destroyed rocks, trees, and Gray soldiers with the same deadly accuracy.

"*Looks like they're bugging out,*" said the voice of Sergeant Balsam over the radio.

"*Affirmative,*" replied Lieutenant Porter. "*Air support's saying the same thing. Sit tight, boys. Continue firing on any targets until I give the word.*"

Shifting his weight so that his body no longer rested atop one of the pouches on his equipment harness, Steverson reached up to wipe sweat from his forehead. "Guess we got lucky, eh?"

"For now," Freeman replied, watching as the *Lisum* craft took another strafing run at the distant ridgeline. "But I wouldn't get too attached to this place if I were you. They know we're here now."

The more he thought about that, the more Freeman decided he was okay with it.

37

The sheer number of flashbulbs was enough to make Andrew Grayson want to raise a hand to cover his eyes, but he forced himself to stand absolutely still, not even to blink in the face of the dozens of cameras presently aimed toward the front of the room.

Christ, I haven't even started and I'm already blind. The bitter thought lingered as he stood at the podium atop the small dais in the Pentagon pressroom. He looked out at the packed assemblage of journalists, military officials, and anyone else able to secure a pass to the briefing, along with—apparently—everyone else on the planet with nothing better to do today. Listening to the uncounted voices, he tried to decipher their overlapping questions, statements, accusations, or whatever else they might be saying. Was it his imagination, or had the temperature increased just in the two minutes that had passed since his entering the room?

Standing beside him at the podium was *Kentelitrul* Aphiledraekodi, a Plysserian officer. The alien soldier, carrying a rank commensurate with that of a general, had been in near total seclusion for months following his covert arrival on Earth. Since then, he had played a vital role in the planning of the counteroffensive on *Jontashreena*, employing his vast knowledge not only of Plysserian but also Chodrecai forces, along with their tactics and their respective strengths and weaknesses.

Holding up a hand to the audience, Grayson gestured for everyone to take a seat. It took several seconds before the reporters and other onlookers settled into chairs or moved to stand against the walls. A low murmur continued for another moment as people leaned close to one another, whispering and nodding toward the stage.

"Ladies and gentlemen, good morning," he said, his voice carrying to the back of the room without benefit of the microphone positioned on a flexible arm at one corner of the podium. "Thank you for coming. I know there have been rumors circulating for hours, and I understand that you've all got questions, and after I offer my opening statement, we'll do our best to provide answers." A brief resurgence met that statement, with reporters rising from their chairs and extending microphones or digital recorders, and Grayson paused again. Once the more tenacious members of the press corps returned to their seats, the general nodded and continued.

"At two-thirty P.M. Eastern Standard Time yesterday afternoon, a combined military force consisting of Plysserian assets as well as those from countries around our own planet launched an aggressive campaign against Chodrecai forces on *Jontashreena*." The room erupted into near chaos as reporters bolted from their seats, simultaneously hurling questions at Grayson, who ignored them and instead reached for the control to activate the podium mike.

"This action," he continued, his voice now amplified over the throng of onlookers, "code-named Operation Clear Sky, is the result of months of planning, coordination, and training. The goal of the campaign is simple: pushing the Chodrecai back from the territory they've occupied on their planet, in the hope that they will in turn be unable to continue their advance against targets there as well as here on Earth. While I can't go into specifics regarding locations where battles are currently taking place, what I can share is that the campaign involves offensive action against multiple targets of varying strategic value." Finally, as if to put the press corps out of their misery, Grayson pointed to one of the journalists seated in the front row—Kirsten Beyer, a reporter for the *Los Angeles Times*. "Yes, Kirsten."

Extending her hand and holding a digital voice recorder toward the podium, the journalist asked, "General, how many forces do you estimate are taking part in the operation, and from which countries besides the United States?"

"I can't give you exact figures," Grayson replied, "because even as we speak, assets are still being moved into target areas. As for individual countries and their level of involvement, again, that's not something I wish to make public at this time." Scanning the crowd, he pointed to Ilsa Bick, an on-air reporter for one of the twenty-four-hour cable news networks. "Ilsa."

A petite woman with short hair and wire-rimmed glasses, Bick rose from her chair. "General, what is the level of the Plysserians' involvement?"

Hoping to get that question, Grayson nodded. "They've been involved at every step of the operation, from concept to execution." He gestured to his Plysserian companion. "*Kentelitrul* Aphiledraekodi has been an invaluable resource throughout the operation's planning phases. He and other members of the Plysserian military command have contributed valuable information which helped us to shape the battle plan and select key targets with high probabilities for success. Other Plysserians have been contributing in numerous other ways. They've trained alongside our armed forces, helped our military enhance their weapons and equipment using their technology, educated us on Chodrecai tactics, and so on. Of course, there also are the portals, which have basically forced us to rewrite the book on how we conduct military operations." He pointed to Howard Weinstein, who wrote for the *Dallas Morning News*, seated two rows back. "Howard."

"General, what sort of progress reports have you received?"

"It's important to understand at this early juncture that the information we've received is incomplete, often sent hurriedly by commanders on the front lines who are continuing to press forward with their objectives. The reports we've gotten to this point are largely positive." The statement itself was mostly true, though the operation was still young enough that Grayson was uncomfortable offering any descriptions of ongoing battles—positive or negative— at this early stage. With so many aspects of the campaign still in flux with respect to the movement of personnel and resources into target areas, as well as the varying levels of Chodrecai resistance being encountered to this point, the general knew that the situation could change in an instant.

Before Grayson could select another reporter, Weinstein raised his hand. "A follow-up, General: Are you receiving any casualty reports yet?"

While he might be reluctant to offer much in the way of concrete information with respect to the operation itself, this was one topic that Grayson had no intention of side-stepping. "Yes, we have. They are preliminary reports, and until they're verified and any next of kin notified, we won't be releasing that information. We've activated casualty assistance centers and field teams to handle these delicate matters in as timely and dignified a manner as possible." He then pointed to Glenn Hauman, a reporter for a news website whose name Grayson could not recall, who was seated near the back. "Glenn."

Hauman, a tall, lanky man, rose from a chair in the last row. He removed his glasses as he held out his own recorder toward the podium, and when he spoke it was in a high-pitched voice. "General, what level of casualties do you estimate will be suffered by this invasion?"

Grayson shook his head. "I'm not going to speculate on that." When that statement drew a general murmur of disapproval from the audience, the general leaned closer to the microphone. "Ladies and gentlemen, we're talking about a combat action on a scale not seen since the Normandy landings. The only difference is that technology has allowed us to attack multiple targets at the same time, coordinating assets from around the world and positioning them at or near key locations on *Jontashreena*."

He had seen other leaders, other presidents, downplay or even appear to dismiss the harsh reality of combat injuries and deaths. That perceived lack of sensitivity was an inexcusable breach of the unwritten contract between a soldier and the civilian leader responsible for sending that soldier into battle. In particular, this was an egregious offense to the families of men and women who volunteered to serve in uniform, and who did so with the tacit understanding that their elected officials would place their lives at risk only for legitimate—even noble—purposes rather than as a means of furthering murky political agendas. Violating this "pact" was more than sufficient to turn a public against its government during wartime. When he accepted the position of JCS chairman, Grayson swore he would never minimize or marginalize the unpleasant truths that were a product of war.

"I'd love to be able to stand here and tell you that casualties will be kept to a minimum," he continued, "but I think we all know how naïve and downright insulting that would be. The best we can do is work toward our objectives, trust our forward commanders to make the right decisions, and support those men and women on the front lines as much as possible." Maybe it was the words themselves, or perhaps it was the tone in which he had delivered them, but the response was enough to give the gathered reporters pause, if only for a second or two. It was enough for Grayson to call on the next journalist with his hand raised, Allyn Gibson from the *Washington Post.*

"General, what kind of timetable are we looking at here? Days? Weeks? Longer?"

"There's no easy answer to that, Allyn," Grayson replied. "We have predictions, of course, but the truth is that plans and predictions and statistics don't mean a thing once the shooting starts. What the American people—no, I'm sorry; let me rephrase that—what the *people of the world* need to know is that we're pursuing this objective not as Americans, or Brits, or Russians or anyone else you want to name. The Plysserians aren't doing this as their own nation, either. We stand together, united in common purpose, acting not only for the future security of this planet but *Jontashreena,* as well, and not just for the Plysserians. There are countless Chodrecai who also want this war over, as quickly as possible and while avoiding as many casualties as possible. But make no mistake: This isn't going to be over tonight, tomorrow, or even next week. War is about two parties pushing one another to the limits of their endurance, and the first one to buckle under that pressure is the loser. People need to know and understand that we could be there for months before we realize our goals."

Or the Grays could dig deep and summon the energy needed to kick all of our asses once and for all. Even as the renegade thought rattled around inside his head, Grayson elected to keep that observation to himself.

The blunt statement brought forth renewed muttering throughout the audience, but Grayson paid it no heed.

Instead, he pointed to Brett Dalton, another on-air talking head from a diffcrent cable news network—one whose coverage more often than not slanted toward the right side of the political spectrum. "Yes, Brett."

Calling forth every bit of the bluster that carried him through his nightly news show, Dalton stood and with hands on hips asked, "General Grayson, what is your overall assessment of the operation at this point, and what are the president's views on the invasion? Obviously she sanctioned it, so far as American troops are concerned. Does she believe we can win?"

Grayson fought the urge to roll his eyes, knowing where Dalton was trying to lead. "The president has been informed at every step of the way and receives constant reports as to our progress. I don't speak for her, but she has expressed supreme confidence in our military as well as those of participating nations. While we are encountering resistance on some fronts, the campaign is being executed without any significant setbacks. Our commanders on the ground assure us that everything is largely proceeding according to plan."

Holy shit on a saltine.

It was all Captain Teri Westerson could do not to speak the thought aloud as she dodged to one side of the narrow tunnel and pressed herself against the cold, unyielding stone wall in time to avoid being run down by a lumbering Plysserian soldier. The Blue uttered something unintelligible as he passed, on his way to some destination or task.

"Pardon the hell out of me," Westerson muttered. She continued down the sloping passageway, which widened as it leveled out before opening into a vast chamber, stuffed nearly to overflowing with personnel and equipment. The cavern, like the tunnels leading from it, was not a natural formation but rather an artificial construct. She had been here only once before, weeks prior to the launch of Operation Clear Sky, touring the bunker and its assortment of interconnected chambers. The complex housed all manner of equipment and weapons, as well as food and other supplies that could—if necessary—make the facility self-sufficient for months. She had been told at that time by the Blue soldier who had provided a tour that the command bunker, one of several subterranean complexes scattered across the *Galotreapiq* continent, was built decades ago, long before tensions between the Plysserians and Chodrecai erupted into full-scale war.

An amalgam of human and Plysserian technology as well as design aesthetic, the bunker was awash in activity. If they were not moving about the chamber, then humans and Blues were manning workstations or overseeing large maps and holographic projections. A massive table at the center of the room depicted no less than eight different holographic displays, along with a plethora of computer screens presenting a host of data. Descending the ramp carved untold years earlier from the stone wall of the mountain housing the complex, Westerson moved from the bunker's entrance to avoid blocking the paths of humans and Blues making their way to and fro as they carried out their responsibilities.

"They need stoplights in here, don't they?"

Turning toward the sound of the voice, Westerson offered a small smile as she recognized Major David Galanter walking in her direction. A lean man with thinning black hair that grayed at the temples, Galanter, like her, was dressed in a combat utility uniform, over which he wore a tactical vest with the front zipper undone. The chamber's low lighting reflected off the handgrip of the M9 service pistol holstered on the vest's left side. She had first met Galanter in the days following the Chodrecai attack in Washington, D.C. At that time, he was commanding the communications detachment for the unit given the responsibility of sweeping the capital and weeding out any Gray soldiers who might have been left behind after the battle.

"I don't think it'd help," Westerson replied, reaching up to unfasten the zipper on her own vest before adjusting the strap of the M470 pulse rifle slung from her right shoulder. Then, she unfastened the chinstrap of her helmet and removed the headgear, tucking it under her left arm. The air here was cool, far more inviting than the summerlike conditions on the surface. She gestured toward Galanter's gear, "Going somewhere?"

The major shook his head. "Just got back, actually. There was a problem with some of the Blue communications equipment topside, so I went with one of their tech people to see if I could help. What brings you here?"

Westerson shrugged. "Not really sure just yet. My bosses were told a translator was needed down here, so they sent me." In the weeks following the Gray offensive, she had volunteered to work with Plysserian soldiers left on Earth, using the technology the aliens had provided to learn the various languages native to *Jontashreena*. It had always surprised her in the months that followed just how many people refused to take advantage of what in essence was a speed-learning program, one far more effective than any of the products offered by late-night TV infomercials. Some of that was based on fear or ignorance, she knew, with people worrying whether the strange technology might have adverse effects on humans. There seemed to be a segment of the population for whom no amount of education or information on this topic was sufficient.

Not that any of that should matter *here*, of all places. Westerson asked, "Am I supposed to believe they don't have anybody else around here who can speak local?"

"We do," another voice responded from behind her, and Westerson turned to see an Army officer dressed in that branch's version of the combat uniform, which was adorned with the insignia of a lieutenant colonel and a name tape that read BENJAMIN. The man, already rather thin, looked tired and gaunt, as though he had not slept in days. His gray-brown hair was disheveled, as was his uniform. "But we're shorthanded, and need all the help we can get."

Nodding in greeting, Westerson said, "Colonel. Captain Westerson, reporting as ordered."

"Good to have you, Captain," Benjamin replied, gesturing for her to follow him.

Galanter said, "I'll see you later," before turning and heading off across the bunker's main floor. Bidding him farewell, Westerson turned to follow Benjamin, who had moved toward the center of the complex and the large octagonal table situated there. Picking up a squat cylinder that resembled an oversized beer can, the colonel aimed the unwieldy object at the table and pressed a large control set into the device. In response to his action, the holographic image before them shifted to show Westerson what she recognized as a three-dimensional topographical map.

"You're here because we had to send a couple of translators up north," Benjamin said, gesturing toward the map, which now spun in a slow counterclockwise motion, angling upward ten or fifteen degrees so that Westerson could make out different terrain features. "This is way up near the northern coastline," he said. "Been in Gray hands for years, but we're starting to beat them back. A Canadian unit was part of the operation sweeping this area. They weren't expected to encounter major resistance, but that intel proved to be worth about twenty pounds of cowshit stuffed into a five-pound bag."

Westerson asked, "And they lost their translator?"

"Ambush," Benjamin replied. "Took out a company commander and two platoon leaders, along with a handful of other troops." He shook his head, frowning. "Lots of battlefield promotions there today. Of course, that's the news pretty much everywhere."

Looking around to see who might be within earshot, Westerson lowered her voice. "How bad is it, sir?"

The expression on Benjamin's face changed, as though he had been caught daydreaming in a junior high history class and was trying to recover. "Sorry, didn't mean to make that seem worse than it is." He waved toward the center of the table, where other maps and images depicted what

Westerson presumed were representations of other areas in which human and Plysserian troops were engaged against Chodrecai targets. "There are twenty-six active operations taking place as we speak. You know that some of those are diversionary actions, designed to draw Gray forces out of position so they can react to situations that are largely manufactured."

Westerson had been given very broad, nonspecific information about the campaign, but most of the information surrounding Operation Clear Sky remained classified at the highest levels well into the counteroffensive's second day. Secrecy clouded much of the invasion's planning and execution, except for those commanders on the ground with troops engaged in combat action, and the brass back here, of course. She knew too that many of the status and situation reports coming back from forward commanders would also not be made available for public consumption, as a security measure. Much of the operation still hinged on human and Plysserian forces to move on targets the Chodrecai either did not anticipate or else could not defend due to poor planning or a lack of resources. It was accepted that the humans and Blues, even working together, could not stand toe to toe with the Chodrecai military might for any extended period.

The key, she knew, was not electing to fight the sheer number of Gray forces, but instead to attack the mind-set, the attitude, that drove the Chodrecai army. In the eyes of the leaders who had devised Clear Sky, the goal was to beat their opponent by breaking their spirit. It was a straightforward plan, seizing or destroying a vast number of key targets scattered across Gray-occupied territory on this continent as well as their own and trying to undermine their confidence, not only in their leaders, but in the Grays themselves. It was a classic battle tactic, with numerous examples of success in the history of both worlds, updated to take advantage of alien technology. The portals allowed the plan to unfold at a pace far greater than if it had relied on conventional transportation. Personnel and equipment were being moved into operational areas with dizzying speed, reducing the wait times for reinforcements and resupply. At the same time, enemy supply and transportation lines were being captured or severed, further hampering the efforts of Gray forces to respond to the numerous simultaneous attacks.

Sounds too good to be true, doesn't it?

Pressing a control on the handheld unit, Benjamin called up a new image, a map of the *Galotreapiq* continent. Westerson counted fourteen blinking red dots scattered across the map. "While the Grays run around trying to figure out what the hell is going on, our main forces are going after these primary and secondary targets."

"And we're winning those battles?"

Benjamin shrugged. "Some of them aren't even battles, but several are proving to be a handful. We think the Grays got at least some reliable intel from somewhere, and were able to anticipate some of our target selections, but not all. Still, we're actually pushing ahead very well, all things considered. There are a few places where we're losing ground, but our thinking is that those are temporary setbacks once we can bring more assets to bear. We're getting reports of lots of casualties, but—and believe me, I absolutely *hate* the way this sounds coming out of my mouth—those are still within the percentages we predicted."

"I understand, sir," Westerson said. How many casualties were suffered on the beaches of Normandy just during the opening hours of June 6, 1944? How many more died in the weeks and months following the opening salvos of the Allied invasion? Would the events now taking place across *Jontashreena*, in both Plysserian- and Chodrecai-occupied territories, reach that level?

"That doesn't mean the Grays aren't putting up a fight," Benjamin continued. "They're determined bastards, I'll give them that." Looking up, he added, "But I'm not telling you anything you don't already know. After all, you were at the Mall."

Westerson nodded. "Yes, sir, I was." Along with hundreds of other Marines and soldiers, she had taken up a defensive position in the heart of Washington, D.C., waiting for the Grays to arrive as part of their three-front assault on Earth a year ago. "It was like World War I. Trenches and waiting for the enemy to advance. The portal wasn't big enough for anything of any appreciable size to get through, otherwise I think they would've kicked our asses all the way to Ohio."

"Well, they're still showing that same tenacity," Benjamin said, pointing again to the map. "This area to the south is supposed to largely be cleared, except for scattered, small groups cut off from their main units for one reason or another. When troops have encountered resistance, it's usually short-lived, since the groups they're finding lack decent weapons or equipment. Still, it was a group like that which hit the unit where we sent the guy you're replacing. Meanwhile, we're taking a number of Grays as prisoners, all of whom have to be interviewed to see if they have any information worth a damn."

Westerson asked, "So, I'm going to be interrogating Gray soldiers?"

"Exactly," Benjamin said, nodding. "Translators who can speak and understand the different Chodrecai dialects are hard to come by."

"When do I get started, sir?" Westerson asked.

"Probably tomorrow." Benjamin placed the handheld pointer atop the table before stepping away and gesturing for her to follow him. "There's a transport convoy bringing us a new batch of prisoners. Most of them won't know much beyond their immediate orders, but there might be one or two hidden in the pack with something more to offer. It'll be up to you to get it out of them."

Westerson chuckled, shaking her head. "A year ago, I was a desk jockey—an accountant in a uniform." Prior to the arrival of the aliens, Westerson's duties were those of a finance officer assigned to a government accounting office located in the basement level of a labyrinthine federal building in Kansas City, Missouri. Fate had conspired to have her join the group of Marine reservists undertaking their annual two-week training refresher at Camp Growding, which had become the focal point for drawing humanity into the war between the Plysserians and the Chodrecai. "Now here I am, on another planet, and all I do is daydream about what I want to do when this is all over."

"And what would that be?" Benjamin asked.

She had purposely avoided dwelling on such thoughts. At infrequent intervals over the past several months, she had tried to reach her boyfriend, Jerry, who had taken his mother and fled the city for his remote hunting cabin in rural Nebraska. Every attempt to track him down had failed, and he had not—to the best of her knowledge—attempted to contact her. Was he still alive? In the beginning, Westerson had thought about how she might go about finding him after the war was over, but would he accept her back into his life? He had disapproved of her decision to stay in Washington during the early weeks of the war as it continued to spill over to Earth. They had not spoken since well before the last major Gray offensive. Even if she survived the weeks or perhaps even months ahead, what would be on Earth, waiting for her?

One thing at a time, lady. One thing at a time.

39

By the time Marty Sloane saw the muzzle of the Chodre-cai pulse weapon, it was too late to do anything except die.

Something grabbed the collar of his body armor, yanking him back and down. An instant later, Sloane felt the rush of disrupted air as the enemy weapon's energy pulse shrieked past. He fell to the ground behind a low wall just as the shot slammed into the side of the massive shipping container behind him, rending the metal with the force of the impact. From somewhere to his left, Sloane heard the reports of weapons fire—human and Plysserian—as his companions took aim at whoever had nearly killed him. Looking up, his vision was filled with the immense gray head of a Plysserian, so close that the sergeant could see where some of the ink in the tattoos covering the soldier's face had started to fade with age.

"Are you injured?" asked the Blue, whom Sloane now recognized as *Zolitar* Ralitreq. One of the soldiers within Javoquek's unit to which he and Lieutenant Gutierrez had been attached for the duration of the current operation, the Blue had become a friend to Sloane in the weeks leading up to J-Day, to say nothing of the long, arduous days following the start of the campaign.

"Just my pride," Sloane replied, grunting the words as he rolled onto his side and placed his back against the low wall.

Ralitreq regarded him with a quizzical expression. "I am not familiar with that component of human anatomy."

Whatever rejoinder Sloane might have offered was lost as more weapons fire shredded the air around them. He crouched by the wall, using it for cover, with Ralitreq lying on the ground next to him, and listened to the sounds of running feet, the lumbering, heavier footfalls distinguishing Blue soldiers from their human counterparts. Shouted orders in English and Plysserian languages echoed in the alley formed by the monstrous shipping containers, which dwarfed even the largest ones Sloane had seen in ports from New York to Hong Kong.

"Come on," he said, pulling himself to his feet and checking his weapon's setting as he moved. Ralitreq mimicked his movements and in short order the pair fell into line with other soldiers moving down the alley. They maneuvered in leapfrog fashion, with soldiers stopping at intersections and aiming their weapons down the adjoining passages, providing cover so that troops behind them could advance. Sloane noted with satisfaction how the human and Plysserian soldiers worked in concert, using hand and arm signals to communicate simple maneuvers as they made their way through the maze that formed the shipping yard's outer compound. The acrid stench of scorched metal stung his nostrils, and a thin veil of smoke drifted through the alley, mute testimony to the catastrophic effects of the indirect fire and bombing raids that had preceded the ground assault. Peering down a few of the narrower alleys revealed debris and other wreckage from where some of the bombs and mortars had missed their marks and taken out shipping containers, rather than landing as intended in the yard's interior compound. More than a few bodies littered the ground in those areas, as well, the remains of Chodrecai soldiers caught unprotected when the bombing began.

A few reports from weapons carried down the passageway, but otherwise the shipping yard had grown oddly quiet. Sloane's eyes moved from left to right across the wide passageway, searching for threats. The containers, which were octagonal in shape for no reason he could fathom save for alien aesthetic, were stacked in formations that provided numerous gaps and other nice hiding places for snipers or anyone else with a weapon and a grudge. Between those gaps, Sloane saw other human and Plysserian soldiers moving forward, clearing every possible hiding place as they maneuvered toward the yard's inner compound.

"Weapon high!" shouted someone, a human from Sloane's unit, just before movement atop one container preceded a shower of pulse fire. One of the bolts struck a Blue soldier, driving him to the ground. The human nearest to him recoiled from the attack, but the next shot found him, the energy pulse driving him into the wall of a nearby shipping container. At least a dozen weapons on the ground leveled fire at the sniper even before Sloane could raise his weapon, the concentrated attack pushing the Chodrecai soldier from his perch and sending him plummeting to the ground, where he landed headfirst in a disjointed heap. Medics moved toward the fallen soldiers even as the rest of the unit continued its advance. A few more turns and fast jogs down narrow passages were all that was needed to bring Sloane to the last row of containers, beyond which lay the yard's interior.

"Holy shit," he said, unable to help himself as he took in his first view of the destruction wrought by the earlier bombing campaign. What might have been a building or central hub of buildings was now a series of smoldering craters. A cloud of dust hung over the scene, slowly settling back to earth with little wind to help dissipate it. Smoke rose from the different craters, and Sloane could see small fires burning inside many of them. The burning remnants of what had once been other buildings or structures littered the area. Several shipping containers on the yard's far end also had fallen victim to the airborne assault, with walls and roofs caved in and their contents now also consumed by fire.

Then there were the bodies, which seemed to be *everywhere*. Intact corpses as well as severed limbs and bodies without extremities littered the ground across the complex, victims either of an explosive shock wave or strewn shrapnel. Human and Plysserian soldiers from Javoquek's unit moved among the carnage, checking for anyone who might still be alive. Sloane heard the occasional shout for a medic, or watched as a soldier knelt down beside a prostrate Gray to check the soldier's condition. Orders in this regard had been explicit, in that anyone found alive in the compound was to be treated as a prisoner unless they presented themselves as a threat.

"What the hell did you guys use?" Sloane asked.

Ralitreq replied, "The ordnance is somewhat smaller than the *Koratrel* device used against your leaders on Earth. It is designed specifically to engage subterranean targets, creating a shaped charge with the force of the blast projected downward."

"I'd say it works," Sloane said, his eyes still taking in the depth and breadth of the enormous crater. "How far down is the blast supposed to be able to go?" When the Blue soldier did not answer, Sloane realized his friend was endeavoring to calculate a figure he would understand.

"Approximately one hundred meters," Ralitreq said after a moment. "Perhaps more. I am still learning how to convert to your units of measure."

Sloane grunted. "I'm pretty sure you'll pick it up before I do." Despite learning how to speak several Plysserian languages with the assistance of the translator headband given to him by Javoquek, the sergeant still struggled with much of the alien vocabulary. He was able to communicate well enough, and most of the Blues with whom he worked had already mastered English along with several other Earth languages. When it came to more complex concepts such as computing mathematical equations or measures of distance or length, Sloane felt as though he were a kid back in junior high school, his face turning red beneath the stern gaze of his algebra teacher as the man handed him yet another homework assignment marked with a failing grade.

Never liked that prick, anyway.

Gesturing toward the crater, he said, "That should've been deep enough to get at the underground chambers, don't you think?"

Ralitreq nodded. "If the aerial surveillance reports we received about this facility are accurate." Those reports, which had included thermal imagery, had picked up the enormous energy signatures being generated on the premises that far exceeded the output one might expect from a simple shipping yard. Further reconnaissance by assets on the ground, including—Sloane noted with no small amount of pride—a team of Army Cavalry scouts, had confirmed the presence of power systems of a type consistent with those needed to operate a portal generator. This information was relayed to Plysserian scientists, *Laepotic* Wysejral among them, who confirmed that the site was one responsible for sending fresh Chodrecai personnel and equipment in support of counteroffensive actions on Earth. Other sites around *Jontashreena* had been identified in similar fashion, and all had been targeted for strikes similar to the one that had decimated this location. Though the Grays had succeeded in mounting some attempts at deflecting the ferocity of the joint human-Plysserian offensive, to Sloane the strategy carried with it all the signs of a desperate, last-ditch gambit—a Hail Mary play.

"At least we were able to save most of the yard itself," he noted. The facility, according to Javoquek, was one of the main freight distribution centers on the western coast of the *Chodrecisilae* continent. Even on *Jontashreena*, whose level of technology and industrialization was estimated at anywhere from two to five generations beyond the most advanced counterparts on Earth, much of the large-scale transport of goods still occurred by sea. Immense carriers, rivaling the biggest supertankers and freight ships traveling Earth's oceans, shouldered the responsibility of transferring cargo to ports around the world. Installations such as this one were vital to the infrastructure of Chodrecai society, and would play important roles in any postwar rebuilding efforts.

"You'd think the portals would make so much of this stuff irrelevant," Sloane said after a moment. Shrugging, he added, "I mean, I know they'd have to be bigger, and many more of them would have to be built, but wouldn't you think, with such technology at your fingertips, sticking cargo on a ship and sending it sailing around the planet would feel a bit outdated?"

Ralitreq said, "There would be a cost for such efficiency. The energy demands for a single portal are considerable. An entire network of them around the world could not help but have a detrimental impact on the planet's natural resources, which have already been stressed thanks to the war and our own unbridled desire to make our lives more convenient, regardless of the environmental as well as the simple monetary cost."

"That has a familiar ring to it," Sloane countered, though he knew he could not disagree with his friend's assessment. The portals currently in use on Earth were necessary, to be sure, but what impact was their use having on his own planet right now? What price would be paid for the role the conduits had played in turning the tables of this war, and what would happen when that bill came due?

A crackle of static snapped in Sloane's ear, followed by the sound of Lieutenant Michael Gutierrez's voice. *"Prairie Dog, this is Sidewinder. You copy?"*

Keying his microphone, Sloane replied, "Affirmative. We're at the center of the compound. What's left of it, anyway."

"We're moving in, opposite your position," Gutierrez replied. Sloane recalled the shipping yard's oval-shaped layout, and how Javoquek had deployed his troops to take the objective. The multiple avenues of approach called for eleven groups, each advancing toward the yard's center from the perimeter security barrier. Aerial recon had revealed a sizable portion of the military contingent to be inside the central structures as well as in the underground cavern beneath the compound. How many of them had fled the subterranean complex once the bombing had started, preferring to take their chances outside on the surface rather than risk being buried beneath tons of rock?

I probably would've done the same thing.

More weapons fire, distant this time, sounded from somewhere ahead of Sloane and to his right, in the vicinity of where he would expect Gutierrez and his team to be. Keying his mike, he asked, "Sidewinder, you okay?"

There was a pause before Gutierrez replied, *"Picking up a few stragglers along the way, hiding in the nooks and crannies. Some are turning and heading back in, probably looking for another exit. Watch your ass."*

Kret Aloquon heard the shouted commands to keep his arms in the air above his head and his hands open to show that he was carrying no weapons. Along with his fellow soldiers, he remained where he stood, offering no resistance and making no moves that might be interpreted as hostile. Maintaining his balance was a struggle as he supported his weight on his uninjured right leg. His other leg was bleeding above the knee, and when he attempted to place his foot on the ground he was greeted with a shock of excruciating pain. Aloquon suspected it had much to do with the piece of charred metal embedded in his thigh.

Before him, Plysserian soldiers as well as smaller, weaker-looking figures moved toward them, weapons aimed and ready to fire. Whereas he understood the orders given by Plysserians, several of them conveyed in his native tongue, he only partially comprehended the instructions offered by their human counterparts. A few of the humans appeared to be speaking in one or two dialects with which he was familiar, but otherwise the sounds they made were little more than gibberish to him.

A human soldier stepped closer to him, the weapon it carried aimed at the center of Aloquon's chest. The human wore a robust head covering as well as a piece of bulky equipment encasing its torso, which Aloquon guessed was meant to offer some form of protection against weapons or explosions. Despite the weapon and other accessories, this human was small and fragile, and Aloquon knew that on any other occasion he could kill the human with little effort. He had seen firsthand the effects of a pulse rifle on their soft, pink flesh, but they also were vulnerable in simple unarmed combat. Aloquon had witnessed the results of such fighting as well.

The human shouted something over his shoulder in what Aloquon recognized as a Plysserian dialect, and a moment later a Plysserian wearing an insignia that identified him as a medical caregiver approached. The caregiver indicated Aloquon's injured leg.

"May I treat your wound?"

Aloquon nodded. Following the caregiver's directions, he slowly lowered himself to the ground, wincing at the bolts of pain coursing through his leg. His hand brushed against the metal shard in his thigh and he could not suppress the cry of pain that action elicited.

"I will administer a medicine for your pain," the caregiver said, reaching out to offer assistance as Aloquon sat on the ground. The human soldier stood nearby, out of reach and with his weapon still aimed at Aloquon.

"Your injuries will be treated, after which you will be taken to a detention area, where you will be fed and sheltered. Do you understand?"

Still feeling the effects of his painful movements, it took Aloquon a moment to realize that the words were not being spoken by the caregiver, who worked in silence to clean the area around his wounded thigh. Looking up, he realized that it was the human who addressed him, its expression unreadable.

"Do you understand?" it repeated, and this time Aloquon nodded in acknowledgment, gratified that the humans seemed to be following the laws of conflict on which Chodrecai and Plysserian leaders had agreed long ago, particularly with respect to the treatment of prisoners.

It seems the reports of the humans and Plysserians working together even at the lowest levels of the infantry are true, after all.

Aloquon noted for the first time that this human appeared better armed and equipped than those he had encountered many cycles ago, during the failed campaign on Earth. The humans he had encountered in the harsh, bitterly cold region into which he had been transported—"*Musk-vah*," according to the briefing he had received prior to entering the portal—were far less prepared, not only for the battle itself, but seemingly even for the environment in which they fought. Their infantry weapons were all but useless against Chodrecai body armor, though they had employed aerial assault craft and armored ground vehicles to surprising effect. In the end, the cold more than anything else had been the deciding factor, eventually forcing the Chodrecai to retreat back through the portal to *Jontashreena*. That naturally had given the human forces even more incentive to fight, which they did with a ferocity that almost made up for their inferior weapons and even their weaker bodies. For Aloquon, that had been the worst part of the entire experience: waiting for his turn to enter the conduit and its relative safety away from the bone-numbing cold and an enemy that had seen weakness and pounced.

Now, it seemed, the humans carried even greater motivation to achieve victory. In truth, Aloquon understood and respected that mind-set. Just as he had joined the military to serve his people and protect his homeland, so too had the human now standing before him. He suspected that the history of both planets was rife with examples of the formidable enemies to be made from those whose primary impetus for fighting was simple survival, or the protection of family. This human, and countless others like it, had responded to the threat posed by the Chodrecai, even if that threat was itself borne only from a similar desire to protect and defend what was held dear. Not only had the humans risen to meet that challenge, they also had seen fit to strike back. How could these aliens be blamed simply for acting just as the Chodrecai had done so long ago?

Formidable enemies, indeed.

40

Smoke hung in the air, obscuring everything beyond a hundred meters. As the convoy of tanks and armored personnel carriers came to a halt and troops disembarked the various vehicles, Ron Hanagan emerged from the back of the LAV—light armored vehicle—and surveyed the area. He coughed despite the scarf he wore to shield his nose and mouth. When he pulled the protective goggles from his face to rest them atop his helmet, his eyes stung and began to water. When he pulled down his scarf, the stench of expended ordnance, burning fuel, and scorched metal assailed his nostrils. Out of habit, he reached up to stroke his brown-gray beard, smoothing the renegade hairs back into place. He could already feel the effects of not trimming the beard during the past several days. It was starting to get scruffy, and his neck itched, though he blamed the knit scarf and sweat for that.

"You're going to want to put that muffler back on," said Corporal Jeffrey Jacques as he stepped from the LAV to stand next to Hanagan. "There's enough crap in the air to give you a dozen different types of cancer." The soldier also wore a scarf and goggles to protect his face, and his uniform and gloves saw to it that none of his skin was exposed. Only the corporal's eyes were visible, through the goggles' tinted lenses. Like the other soldiers in his unit, Jacques carried a new C8AA1 assault rifle slung from his shoulder in such a manner that the weapon hung across his body, allowing him to rest his right arm along its barrel. The rifle was a variant of the weapon developed by American arms technicians working in concert with Plysserian engineers, using technology provided by the alien benefactors. Hanagan had seen the rifles in action during familiarization fire exercises, watching with no small amount of fascination as they obliterated their man-sized targets.

"Correct me if I'm wrong," Hanagan said, smiling as he wiped grit from his eyes before replacing the goggles and scarf over his face, "but don't you smoke something like a pack and a half of cigarettes a day?"

Jacques shrugged. "The devil you know. You have to wonder what kind of noxious crap is in the stuff we're breathing now. Our gonads will probably be glowing in the dark by the end of the week." Even with the scarf covering his mouth, Hanagan could tell when the corporal smiled. "That could make for one hell of a conversation starter with the ladies at the clubs."

Chuckling, Hanagan shook his head. Despite the age-old mantra about journalists maintaining objectivity and a professional distance from the subjects of their reporting, he had from his first day taken a liking to Jacques and many of his fellow soldiers from Company D, 2nd Battalion, Royal Canadian Regiment, Canadian Land Force Command. The operation in which the company was taking part—seizing this Chodrecai air base—was being conducted as a joint venture between Canadian, American, Japanese, and Plysserian forces. Hanagan was one of five embedded journalists traveling with the troops, and when the Canadian correspondent was asked by his news network to cover the movements of the Blue units, Hanagan and his fellow American reporter flipped a coin to see who would go with the CLFC contingent. Excited at the opportunity to observe a different aspect of military operations from what he had seen during his brief tours with American units in the Middle East back on Earth, Hanagan at first had wondered what he would encounter as an American reporting on the activities of a Canadian unit. His concerns were unfounded, as Jacques and his companions had never once made him feel like an outsider.

A light breeze was helping the smoke to dissipate, and Hanagan was able to make out the remnants of what likely had been a massive hangar, now reduced to crumpled heaps of burning rubble. All around him, the dull gray surface of the tarmac was pitted with craters, some of them still smoldering. Other buildings were in various states of collapse, flames shooting from windows or through their roofs. Scattered about the tarmac were dozens of bodies in varying degrees of grisly ruin, as well as the scorched hulks of dozens of *Drakolitar* attack craft. Hanagan had seen more than his share of the intimidating fighters during the Chodrecai attack on Washington, standing in mute shock as the alien vessels tore through American and Canadian jets and helicopters with alarming ease. It therefore was gratifying now to see many such vehicles reduced to molten flotsam where they could no longer inflict such horrific damage.

"They really hammered this place, didn't they?" said a female voice from behind them, and both men turned to see Stephanie Maguire, Hanagan's photographer and video camera operator. Even buried beneath camouflage utilities, body armor, and helmet with goggles and scarf, she still somehow managed to look feminine and even attractive.

Jacques nodded in greeting as Maguire moved to stand with them. "Even the canaries can strap on a pair and get it right every so often." He smiled again at his invocation of the rather insulting nickname infantry soldiers used when

referring to their Air Force brothers and sisters. Though
Hanagan had heard the term employed on several occasions by different members of Company D, he would never
think to use the term himself. Although such good-natured
trash talking was accepted by those in uniform as part of
the military lifestyle, it rarely was tolerated in civilians or
other onlookers. "Of course, the Blues helped them with
the heavy lifting, not that they'd man up and admit anything like that."

From what Hanagan had learned from the company
commander, the air base was one of the first targets selected
during the planning stages of Operation Clear Sky. It was
important on several levels, first and foremost being its cen-
tralized location within the largest Chodrecai-occupied
zone on the *Galotreapiq* continent. Built here after the region was seized by the Grays years earlier, the base was the
primary launching point east of the *Margolitruul* Mountains
for combat operations as well as resupply and personnel
transport missions. Capturing or rendering the facility unusable by the Grays was one of the counteroffensive's main objectives for liberating Plysserian territory. It also was hoped
that the base, once the war was over, might be retooled for
use as a civilian facility to aid in reconstruction efforts.

*It's a fixer-upper now, but with any luck, Plysserian pas-
sengers will be losing their luggage here in no time.*

"Steph, grab the camera," Hanagan said. "We should
probably get as much of this as we can before they start
sweeping the area." Real-time reporting from the field for
simultaneous broadcast back on Earth was not an option.
Even if a portal was available and operating nearby, the
impossibility of transmitting conventional communications through a conduit made it necessary for Hanagan and
Maguire to edit their footage before handing over a digital
video disc to the company's communications crew, who

would then see to it that the information was relayed to one of the command bunkers for packaging with other messages to be sent back to Earth.

Surveying the area again, Hanagan shook his head. "Of course, by the looks of things, the Air Force didn't leave us much to work with."

Maguire released something approximating a snort. "Yeah, maybe, but I wouldn't count out a few stragglers hiding out around here. They can be sneaky bastards when they want to be." Turning to head back to the LAV, she said over her shoulder, "I'll get the gear. Try not to interview any Grays before I get back."

Nodding in agreement, Hanagan knew that the woman spoke from experience. Originally from the small town in southwest Missouri that had been the site of the first known encounter between humans and the Chodrecai in the United States, Stephanie Maguire at the time was a photojournalist working for one of the local television stations. Footage she had captured of the aliens during those initial days had garnered her the attention of her station's broadcast network, catapulting her from obscurity to the national spotlight at light speed. Anyone who might think she had advanced on looks alone need only watch her in action while on assignment. Hanagan had worked with her from the moment she arrived in Washington. In addition to being a first-rate photographer with a natural eye and good instincts, she was just hungry—eager to succeed, and possessing what she described as a new lease on her life and career. That, Maguire chalked up to finally being rid of the reporter from her hometown with whom she often worked, who in her words was a "useless small-peckered asshole."

Hanagan liked her from the start.

Turning to look ahead of where his and the company's other LAVs had come to a halt, Hanagan saw a row of

Leopard 2A6s, the principal battle tank of the CLFC, along with a complement of American M1A2s and a squadron of Plysserian *Jenitrival* armored assault vehicles, making their way across the expanse of open, uneven terrain. Hanagan knew from watching the units in action during the past few weeks that the mechanized infantry assets were spreading out, establishing a perimeter around the base from which a more comprehensive security sweep of the area would be conducted.

"You think we'll stay here tonight?" he asked, glancing at Jacques.

The corporal shrugged. "Probably. You'd think the Grays would be sending somebody to check on this place, verify they lost it, or maybe even try to get it back. I'm betting we'll be sticking around here for a bit, until they can free up a permanent garrison to relieve us." He shook his head. "Given how important this place is supposed to be, you'd think they'd have fought harder to hold on to it."

Hanagan replied, "Well, maybe the Air Force just did too good a job pushing them out."

"Don't let anyone hear you say that out loud," Jacques countered, laughing. "You'll find yourself walking home." He held up a hand. "Just you, by the way. The lady can still hitch a ride."

As he was preparing an appropriate retort, Hanagan felt the words die in his throat as his eyes caught movement from ahead of the convoy. It took him a moment to make out what he had seen through the still-lingering smoke, but then the source of the movement revealed itself.

"Holy shit." It took Hanagan an extra second to realize that he and Jacques had said the same thing at the same instant.

Dozens of Chodrecai, most of them soldiers by the looks of their clothing, were walking directly toward the nearest

Leopard. They carried no weapons that Hanagan could see, and as they advanced he noted that many of the Grays wore clothing that had been reduced to tatters. They all walked with their hands held above their heads in an obvious gesture of surrender. Had they learned that gesture from humans they had encountered and possibly captured or killed?

Stop asking stupid questions, you moron! Where's your fucking camera?

"Steph!" he called out, looking around for Maguire and finding her standing to his left, camera on her shoulder and aimed at the columns of approaching Grays.

"Already on it, Boss," she said, not moving her eye from the camera's viewfinder.

In the distance, Hanagan could hear various shouts of alarm, but no weapons fire, even though dozens of soldiers were running toward the gathering with weapons raised. In seconds the Grays were surrounded, and there was more yelling as they were herded closer together. Someone was talking through a speaker system, probably the company commander using the communications setup in his lead vehicle. He issued orders in English for the Grays to maneuver into a single column and wait for further instructions. Another voice, presumably repeating the directives in what to Hanagan's ear sounded like a Chodrecai dialect.

"Well, you don't see that every day," Jacques said, shaking his head in obvious wonderment.

Reaching into a pouch of his equipment harness, Hanagan retrieved a digital recorder and activated it. "No sooner did we arrive at the air base," he began, trying to order his thoughts into something approaching what he might say when he began the process of editing the footage Maguire was shooting, "than numerous Chodrecai soldiers emerged from the wreckage of the bombed-out facility with their hands raised in surrender. I'm watching dozens of Grays being taken into custody without a single shot being fired. I'm reminded of stories I heard from fellow journalists who covered American combat actions during the first Gulf War, when demoralized units from Iraq's Republican Guard surrendered to anyone who might offer them a hot meal. It remains to be seen if we're seeing something like that here and now."

His finger pressed the pause button, after which Jacques said, "You make it look so easy, just rattling stuff off like it's nothing."

Hanagan gestured toward the assemblage of Chodrecai, who continued to heed instructions given to them without the slightest hint of rebellion or subterfuge. "They're the ones who're helping us make it look easy. How many do you think there are?"

"About seventy," Maguire said, not moving from the camera. "Give or take a couple. They were hard to count when they were just moving around out there."

Had their spirit simply been broken by the aerial bombardment? Hanagan had no way of knowing how many casualties had been inflicted during that operation. Had the survivors simply seen the futility of continuing to resist the encroachment of human and Plysserian forces?

It can't possibly be this easy.

The proceedings were continuing to unfold. Stephanie Maguire was acquiring first-rate video footage of the mass surrender. Corporal Jacques was communicating with his platoon sergeant and making inquiries about conducting security patrols just to make certain the Grays' action was not some kind of feint or trap.

That left Hanagan himself, who with no small amount of anxiety was standing in stunned silence, waiting for the other shoe to drop.

41

The soft alert tone roused Aziletal Iledisavo from fitful slumber. Lifting his head from the sleeping platform, he craned his neck to see the computer interface perched atop his desk. According to the chronometer display, the device had awoken him at the prescribed time, but to Iledisavo it felt as though he had closed his eyes mere moments ago. He felt no more rested than he had prior to his reluctant decision to take a brief respite within the private confines of his office.

He decided it was a good thing that he had not even bothered to remove his boots, though he reminded himself that he had managed to pour himself a glass of *secratichal* prior to retiring. The glass sat empty on the window shelf next to where he slept, the drink's pleasantly sour aftertaste still lingering in Iledisavo's mouth. His personal physician would doubtless disapprove, having warned against overindulging with the spiced beverage while taking medication to regulate his circulatory system. Iledisavo initially had balked at the younger officer's overprotectiveness, but eventually had relented, just as he had complied with the physician's demand for him to take a brief rest period. Disregarding a medical officer's recommendations was sufficient to be relieved of duty, and he could not allow that to happen, not at this critical time.

Though it is tempting. The tired thought echoed in his mind, and with a grunt of resignation Iledisavo pushed himself from the sleeping platform and onto his feet.

A soft chime echoed in the room, followed by the voice of one of Iledisavo's aides speaking via the communications system. "Jenterant, *First* Dekritonpa *Lyrotuw has arrived and requests your presence.*"

"Of course he does," Iledisavo said to no one. In the cycles that had passed since Hodijera Lyrotuw had been transferred from the First *Dekritonpa*'s official residence to this secure command-and-control facility—buried hundreds of *cenets* beneath the surface of a remote mountain range near the center of *Chodrecisilae*—he had demanded constant status updates on the numerous engagements taking place between Chodrecai military forces and those of the humans and Plysserians. Seemingly capable of forgoing sleep for cycles at a time, the First *Dekritonpa* demanded new information regardless of the time of day or night, preferring instead to venture to the bunker's command center rather than have messages relayed to him through communications channels. Of course, Iledisavo held no illusions that the First *Dekritonpa*'s network of assistants and informants also did their best to keep him apprised, as well. Though Iledisavo could appreciate and even respect Lyrotuw's decision to directly involve himself with the military situation as it evolved—with every shift of the wind itself, it seemed—there was a point where being engaged deteriorated to simply becoming an obstruction. In Iledisavo's mind, First *Dekritonpa* Lyrotuw had made that transition cycles ago.

Without bothering to respond to his aide's call, Iledisavo straightened his uniform more from force of habit than out of any desire to appear presentable before Lyrotuw, and exited his office onto the command center's main floor. As he always did upon entering the chamber, he paused and took in the scene before him, glancing at those computer monitors and status indicators in his field of vision and looking for anything out of the ordinary. All around him, soldiers and civilian technicians were engrossed in their duties, sifting through information being sent to the bunker from a network of command centers across the planet, which in turn were receiving updates and situation reports from field commanders currently engaged against the enemy. There was a constant hum of activity permeating the air, a buzz of purpose as his staff labored to coordinate the numerous facets of the ongoing military campaign.

"*Jenterant*," called the now quite familiar voice of Hodijera Lyrotuw, and Iledisavo turned to see the First *Dekritonpa* walking toward him. With him was *Nomirtra* Farrelon, one of the officers who had made the transition from the staff once overseen by Iledisavo's predecessor, Lnai Mrotoque, and for whom Iledisavo had held little regard.

Rather than the flowing, colorful robes of office he might wear on any other occasion, Lyrotuw now was dressed in a drab single-piece, formfitting garment of the type often worn by technicians servicing crew-served weapons or assault craft. Iledisavo noted that the garment was insufficient to contain the First *Dekritonpa*'s ponderous bulk. It also was not an actual uniform, a small yet important distinction for which Iledisavo was grateful. Though Lyrotuw fancied himself a "voice of the people" and an ally to the military forces, and despite being one of the most vocal supporters of continuing the conflict with the Plysserians, he himself had never served. To his credit, he always had stated that point whenever putting forth legislation or other policies that impacted the military, but that still was not enough to convince many skeptics, Iledisavo among them, that Lyrotuw truly held the welfare and best interests of the Chodrecai people—including the military—as his foremost priorities.

If he did, would we be facing utter defeat at the hands of our enemies?

"First *Dekritonpa*," Iledisavo said in greeting as he gestured toward the massive status table at the center of the room. The table was encircled by a sloped, polished parapet, into which had been embedded computer interfaces and other control pads to direct the display monitors and holographic emitters installed into the table's surface. Reaching for one of the control pads, Iledisavo entered a string of instructions to activate a holographic display illustrating a three-dimensional map of *Jontashreena*. Touching several controls in sequence shifted the image to show the planet's two major landmasses, *Chodrecisilae* and *Galotreapiq*, along with several smaller territories claimed by either side. Regions currently under Chodrecai control were colored red, while those belonging to the Plysserians were shaded blue. A glance at the map told Iledisavo that the configuration was the same as it had been earlier in the day. He suspected that would change as status reports continued to be received at irregular intervals from military commanders.

"I understand that our forces at the weapons facility near Narispental were able to withstand an attack?"

It seems he gets his information from multiple sources, after all, Iledisavo mused, pausing to eye Farrelon, who despite his content expression had the good sense to remain silent. Again touching the control pad, he called up another display, this one depicting a re-creation of a situation report sent by the commander of the installation in question. "Yes, *Dekritonpa*. Our forces were successful, this time, but I do not expect they will be so fortunate during the inevitable second attempt." Before Lyrotuw could respond, the *jenterant* pressed another control and retrieved yet another report. "According to information we received prior to the attack, the facility is a primary target in their overall campaign." That made sense to Iledisavo, given that the installation served as a major supply hub not only for weapons and the means to arm and repair them but also for a broad range of equipment and other items required by deployed forces.

"What are you doing in response to this, *Jenterant*?" Lyrotuw asked, his tone neither accusatory or mocking.

Before Iledisavo could respond, Farrelon retrieved a handheld pointer from the table and used it to indicate an area of the map adjacent to the region where the weapons facility was located. The *nomirtra* replied, "We are attempting to redeploy forces from the air base at Wlentripan to supplement those already at Narispental."

"That location is also expected to come under attack," Iledisavo added, this time ensuring that Farrelon understood from his own stern expression to refrain from further speaking without permission. Returning his attention to Lyrotuw, he said, "The simple truth, First *Dekritonpa*, is that we are overextended in some of these areas."

Were all things equal, the ability of Chodrecai forces to control so many areas within Plysserian territory—with those regions in turn connected by means of conventional air and ground transport—would be considered an advantage. The massive campaign conceived and overseen by Iledisavo's predecessor had proven most successful in giving the Chodrecai immovable footholds on the *Galotreapiq* continent. Attacking the coastal realms and moving inward, forces had claimed territory at an impressive rate, occupying civilian population centers as well as military installations from which Plysserian forces were compelled to retreat. Using abandoned or captured Plysserian air bases, Chodrecai attack craft were able to launch sustained airborne attacks against inland targets.

The Plysserians staged counteroffensives, of course, both on the ground and from the air, but military leaders even-

tually discarded that strategy in favor of fortifying defenses
farther inland as well as guarding the continent's opposite
coastline, lest they fall victim to a massive enveloping maneuver. From there, the war, at least as it was being fought
on *Galotreapiq*, deteriorated to little more than a holding
action as Plysserian forces struggled to rearm, rebuild, and
reorganize. In the interim, uncounted thousands of Plysserian civilians fell under Chodrecai authority, forced to work
in factories or military installations in order to support the
Chodrecai army, which now was firmly embedded within
captured Plysserian territory.

The portals changed all of that.

"In conventional terms, and even with the losses we have
suffered," Iledisavo continued, "we still would possess an
advantage. However, the portals from Earth offset much
of that benefit." The conduits' ability to deliver personnel and equipment anywhere in the world far outweighed
any ground or air superiority the Chodrecai military might
possess. He again pointed to the map. "With the portals,
they can transport resources from one point on our planet
to the humans' world, and then redeploy them back to
Jontashreena through another conduit to a different location
here, in moments. By doing so, they sever connections between important locations, cut off supply lines, and hamper
our ability to move forces over ground. We have attempted
to replicate this tactic, but we lack the detailed information
of vital targets on Earth. Even if we were to use a similar approach to send forces to Earth and then transport them back
here to different locations, we lack the knowledge necessary to calculate conduit endpoints here on our planet." He
sighed. "The humans have profited from Plysserian counsel
with respect to our planet, and they have worked together to
construct what is an impressive battle strategy."

"You sound defeated, *Jenterant*," Lyrotuw said, and for

the first time Iledisavo heard a hint of disdain in the First *Dekritonpa*'s voice.

He shook his head. "I merely state the facts, *Dekritonpa*. At present, though we possess superior numbers, the simple fact is that we cannot respond to all of the various attacks against our positions in a timely fashion. Those who orchestrated this campaign have to know that. It is the logical explanation for the pattern and timing of the various assaults. The effect against our forces has been devastating. We are receiving numerous reports of units surrendering their positions after offering little or no resistance. Commanders in forward or isolated areas know that we are unable to reinforce them and that defeat is inevitable, and they are choosing to lay down their arms in the hope of preventing unnecessary casualties."

"That's tantamount to treason!" For the first time, Lyrotuw's voice rose above the omnipresent drone of activity enveloping the command center. Glancing around, Iledisavo saw the concerned faces of subordinates turning in his direction, their attention attracted by the First *Dekritonpa*'s outburst.

"No, it is not," he countered, keeping his own voice calm. "Under the agreements we have established, soldiers are not expected to sacrifice their lives in battle if a commanding officer feels the situation is untenable. Anything else is the convention of fiction, *Dekritonpa*. Soldiers who surrender are required to be treated with care and compassion—food, shelter, medical attention. There is nothing to be gained by needlessly forfeiting lives to a hopeless cause."

Aware that their conversation was being overheard, Lyrotuw leaned forward, all but hissing between gritted teeth. "You call our survival a hopeless cause?"

It was an effort for Iledisavo not to reach across the table and choke the life from the First *Dekritonpa*. He was not accustomed to being addressed in this manner, and certainly not in front of a subordinate. The expression on Far-relon's face—masked and fleeting though it might have been before the *nomirtra* turned his head—still was enough to further irritate Iledisavo.

"*Nomirtra* Farrelon," Iledisavo said, "collect the latest situation reports from the forward command centers and bring them to me." It was a weak order, one intended solely to remove Farrelon from the immediate vicinity if even for a short time, but Iledisavo did not care. He knew that the younger officer, working as a military attaché to Lyrotuw long before the latter's ascension to the role of First *Dekritonpa*, had developed a close working relationship with the leader. Not for the first time, Iledisavo wondered just how far that association went, and to what lengths Farrelon might go to preserve whatever political capital his affiliation to Lyrotuw provided.

Though Farrelon appeared reluctant to carry out the order, he instead nodded. "Yes, *Jenterant*," he said, turning and leaving Iledisavo and Lyrotuw alone at the table.

"You do not like *Nomirtra* Farrelon," the First *Dekritonpa* observed. "In my experience, he is a fine officer with much potential."

"He is an opportunist," Iledisavo replied, "and that is fine, so long as it does not interfere with his duties or my ability to carry out mine. Now, as to your concern that I might find our cause hopeless, I say only that we cannot survive if we throw away the lives of those sworn to defend us, *Dekritonpa*." Though he and Lyrotuw had disagreed on previous occasions, this was the first time the leader had taken any disputes to such a level. Iledisavo at first reasoned that the behavior was a consequence of the stresses Lyrotuw was under, trying to govern the Chodrecai people through a crisis that seemed to be deteriorating with every passing cycle. Was there something more here?

Drawing a deep breath, Lyrotuw reached up to wipe his pronounced brow. "What do you suggest we do, *Jenterant*? Surrender?"

Iledisavo conceded that such was not a desirable option. He still possessed formidable forces, which might conceivably continue to withstand the ongoing human and Plysserian attacks, but for how long? Looking at the map, he imagined various scenarios whereby the proper allocation of forces might give them an advantage, at least for a time. But how much time would be required for the enemy to adapt their strategy in order to counter any new defensive schemes he might imagine? Could the engineers laboring frantically to understand the transference technology be able to do so in time for it to be of any use? Despite such misgivings, he could not in all honesty say that the fight was lost. A surrender now likely would spare countless lives on both sides of the conflict, but what did the Chodrecai stand to lose if their leaders allowed them to be subjugated by the very people who initiated this war so long ago?

"I see it in your eyes, *Jenterant*," Lyrotuw said, his tone of voice returning to that of the professional politician. "You think we might prevail, despite these setbacks."

Iledisavo shook his head. "No, *Dekritonpa*, I cannot say that with any degree of confidence, but nor can I say that we are destined for defeat. There is a possibility of our being able to reverse the battle, but I am uncertain as to its likelihood for success."

That was sufficient for Lyrotuw. "Then we press forward."

With no small amount of reluctance, Aziletal Iledisavo acknowledged the order, wondering as he did so whether this day might well mark the beginning of the end for the Chodrecai.

42

"Group Twenty-one, move to the ready line. Group Twenty-one to the ready line. Stand by for transport!"

The master sergeant's voice boomed across the open expanse of the hangar as he strolled past groups of soldiers. He never broke stride, walking in a straight line down the center of the long, narrow hangar as subordinates scrambled to get out of his way.

"That's us," said Leading Private Yoshida Hideaki to his friend, Private First Class Sasaki Masato. As their companions busied themselves with picking up their packs and weapons, Yoshida took one last drag of his cigarette before dropping it to the concrete floor and mashing it beneath his boot. Then, because he did not wish to invoke the wrath of the master sergeant or some other officer or senior enlisted soldier, he retrieved the butt, stripped it until it was little more than confetti, and placed the litter in his trouser pocket.

"You really·should stop smoking," Sasaki said as he hefted his pack onto his back and tightened the shoulder straps, adjusting and situating it until he was comfortable.

Yoshida shrugged. "I'll stop when we get back." While smoking was frowned upon in the service, it had not yet been officially forbidden. Yoshida knew the habit was unhealthy, but it was a holdover from the aimless, almost criminal lifestyle that had characterized his late teenage years, before his father convinced him to seek the structure and discipline that came from joining the Self-Defense Forces. He supposed the connection to his former life was reason enough to quit, but to this point he had been unable—unwilling, in reality—to summon the willpower necessary even to keep himself from buying a new pack.

With their gear situated on their backs, helmets donned, and weapons slung over their shoulders, the pair fell into line behind fellow soldiers and began moving toward the designated assembly point, the "ready line" for groups preparing to be deployed to the alien planet by way of the outlandish interplanetary portal. That such a gateway had been built within the confines of this hangar was still difficult to believe, despite everything Yoshida had learned about the aliens and their war in the year since their arrival on Earth.

Reaching up to wipe sweat from his forehead, Yoshida said, "I hope it's cooler where we're going." The air was stifling inside the hangar, one of several at the west end of the expansive tarmac that was one of the dominant features of Kadena Air Base, the largest American military base on the Japanese prefecture island of Okinawa and the focal point of American airpower in the Asian-Pacific region. With no discernible environmental control, the structure's interior appeared to have been left at the mercy of the Okinawan summer's typically brutal heat and humidity.

"I still can't believe we're doing this," Sasaki said, falling into step beside Yoshida. "Even though it makes sense, considering all of the training they put us through."

Yoshida nodded. "I wonder how long they've known they'd be sending us. You know people will protest what we're doing." He remembered news reports from months ago, speculating that units of the Japan Self-Defense Forces might be deployed to points around the world or even—

according to some of the more extreme theories—sent to the alien planet to fight. The unchecked conjecture on the part of the media naturally had fueled a storm of protests throughout Japan, with many people believing the notion of military forces engaged in any capacity beyond the country's boundaries was a violation of legal doctrine dating back more than sixty years.

Following Japan's defeat at the end of the Second World War, nearly every vestige of the nation's military culture was eliminated, and an article written into its new constitution specifically prohibited the existence of any military forces capable of participating in war. The Japanese government modified that stance in the early 1950s, authorizing the creation of a small, civilian-supervised military force, whose primary mission was internal defense, security, and disaster relief. Aggressive armed action was expressly forbidden. From the time of its inception, the JSDF maintained its focused mission, rarely deploying beyond Japanese borders and only then to participate in United Nations–authorized peacekeeping and humanitarian assistance efforts. Though forces were sent to Iraq at the request of the United States to support reconstruction initiatives, even that action did not stray too far from the organization's mandated mission. Only now, with the entire world facing a global threat, were Japanese soldiers for the first time being sent to participate in offensive combat operations. As part of the planning for Operation Clear Sky, infantry units from the force's Northern Army had traveled to Okinawa, where they in turn would transport to the alien planet alongside their American counterparts.

While Yoshida Hideaki understood the historical significance of what he and his fellow soldiers were about to do, that did not ease the anxiety he now felt. Having enlisted two years earlier, not a day had passed that he was not reminded of the JSDF's role. How would the civilian populace, which had become accustomed to the country's all but pacifist culture, react to this sudden sidestepping of a cherished cornerstone of modern Japanese society?

If we're lucky, we'll make it back to see what happens.

Shifting his pack higher on his shoulders, Yoshida adjusted the sling of his rifle. He raised his head, trying to see above the parallel columns of soldiers that now stood in the hangar's staging area. At the structure's far end, he could see the massive generators that he now knew was used to power the machines responsible for creating the portal that would connect Earth to the alien planet. Though he had watched the portal generation in action several times since his unit had arrived at Kadena, he had yet to tire of the sight. Just trying to fathom the idea of harnessing the incredible energies required to establish the conduit was enough to make his head spin. He had watched fellow soldiers disappear through the portal, and now Yoshida's heart hammered in his chest in anticipation of taking that journey with his unit. His platoon leader had informed them that the process was as quick as it was painless, taking scarcely a moment to make the transition between planets. They would not be marching directly into battle, but rather arriving at a staging area from which the soldiers would board Plysserian transport craft for movement to the area of primary combat operations. The strategy had proven successful in the human-Plysserian campaign in the weeks since the start of Operation Clear Sky.

"This is it," Sasaki said, and Yoshida heard the faint tremble of fear in his voice as his friend pointed ahead of them just as a deep rumbling sound reverberated through the hangar. Looking past his fellow soldiers, Yoshida saw the pair of immense generators being powered up, with a series of indicators flaring to life as they were activated. He glanced at his watch, noting that twenty-seven minutes had passed since the generators had been disengaged, a requirement given the stress the machines underwent every time a portal was created. During previous iterations of this exercise, the cooldown period had taken between thirty and forty minutes. Had the engineers responsible for keeping the generators operational found a way to increase the efficiency of the process, or were they cutting corners in the name of expediency, trying to get as many troops as possible through the portal? If it was the latter, what was the danger potential from such a practice?

You worry about the wrong things, Hideaki.

Feeling his exposed skin tingling as a bright flash erupted at the end of the hangar, Yoshida watched a circle of energy form from nothingness. As it had during the previous activations, the sound of energies colliding and being harnessed to create the portal was uncomfortably loud in the hangar's enclosed space. He squinted as he raised his hands to cover his ears. Beside him, Sasaki mimicked his movements. Near the portal itself, he saw someone, an older, noncommissioned officer, wave an arm toward the assemblage of troops before him, signaling for the group to advance forward. In groups of ten to fifteen, soldiers began stepping up to and through the portal, their bodies absorbed by the swirling vortex of color. Yoshida looked to Sasaki, swallowing as he felt his throat beginning to tighten.

"Here we go, my friend."

Sasaki affected a nervous smile. "See you on the other side."

A rush of sudden movement from the portal caught Yoshida's attention and he turned in time to see soldiers scattering away from the conduit as something emerged from it. It was a sphere: large, perfectly round, and made of some type of gleaming cobalt metal. The way light reflected off its surface, to Yoshida it appeared to be nothing more than a massive sphere of brilliant blue water.

"Hideaki," Sasaki began, and Yoshida felt his friend reach out and grab the sleeve of his camouflage uniform jacket an instant before everything disappeared in a flash of hot, white light.

43

Teri Westerson entered the command center at a full run, nearly barreling into and over a hapless airman with the misfortune to be walking past the tunnel entrance as she emerged from the passageway. She barely made it inside before the protective blast door cycled shut, sealing off the chamber. Pausing to catch her breath, she placed a hand on the arm of the airman.

"Sorry about that," she said, loud enough to be heard over the alarm Klaxons wailing across the chamber.

The younger man offered a feeble smile. "No problem, ma'am."

"What the hell's going on?" Westerson asked. "Why the alarms?"

His already pale face appeared to lose whatever color it possessed as the airman cleared his throat. "We're in lockdown mode, ma'am. There's been an attack, on Earth. A couple of them. The brass is worried that the Grays are gearing up to punch back after all the ass-kickings we've been giving them."

Westerson's mind was still processing the airman's first statement. "Attack? Where?"

The airman replied, "The southwestern U.S., somewhere in England, and Okinawa. That's all I know, ma'am. Details are still coming in." He nodded toward a grouping of workstations at the far end of the chamber. "I'm sorry, Captain, but I need to get back to work."

Still trying to comprehend what he had just told her, Westerson gestured for the harried young man to return to his duties. Now standing alone near the blast door, Westerson took stock of the command center. Men and women—humans as well as Plysserians—manned every desk and control station. Other personnel moved between the stations, and several others stood around the octagonal situation table at the center of the chamber. Among the faces staring at the table's myriad displays was the one she had hoped to find.

"Colonel Benjamin!" she called as she started across the room toward him. Darren Benjamin looked up from the table at her approach, his distraught expression giving Westerson pause. "I just heard what happened."

Benjamin nodded, reaching up to wipe his forehead. "We're only getting sketchy reports, but from what we've learned so far, it looks like three sites were hit, each of them housing a portal generation facility. White Sands in New Mexico, RAF Cottesmore in England, and Kadena Air Base on Okinawa."

Feeling her jaw slacken, Westerson reached for the table to steady herself without thinking. "Jesus Christ. How bad?" Even though she had come here to tell Benjamin of information she had obtained from one of her interview subjects—information she had attempted to corroborate by questioning other detainees—none of that seemed to matter as she considered the scope of what Benjamin had just reported.

On the opposite side of the table, *Malitul* Grotilequtem, a Plysserian officer Westerson recognized as an advisor to Benjamin and other officers assigned to the command bunker, replied, "It appears that *Koratrel* mass-casualty weapons were used in all three attacks. These would have been the same model of explosive as that used at the site of the peace summit on Earth."

"All three bases have three-hundred-meter-wide holes in them," Benjamin added. "No word yet on casualties, but when you figure that all three were staging areas for troops to be brought here from Earth, that number's going to be huge."

Holy shit.

Westerson knew that the targeted bases were but three of the dozens of sites scattered around the world acting as rally points for personnel and materiel to be transported via portals from Earth. "How did the Grays know where to attack?"

Grunting in obvious irritation, Benjamin replied, "Would you believe they had good intel?" He touched a control on a pad embedded into the side of the situation table, and a three-dimensional map appeared above its surface. Westerson was surprised to recognize a computer-generated map of the United Kingdom on Earth. "According to one of the Chodrecai officers we interrogated downstairs, there are several cells of Gray scouts and soldiers scattered around the world, collecting intel until such time as they can find a way to get that information into the hands of superior authority." He pressed another control and the map zoomed in to highlight an area of southeastern England. "One such cell was found operating in a little village near Sussex. Believe it or not, they were being harbored by members of an activist group sympathetic to the Grays. Ironic, huh?"

Westerson shook her head, finding the story difficult to believe. "These Grays managed to collect info on our operations from some house in the middle of nowhere?"

Another colonel, a stoop-shouldered, balding man she did not recognize, and wearing an Army combat uniform with a name tape that read COLLINS, replied, "They had some help. A few of the activists were either prior military or prior government service, and some of them still had the means to access secure government computer networks. From what we know, the Grays just let them do all the hard work, then killed them before moving on."

"And that worked?" Westerson asked.

Benjamin nodded. "Well enough. They were able to find information on at least half a dozen portal sites, and managed to meet up with a Chodrecai unit who in turn got that information back through a portal the Grays controlled. Once Operation Clear Sky began and conduits started opening across *Jontashreena*, Gray units had enough information to launch strikes of their own. The endpoints on Earth were just random targets; the Grays couldn't have known where the bombs would end up."

"I guess we got lucky that Gray officer was willing to spill his guts like that," Westerson asked.

Shrugging, Benjamin replied, "Not when you think about it. Grays have been surrendering left and right, especially in the last couple of weeks or so. They might still have us outnumbered, but Clear Sky operations are largely succeeding in severing supply lines and cutting units off from each other. We have air superiority over most of Plysserian territory, and about sixty percent of Gray zones. Assuming they don't pull some kind of magic rabbit from a hat or their ass, it's only a matter of time."

Collins added, "The Blue scientist overseeing all of the transport operations—Wysejral, I think that's how you say it—has already initiated procedures to reconfigure all remaining portal sites to secondary destination points. At least the damage the Grays were able to do can be mitigated to an extent. Still, it's going to take time, and it also affects the ability of assets to link up with troops already on the ground. We're coordinating that effort as best we can from here."

"Despite the losses you have sustained," Grotilequtem said, "we still retain a sufficient number of uncompromised portal sites to prevent this from being more than a temporary setback."

Bristling at the apparent callousness of the Plysserian officer's words in the face of however many troops and support personnel had been lost at the three attacked locations, Westerson nevertheless forced herself to maintain her bearing. Instead, she looked to Benjamin. "Colonel, I think I've got some information that will help us." Reaching for the trouser cargo pocket along her right thigh, she extracted a Plysserian portable computer data storage plate. About the size of a piece of paper folded in half, it possessed the thickness of a typical magazine. The data plate featured a connection port at one end, and Westerson inserted it into a slot next to the control pad near Benjamin. "Courtesy of another of our Chodrecai guests."

Benjamin tapped a control on the pad, instructing the table's computer interface to access the data plate, and the holographic image of a topographical map appeared above the table. The map's primary feature was a range of mountains, depicted by the computer representation as rows of jagged lines nearly superimposed upon one another.

"The *Hneri* mountain range," she said, recalling what she could from the hasty notes she had written in the moments after her interview with the Chodrecai detainee.

Malitul Grotilequtem said, "I am familiar with this region. It is largely unpopulated, located a short distance inland from the *Sembrakre* Ocean, what you would call the eastern coastline of the *Chodrecisilae* continent."

Nodding, Westerson said, "It's also believed to be the location of the primary command-and-control headquarters for the leaders of the Chodrecai military."

There was silence around the table for a moment before Collins said, "Are you sure?"

"Well, I didn't take the Gray's word for it, if that's what you're asking, sir." Reaching for the control pad, she tapped a new string of instructions. In response to her commands, a flurry of images began to appear next to the map. "This is high-altitude reconnaissance footage of the area, as captured by Plysserian surveillance craft." She paused the rush of data, selecting one image and expanding its size before keying another control. Now the single picture showed the computer-generated representation of a mountain, with areas of the impressive geographical formation highlighted in glowing red. "These are energy signatures captured by thermal detection. They're definitely artificial. Somebody's got a nice pad there."

"Jesus," Collins said. "If this intel is right, then—"

"If we could capture or destroy that facility," Grotilequtem added, cutting him off, "it could inflict significant, perhaps even irrevocable damage to the Chodrecai military command structure."

Westerson smiled. "It gets better. According to my detainee—and he admits this is an unconfirmed rumor—the Chodrecai First *Dekritonpa* has also been moved to that location because of its superior security features."

"God damn, people," Benjamin said, his eyes wide with disbelief. "This could be it. We can break their backs right here."

"There's no way that place won't be defended by any and every Gray soldier they can find," Collins said, waving toward the display and shaking his head. "We're better off dropping a nuke on the mountain and being done with it."

"That is not an option," Grotilequtem replied, his voice firm. "The use of such weapons has been forbidden by both our peoples. It also is likely that such a complex, buried as it is within the mountain, is almost completely self-sustaining. There is a strong possibility that large numbers of civilians—refugees, the families of the First *Dekritonpa* and other high-ranking civilian and military officials—are harbored there. Any military action against the facility has to take into account the risk to noncombatants. My superiors will stand for nothing less."

Benjamin snapped, "The Grays didn't seem too worried about noncombatants when they dropped a bomb on Geneva."

Grotilequtem nodded. "That is correct, and it is unfortunate, but you must remember that my people lost many of our leaders in that tragedy, as well. If we are to have any hope of ending this war sooner rather than later, then the First *Dekritonpa* must be made to surrender and order Chodrecai forces to stand down."

"That's going to be a tough sell to the president," Westerson said, "not to mention other Earth leaders." Of course, she knew that was a moot point. Plysserian civilian and military leaders had been calling the shots for weeks now, in accordance with the agreements reached between the Plysserian government and those of the Earth nations involved in the campaign.

Looking away from the map and directing her gaze to Grotilequtem, she added, "I know it's your planet and all, but we're not going to stand by while the Grays lob more bombs like that at us. You'd better hope your plan works, because if it doesn't, you can be sure our president will order us to turn that mountain into a hunk of glass."

44

Colin Laney spit out the chunk of pulp he had bitten from the strange fruit, grimacing at its sour taste. "What the hell is this?" he asked, reaching for the tube of his camel bag and taking a greedy gulp of water.

"It is called a *paola*," replied Kel, who stood nearby holding another specimen of the exotic-looking fruit in his massive hands. "It has been a favorite of mine since childhood."

Swishing water around in his mouth and trying to ease the fruit's lingering aftertaste, Laney shook his head. "It's like a lemon on Viagra." He pushed a gentle, probing finger past his teeth, checking to see if juice from the *paola* might actually have eaten a hole through his tongue.

"Be careful with those," said Sergeant Russell, from where she sat inspecting her M470 rifle in the shade of a large tree, which in Laney's mind looked as though it might have sprung from the pages of a Grimm's fairy tale. "They are without a doubt an acquired taste."

"And don't eat too many of them either," DiCarlo added as he crossed the ground toward them. "Otherwise, the next time you take a leak, the enemy will hear you screaming. From space."

That was enough to convince Laney, and he promptly dropped the *paola* to the ground. "Don't worry." Casting a wary eye toward Kel, he asked, "You could've warned me about that part, you know."

The Plysserian's face was unreadable. "Having observed the *paola*'s effects on the human digestive system, I know that is not a fatal condition. Indeed, when DiCarlo and Russell consumed the fruit in moderate quantities, it proved most helpful in alleviating the initial waste elimination difficulties they suffered when they began eating food indigenous to my planet."

"And that's really more sharing than I was hoping for," said Lance Corporal Thorne, who had taken advantage of the lull to lie down on the ground beneath the branches of a neighboring tree, using his pack for a pillow. With his boonie hat pulled down over his eyes and having lain motionless for nearly an hour, Laney had figured Thorne was sound asleep.

For his part, DiCarlo chuckled as he sat down next to Russell, unslinging his rifle and removing his helmet to place them atop the pack he had left on the ground near Russell's. Reaching for a pouch attached to his tactical vest, he extracted a cigar, which he stuck in his mouth but did not light as he reclined against his pack.

Grunting in agreement, Laney said, "Well, I'll never complain about MREs again." He reached up to scratch his throat, his fingertips brushing across the thick stubble he found there as well as along his chin and jawline. The nearly two weeks' worth of beard growth had been itching for several days, a condition exacerbated when he perspired, which he had been doing a lot lately. With no small amount of reluctance, he raised his left arm, all but recoiling at the smell of his own body odor. A check of his hands showed dirt beneath his fingernails and caked into his pores. Though he had washed his hands and face when circumstances allowed, he was still filthy. It had been weeks since his last bath, and almost a month since he had slept in anything more than his sleeping bag—or even just a hole in the ground. "What I wouldn't give for a shower and a shave. They always made us shave in the field during boot camp and MCT."

"Welcome to the real war," DiCarlo said, folding his arms across his chest as he chewed on the end of his cigar. His face also bore several days' worth of stubble, and his and Russell's uniforms were as dirty as Laney's own. "You want to drink your water, or use it to make your face look pretty?"

"I'm with him," Russell said, punctuating her statement by slapping a new power cell into the stock of her M470, the action similar to that of inserting a magazine into a conventional assault rifle. She turned to DiCarlo, gesturing toward Laney with her free hand. "After a month of running around and lying in the dirt and mud, a hot bath and a hot meal sound pretty good right about now." Reaching for the MRE packet she had pulled from her backpack, she held it up for emphasis. "There's only so many of these things a girl can eat, you know."

"There's always the *paolas*," DiCarlo said, smiling around the cigar.

Laney turned away from the exchange, not wanting either Marine to see that he recognized their verbal jousting for what it was: the playful banter of two people in love. Though both took pains not to leave too many clues for casual observers, there could be no mistaking the bond they had forged. It was not hard to imagine DiCarlo and Russell becoming attached to each other—rules and regulations be damned—after the months they had spent here, living and fighting in the company of Kel and their other Plysserian friends. Setting all of that aside, it also was obvious from his observations that the pair worked well together, having fashioned a form of spoken and nonverbal shorthand that was of particular use while in the field. Their familiarity with Kel and other Plysserians as well as their knowledge of the terrain, including which fruits and plants were edible for humans, also were valuable commodities. That they also had feelings for one another served only to enhance the other aspects of their relationship.

If these two finding each other is one of the decent things to come out of this mess, then more power to them.

Leaning back on his own pack and enjoying the shade of a tree adjacent to the one DiCarlo and Russell lay beneath, Laney allowed himself to relax as he regarded the massive water processing and distribution plant before them. Several Plysserian *Lotral* troop transports and *Lisum* attack craft rested on the grounds near the facility's main entrance, and Laney watched as human and Plysserian soldiers moved about the area, talking to members of the plant's workforce or inspecting the security barrier as well as various pieces of equipment.

Originally a Plysserian facility, it had been taken over by Chodrecai forces during one of the more recent skirmishes between the two powers, remaining in their control after Blue troops were ordered to retreat from the area. According to Kel and the information he had obtained from Javoquek, the plant was tasked with supplying potable water for the populated sections of the surrounding valley, drawing source water from underground springs and channeling it via a complex system of aqueducts to nearby villages and small towns.

Given the terrain and the paucity of water sources in this region, the plant was a valuable asset not only for the military but also as part of any postwar reconstruction efforts. With that in mind, DiCarlo and his team had been given strict instructions not to repeat the tactics used at the Chodrecai fuel depot. While they were to avoid as much as possible damaging the plant itself, the Gray military presence in the area was fair game.

Dispatching that military contingent had been a straightforward task. The unit consisted of a cadre of Chodrecai soldiers who oversaw the plant's security as well as the civilian Plysserian workers tasked with operating and maintaining the facility. The Grays had constructed a cluster of small buildings to serve as headquarters, barracks, and storage for weapons along with other supplies and equipment, which resided outside the plant's perimeter due to a lack of space within the compound itself.

It was awful nice of them to do that.

With the assistance of laser rangefinders—one of which Laney had operated while working with Russell—another couple of missiles had been delivered via mobile launchers brought from Earth as part of the larger materiel staging effort for Operation Clear Sky. The Chodrecai encampment was reduced to burning rubble in seconds. Those Grays not in that area at the time of the attack found themselves outnumbered by a newly energized Plysserian workforce, and the rest had worked itself out with little effort. Laney and his teammates had observed that bit of business from the safety of their concealed perch among the rolling, forested hills surrounding the plant. There was something gratifying about watching the civilian workers, at the mercy of the enemy soldiers for who knew how long, turning the tables on their oppressors. While the methods of rebellion were not for the squeamish, Laney could not bring himself to disagree with what he had observed.

Payback's a bitch.

Laney did not realize that his eyes had closed until the sounds of approaching footsteps jerked him to a sitting position. Blinking rapidly, he saw two men—one Caucasian, the other African-American, wearing U.S. Army camouflage uniforms as well as tactical vests, helmets, and weapons—walking toward them. His eyes caught sight of the captain's insignia on the African-American man's uniform, and he promptly began pulling himself to his feet.

"As you were," the captain said, raising a hand to halt Laney's movements. Glancing over his shoulder, Laney saw that while Russell, Thorne, and even Kel stood at the officer's approach, DiCarlo had pulled his own boonie hat down across his eyes, the cigar in his mouth resting against the cover's wide, floppy brim. Had he fallen asleep that quickly?

A subtle nudge from Russell's boot woke him, at which time the sergeant major sat up, his expression one of irritation until he saw the captain and his companion, who wore the insignia of a first lieutenant. "Sorry about that, sir," DiCarlo said, offering a disarming grin. "Old man has to have his nap, and all that."

The captain, whose uniform name tape read HAWKINS, nodded, and his entire face seemed to stretch to accommodate his broad smile. "I'll let you get back to that in a minute, Sergeant Major. My unit's secured the plant, and we're moving in a fresh crew of Plysserian engineers to mind the store while we interview the employees. From the looks of things, about ninety-five percent of the equipment is functional, and I've already been told the rest can be repaired or replaced without any major problems. I just wanted to tell you and your team how much we appreciate what you did here. It sure makes it easy on us when you do all the heavy lifting. I kind of wish I was getting to run around and blow shit up like you are."

"It has its perks, sir," DiCarlo said. Turning, he waved toward Laney, Russell, and Thorne. "But it was all them. I don't pretend to understand any of that high-tech mumbo jumbo. I'm hoping one of them can help me program my VCR when we get back."

"VCR?" Laney asked, unable to help himself. "They still make those?"

"At ease, Marine," Russell said, her tone one of gentle warning but her expression belying whatever weight her mock rebuke might have carried.

For his part, DiCarlo hooked a thumb in Laney's direction. "I rest my case."

Hawkins's laugh was loud and boisterous, emanating from deep within him. After a moment, he cleared his throat. "I just came up here to let you know that your team's being rotated back to the rear. You're being reassigned to a new mission, but first you get a couple of days' worth of decent sleeping and eating."

"Any idea what our next mission will be, sir?" DiCarlo asked.

The captain shook his head. "Above my pay grade, Sergeant Major. Even my friends back at command aren't talking. That should tell you something."

"Something big," DiCarlo said, his expression falling. Then he nodded. "Understood, Captain. Do we have transport back to the rear?" By way of reply, Hawkins gestured to his companion, who stepped forward and nodded.

"Lieutenant Drew, Sergeant Major. I've got a Blue transport heading back in about an hour. You're all booked on it."

"Outstanding, sir," DiCarlo replied. "Much obliged." Looking to Hawkins, he asked, "Any updates on the big picture, Captain?"

"Bearing in mind that my intel is a couple of hours old, everything I'm hearing says that we've definitely got the Grays back on their heels. They've pulled back from several key objectives, but a few targets to the south are still being heavily defended. From everything we can gather, they're trying to get organized and move assets to support those that have been cut off or caught off guard. Still lots of ground to cover, but we look to be making decent headway."

Awesome, Laney thought. The success of the campaign had relied heavily upon the overt, seemingly chaotic nature of the opening attacks to push the Chodrecai off balance and keep them reeling while human and Plysserian forces moved into position on strategic military and civilian targets. Sheer audacity coupled with surprise during the first weeks of the campaign, working in tandem with the Grays' depleted reserves and the decentralized manner in which they currently occupied Blue territory, was proving to be the offensive's greatest advantage.

"You'll love this, too," Hawkins continued. "We're starting to get reports of Gray soldiers surrendering by the truckload. A whole squad gave themselves up to the crew of a field mess hall earlier this morning. By the looks of things, Grays are scattered all over the place, either with intermittent or nonexistent contact with anybody in authority, and a lot of these guys are electing to hand themselves over." He shrugged. "I guess they figure they'll at least get fed or something."

"They might change their minds once they taste field rations," Russell quipped, holding up for emphasis the MRE she still held in her hand.

"Point taken," Hawkins replied, again smiling. "Anyway, you're all set. Thanks again for all you—"

The captain's next words were drowned out by the whine of energy an instant before Lieutenant Drew's head vanished in a spray of blood, shredded muscle, and shattered bone that washed across Hawkins.

Jesus Christ! Laney was diving for cover before the hapless lieutenant's body fell to the ground. The Marine's hand tightened around the barrel of his M470 as he rolled over his pack, verifying that the rest of the team was doing the same. He was still trying to bring his weapon around when he heard more shots from behind him, and he turned to see Thorne firing on the run, advancing on a clump of vegetation surrounding the base of several tall, overgrown trees.

"Geoff!" Laney shouted. "Wait!"

The Marine paid no heed, his attention focused on the thicket as he continued to fire. Thorne maneuvered behind the wide trunk of the tree Russell had been using for shade, laying the barrel of his rifle against the bark and firing again. Without missing a beat, his right hand moved to the M203 grenade launcher that had been fitted to the hybrid weapon and pulled the trigger. There was a dull thumping sound as the grenade was fired, followed by a compact explosion that tore the thicket apart, sending dirt and branches and whatever else scattering in all directions. A body lurched into sight from behind the tree, a Chodrecai soldier, staggering as it carried its own weapon in one hand while the other pressed against an injury to its shoulder. Blood ran from numerous wounds, and the soldier was able to stumble only a few steps before it collapsed to the earth. It fell in a disjointed heap and did not move.

"Son of a *bitch*!" Hawkins shouted, fury lacing every word. He made no move to wipe away any of the blood or other bits of Lieutenant Drew stuck to his uniform as he stood over what remained of the slain officer's body.

Laney ran up toward Thorne, nodding for the other Marine to move right as he went left around the now burning thicket, verifying that the Gray had been alone.

"Clear," he called out, keeping his rifle to his shoulder as he sighted down the barrel and swept the weapon from left to right before him, searching for threats. "Looks like he was alone." Even as he spoke the words, every tree and bush now looked to him like a potential place of conceal-ment. "Damn it, we secured this area hours ago." He waved the M470's barrel toward the dead Gray. "Where the hell did he come from?" Dropping the rifle from his shoulder, he shook his head, the reality of what had just happened only now beginning to sink in.

That bastard was watching us. Watching us the whole time.

"Nice job, Thorne," DiCarlo said, his expression con-veying that he knew the compliment rang hollow in the face of what had just happened. Russell, though she looked somewhat shaken, also appeared to Laney more angry than scared. Behind them, Hawkins had regained his bearing and now was talking into his radio, calling for medics to re-trieve Drew's body and for security patrols to make another sweep of the area.

A metallic rattle caught Laney's attention, and when he looked down at his rifle he realized that his hands were shaking. How close had he come to being killed? How long had they let their guard down? Yes, the area had been deemed secure, but the nature of combat was how quickly it began or ended, was it not? Peaceful conversation and the elation of knowing they were heading back for some well-deserved rest had taken only heartbeats to revert to madness.

Welcome to the real war, sport.

45

His eyes focused on the targeting scanner, Major Kung Jae Paik watched as the trio of overlapping multihued circles danced over and around one another. Constricting toward the center of the screen with every passing instant, the circles became one and glowed a bright crimson, the action accompanied by a telltale alert tone informing him that his target had been acquired.

"Fire," he ordered, his voice calm and composed.

Seated to his left at the weapons station in the cockpit of the *Jenitrival* armored assault vehicle, the young soldier serving as his gunner pressed several oversized controls in a prescribed sequence. The vehicle's reaction was immediate, the cramped cockpit's array of computer screens, status indicators, and backlit controls flickering or fading as energy from the *Jenitrival*'s onboard power plant was diverted to the weapons. Kung felt the entire vehicle tremble around him as its four pulse cannons erupted in a synchronized firing pattern. Diverting his attention from the targeting scanner to a display screen receiving feeds from a pair of cameras mounted atop the vehicle, Kung watched the quartet of pulse blasts tear into their target. In this case it was a fortified bunker, barely a sliver of metal visible aboveground from the reinforced compartment built into the base of the mountain. Even at this distance, the energy pulses found their mark with unerring accuracy, ripping through the bunker and the surrounding rock and dirt and chewing massive holes into the sloping, uneven terrain.

Near his right hand, the firing computer was searching for new targets even as Kung manipulated the controls to maneuver the *Jenitrival* over the broken ground. Learning to drive the Plysserian assault vehicle was a skill he had acquired in only a few short weeks, aided by his expertise with T-72s and other tanks spanning twenty-five years of service with the Korean People's Army. Though the controls were different—designed as they were to accommodate Plysserian physiology—he had seen enough variation in the tanks and other vehicles of Earth's various military forces that adaptation proved straightforward. The main difference was that the alien vehicle's cockpit seated only two crew members, rather than the three or four to which Kung was accustomed. Still, now that he had mastered the intricacies of navigating the *Jenitrival*, he found it easier than driving his own car.

It also was far more rewarding.

His gunner turned in his seat, swiveling from the weapons control so that he could better oversee the vehicle's navigational systems as well as its array of status indicators. Pointing to one computer screen, which depicted a topographical map, the gunner said, "Sir, the formation is breaking up."

Without taking his eyes from the navigational screen that was his only window to the world outside the *Jenitrival*, Kung nodded. "Understood." Given the terrain and the placement of enemy fortifications, maintaining any sort of rigid formation as the platoon of *Jenitrival* vehicles pressed forward was impractical.

Something punched the side of the tank, and the entire vehicle lurched up and to the left. Kung grabbed the control console to steady himself, and his gunner gripped the safety handle above his head as the *Jenitrival* settled itself. Kung tapped the acceleration control and felt himself pressed into the cockpit's unpadded seat as the vehicle lunged forward, its power plant whining in response to the added exertion.

"Stand ready to fire on my command," he said, checking the status of the targeting computer. Glancing at the display screen depicting his tank's location relative to the other fifteen vehicles participating in the forward push, he noted that the wedge formation indeed was breaking up. His platoon, along with three others that, like his, consisted of assault vehicles manned by human as well as Plysserian crews, had faced little resistance over the several kilometers of mostly open ground separating the forest at the base of the mountain from the landing site where the portal had deposited them. They had encountered token enemy opposition since arriving in the region, and Kung had seen more Chodrecai soldiers and vehicles retreating or simply fleeing the area rather than face the oncoming attack.

Was Gray morale and conviction so bad that they simply were giving up? Had their fighting spirit truly been crushed? Experience tried to tell Kung it could not be so easy. He had fought the Chodrecai on several occasions as he defended his home country, and therefore knew firsthand how tenacious and unyielding they could be. Though the joint human-Plysserian campaign seemed to be producing favorable results, with Gray units on the run or scrambling to hold in the face of the overwhelming multifront counteroffensive, Kung knew there was no enemy more formidable than one that had been cornered, stripped of all options, and left with nothing to lose. Of the Chodrecai forces they were likely to encounter, many now were cut off from higher authority and left to their own devices without hope of reinforcement or resupply.

Fueled by this belief, those in charge of coordinating the massive campaign had opted for a single, bold strike against what was believed to be a key enemy stronghold, the capture or destruction of which might result in an accelerated end to the war. The tactic was as aggressive as it had been quickly planned, with military leaders from each of Earth's military forces collaborating with Plysserian counterparts to devise a strategy that would coordinate air and ground assets against the objective.

Kung considered it sound thinking, but he also knew the potential risks. With human and Plysserian forces pushing inward from all directions, slowly yet inexorably drawing tighter the defensive perimeter encircling the supposed enemy nerve center, the soldiers tasked with turning back any enemy advance would view themselves as the final protective line. This would make them desperate, perhaps even reckless, and most definitely dangerous.

The now-familiar alert tone sounded again in the cramped cockpit, and Kung glanced to the firing computer's status display. Another target had been acquired.

"Fire!" he yelled over the whine of the *Jenitrival*'s power plant. An instant later the vehicle bucked beneath him as his gunner loosed another salvo, the results of which Kung did not see, as his attention was pulled to yet another indicator. "Incoming!" He was able to shout the warning a heartbeat before something slammed into the front of the tank. The vehicle shuddered, its metal shell groaning in protest as it absorbed the brunt of the attack. There was no time to recover as another energy pulse hammered the *Jenitrival*, and it was all Kung could do not to be bounced from his seat and slammed headfirst into the cockpit's low ceiling. His fingers moved almost of their own volition, directing the tank to change direction even as he applied more speed. The shots now were coming faster and faster, beating against the outer hull and sending reverberations directly into his skull. Several different alert tones echoed in the cockpit, including that of the targeting scanner, and his gunner already was acting without waiting for instructions, doing his best to lay down some form of suppressive fire even as Kung fought to maneuver the vehicle out of danger.

The Grays indeed were putting up a fight.

Kung expected no less.

"Light 'em up, Ozzy."

Though onboard inertial damping systems prevented him from feeling the effects of the steep dive into which he had just maneuvered the *Lisum* attack craft, Chief Warrant Officer Chuck Roland still leaned into the turn. Through the windscreen, he saw the orange-brown-green ground rushing up at him as he leveled out an instant before his copilot, Osvaldo Garcia, tapped the controls to unleash the ship's forward pulse cannons. Garcia's aim with the alien weaponry was right on target, and a barrage of energy pulses ripped into the battery of ground-based antiaircraft guns now visible along the side of the mountain. A trio of explosions highlighted the gun mounts, shredding them and twisting the metal so that the weapons themselves toppled or simply were consumed by the blasts. Fire and smoke roiled into the air even as Roland maneuvered the *Lisum* back into the sky.

"Nice shooting." Though he did not take his eyes from his console, he could still sense when his copilot smiled, imagining the light from outside the window reflecting off the man's impossibly white teeth.

"Nice flying," Garcia replied.

Roland nodded. "God damn, but this is a sweet machine. I don't know how the hell I'll ever go back to Black Hawks after this."

As though in reply to his musing, the ship shuddered, and Roland felt the vibrations coursing through the deck plates and into the pilot's controls.

"Uh-oh," Garcia said as an alarm sounded in the cockpit. "The natives are getting restless."

Frowning, Roland checked the array of external sensors and saw the source of the threat. Another pair of antiaircraft cannon had risen from concealment along the mountain's southern face. "Shit, how many of those things do you think they have?"

"Well," Garcia said, his attention on the *Lisum*'s weapons system, "if I'm the highest-ranking son of a bitch, then pretty much every one I can get my grubby little paws on."

Roland nodded in agreement. If the intel reports were accurate and this mountain did in fact house a vast underground Chodrecai command-and-control complex, then it went without saying that it would be well defended, but how far did that descriptor extend? Though high-altitude recon imagery had pinpointed what looked to be weapons emplacements along each of the mountain's sides, it already had become obvious that even thermal detection had not located all of the concealed positions. Roland remembered what he had been told about the antiaircraft weaponry, and how it likely was camouflaged beneath thermal shielding and almost certainly operated on some type of automated tracking system, using fire-control and threat detection computers to locate and engage targets. There was no other way to explain the uncanny accuracy of the weapons, which already had claimed at least three Plysserian attack craft in the opening moments of the air assault. However, it also had become obvious that those casualties had come when the luckless fighters had flown close enough to the mountain to be targeted by multiple weapons emplacements. So far as Roland could tell, a single cannon was not sufficient to bring down the fast, agile *Lisum*s. If he could avoid being simultaneously targeted by two or more positions, he should be okay.

Piece of cake, right? Roland knew it most certainly was not an easy proposition, particularly when one considered that his mission, along with that of the other *Lisum* pilots, was to engage the automated weapons and keep them occupied, so that they could not be used against the lines of infantry and mechanized ground assault vehicles currently converging on the mountain complex.

"We're being painted!" Garcia said, almost shouting as he pointed toward a threat assessment display. The image on the screen turned bright green and was blinking, indicating imminent danger to the craft. Going against instinct and years of training, Roland did not fight the *Lisum*'s navigational controls, instead allowing the attack craft's onboard computer to process the information from the threat recognition system and make its own choice as to evasive action. Beyond the windscreen, the earth fell away and was replaced by cloudless sky as the ship arced upward, clawing for altitude and distancing itself from immediate danger.

I'm never going to get used to that.

The computer turned off the alarm, telling Roland that the threat had passed. He once more took control of the craft, consulting the navigational displays to orient himself as the weapons systems searched for new targets. Once more the ground far below filled the window, and he caught sight of several other *Lisum* ships maneuvering above the mountain. He saw other craft as well: the uncomfortably familiar horseshoe shapes of Chodrecai *Drakolitar* attack fighters.

"Look sharp, Ozzy. We've got company up here."

Looking up from his console, Garcia peered through the window. "Aw, shit. I hate those pricks."

Roland sympathized with the sentiment. He and his co-pilot had seen the enemy craft in action before, back on Earth during the Gray attack on Washington. One of the damned things had blown their Black Hawk practically out from under them with a single shot, the helicopter possessing no defenses against the advanced alien weaponry. That incident had cost the lives of his crew chief as well as two of the soldiers loaded in the troop compartment, killed before even getting a chance to join the massive battle that had erupted on the historic grounds of the nation's capital.

That shit ain't happening this time.

Without being asked, Garcia tapped a string of instructions into the control pad of the threat assessment monitor's oddly sized keypad. "Says here there's only half a dozen of them. Hell, we outnumber them five to one."

Roland was not convinced. "Intel said there were only two dozen gun placements on the mountain. Wanna lay odds there aren't a few more of those fighters waiting in reserve?"

"Sucker bet," Garcia replied.

The speaker in Roland's helmet crackled, followed by the voice of *Malitul* Cejapoqrit, the attack squadron's commander. "*Attack Flight One, this is the Flight Leader. We are encountering increased enemy resistance, both on the ground and from the air.*"

"Thanks for the update," Garcia said.

"*Our instructions are to maintain attack posture and continue engaging all targets of opportunity. Ground assault forces are making advances, but they are being hindered by the weapons emplacements as well as infantry forces that have assumed defensive positions along the base of the mountain. Our priorities are the larger weapons.*"

"It's days like this that I remember why I became a pilot," Roland said. Though he and the rest of the attack squadron had not been briefed on the specifics of the ground attack, he was experienced enough to know what such an assault would mean for the human and Plysserian infantry forces currently deployed in support of that effort. "You just know those poor bastard grunts are eating some serious shit right now."

46

The pulse cannon tracked its target with horrific speed, pivoting atop its mounting, locking onto Jaxon Kelly, and firing before the corporal could take the first step toward concealment.

"No!" Angus Feder yelled, too late to do anything except watch his friend disappear in a haze of concentrated energy and blossoming red rain. Primarily intended for aircraft and armored vehicles, the pulse cannon was far more powerful than the rifles carried by foot soldiers. At a distance of less than thirty meters, the Plysserian body armor Kelly wore was no match for the energy discharged by the cannon. From where he hunkered behind a grouping of small, partially buried boulders sticking out from the base of the mountain, Feder felt his exposed skin peppered by bits of whatever remained of Kelly's body. The rest of it spattered across the rocky slope, slickening it with blood, chunks of bone and muscle tissue, and shards of what might once have been the man's uniform and equipment.

"Where the fuck did that thing come from?" shouted Cooper Harris from where he had thrown himself into a small depression to Feder's right.

"Concealed placement," Feder called back. "Damned thing didn't show up on the thermal pictures. Fuck!" With barely restrained fury he wiped pieces of Jaxon Kelly from his uniform. The corporal had been a good trooper, someone you could trust with your life. He had died doing what he loved, but no one deserved to go out in such grisly fashion. Feder wondered if the man had even seen or felt what had killed him.

Here's hoping you were spared that, mate.

Looking to his left, Feder saw other soldiers sixty or seventy meters away, advancing farther up the slope, using whatever cover they could find to keep between themselves and the pulse cannon. Elsewhere along the ridgeline, the occasional lumbering figure of a Chode soldier moved between trees or rocks, firing on the run while working to evade its human or Plysserian adversaries.

Why not shoot at them? Feder wondered, considering the cannon mount. Did the thing just not care about anything outside a prescribed range? That made as much sense as anything else, he decided. Glancing quickly around the side of the boulder that protected him, he saw that the weapon's muzzle had angled back toward the sky. The air hummed as it pivoted, turned, and fired shot after shot in rapid succession. Peering through the forest canopy overhead, he caught sight of both Plysserian and Chodrecai fighter craft streaking through the air, engaging each other as well as targets on the ground. Sighting in on the latter was made somewhat difficult by the forest cover ringing the base of the mountain, but Feder was not about to put his faith in the relatively scarce foliage to protect him.

"We can't stay here," he said to Harris as well as the other soldiers coming up the slope behind and to either side of him. "We need to keep moving."

"You first, mate," Harris said, and when Feder looked at him he saw his friend's grim, resigned smile, the one he always seemed to wear when the going got tough.

Of course it could not be so easy. They had waited as

mechanized infantry units and squadrons of attack fighters pummeled the ground around the mountain in a concerted effort to soften the lines of Chodrecai defenses. Aerial reconnaissance images had revealed the locations of numerous bunker and weapons placements as well as a few openings that suggested entrances. According to the tactical map in Feder's shirt pocket, his unit was not that far from one such aperture. Whether they were natural cave formations or artificial ports designed to look natural was anybody's guess. Feder could not care less, just so long as one of those holes led into the bowels of the mountain and the enemy command center believed to be buried within.

In the distance, he could hear the telltale sounds of human and alien weapons discharging. Despite the first wave of attacks by air and armored ground assault vehicles, the dozen or so battalion-sized units of soldiers dispatched by transport craft to sweep the area on foot were encountering resistance. There was no way to gauge the level of that opposition, but their mission orders had warned them to be prepared for a significant defensive effort on the part of the Chodes.

And on top of that, they've got these fuckin' monsters parked at every door.

Feder stuck his head out from around the rocks, trying to get another look at the pulse cannon, and his efforts were rewarded by the weapon angling its gaping muzzle lower as it swiveled in his direction. He pulled back an instant before the cannon cut loose with another salvo that chewed away chunks of the boulder he hid behind.

"Might want to be a bit more careful," Harris called out, and Feder watched as the sergeant inched his way to a point where he could see the oversized weapon. When the thing did not attempt to shoot him, he looked to Feder and shrugged.

"Sudden movements maybe set it off?" Feder suggested.

Slowly—millimeter by millimeter, it seemed—he maneuvered until he could see around the boulder with one eye. The pulse cannon had returned to searching for airborne targets.

"Fuck the cannon itself," Harris said. "It's the mount that looks vulnerable." He moved his Steyr A99 into position next to his face, sighting down the barrel and firing. Feder saw the rifle buck against the sergeant's shoulder an instant before he heard the sound of its energy bolt slamming into something metal. Peering once again around the boulder, he saw scorch marks where Harris had hit the cannon's base. In response to the attack, the weapon cycled back down and aimed in Harris's general direction, unleashing yet another devastating salvo. Harris was able to duck back into the depression before the cannon fired, and Feder watched as dirt and rock were flung into the air mere meters from where his friend cowered.

"I think it knows that's its weak spot." Feder grumbled, more to himself than anyone else. "This shit isn't getting us anywhere." Keying his radio, he snapped into his microphone, "Lieutenant, we've got a problem up here. Fucking ack-ack gun has us pinned down."

"*Already on it,*" replied the voice of Lieutenant James Swallow, the platoon leader who had replaced the late, lamented Michael Schuster. "*Keep your heads down there, boys.*" A moment later Feder heard the sound of something approaching from high overhead. The whine of an engine was growing louder with every passing second.

"Holy shit," Feder whispered, before shouting in a louder voice, "Incoming!"

A high-pitched shriek of energy sliced through the air just before something slammed into the mountain, the force of the impact coursing through Feder's boots. He had no time even to curse in surprise before he heard a second wail, followed as quickly by a third. The howl of the engine changed pitch, and Feder looked up to see the silhouette of a *Lisum* attack craft angling into the air. Then that was forgotten as something exploded from up ahead of them. When Feder poked his head around the boulder this time, he saw the cannon falling inward upon itself, the mounting base and the surrounding structure collapsing as the entire assembly fell into the newly created hole in the rocky, broken earth.

"Hot damn!" Harris called out in unabashed jubilation. "We're in business now!"

The message was spreading as soldiers all along the slope rose from their various places of concealment and continued their advance up the mountain. A shadow fell across Feder, and he looked up to see the hulking figure of *Zolitar* Niilajun standing over him. The Blue soldier cradled his pulse rifle in one hand, and with the other he reached toward Feder.

"Christ, Niles," Feder breathed, relieved to see the massive Blue's broad face. "Am I happy to see you."

"Are you injured?" the Blue asked, extending his hand. The expression of concern was evident even on the normally unreadable soldier's face.

Feder shook his head as he took the proffered hand. "I'm fine." Then, looking down at his bloodstained uniform, he added, "The blood's not mine. It's Kelly's."

"I am sorry for your loss," Niles said. "Corporal Kelly was a fine soldier."

Nodding, Feder allowed the Blue to pull him to his feet. "That he was, mate. That he was." Looking around the immediate vicinity, his eyes came to rest on the smoldering remnants of the pulse cannon. "Think there're any more of those things sticking in the ground?"

"It is a distinct possibility," Niles replied, before pointing through a stand of trees ahead and above them on the slope. "There," he said. "Do you see it?"

It took Feder an extra moment to discern what the Blue meant. Beyond the trees, there was what he at first thought was simply more of the slanted ground, rising upward at an ever-increasing angle the farther up the mountain they traveled. Then he saw it: a dark hole set into the pale brown rock.

"I'll be damned," he said. Glancing over his shoulder, he saw Harris walking toward them, rifle at the ready. "You see this?" he asked, before pointing uphill.

Harris nodded. "Well, there we go, then."

Several minutes passed as the unit, with Niles, Harris, and Feder in the lead, crossed the expanse of broken terrain, their progress slowed as they remained watchful for the appearance of any more pulse cannons. When none appeared as they closed on the now quite visible cave opening, Feder finally allowed himself to relax, but only the slightest bit.

Reaching for his radio mike, Feder keyed the unit. "Lieutenant, this is Feder. We've got eyes on the entrance. Looks like a cave, but the closer you get, the more you can tell it was carved out by some kind of machine."

"Out-fucking-standing," the lieutenant's voice echoed in his ear. *"Looks like we've got the Chodes on the run, at least in this sector. Keep your eyes open, though. There might be stragglers about."*

The muzzles of their rifles leading the way as they climbed the last few meters, they arrived at the entrance. It was not large, perhaps no bigger than two Blue soldiers standing side by side, and when Feder ran his hands along the rock wall his fingertips registered the smoothness of the surface. *Definitely artificial.*

"Doesn't seem wide enough to be of any real tactical use," Harris said.

"Shit," Feder countered, "I've got a friend in the States

who fought in Vietnam. Let him tell you the stories about the fucking tunnel rats they dealt with, assuming you can get enough liquor in him to open up about it."

Stepping closer, Harris angled himself so that the muzzle of his Steyr pointed down the mouth of the entrance and into the darkness of the tunnel beyond. "Well, anybody want to see where it goes?" If he was worried about the level of Chode resistance they might still encounter, he chose not to show it. Not that it mattered, anyway. The mission objective was straightforward.

Feder nodded. "Let's do it."

DiCarlo saw the enemy soldier just as the transport's rear hatch cycled open. The Gray's pulse rifle was aimed directly at him.

"Shooter at one o'clock!"

Standing to DiCarlo's right, Javoquek was faster than the Gray, his pulse rifle coming up and firing without any true attempt to aim. DiCarlo winced at the near-deafening report of the weapon's discharge even as he saw the enemy soldier take the shot high in the chest. It was enough to knock the Gray off his feet, and Javoquek was firing again even before the soldier fell to the ground. DiCarlo saw movement to his right and brought up his M470 as another Gray popped his head out from behind a large boulder. He saw the muzzle of the soldier's pulse rifle but ignored it, letting loose a barrage of fire that forced the Gray back into hiding.

"We're coming in hot!" DiCarlo shouted for the benefit of the transport's other passengers. They had been told to prepare for active resistance from the moment they entered the landing zone, and as such the transports themselves would not actually land. Instead, the craft would hover slightly aboveground, allowing the troops to disembark by jumping the meter or so to the unyielding rocky plateau that served as their landing site. DiCarlo studied the area, noting how dirt seemed to have been blasted away to reveal smooth rock beneath. Identified from aerial recon imagery as a possible entrance to the subterranean complex believed to lie beneath the mountain, the patch of relatively flat terrain—perhaps fifty meters in diameter—was an ideal location for small landing craft.

The rear of the transport settled to a point just above the plateau, and with a final nod to Javoquek, DiCarlo stepped from the landing platform, his boots finding purchase on the rock. Rifle up and ready, with its muzzle trained on where he had last seen the Gray soldier, he moved forward, clearing the way for the human and Plysserian soldiers behind him. He sidestepped to his left, noting from the corner of his eye that Javoquek mirrored his actions as the Blue officer traced a path around the plateau's right side, followed closely by Colin Laney and Lance Corporal Thorne. He heard the bursts of other weapons but ignored them, forcing himself to stay focused on potential threats within his own field of fire. Pulse pounding in his ears, he maneuvered toward the boulder, hunting for the Gray soldier. A glance to his left confirmed that he was nearing the edge of the flat and the steep drop-off beyond it.

"Watch your feet," DiCarlo called back over his shoulder. "That first step's a bitch."

Air whipped around him as the transport, having disgorged its passengers, lifted away from the plateau and pivoted on its axis before angling upward into the sky. Movement to his right confirmed the approach of another inbound craft, this one also loaded with human and Plysserian troops. If all went to plan, two more transports also would offload personnel in support of the mission to which Javoquek and his unit had been assigned: finding the mountain complex's command center, if it was here.

"Clear on this side!" Javoquek called out from the plateau's opposite side, but DiCarlo ignored it, concentrating instead on the area directly in front of him. The face of the stout mountain extended upward only a few hundred feet, DiCarlo guessed, and near the rock wall were piles of boulders stacked far too uniformly to be a natural formation. Some of the rocks had withstood the pounding of the earlier aerial assault, bearing scorch marks or deep ruts and pits where pulse cannons had torn into them. A hint of gray was visible to one side of a smaller boulder, and when DiCarlo moved closer he saw that it was the leg of a prone Chodrecai soldier. Once he reached the alien he saw that it was in fact dead, a significant portion of its head having caught the full brunt of a pulse blast.

"Nice shooting, old man," Russell said from behind him. "Good to see you haven't lost your touch."

"Yeah," DiCarlo said, turning away from the grisly sight and looking up the side of the mountain. From the pictures he had seen, he knew that the top featured a plateau, likely home to a larger, fortified landing area. Other units were being dispatched to that location, just as hundreds of soldiers currently were working their way up on all sides from the mountain's base. The strategy was not without hazard, particularly in the case of Javoquek's team, as they had for all intents and purposes inserted into an area likely to be surrounded by enemy soldiers. However, reports of only scattered resistance up and down the mountain, coupled with favorable air, indirect fire, and mechanized infantry support, were enough to convince Javoquek that the risks were acceptable.

And I was just stupid enough to want to go along. Indeed, DiCarlo and his team had been enjoying their second week of downtime at one of the several base camps established by human forces around the planet. They had earned their rest, but the entire group—DiCarlo included—had volunteered for this new mission.

Feeling a tap on his shoulder, DiCarlo turned to see Russell standing behind him, her arm outstretched as she pointed to something off to his right. He looked in that direction and saw what she meant.

"Now we're talking," he said, seeing the narrow opening between two large boulders. The gap was partially obscured by a hefty hunk of foliage, making it almost invisible unless viewed from a proper angle. "Good eyes," he said to Russell before turning and seeking out Javoquek. Once he had the Blue's attention, he pointed toward the opening. Then human and Plysserian led their respective columns around the edge of the plateau, working toward the mysterious hole set into the mountain's face. It was not until he closed to less than fifteen meters that DiCarlo noted something smooth and metallic set into the rock: a reinforced hatch, if his guess was right.

"What do you think of that?" Russell said, her voice low and tight.

"I think we just found the goddamned Batcave," DiCarlo said, keeping his rifle's muzzle trained on the hatch. He saw no signs of a lock or other mechanism by which the door might be opened. "Sealed from the inside, maybe?"

"You'd think there'd be some way to open it from out here," Russell said.

Moving to stand next to them, Javoquek replied, "There is." He was brandishing a *Bretmirqa*, a stout, ugly weapon that was the Plysserian equivalent of a light antitank weapon or other portable rocket launcher. He paused, looking to DiCarlo with what the sergeant major had come to know as the Blue's version of a wry grin. "Unless you have another suggestion."

DiCarlo smiled, making a show of gesturing toward the hatch. "Yeah. I suggest we all move the fuck back."

47

Multiple alarms echoed throughout the command center. Alert indicators flashed at every workstation, and personnel were scrambling to react to the numerous warnings and status reports demanding their attention. Standing in the middle of it all, Aziletal Iledisavo watched the barely restrained chaos threatening to engulf the chamber despite his people's best efforts to maintain some semblance of control.

"We have multiple breaches, *Jenterant*," reported *Nomirtra* Farrelon from where he stood near one workstation. "Enemy soldiers have entered the complex. Our soldiers are trying to fight them back, but at this point they are outnumbered. The command chamber is secure, but I suspect that is a temporary situation at best."

His demeanor a mixture of rage and fear, First *Dekritonpa* Hodijera Lyrotuw stepped closer to Iledisavo. "We must evacuate!"

The *jenterant* shook his head. "Even if we could reach a transport, we likely would be shot down moments after departing." From the reports he had received at a constant, rapid pace since the first attacks began, Iledisavo knew that the combined human-Plysserian force currently moving into the mountain complex already had disabled the majority of the exterior automated defenses. What few *Drakolitar* were available to strike at inbound enemy craft from the air also had been damaged or destroyed during the aerial bombardment and ship-to-ship engagements that had preceded the ground assault.

Iledisavo's answer appeared to do nothing save further enrage Lyrotuw. "We cannot simply do nothing. Surely you have some sort of procedure to follow for a situation like this."

"There is the Final Directive, *Jenterant*," Farrelon said, his tone suggestive.

Shaking his head, Iledisavo could scarcely believe his subordinate would even suggest such a course of action. "That protocol was abandoned long ago." The Final Directive, drafted even before the war had begun, called for the wide spread use of mass-casualty weapons against key Plysserian population centers. Naturally, the Plysserian government had their own version of this gambit, as well as a counterpoint to any such initiative the Chodrecai might employ. The results would be catastrophic, rendering large portions of the entire planet uninhabitable and likely dooming any survivors to a long, slow death, if not from radiation poisoning, then from simple starvation as food sources dwindled and whatever civilization remained crumbled to dust.

To his credit, Lyrotuw seemed appropriately repulsed at the notion. "No, we cannot do that, but do we not have a protocol for selecting key military targets?" He pointed to the computer-generated image of Earth hovering over the massive table at the center of the chamber. "And what of the humans? Do we not at least attempt to strike at them further before throwing up our hands in surrender? Surely if they see their world as vulnerable to our weapons, they will withdraw, if only for a short time."

"The enemy is in our midst, *Dekritonpa*," Iledisavo replied. "They know we are here, and they will not stop until they have reached their goal." At Lyrotuw's behest, he already had ordered the use of *Koratrel* weapons, deploying them through three portals known to be controlled by the humans. The effects of those weapons were but temporary, as the humans demonstrated once again how they could adapt even in the face of such catastrophic setbacks.

For no other reason than to gauge Lyrotuw's reaction, Iledisavo said, "Of course, I could order the destruction of this facility before they are able to capture it."

It took a moment for comprehension to dawn on the First *Dekritonpa*'s face before his features paled in fright. "You mean, with us still inside?"

"It would prevent our capture, *Dekritonpa*," Iledisavo said. "However, there are far too many civilians taking shelter here. I refuse to sacrifice noncombatants for the sake of some corrupted notion of honor or courage." Shaking his head, he drew a deep breath, releasing it slowly as he resigned himself to the inevitable and perhaps wiser course. "At this point, surrender is the most viable option."

"Surrender?" Lyrotuw repeated, all but spitting the word. "And yet you have the temerity to speak of honor or courage?" He pointed an accusatory finger at Iledisavo. "You have disgraced yourself and your uniform since taking command of my military. At least Mrotoque, feebleminded sycophant to Praziq that he was, understood the need to demonstrate strength to all who would challenge us. Instead our soldiers run and cower from our enemies, just as we hide in this oppressive hole. I should never have—"

"*Dekritonpa!*"

Farrelon's shout was enough to silence Lyrotuw, but the expression on his face told Iledisavo everything that remained unspoken.

No, he thought, his eyes widening in horrific realization. *It cannot be true.* Was the First *Dekritonpa* responsible for Lnai Mrotoque's death, which until now had been blamed on the same mysterious extremist faction believed to be responsible for the devastating attack on the Earth peace gathering? While Lyrotuw had condemned the incident in public, it had not swayed him from pursuing his original agenda, that of recontinuing the war against the Plysserians and the humans in the hope of securing Earth's vast resources to aid in the reconstruction of Chodrecai society. Still, was he capable of such mindless, callous slaughter? Was Lyrotuw willing to sacrifice thousands of lives in order to follow a political agenda?

Of course he is. The thought rang in Iledisavo's mind as he stared at the First *Dekritonpa.* "You." He said nothing else, the single word carrying sufficient meaning that Lyrotuw's expression grew fearful.

Any doubts as to where Farrelon's loyalty might lie were erased when he reached for the *Misabril* sidearm holstered at his hip. Despite his greater age, Iledisavo still was faster than the younger officer, crossing the distance separating them in a pair of strides and gripping Farrelon by his throat. The *nomirtra* cleared the weapon from its holster, but Iledisavo knocked it away with his free hand. Farrelon's eyes were wide with terror and he began fighting back, lashing out with hands and legs in an attempt to shake loose his attacker. Iledisavo's response was to grip the *nomirtra* even harder, feeling his fingers dig ever deeper into the other officer's throat. Reaching up with his other hand, he jerked Farrelon's head to one side and the sound of snapping bone was audible even over the noise of the nearby computer consoles. His body sagged in Iledisavo's hands and the *jenterant* released his grip, letting the now-dead Farrelon drop to the floor. Without giving the traitor a second thought, Iledisavo bent to retrieve the deceased officer's sidearm.

Consumed by shock, Lyrotuw stood rooted in place, his features a mask of revulsion at the raw savagery of what had just occurred. Looking to Iledisavo, his mouth opened, trying to form words, but the *jenterant* paid him no heed. Despite the emergency situation that all but consumed the command center, officers and other military and civilian personnel stood motionless, watching the scene unfolding before them with fascination, uncertainty, and fear.

"First *Dekritonpa* Lyrotuw," Iledisavo said, raising his voice so that everyone in the room heard him, "I accuse you of treasonous acts against the Chodrecai Territorial Confederation, including the murder of First *Dekritonpa* Vahelridol Praziq as well as *Jenterant* Lnai Mrotoque. I further accuse you of ongoing acts of aggression against the Union of Plysserian Allied States and the people of the planet Earth, by undermining First *Dekritonpa* Praziq's wish to pursue peaceful negotiations, and electing instead to continue the war under false pretenses."

He paused, hearing the murmurs of shock and disbelief washing over the collection of bystanders. For his part, Lyrotuw seemed ready to flee, his eyes darting around the room, looking for someone who might come to his aid. Stepping closer, Iledisavo regarded him with undisguised loathing.

"How do you answer to these charges, *Dekritonpa*?"

Lyrotuw's mouth opened, but the first word never emerged before Iledisavo raised the sidearm in his hand and fired.

In what had long ago become habit, Ron Hanagan followed close behind Corporal Jeffrey Jacques as he and the rest of the soldiers from Company D made their way deeper into the subterranean complex. Even though scouts had cleared the area, no one was taking any chances, and Hanagan knew better than to stray too far from Jacques, as the corporal had become something of a good-luck charm in the weeks they had spent together.

"Are you getting this?" he asked, calling over his shoulder to where Stephanie Maguire was walking behind him.

"Got it," Maguire answered. She moved without pressing her eye to the viewfinder of the video camera she carried on her shoulder, instead allowing the unit to record images as the company progressed down the wide, dimly lit corridor. The passageway's floor as well as its curved walls and ceiling were smooth, as though bored out of the rock by some immense drill. Light fixtures set into the ceiling illuminated the tunnel, revealing hatches set into the rock walls. Some of the doors opened when tested by soldiers, after which the young man or woman investigating the particular hatch announced the chamber beyond as clear or secure.

The most prominent evidence of Chodrecai occupation came in the form of bodies along with discarded weapons and equipment. Hanagan imagined he could still feel the residual heat of the weapons fire that had been exchanged here. The odor of sweat and blood was everywhere, along with the scent of scorched rock and metal. According to Jacques, the firefight that had raged here less than an hour earlier had been brutal. That much was apparent by the number of fallen soldiers—Chodrecai, Plysserian, and human—the company encountered as it moved forward.

Whereas most of the human corpses they passed were shrouded with the nylon rain ponchos each soldier carried, the Chodrecai and Plysserian bodies remained uncovered in accordance with their customs when it came to the handling of the dead. Instead, their bodies were arranged—when possible—with legs straightened and with hands clasped atop the chest. Human soldiers had been briefed on proper handling of alien remains, and Hanagan had observed more than one human coming to the aid of a Blue counterpart to render appropriate assistance, regardless of whether the fallen soldier was enemy or ally. Maguire recorded footage of such instances as she was able, both journalists convinced that this was a necessary, if heart-wrenching, side of the war that must be documented. If nothing else, Hanagan hoped the images might lend proof to the notion that human and alien could work together despite the differences that had conspired to consume them.

Following Jacques caused Hanagan to step around the body of a fallen human, and when he glanced down he noted that the uniform was of the variety worn by British soldiers. Hanagan nodded to himself in understanding, knowing that a British unit had taken the lead in securing this area of the complex. A patch above the man's pocket read FREEMAN. Though he had been positioned like the other fallen, there was no poncho to cover him. Without thinking, Hanagan reached into a pocket of his rucksack and withdrew his own poncho, rapidly unfolding it and laying it across the soldier's body.

I'm sorry.

From the fragmented reports Jacques had been able to offer him, Hanagan knew that the assault on the complex—rumored to be a vital command-and-control center of the Chodrecai military—was proving successful. Human-Plysserian units had engaged Gray forces all across the base of the mountain that allegedly concealed the facility, pushing through whatever opposition could be mounted. Casualties were significant, but whereas the humans and Plysserians benefited from continuous reinforcement, the Chodrecai were turning out to be little more than pockets of last-gasp resistance. It was but a smaller representation of what was taking place across *Jontashreena*, with the Grays buckling beneath the weeks of unrelenting pressure mounted by the combined human-Blue forces.

Ahead of him, Hanagan saw a soldier at the front of the column come to a halt, raising his right hand and forming a fist. Paying heed to the silent signal to stop, the rest of the company passed the message down the ranks, and Jacques turned toward Hanagan while pressing his left hand against the radio headset affixed to his left ear. "We're holding up here for a minute," he said for Hanagans and Maguire's benefit. "The Brits up ahead have found some kind of reinforced hatch."

"Do they think it's the command center?" Maguire asked.

Jacques shrugged. "Beats me. It's not like they'd tell us grunts that much." He smiled. "You two should really be up front with the officers. That's where all the fun is."

"We came this far together," Hanagan replied, returning the smile. "Seems only fair to finish it the way we started." He paused, considering what he had just said. While it appeared the push to secure the mountain complex was proceeding apace and unlikely to encounter significant opposition, he knew there still remained much to do. Not the superstitious type, he still could not help but wonder if he might just have jinxed the whole damned thing.

He flinched as the air around them crackled with static that filled the passageway. "What the hell is that?" he asked, feeling his heart rate increase. Behind the static was a low, constant hum, which rose in pitch for several seconds before fading altogether.

"Tell me we didn't just trip some kind of booby trap," Maguire asked, her expression one of worry.

As if in response to her question, a voice boomed through the tunnel, bouncing off the walls. At first Hanagan thought it to be indecipherable gibberish, but then realized what he was hearing was someone speaking in a native Chodrecai language.

"What's he saying?" Hanagan asked, a moment before his eyes widened in understanding. Though his grasp of the alien dialects was weak, he still was able to comprehend various words and rudimentary phrases. Two words in particular demanded his attention.

. . . *our surrender?*

48

Despite the voice speaking over the communications system telling Chodrecai soldiers to lay down their arms, there were at least a few Grays uninterested in going out or anywhere else without some kind of fight. Unfortunately for Colin Laney, several of those rebels were in front of him.

"Get back!" DiCarlo shouted, pulling Colin with him into the connecting corridor from which they had emerged into the larger passageway. Weapons fire echoed in the wider tunnel beyond, which to Colin looked like some kind of thoroughfare, large enough to accommodate vehicles and heavy equipment. He likened it to what he thought he might find if he ever had the opportunity to tour the interior of Cheyenne Mountain in Colorado, home to the North American Space Command. That facility had been depicted in various forms on television and in films, and Russell suspected it looked nothing like what the Department of Defense had allowed to be broadcast with respect to that tightly controlled facility.

Then another pulse blast tore into the rock a few meters in front of him, and Colin forgot all about such inane musings.

"They're dug in, all right," a voice said from across the tunnel, and Russell looked up to see Sergeant First Class

Marty Sloane crouched at the mouth of another adjoining passageway. Next to him knelt Lieutenant Michael Gutierrez and a Plysserian soldier he did not recognize. Upon making eye contact with him, the sergeant cast a perfunctory wave in his direction. "Anybody got any ideas?"

At the far end of the tunnel, where it appeared to intersect three other similar passages, at least half a dozen Gray soldiers had formed a last-ditch barricade from whatever vehicles, packing containers, furniture, and other detritus they could collect in the time available to them. The enemy soldiers had fashioned the barrier so that they could fire from behind it without exposing themselves, the muzzles of their pulse rifles protruding from slits or other openings in the makeshift fortification.

"We could try Javoquek's door opener," said Colin Laney from where he crouched behind Russell.

Standing next to DiCarlo, Javoquek said, "It would require too much time to aim. From their protected positions, they likely would neutralize any such threat with ease."

"I've got a better idea," DiCarlo said, gesturing for the Plysserian officer to hand over the *Bretmirqa* launcher. Taking the weapon, he inspected it to see that it was loaded and ready to fire.

"What the hell are you doing?" Russell asked. Though DiCarlo glared at her with an expression that seemed to warn her away from any attempts at insubordination, Colin could see that she did not care about any pretense of protocol, her eyes pleading with him to answer her question.

DiCarlo shrugged. "I'm getting tired of this shit, is all. Hang on." Without another word, the sergeant major stepped as close to the mouth of the tunnel as he could without exposing himself to enemy fire. Raising the *Bretmirqa* to his shoulder, he angled the muzzle of the hefty weapon well above where he might aim toward the barricade and pressed the firing control. A dull *thump* echoed in the narrow passageway as the launcher fired, followed an instant later by the wash of detonation as the explosive impacted against . . . whatever the hell DiCarlo had shot.

As the echo of the explosion faded, Colin heard a new rumbling sound, channeled through the tunnel wall behind him as well as the floor beneath his boots. He heard the impact of something heavy falling to the ground, and when he looked toward the passageway he saw clouds of dust billowing across the open floor.

"What the hell did you do?" Colin asked.

DiCarlo did not respond but instead ducked back into the tunnel as, on the far side of the thoroughfare, the Plysserian accompanying Sloane and Gutierrez mimicked the sergeant major's action, aiming his own *Bretmirqa* at a steep upward angle. This time, Colin understood. DiCarlo had fired at the ceiling, dislodging rock so that it might fall upon the enemy position. A second later, another resounding explosion washed through the tunnel, followed by an additional round of cascading stone from the damaged ceiling.

"A cave-in?" Colin asked, smiling in surprise and approval. "That's pretty fucking harsh."

"Beats taking a pulse rifle up the ass," DiCarlo said before nodding to Javoquek, who in turn rose to his feet and stepped into the corridor, weapon at the ready. DiCarlo followed, with Russell behind him and Colin shadowing her. Across the hallway, Lieutenant Gutierrez followed suit, hugging the wall to his right as he led his team into the corridor.

Dust and debris now littered the passageway, obscuring Colin's vision and stinging his eyes. He blinked away tears but did not reach to wipe his face. While the impromptu avalanche had not completely destroyed the barricade, it nevertheless had caused significant damage. Huge chunks of rock, some as large as a sport-utility vehicle, now lay amid or atop the items and scrap material used to form the barrier. The stock of the M470 to his shoulder, Colin moved the weapon's barrel in an arc across his body as he examined the wreckage, searching for signs of anyone who might have survived the blast.

"Got one," said a voice, and Colin realized it was Sloane an instant before the sergeant fired. It was a single shot, striking the prone Chodrecai soldier where he lay among the twisted remains of what had once been some kind of packing container. The Gray slumped, the rifle in his hands falling from his grasp and clattering across the debris surrounding his body. Around Colin, members of both Javoquek's and Gutierrez's teams began to fan out, inspecting the crude barricade in search of other survivors.

Ahead of Colin, Javoquek looked back over his shoulder. "DiCarlo. Gutierrez. Do you see this?"

Beyond the now-wrecked barricade was what Colin took to be a massive metal hatch, larger than anything they had yet encountered since entering the complex. A control pad was set into the wall next to it, along with what she recognized as a panel for interfacing with an internal communications system.

"Now, that is one big fucking door," DiCarlo said. "I don't think that grenade launcher's gonna get it done this time."

"It is a reinforced pressure hatch," Javoquek replied. "It likely means that the chamber beyond is equipped so that it can be completely isolated from the rest of the complex, to include its own power and environmental systems."

"Like a fallout shelter?" Russell asked. Then, as though realizing Javoquek would not understand the reference, she added, "A hardened room, designed to withstand explosions, extreme weather events, things like that?"

The Plysserian nodded. "That is correct. Such facilities are commonly used among high-ranking military and political officials. If this is such a construct, then it likely is the control center we seek."

"Should we knock or something?" Gutierrez asked, his weapon still aimed at the door.

"It is unlikely that we will be able to penetrate this door with our weapons," Javoquek said. "We will need either larger explosives or a drill of some kind."

As Russell was stepping around some of the debris littering the floor, angling for a closer look at the control panel, Colin saw a shadow move to her left. She had not seen it, just as she did not see the muzzle of the Chodrecai pulse rifle aiming at her from amid a pile of wreckage. It trembled, as if its owner held it in unsteady hands, but at this distance and regardless of her body armor, a single shot would be fatal.

"Look out!"

There was time only to—

The weapon roared in Russell's ears the instant before something crashed into her from behind. Then she felt the impact of something slamming into her body armor, pitching her across the floor where she landed atop a mound of the rubble. Something wet splashed across her face and neck, in her mouth and her eyes, but she could only cringe as numerous voices shouted before being drowned out by the reports of countless pulse rifles. Clamping her eyes closed, Russell rolled off the wreckage where she had landed, every movement like fire in her rib cage. Stars danced inside her eyelids, and when she tried to breathe she tasted bitter copper dust.

"Belinda!" a voice—DiCarlo's—shouted before she felt hands on her body. They moved quickly, and she realized they were checking her for injuries. Reaching up, she wiped at her face, and when she opened her eyes she saw that her hand was covered in dark blood.

"Take it easy," DiCarlo said, his words calm and soothing. "It's not yours. I think you're okay."

Buoyed by DiCarlo's voice and the look of concern on his face as he looked down at her, Russell tried to sit up, but the motion sent fresh fire shooting along her side. Looking down, she saw that the left flank of her body armor was partially dented. *God damn, that hurts.* "What happened? Who . . . ?"

The words died in Russell's throat as she turned and her eyes fell across the body lying on the rubble-strewn ground. It wore a Marine's camouflage fatigues, but its head and parts of its upper torso were missing. Blood ran freely from the ghastly wound, and the fingers on the body's right hand still twitched.

Laney.

"Oh, God," she said, her stomach lurching as she was overcome by the need to vomit. The bile rushed up her throat and pushed past her lips, spewing across her lap. DiCarlo, of course, moved not one iota, his hands remaining on her shoulders as she retched.

"It's okay," he said, the words barely a whisper.

"What . . . what happened?" she asked wiping her mouth with the back of her hand.

"He pushed you out of the way," DiCarlo replied, without embellishment. "You took some of it, but he got in front of the worst of it. It was over before the rest of us knew what was happening."

Her eyes stinging with fresh tears, Russell almost did not hear the metallic click from somewhere behind her. It echoed in the passageway, with DiCarlo and the rest of the soldiers scrambling to react as a low hum became audible.

Despite the pain in her ribs, Russell managed to turn herself enough that she could see the massive door at the end of the tunnel beginning to open. In response to that, DiCarlo, Javoquek, and the others aimed their weapons at the hatch, stepping back to give themselves maneuvering room. Reaching for her own rifle, Russell winced in pain as she pulled herself to her feet, bringing the weapon to her shoulder and sighting down its barrel at the door. She heard the sound of escaping air as seals were retracted, and seconds passed as the hatch cycled open with agonizing slowness. As suddenly as it had begun, the door ceased moving, having spiraled open just enough to allow a single figure to emerge.

It was a Chodrecai, an older male, dressed in a senior military officer's uniform. Unarmed—it seemed—the Gray held its hands away from its body as it stepped into view. When he spoke, he did so in a Chodrecai language, and Russell realized his was the same voice they had heard moments before over the communications system.

"What the hell's it saying?" Gutierrez asked, the barrel of his M470 trained on the Chodrecai soldier's chest.

As if in response to the sergeant's query, the Gray shifted to speaking halting, broken English. "I am *Jenterant* Aziletal Iledisavo, supreme leader of Chodrecai military forces. As I stand before you, I have already communicated to my subordinate commanders to cease hostilities and to relinquish all weapons." He gestured toward the bodies scattered in the passageway before him. "Let these be the last regrettable casualties of a war started generations ago for the wrong reasons, and that has continued unabated for far too long. My only request is that my people be treated with compassion as we strive to move past that which has consumed us all. I am authorized on behalf of my superiors to offer the unconditional surrender of the Chodrecai Territorial Confederation."

Tomorrow

49

The images on the plasma screen television hanging on the forward wall of Bruce Thompson's office were muted, which was fine with him. He did not require the audio feeds to tell him what he already knew, or what he could glean from the broadcasts being received from around the world. The content largely was the same; only the way in which it was presented varied as different news outlets broadcast reactions to the news of the Chodrecai surrender. Most of the talking heads now were repeating themselves, anyway, waiting as they were for any new details to be released, be it from official sources or anyone else who had something to say. The cacophony of information had degenerated to a dull buzz, for which Thompson had no use.

His tie loosened and his uniform jacket hanging on a hook on his bathroom door, Thompson reclined in his high-backed leather chair with his feet perched atop his desk. He had even removed his polished black shoes, luxuriating in the casual tossing aside of rigid military protocol. After this many months, he figured he had earned himself the minor rebellion.

And those who don't agree can kiss my old, wrinkly ass.

His left hand held a glass of his favorite brand of single malt scotch. A cigar, one of the richly flavored blends preferred by Sergeant Major DiCarlo, smoldered in a nearby ashtray in flagrant defiance of however many Pentagon anti-smoking ordinances there might be at the present time. His right hand held the remote for the plasma TV, using the device to scan through the hundreds of channels received via the Pentagon's satellite television system. With the assistance of a younger, smarter aide well versed in the complex nature of modern consumer electronics, Thompson had configured the television to mimic most of the functions of the Situation Center's map wall. He rarely used the screen in this fashion, preferring instead to sit among his people in Op04-E's main operations area and gather their reactions, suggestions, and other observations with respect to the constant stream of information the group received. However, given his current predilection for flouting rules and regulations, he had chosen a wiser course and opted to recuse himself within the relative privacy of his office.

"Want to see if there's a game on or something?" asked Tommy Brooks from where he sat on the leather couch along the office's left wall. He held his expression for several beats, after which he released a tired grin. Like Thompson, the large, dark-skinned man had removed his uniform jacket and loosened his tie. His feet rested atop stacks of reports and binders covering the surface of the low-rise coffee table positioned before the couch. A nondrinker in all the years Thompson had known him, Brooks held a bottle of water in his right hand.

"You know," Thompson said after taking a sip of his scotch, "it occurs to me that I can't remember the last time I watched a decent football game or a good movie, or even a bad movie. I can't remember the last time I read something that wasn't a status report or didn't come with a DoD label or stamp on it."

"Me neither," Brooks replied, "but I'm betting it wasn't

this calendar year, whatever year this is. Hell, what *day* is it, anyway?"

"Tuesday," Thompson replied, then frowned. "I think." Shrugging, he decided he did not care one way or another, and instead elected to take another drink.

After a moment, Brooks said, "We could probably go home, you know. You could even pack up and head to one of those cabins in Montana you used to talk about all the time."

Thompson nodded. "It's a fishing camp, and I *have* thought about going out there, thank you very much." What he did not say—what he did not want to say—was that, in many respects, none of what they currently were experiencing felt real to him. For more than a year, without meaningful diversion of any sort, he had come to view the Pentagon, Op04-E, and this office as his home. On those rare occasions—once or twice a week, at most—when he had permitted himself a brief respite, his house had felt empty, even alien, and every moment he spent there seemed to him a violation of the duties and responsibilities with which he was entrusted. Intellectually he knew that was not the case, just as he knew the importance of resting his mind as well as his body from the demands of his job. None of that stopped the illogical sensation of being derelict in his duties from clouding his feelings as he lay awake at night, particularly after Operation Clear Sky had commenced. During the past weeks as the campaign unfolded, there were many nights when he didn't even leave the Pentagon at all. In the final days, with so much happening so quickly as Chodrecai forces seemingly to further deteriorate with every passing hour and victory seemed inevitable, Thompson rarely left the Op04-E's environs, lest he miss some major development.

Now all of that was behind them.

"I know what you're thinking," Brooks said, pointing at him with the index finger of the hand he used to hold the water bottle. "But you're wrong. It's over. We won."

Shaking his head, Thompson took another sip of scotch. "It's not that simple. It wasn't over the day after the Germans surrendered, or even the Iraqis. The war might be over, but we've still got a lot of work to do."

"And it's going to be there tomorrow," Brooks countered.

"Well, we agree on that much, anyway." Seizing the Chodrecai command bunker and forcing the surrender of its civilian and military leadership had cut short what might have been a long, costly campaign. Though major combat had ended and a formal cease-fire declared, mop-up operations would be in play for days, if not weeks. Small skirmishes still were being reported, either because some forces had not yet received word of the cease-fire or because rogue units had taken it upon themselves to continue the fight. There still remained any number of resistance cells, on *Jontashreena* and Earth, requiring attention.

And what of reconstruction? Repairing the infrastructure of both Chodrecai and Plysserian societies would take years. Earth also faced its share of work. In addition to the staggering yet accidental damage inflicted upon southern China during the initial weeks of the war, there were mammoth craters at installations in New Mexico, Okinawa, and England—portal generation sites attacked by the Grays. Casualty figures were still being computed, and though Thompson knew that whatever the final number might be, and while that total would still be far too many, he shuddered to think of the results of such an attack upon a more densely populated area like Los Angeles or New York City. Television talking heads had still managed to find something about which to endlessly drone, stressing the cruel irony of New Mexico—formerly the site of early and extensive nuclear bomb tests—being the victim of such over-whelming devastation.

Despite all of that, the physical damage the conflict had exacted on this planet was minimal compared to that visited upon *Jontashreena*, where the effects of ramping up a global war machine would be far-reaching and long-lasting. There also remained the need to stabilize those governments that still had not recovered from the loss of numerous political leaders. While relations may have improved between nations that once viewed one another as adversaries, new strains and stresses now existed between former allies. Thompson suspected those issues would be resolved soon enough, but for a time he knew there would be much rhetoric and posturing as various rival leaders sought to position themselves to take advantage of whatever global cooperative spirit had emerged from fighting the Chodrecai.

Same shit, Thompson mused. *Different day*.

"Nothing's going to happen in the next couple of weeks that can't happen with you fishing somewhere," Brooks pressed. "Hell, it'll take that long for the leaders on all sides to decide on the place settings for the negotiating table. I can run the store just as well as you can, and I'm thinking I can run it from my cell phone and laptop while I'm sitting on a beach in the Caymans."

Thompson chuckled at the imagery that evoked. "I never pictured you for the loud-shirt, rum-drinking, beach-walking crowd, Tommy."

"Well, there's a first time for everything, and I figure the time's right for me to check out what I've been missing all these years. I'm not getting any younger, that's for damn sure." He held up a paper napkin he had retrieved from Thompson's small wet bar and set it beneath his water bottle to protect the coffee table from condensation. "See this? This is more material than you'll find on any bikini on any girl walking around down there. Why the hell I didn't move there years ago, I'll never know."

"You're a dirty old man, General."

Brooks nodded. "Roger that," he said, and both men laughed at the remark. It was the first good laugh Thompson could remember having in what seemed like forever. He relished the sensation, feeling the weight of his responsibilities beginning to lift from his shoulders. He had scarcely dared to hope that a day like this might come, when he could sit and enjoy the company of his lifelong friend and rejoice in the knowledge that they had traversed the darkness and uncertainty of war and emerged into the light of what looked to be a new tomorrow.

Waxing poetic again? Must be the scotch.

A knock on the door quieted their revelry, and Thompson looked up. "Come in." The door opened to admit Nancy Spencer. Her hair once again was secured in its ubiquitous ponytail, but she was dressed in faded blue jeans and a dark red button-down blouse. Thompson could not recall ever seeing her sporting such casual attire. This in itself was cause for celebration. Despite her looking as tired as Thompson felt, Spencer nevertheless still carried that quiet sense of authority and confidence he had always respected.

"Good afternoon, gentlemen," she said as she stepped into the office, closing the door behind her.

"Nancy, grab a chair," Thompson said, indicating one of the chairs situated before his desk. "General Brooks and I were just discussing various forms of debauchery with which to entertain ourselves when we take our well-deserved vacations."

Without missing a beat, Spencer replied, "I've seen the pictures of your last vacation, sir. Trout really aren't that debauched. You might want to try something else." As she spoke that last part, her eyebrows bobbed, and the hint of a smile teased the corners of her mouth. The suggestion was obvious, even to somcone as long out of practice as Thompson.

"Fair enough," he said, clearing his throat. "What can I do for you?"

"The president has requested your presence at the White House at oh eight hundred tomorrow," Spencer replied. "There's a press conference or some kind of dog and pony show, and she wants to personally thank you for . . . you know . . . whatever it is you do here."

"When somebody finds out what that is, I hope they tell me." Thompson grimaced at the notion of having to stand before cameras at the president's side, accepting whatever platitudes she had planned for him. He gestured in the direction of the Situation Center. "She should be thanking them. They're the ones who did all the hard work."

"Yeah," Brooks said, "but all of them can't fit in the White House pressroom. So, you accept her thanks, then you come back here and give the rest of us raises, bonuses, new carpeting in our offices, whatever."

"Now we're talking," Spencer said, crossing her arms. "Taupe's always been my favorite color, if you're making note of these things."

Holding up his hands in mock surrender, Thompson closed his eyes. "All right, all right. I give up." To Spencer, he said, "Please send my respects to the president, and inform her that I'll be there."

Spencer smiled. "Don't worry. She knows how much you hate these sorts of things. She promised she'd only keep you as long as absolutely necessary, after which you're free to take that vacation you keep putting off." Her statement was punctuated by Brooks's chuckle.

"Let me guess," Thompson said, pausing to drain the last of the scotch from his glass. "You can run your office from your phone while you're sitting on a beach or beside a pool somewhere."

Shaking her head, Spencer regarded him with a disapproving scowl. "Screw that." She held up her phone. "I'm backing over this thing when I drive home tonight."

For the first time, Thompson allowed himself to consider what lay behind his friends' good-natured teasing, seeing past the verbal jousting to their genuine concern for his well-being. It had been a long, arduous journey to where they now stood, poised to embark on a new chapter of history unlike anything humanity had ever before faced. Maybe, he decided, that journey could wait for a little while—a few weeks, at any rate.

He smiled as he regarded Spencer. "Tell me something, Nancy. Ever been to Montana?"

The first rays of *Jontashreena*'s sun were beginning to peak over the horizon when Russell heard footsteps behind her. Looking over her shoulder, she saw Simon DiCarlo walking down the paved footpath toward her. In each hand he carried a metal cup, and he smiled as he caught sight of her studying him.

"Real coffee," he said, gesturing with the two cups. "The good stuff, too. It sucks to have to admit this, but Army field cooks always knew how to make better coffee than the Corps." Reaching her, he offered her one of the cups before lowering himself to the ground next to her, leaning against the smooth side of the boulder she had selected as a backrest. Like her, he wore clean combat utilities, having benefited from a hot shower and a shave, thanks to the camp erected at the base of the mountain. It had been decided that the captured Chodrecai command bunker would serve as a base of operations for human-assisted operations in this region, at least for the short term. From where she sat, Russell could see the rows of olive drab general-purpose tents that would serve as homes and even offices for the units stationed here until more permanent facilities could be constructed.

Taking the coffee, Russell held it to her nose and inhaled, savoring the rich aroma. "Thanks," she said before taking the first sip. It was hot, but not so much to take away her enjoyment.

"They'll be serving morning chow in a bit, if you're hungry," he said.

Russell shook her head, holding up the coffee. "Nah, this is good."

"Real eggs, real bacon, real pancakes," DiCarlo said, teasingly pressing the point. "Did I mention the bacon?"

She laughed, taking the opportunity to shift to a more comfortable position. The action made her wince, and she reached with her free hand to her right side.

"You okay?" DiCarlo asked.

"Fine." With a grunt, she settled back to the ground, this time leaning against his left arm. "Still tender, is all. I'll be okay." She paused, her thoughts turning—as they had countless times over the past days—to Colin Laney and what he had done for her. The image of that horrific moment had played and replayed in her mind during the past two days, refusing to fade.

As if comprehending her thoughts, DiCarlo said, "You know it's not your fault. Laney knew exactly what he was doing. It takes a special sort of person to do what he did. We all think we'd do the same thing under the same circumstances, but the truth is that most people wouldn't. He didn't hesitate, and you're here because of that. I'm just sorry I didn't get a chance to thank him."

Nodding, Russell wiped away a tear as she stared at the contents of her coffee cup. She knew DiCarlo was right, and that the young Marine had acted deliberately in the hope of saving her life, likely with the full knowledge that he was forfeiting his own. It was the greatest gift any person could offer another, and Russell now found herself contemplating whether she was worthy of such a noble, heroic gesture. As soon as the errant thought crossed her mind, she forced it away, refusing to let it take root in her consciousness. She could never entertain such thinking, not even for the briefest of moments, if Laney's gift was to have any meaning. Russell now held a responsibility, an obligation, to ensure the life she lived remained worthy of his sacrifice.

Thank you, Colin.

After a few more moments spent in silence, during which they continued to watch the sun pushing its way past the horizon, DiCarlo said, "You know, we don't even have to stay here. I can put in a word with the unit commander and get us on a shuttle to the nearest portal site. We can probably be back on Earth in time for dinner." He stopped, his expression changing to one of disbelief as he shook his head. "I don't think I'll ever get used to saying something like that."

Russell shrugged. "What's the rush? The portals aren't going anywhere. We've got all kinds of time." She had heard late the previous evening about a notion fielded by the Chodrecai and Plysserian civilian leaders, offering to permanently close all remaining portals and to have the equipment responsible for their generation disassembled. The offer was politely refused, with President Valenti and other world leaders convincing their counterparts on *Jontashreena* that a policy of isolationism was not in the best interests of either planet. Trust obviously remained an issue, to say nothing of the lingering resentment harbored by people on both sides of the conflict. While many challenges lay ahead as the civilizations of both worlds struggled to heal, it made sense that the journey would be easier if it was taken together.

"To be honest," DiCarlo countered, "I've pretty much had my fill of this kind of thing. I've been doing it since before you were born, for crying out loud." He waved toward the camp. "We're going to have people here for months, if not longer."

It was true, Russell conceded, that postwar efforts would continue for some time. Reconstruction would soon be getting under way across both planets. The search was ongoing for any surviving perpetrators of the attack on the peace summit in Geneva. Russell had seen news reports in which members of *Jontashreena*'s civilian populace had called for war crimes tribunals to prosecute suspects from both sides of the conflict. Despite the ongoing turmoil, numerous promises had already been made, and many visions were being outlined for healing *Jontashreena* as well as those who had weathered generations of global war.

"I was thinking," she said after a moment, "that I'd like to stay here, at least for a while, and help Javoquek." The Plysserian officer had been given the enviable assignment of overseeing the rebuilding of several schools and other public facilities in his home city on the *Galotreapiq* continent. Until stability had been achieved and the cease-fire was recognized and obeyed by everyone, it was felt that deploying military units to affected regions would offer an added sense of security to those already living in such areas, while allowing units to respond to incidents in timely fashion. Part of the task would require the recruitment of local residents to serve on construction teams, as well as demolition and cleanup crews to tear down unusable structures and remove rubble and other war-related debris that had accumulated over the years. Workers were needed in cities and other population centers across the planet to serve in every imaginable capacity where physical labor was concerned, and volunteers were turning out in droves—Plysserian, Chodrecai, and human. Many members of Earth's various military contingents, representing every nationality Russell could easily name, were among those requesting temporary and even permanent assignment to the rebuilding efforts on *Jontashreena*. She had heard talk around the camp of people bringing their families here from Earth. Perhaps some, like her, felt the need to contribute in some tangible way to the healing process.

"Well," DiCarlo said, leaning against the rock and rubbing his chin, "I suppose it'd give you material for another book, wouldn't it?"

Smiling, Russell sipped her coffee. "Yeah, I guess there's that, too." She thought of the pair of notebooks lying beneath the pillow on the cot in her tent, the latest such tomes in the collection she had amassed since the first days of the war. Their pages now were almost filled with notes, ideas, random scribbles, and anything else she had channeled from her brain onto the paper. There was a story to be told from all of that, once she found a way to make sense of it. It seemed to her that such a story would be better served if it retained the type of firsthand knowledge and experience that had carried her to this point.

Russell rested her head against DiCarlo's shoulder, and they watched in silence as the first rays of sunlight lanced across the faces of the surrounding mountains. The valley was bathed in a warm orange glow, the light of renewal and promise.

Finally, DiCarlo said, "I guess there's no rush to go home. It'll be there, right?" He shrugged. Though he would never say it aloud, Russell knew he had no compelling reason to return to Earth—no family, no one waiting for him. She sensed him pondering that thought, and perhaps even trying to contemplate some deeper meaning it might be hiding. Leaning closer, she raised her face to his and kissed him on the cheek.

"If you've got nothing better to do, I wouldn't mind the company."

DiCarlo looked down at her with a wistful smile. "Keep you company? If that's code for something fun, I suppose I could do that."

She laughed, pressing into him. Now blessed with all the time two worlds could offer, they could do whatever they wanted.

The war was over.

ACKNOWLEDGMENTS

The first round of thanks goes to my editor at Pocket Books, Jaime Costas. My ears rang in disbelief for days after she called to tell me that she wanted to edit a sequel to *The Last World War*. She's been patient, gracious, and enthusiastic throughout the process, and I am supremely grateful for her faith and support of this project.

Thanks also are due to Marco Palmieri, formerly of Pocket Books, who during his tenure became a mentor to me and also remained a steadfast champion of me and my work. Though he always gave me the straight dope whenever I asked about commissioning an *LWW* sequel, he never stopped exploring ways to make it happen. Jaime did the heavy lifting so far as shepherding this project through its development and getting it into your hands, but Marco laid the groundwork for what became the book you've just finished reading.

To the countless fans who've sent letters or talked to me at conventions and book signings over the years, I once again offer my eternal appreciation. I never thought the first novel would ever enjoy any sort of success or longevity, and it's been heartwarming to read comments from readers who took the ride with me. Make no mistake: This book is here because of you.

Finally, there's my wife, Michi, who as always remains at my side as we navigate the often tumultuous waters of parenthood, jobs, and just life in general. Her support and love are unwavering, and though it might sound clichéd to say I could not have done this without her, I'll take the hit and say it anyway. Love ya, babe.

ABOUT THE AUTHOR

When he's not writing, Dayton Ward is a software developer, having become a slave to Corporate America after spending eleven years in the U.S. Marine Corps. When asked, he'll tell you that he joined the military soon after high school because he'd grown tired of people telling him what to do all the time.

Whoops.

In addition to the numerous writing credits he shares with friend and coauthor Kevin Dilmore, Dayton is the author of the science fiction novels *The Last World War* and *The Genesis Protocol*, the *Star Trek* novels *In the Name of Honor*, *Open Secrets*, and the forthcoming *Paths of Disharmony*, as well as short stories in the first three *Star Trek: Strange New Worlds* anthologies, *Kansas City Voices* magazine, the Yard Dog Press anthology *Houston, We've Got Bubbas!*, and the *Star Trek: New Frontier* anthology *No Limits*. He also served as editor for the anthology *Full-Throttle Space Tales: Space Grunts*, published by Flying Pen Press.

Dayton currently lives in Kansas City with his wife, Michi, and their daughters Addison and Erin. He was born and raised in sunny Florida and though he has lived all over the country and even overseas, Dayton maintains a torrid long-distance romance with his beloved Tampa Bay Buccaneers.

Find out more about Dayton at his official website: www.daytonward.com.